$3.75

Portrait in Smoke

I stood there, holding the gun, frozen to the spot. Krassy turned quickly and ran toward the archway leading to the hall. Then I realized she was screaming.

I stared at the quiet figure in the chair. The hair was the bright color of catsup now, like a bottle had been emptied over the top, and was draining with slow inevitability down the upholstery. Then I became conscious that several other people had entered the room.

I knew I had to get out fast.

The Tooth and the

Late at night, I'd sit in my the best possible method with which to kill him. While I would have enjoyed strangling him with my hands, making it as painful and lingering as possible, I realized such a plan had a drawback. Although Humphries was twenty years older than I, he was also larger and possibly stronger. But I liked to consider it anyway—as well as guns, knives, blunt instruments, and all their variations.

However, I was also determined to escape the consequences after I had murdered him. I hoped to escape the law, and with this in mind I began planning.

ATTENTION: ORGANIZATIONS AND CORPORATIONS

Most HarperPaperbacks are available at special quantity discounts for bulk purchases for sales promotions, premiums, or fund-raising. For information, please call or write:
Special Markets Department, HarperCollins Publishers, 10 East 53rd Street, New York, N.Y. 10022.
Telephone: (212) 207-7528. Fax: (212) 207-7222.

BILL S. BALLINGER

PORTRAIT IN SMOKE

THE TOOTH AND THE NAIL

HarperPaperbacks
A Division of HarperCollins*Publishers*

If you purchased this book without a cover, you should be aware that this book is stolen property. It was reported as "unsold and destroyed" to the publisher and neither the author nor the publisher has received any payment for this "stripped book."

This is a work of fiction. The characters, incidents, and dialogues are products of the author's imagination and are not to be construed as real. Any resemblance to actual events or persons, living or dead, is entirely coincidental.

HarperPaperbacks *A Division of* HarperCollins*Publishers*
10 East 53rd Street, New York, N.Y. 10022

Portrait in Smoke copyright © 1950 by William S. Ballinger
The Tooth and the Nail copyright © 1955 by William S. Ballinger
All rights reserved. No part of this book may be used or reproduced in any manner whatsoever without written permission of the publisher, except in the case of brief quotations embodied in critical articles and reviews. For information address HarperCollins*Publishers,* 10 East 53rd Street, New York, N.Y. 10022.

A hardcover edition of *Portrait in Smoke* was published in 1950 by Harper & Row, Publishers, Inc. A hardcover edition of *The Tooth and the Nail* was published in 1955 by Harper & Row, Publishers, Inc.

Cover photographs courtesy of Archive Photos

First HarperPaperbacks printing: November 1993

Printed in the United States of America

HarperPaperbacks and colophon are trademarks of HarperCollins*Publishers*

10 9 8 7 6 5 4 3 2 1

PORTRAIT IN SMOKE

ONE

If I shoot off my mouth to the wrong guy, I'm a goner.

And besides, who'd believe me?

But the whole thing doesn't make sense. It doesn't make any sense at all. I been thinking about it and talking it over with myself. And then on top of that I get dreams. And it still doesn't add up. I can't understand why it happened. I go over the whole thing, step by step, and then after a while it gets hazy. It's like trying to paint a picture with a bucketful of smoke.

At first the picture of Krassy starts out clear and distinct. Then the edges move a little and it starts to get fuzzy. Then all the lines overlap and the edges curl up and start forming crazy whirls and swirls . . . and you don't have a picture anymore. I try to take my mind and grab the lines and pull them back straight, but the lines are really smoke and they slip away. And then all I have is hazy blue smoke which stretches all over the picture.

That's the way it is, and maybe I'm making it up in my mind. About the smoke part, I mean, because the day it started was a smoky, hazy Chicago day. Smoke from the factories sifts in and mixes with the damp lake air, and it lies in soggy, gray felt blankets all over the city. Then the damp air turns into a fog, and the smoke mixes with it, and then the mixture hangs suspended and motionless and everybody goes around saying, "Christ, what a day!"

The smoke and fog cuts off the tops of the great big beautiful buildings down in the Loop . . . but it doesn't touch the real Chicago. Not the dirty, little two- and three-story buildings which straggle along as far as you can see. And the smoke doesn't make any difference to the stinking little shops with hand-drawn cardboard signs in their windows advertising bicycles repaired, men's clothing slightly used—50 percent off, dresses cleaned while-U-wait, swap your old furniture here. Or all the neon signs advertising billiards, taverns with beer on tap, girl shows . . . the most beautiful girls in town, hotel rooms walk up two flights to the lobby.

Sometimes the smoke hangs from rusty iron fire escapes which stick out from the second stories over the street. Their end steps balance in the air, and when the signs are turned on, they throw crazy patterns and shadows on the patched sidewalks. The smoke covers a lot of things, but it doesn't cover it all.

Anyway, it was that kind of a day when I got a message that my grandfather, old Charlie April, had died and left me twenty-five hundred bucks. I went into a little bar down the street and put a couple drinks inside me and thought about the old man and tried to feel sad. But I couldn't feel too bad. I'd always sort of hated his guts because he was a mean old bastard.

He was the only living relative I had, and when I was a kid I'd lived with him. He'd worked as a fireman on the Erie Railroad and every so often he'd get liquored up and get into a fight at the end of his run. Sometimes he'd still be mad when he came home. Maybe just pounding things with his fists made him feel better. I don't know. Anyway, one night he came home, drunker than hell, and knocked my brains half out. I left home.

I was fifteen.

I came to Chicago and started working around. Finally, I landed a job with the International Collection Agency; it wasn't much of a place to work but I stayed on. Mostly I wrote threatening letters to deadbeats who wouldn't pay their bills and traced skippers and dunned suckers.

It didn't add up to more than forty or fifty bucks a week, which meant a room on the third floor of a walk-up. There was a cheap dresser and a brass bed with a faded, old linoleum rug on the floor. In one corner there was a beat-up bridge lamp, and a sagging overstuffed chair. In another corner, I had me a washbowl, bolted to the wall. It had only one tap that worked and petered out a weak stream of water. Down at the end of the hall was a can which ten people all tried to use at the same time.

I used to lie on my bed and trace pictures in the designs caused by the tears in the rotten old green shade at the window. The dusty sunlight coming through the holes made all kinds of different patterns which you could change by shutting one eye and then the other. Sometimes you could do it by moving your head just a little bit. The walls to all the rooms were so thin that the only privacy you had was sitting around with your own thoughts. But I didn't have much choice, so I kept on living there and working with International Collections.

Then I got word about Grandpa April's insurance, and for the first time I felt maybe I had a chance to make a break.

The union buried the old man, and I went over to Indiana for his funeral. I didn't feel sad or unhappy because it'd been ten years or longer since I'd seen him. Nobody was at the funeral except the undertaker and me. He was there because he'd been paid, and I was there because I was the only one left.

All the way back on the train I kept thinking about that twenty-five hundred bucks and what the hell I could do with it. I knew damned good and well I'd shoot all the dough if I kept it around where I could get my hands on it.

So I decided I'd try to buy some kind of a business with it.

But for twenty-five hundred bucks you don't buy much. When I got back to Chicago, I started nosing around and heard of an old guy by the name of Clarence Moon who wanted to sell his collection agency. I figured it was better than a hamburger stand, or a leased gas station, because it was at least the kind of a business I knew something about. I went to see him.

Clarence Moon was a big, fat slob of a man about seventy years old. He was completely bald except for a fringe of long white hair which hung just in front and in back of his ears. The top of his head was so dirty you could see white streaks on the skin where he'd scratched with his fingernails. He had a little two-room office located in an old loft building down by the Civic Opera building.

There wasn't anything in the front office except a decrepit old desk, covered on top by a cracked piece of glass; a swivel-backed desk chair, and one straight wooden chair for clients. An aged 1929 Underwood typewriter stood on a small table by the side of his desk. In the back room were a dozen green filing cabinets, each with three drawers. Stacked on top of the cabinets and in the corners were old clippings, magazines, and correspondence. I sat down on the straight-backed chair while the old man sized me up. I sized him up back. He was a rummy . . . if I ever saw, or smelled, one.

"My name is Dan April," I finally said. "I understand you want to sell out."

The old man pawed at his vest and tried to button it. There were only three buttons on it, and beneath, his belly bubbled and rolled. "I've considered the possibility," he said. "That is, if I find the right party."

"Nuts," I said, "you'll be lucky to sell out to anybody. How much you asking?"

"I want thirty-six hundred dollars," he replied. He shot a quick glance at me, then dropped his eyes and started fiddling with his vest buttons again.

I thought it over. A collection business is a funny thing. You get paid just for the bills you collect. But even so, if no one gives you overdue bills, you don't have a business. Once you get a company sending you their bills to collect, if you do a pretty good job, you keep getting their business year after year. There's nothing to buy like machinery or merchandise; you don't have to worry about dealers, or outlets, or any other damn thing. You just get the chance of doing business for the same old accounts.

"How long you been in business?" I asked Moon.

"I've been here for thirty-five years," he said proudly. Again he started fumbling with his vest and I could see he had the shakes bad.

"Go ahead and have a drink," I told him.

"I don't drink during office hours," he said with pride. Then his pride punctured and ran out of him like dirty water. "However, my arthritis has been bothering me lately, and I think I'd better have a short one." He made a grab for his desk drawer and hauled out a bottle of Old Culpepper. He twisted the cork out and dropped it to the floor and took a long haul. Then he reached down, picked up the cork and handed the bottle to me.

"No, thanks," I said and watched him put the bottle away. "How many accounts you got?" I asked.

He started to answer me a couple of times and stopped before a word got out. He wanted to lie to me, but he didn't have enough nerve left to try it. Finally he said, "Six. Six steady ones that is. I used to have thirty-six. But since I've been . . . ill, I've only been able to handle six."

I knew what that meant. Moon had lost thirty accounts because he'd been too damned drunk to handle them. But if six accounts still stuck around with him, that meant they'd probably stick with me, too.

"How about letting me see your books?" I asked him. He pulled out the middle drawer and handed me an old, dog-eared ledger. All it contained was a column of figures with dates of collection. At the end of each month was a gross total. I looked in the back of the book and for the year before he'd done enough to gross himself three thousand dollars. Leafing back through, I saw he'd made fairly regular entries for half a dozen small firms, which made up the bulk of his business.

We sat around and I asked him some more questions. His business wasn't worth very much and he knew it. Finally, I got up and started to leave. "Look," I said, "I'll give you two thousand bucks for what you got left."

He started to protest.

"Skip it," I told him. "I'll call you tomorrow and you tell me then. Take it or leave it." I went out the door just as he made a dive for the drawer with the bottle of liquor.

I knew then . . . he'd take it.

That night I went to bed and did some figuring. I figured that with plenty of work, I could build the business back up to making a few bucks. Even if I didn't do any better than the old man, I'd still break even. When I finally went to sleep, I dreamed most of the night and got my dreams all mixed up between old Charlie April and Clarence Moon. In the morning I'd quit hating old Charlie and I felt sorry for Moon the rummy.

I had breakfast and went to a phone and called Moon's office. I knew I was a sucker, but I felt sorry for the old guy, and I couldn't help myself. "Look, Moon," I said, "I been thinking it over and this is my last offer. I'll pay you two thousand cash now . . . and another thousand in one year."

The old man swallowed on the other end of the line. "All right, my boy," he said, "the Clarence Moon Collection Agency is yours."

TWO

PART I

I walked down to State and Van Buren where International Collections is located. I got in the office an hour and a half late. The girl at the switchboard said, "Jeez, Danny, you're going to catch it! Crenshaw's been looking all over for you." I took off my coat and hat and left them in the reception room.

Sitting down at my desk in the main office where five other collectors were all busy, I started cleaning the desk out. It didn't have much in it, but I wanted to clear out of the place completely. Crenshaw, the office manager, saw me and came barreling up.

"Where the hell you been, April?" he shouted.

"Around," I told him.

"Around!" and he laughed through his nose. "You better be around here more, if you expect to be *around* here!" He waited for a laugh. It didn't come.

"Very funny, Crenshaw," I told him. "But personally you give me the creeps."

He stopped like he'd been shot and turned red. He opened his big, ugly mouth to bellow.

"Shut up!" I said. "For five years I've wanted to kick you in the middle of your big, fat lardass. Now's a good time to do it."

The office was still. Crenshaw backed away with his butt up against a desk. I pushed my personal belongings into my pockets and walked out to the reception desk. In the doorway, I turned around and looked back. No one had moved. I waved to Bud Glasgow, whose desk had been next to mine, and went out.

When I got to the Clarence Moon Collection Agency, the old man was gone. He hadn't taken anything out of his desk except the bottle. On top of the desk was the door key and a note typed on the Underwood:

> DEAR MR. APRIL:
> I'll be in for my money tomorrow. Good luck.
> Sincerely,
> CLARENCE MOON

In one of the side drawers of the desk, I found a stack of correspondence going back maybe three months. I sat down at the old typewriter and started answering it.

That night, after dinner, I went back to the office and began going through the old green file cabinets in the back room. They were jammed with years-old correspondence and data cards. For each collection that comes up, a card is filled out containing as much information as is known about the person you're trying to collect the dough from. Where he lives, if he's married, his age, where he works, how much salary he makes, what his reputation is, credit rating if any, the kind of merchandise he usually owes money for, and stuff like that. If a guy is constantly back in paying his bills, the cards are kept up to date for each collection.

From the data cards, a collector can usually tell how rough it's going to be to collect his dough. Also they save a hell of a lot of time digging up information.

Old man Moon had saved every damned data card since he'd been in business. Most of them were out of date, and in the last few years his information had been skimpy and his writing more shaky. The cards weren't filed in any particular order, but they were roughly grouped together by years. It was a long, tough job going through those files, trying to pull them together and throwing out all the trash. Every night for a month I went back and worked for hours on the files.

One evening I started working on a file which was ten years old. A couple hours later, I pulled out a data card which had the name "Krassy Almauniski" on it. Clipped to the card was a faded newspaper story, with the picture of a young gal in it.

She looked out from the picture with a special, proud smile on her lips. I laid the picture to one side, then picked it up again and studied it closely. Her eyes were light, either gray or blue, but heavily lashed and her blond hair was in thick braids around her head. There was a certain dignity to her I can't explain. She was very young and without a doubt one of the most beautiful girls I've ever seen.

Under the picture was the story. It read:

Miss Krassy Almauniski, 4120½ South Hempstead, today was announced the winner of the *Stockyard Weekly News* beauty contest. Miss Almauniski, who was selected from over thirty entries, will receive one hundred dollars from the *Stockyard Weekly News*, a beautiful, fitted leather traveling case from Browser's Trunk and Leather Company, a new suit from Solomon's Dress Shoppe, a stunning hat and coat from Edna Mae's Thrifty Shoppers Mart, a permanent wave and manicure from the Glamour Beauty Salon, a five-dollar book of taxi coupons from the Red-Top Taxi Company, and a case of beer from the Deep Well Brewing Company.

Something about that picture started a memory clawing and scratching around in the back of my mind. There was something sad about it . . . something unhappy . . . and I couldn't place it at first. And then in a rush I had it! The memory, that is. It went back to the first summer I'd arrived in Chicago and I was still just a kid, plenty broke and plenty lonesome in the big city, but I was growing up fast. For the first time I was becoming conscious there were girls in this world, and it would be nice to know some of them. But I didn't know anybody yet who could introduce me to them, and I was still too shy of them to try to pick one up on my own.

But a guy can dream.

Well, it was in the summer . . . a blistering, hot Illinois night. There wasn't the stirring of a breeze, a breath of wind except along the lake front. The beaches were jammed with families, and kids, and couples just sitting in the sand. Waiting for a cool breath of air to come in across the lake, or waiting for the night to end, or just waiting to fall asleep. A lot of the older women had taken off their dresses and were waiting, quietly, in their slips and thinking about going back to their walk-up, oven flats and the washings and things they had to do the next day. Their husbands were stripped to the waist, and maybe they were thinking about their factories and benches. I don't know.

But I couldn't sleep, either, that night in my two-by-four room. So I'd walked up to the North Avenue beach, and along the concrete breakwater which sticks out like a crooked arm. I sat down, and swung my feet over the side and sat there hot and uncomfortable and lonesome. I looked out across the lake, and occasionally the lights of an excursion steamer would show far out. And dotted as if they were fireflies, would be the lights of the small, private boats and occasionally I'd hear some music from a radio coming across the water from a boat, and once in a while voices and laughter.

And as I sat there, I began to hate the boats, and the guys who could afford to have them, and the beautiful dames riding on them. And I thought about shagging errands for two bits, and delivering telegrams for a dime, and unloading vegetables for trucks at thirty-five cents, and all the things I'd been doing to try to keep alive.

Little by little, my eyes got accustomed to the darkness, and I noticed a girl sitting on the breakwater . . . maybe ten feet away from me. She had her legs drawn up in front of her, with her arms clasped around them, and her chin resting on her knees. She was staring off across the water, too, as if she were waiting for something . . . or seeing something. She was absolutely motionless. I don't know if she'd been there when I walked by; maybe she had, and in the darkness I hadn't seen her. Or perhaps, she'd come along afterward, and had been so quiet I hadn't heard her. But when I first saw her, it gave me a start.

I couldn't see her features distinctly, but even in the darkness, I knew she was young and pretty, and probably about my age. I kept glancing over at her and I wanted to say something, but she didn't even seem to know I was sitting there, and she kept staring out over the lake. I tried to think of something clever to say . . . of introducing myself . . . of striking up a conversation. But not only could I think of nothing to say, I was embarrassed by the prospect of her scorning my clumsy advances, and perhaps calling the park police.

So I sat there, more conscious of her by the minute, and wondering what to do about it. Then silently, and in one swift, easy motion, she swung to her feet and started slowly to walk down the breakwater to the beach. Without hesitation, I was on my feet and following her . . . at a respectable distance. She walked down the breakwater to the beach, and followed the winding, crowded walk to the underpass across the Outer Drive. As I followed her, crazy thoughts ran through my mind . . . like walking up beside her, taking her arm without saying a word. Or asking her if I could drive her home . . . but I didn't have a car. I could see her naked back, white in the darkness ahead of me, and even then I was conscious of the swing in her walk as she went down the hollow, vibrating underpass. She came up on North Avenue, and continued west toward Clark Street. Two blocks away, on the corner of Clark and North Avenue, is a big, cheap drugstore, and she turned into it. I stopped outside the door, while she climbed on a stool at the soda fountain and ordered a Coke. In the light of the store, I really saw her for the first time. Around six-teen, and beautiful as hell, with long, braided golden hair. She was wearing a cheap, faded blue cotton dress, with no back; the dress had been washed so many times, it had reached a light, delicate blue color . . . lovely with her hair. I knew that color of blue, all poor families know it too well. And I could tell that she didn't live near the beach, either, because her arms and back wore only a soft tan, the kind of a tan you pick up just going outdoors, and not living on the beach.

As I stood there watching her, I could see the soda jerk talking with her, and she smiled back at him. I was jealous of the guy, and would have given anything to be able to talk to her and receive a smile. He didn't ring up the sale of the Coke, and when the girl offered him the money, he grinned and waved it away. She got down off the stool, and headed toward the door. Quickly I turned my back, and stared into a window while she passed behind me. Then I heard her feet break into a quick, little run and as I swung around, I saw her scrambling aboard a streetcar headed for the Loop. For just a sec-ond, the possibility of catching the car, too, flashed through my mind. And then I let it die. I couldn't afford to waste the carfare. Tomorrow, I still had to find a job.

Well, that was the one and only time I ever saw her. But for a long time afterward, I thought of her many times. Who was she? Where did she live? How could I meet her? I never found out. I never saw her at the beach again. Lots of times, I built up ideas in my mind, and I worked out what I'd do if I ever saw her. And some-times I'd make up the fact that I had a lot of dough, and I'd see myself dancing with her, and I was dressed in a pair of white flannel pants, with a double-breasted blue coat, and was wearing black and white shoes . . . and she had on a long evening gown, and we were some-where very fancy . . . and stuff like that.

Dreams die hard when you're just a young punk, and I kept remembering that girl for a long time afterward. Even after I'd met other gals and found that lots of things can just rub off. After a while, I maybe thought back on me, and my actions and what a jerk I'd been about being afraid to meet her. And finally I forgot about it completely. I hadn't thought of her in years.

Until I saw that newspaper clipping!

Even then, I couldn't be sure it was the same gal. I'd only seen her once, and the details and memory had faded. But there was something about Krassy Al-mauniski, and the girl at the beach, which brought back the old memory. And then suddenly, I found that I hadn't forgotten it at all. I picked up the clipping again.

The story was dated March 31, 1940. I picked up the data card attached to the clipping and read the date the card had been filled out; it was September, 1940, nearly six months after the story. On the data card was a list of merchandise which she had bought, including irons, ra-dios, traveling bags, watches, jewelry . . . not expen-sive . . . and clothes. The total was over $1,200, which is a good pile of bucks. I whistled to myself when I saw the amount, but I whistled more when I saw the card had been marked "paid in full." Maybe it was a hunch, or maybe it was just damned curiosity, but something made me look for the old 1940 ledger.

I finally found it jammed away in the bottom of the lower drawer in a file cabinet. I turned to September and looked down the list of payments received in that month. There was no payment listed for Krassy Almauniski, and she wasn't listed in October, November, or December. But the card said she'd paid in full.

I shrugged. What the hell. The bills were outlawed now, and I set her card to one side, but I put her picture in my pocket. The rest of the evening I spent on other cards, but I couldn't get Krassy Almauniski out of my mind. I decided the next day I'd call Moon and find out what he knew about it.

When I opened my eyes the next morning, she leaped immediately into my mind. Old man Moon had been in a month before to pick up his dough, and had left a phone number at his rooming house to call in case I wanted to reach him. I called his number, and a surly, bitchy voice told me the old man hadn't been home in weeks. I hung up the phone and went down to the office. Several times during the day I pulled the clipping out of my pocket and looked at her picture. Always, her calm eyes smiled back at me, and I found myself trying to read thoughts into them. I cussed my curiosity up and down and then decided I'd go out to 4120½ and see her. I could always pretend I was on some kind of business.

Forty-one twenty and a half South Hempstead was a stinking, narrow little house sandwiched in between two larger but equally crummy houses. Ramshackle wooden steps ran from the sidewalk to a little porch high up on the face of the house. A rusty iron pipe railing followed the stairs. The windows facing the street, under the steps, had been boarded up and stared blankly. The entrance to the house was through a battered doorway on the perching porch. Once the house had been painted, but years of smoke and soot had rotted its complexion like smallpox. A red brick chimney poked weakly through the middle of the roof, and rusty, corroded troughs clung scablike under the eaves.

I climbed the stairs and knocked at the door. The windows, on each side of it, were smeared and greasy. Then I saw a curtain twitch for a moment. Finally the door opened and a woman with tremendous bulging hips and thickly knotted ankles looked at me suspiciously. She had on an old housecoat wrapped loosely about her, and you could see her huge, deflated balloon busts bounce against her belly.

"I no want," she said and started to close the door.

"Hold it," I told her. "I want to talk to you."

"I no want. I no buy," she replied and shoved the door against my hand.

I kept it open. "I want to talk to Krassy Almauniski," I told her. Her tiny, suspicious pig eyes regarded me sullenly. She raised a red, chapped hand, with big purple veins on the back of it, and pushed her dirty gray hairs over her ears.

"No Almauniski here," she said.

I reached in my pocket and pulled out a dollar bill. Five bucks would've made her suspicious. I handed her the dollar and said, "I want to talk to Krassy Almauniski. I want to give her a job."

The old hag took the buck and shook her head.

"Is her father and mother here?"

"No Almauniski here," she repeated. "Almauniski die back ago."

"Her father died?" I asked.

She nodded her head.

"Where's her mother?"

"No mother," flatly.

"What happened to Krassy?"

The woman shook her head, and shrugged. "No Al-mauniski here," she repeated.

I gave up and walked down the stairs to the street. I hauled out Krassy's picture and looked at it again. It seemed impossible that anything as beautiful could have come out of a cesspool like the house above me. My next move was obvious. I walked down Hempstead and stopped at the first dive I came to; going up to the bar, I ordered a beer and took the glass back to the phone booth with me. There I looked through the classified telephone directory under "Publishers—Newspapers." I found the *Stockyard Weekly News* listed and tucked the address away in my mind. Finishing the beer, I hiked over to the newspaper office. It was about five blocks away.

The *Stockyard Weekly News* was located in a small, two-story brick building. The building was split into two parts by a concrete dividing wall straight through the middle. On the ground floor, the right side of the building was occupied by a barbershop, with a take-out liquor store in back of it. Separated by the concrete partition, the newspaper was located in the left side of the building. Upstairs, on the second floor, it looked like there might be a few ratty rooms and apartments.

I walked in the door of the paper, and about six feet inside it there was a dirty, scarred counter running the width of the narrow office. Hanging on one end of the counter was a swinging gate on sagging hinges. Back of it was a roll-top desk, a long battered office table piled high with bound copies of the paper. A shoulder-high partition of clapboard partly concealed an ancient flat-bed press, and several type cabinets.

A young guy maybe twenty-seven or -eight was seated

at the desk clipping stories from exchange papers. I walked up to the counter and he looked up at me.

"Is the editor in?" I asked.

"I'm the editor," he said. Slowly he got to his feet and slouched over toward me. When he got up next to me I could see he was tough. Plenty tough. He had a swarthy skin and a nose that had been broken and never set. His hair was slicked back and heavily oiled and I could smell lilac water in it. He placed his hands, palms down, on the counter and hunched his shoulders over it. "Anything you want?" he asked.

"Yeah," I said, "I want some information. The best place to get information is from an editor. That's why I'm asking you."

I could see him relax a little under the blarney. "What you want to know?"

"I'm trying to locate a girl named Krassy Almauniski," I told him. "Do you know her?"

"What you want to find her for?" he asked.

"She took out an insurance policy about ten years ago," I said, "and dropped it after a couple years. Anyway, she's got a small refund coming and we'd like to get it off our books. So far we've been unable to find her."

Finally he said, "I haven't seen her in ten years."

"Did you know her?" I asked.

"Yeah," he said, "I knew her."

"She won some kind of a beauty contest with this paper, didn't she?"

He laughed shortly. "Sure," he agreed, "she won a beauty contest. My old man was editor of the paper then. Me? I worked around the shop here after school. I knew her." He picked his hands up from off the counter and shoved them in his pockets. "What's your name?" he asked.

"April," I told him. "Danny April. What's yours?"

"Mike Manola," he told me.

"Does she have any relatives living?"

"No. Her old man was a crazy Pole who was living with some dago bag. He got killed out in the Gary mills a couple years after she disappeared. The old bag is still living at the same place, but there's no other family I know about."

"When was the last time you saw Krassy?"

"The day she won the beauty contest, here. She came to the office, collected her . . . prizes and left. I haven't heard of her since."

"She win some good prizes?" I asked.

He dropped his eyes to the counter and studied it a moment before replying. "Yeah," he said flatly, "she won some good prizes." He turned around and walked back to his desk.

He was through talking. I left the office. Down the street, I resisted the temptation to take another look at Krassy's picture. By now, I could see her face each time I closed my eyes.

Two

P A R T I I

Krassy Almauniski opened her eyes and stretched in her bed. She stiffened motionless for a moment before slowly relaxing again. "March seventeenth . . . St. Patrick's Day," she told herself with satisfaction, "my birthday!" She jumped from bed and walked across the bare floor to a small mirror which hung by a wire from a hook in the wall. She unbuttoned the faded man's silk shirt, which hung nearly to her knees, and pulled it over her head.

"Starting today," she told herself, "things are going to be different."

At seventeen, she had the figure of a mature woman. She had been that way since she was fourteen. Leaving the man's shirt on the floor, she slipped into her overcoat and tiptoed quietly into the hall. She heard the heavy turning of bodies in the next bedroom and then the rhythmic rattle of the bed. She stood motionless for a moment. "Oh, God!" she said softly, "they're at it again."

She hurried into the tiny, dirty toilet. Turning on a thin stream of water, to keep it quiet, she quickly washed her face and hands, hoping her father wouldn't hear her.

"He's busy," she told herself, "busy with Maria." She gathered her coat around her and sneaked silently back into her room. Her father and Maria were still rustling in the other bedroom.

Quickly she started dressing. As she shrugged into her cheap, pink rayon brassiere, she winced with pain from a large, red bruise on her breast. "Damn Mike Manola," she cursed, "goddamn him." But as she swore, she realized she must be careful with Mike, not make him sore, not make him angry enough to withdraw his support. She needed Mike Manola, even if it meant standing in dark doorways while he kissed and pawed her.

"You don't like me," Mike had accused her.

"Sure I like you, Mike," she'd replied.

"Then why don't you break down?" he asked.

"I like to kiss you. . . ."

"Kissing is kid stuff," Mike said and pulled her to him in the darkness. She had felt his hand working its way up the outside of her thigh, then across her stomach. In strained terror, mingled with a wild anticipation, she'd waited for his hand to continue moving . . . until it had cupped itself around her breast. In the blackness of the doorway, she'd felt Mike's body probing against her. Suddenly he bit down on her lip, and his hand tightened around her breast.

"Don't, Mike . . . don't . . . please." She tore her

mouth away from his and tried to separate their bodies. Mike had pulled away in the darkness, but his hand still grasped her breast.

"Why not, Krassy . . . why not?" Mike whispered breathlessly.

Suddenly the words spat from her mouth. "I can't stand it! I hate it . . . your hands make me sick!" Mike's fingers had clenched together, with a terrible anger, and she had screamed in pain. Then Mike had dropped his hand and turned out of the doorway. All the rest of the way home, her breast had throbbed with the fire of Mike's bruise.

Now completely dressed, Krassy slipped back into her coat and hurried toward the stairs. A creaking board shattered the stillness, and her father's voice stopped her.

"That you, Krassy?"

"Yes, Paw," she said.

"What you doing up so early?"

"I got to get to school early today," she said. "Besides this is my birthday and Mike Manola wanted me to meet him at the drugstore."

"You stay home for breakfast!"

"Mike wants to buy my breakfast, Paw," Krassy replied. "It's for my birthday!" Without waiting for his reply, she hurried down the stairs and into the street.

At Miller's Drugstore she found Mike sitting at the counter waiting for her, his face still sulky from the disappointment of the night before. Krassy climbed on the stool beside him and patted his arm. "It's swell of you to buy me a birthday breakfast," she told him.

"Yeah," he agreed, "I must be nuts. There're plenty

gals who'll give a guy a little break for being nice to 'em. Jesus! I must be outta my head."

"You help me win the beauty contest, and you won't be sorry, Mike," Krassy whispered with a promise heavy in her voice.

Mike was doubtful. "Is that a promise?" he asked surlily.

"Sure, it's a promise, Mike."

"Oh, sure . . . sure, just another come-on," said Mike. "The minute I start trying to love you up a little, I get all the thanks in the world!" His voice mimicked her " 'I can't stand you . . . yatty, yap!' "

"Not this time, Mike," she said. "And you'll be the very first boy who's ever touched me."

Mike heartened visibly. "Christ!" he said. "Well, how about breakfast . . . anything you want."

Krassy looked at his dark skin, with his arrogant nose, and white smile. "It won't be so bad," she told herself. "Anything will be better than what I got!"

"Come on, Krassy, order up," urged Mike.

Krassy ordered the Number One Breakfast, with tomato juice, two eggs, two strips of bacon, toast, marmalade, and coffee. It cost forty cents. Mike doubled the order.

After breakfast they caught the streetcar to the high school. On the way, Mike explained his strategy.

"This whole beauty contest is just an advertising promotion my old man dreamed up," he said. "It's just to help him sell more ads. He gets stores to give away prizes to the winner. For a couple of weeks he builds it up in his paper. He furnishes the stores with ballots and every customer gets one vote for every ten-cents worth of merchandise they buy. The customers vote for whoever they want as beauty queen. Then when it's all over, the stores buy more ads to congratulate the winner."

"I don't care," said Krassy, "I want to win it."

"Don't worry," said Mike, "you can't lose. My old man will make me count the ballots, because he's too damned busy to do it himself. I'll have all the extra ballots I need right at the office, so if you don't win when I count the votes . . . I'll fill out extra ballots until you do." Mike threw back his head and laughed. "It's a pushover!" And then more soberly, "But don't let my old man catch on. He'd murder me!"

"I think you're wonderful," said Krassy. She tucked her hand through his arm and pressed her hip slightly against him. She could see him start on the seat. Krassy smiled secretly. "Soon," she said, "soon. . . ."

After school, Krassy hurried home. Dunc Tingle walked part of the way from the car line with her.

"How about going to a show Saturday night?" he asked. Tingle was a tall, skinny boy with pinkish red hair, and tight, coal-black eyes.

"I can't, Dunc," said Krassy, "I got to see Mike."

"You going steady with Mike?"

"Sort of," admitted Krassy.

"You're going to end up back of the old eight ball with a guy like that," said Dunc.

"If I do it's none of your business," said Krassy and turned quickly away. But deep inside her, she was smiling. "I won't end up back of the eight ball with Mike . . . or any other man," she thought. "They're easy to handle if you know how. Why, look at Paw and Maria. Ever since Maria moved in, big and fat and sloppy, all Paw does is sit around that stinking kitchen drinking wine and getting charged up. Then he takes Maria to bed and makes love to her all night. Sex must be awful damned important to a man. That's all any man thinks about!

"With Mike helping me, I'm bound to win. Then I'll get out of here. I'll go away where nobody knows me or knows Paw . . . and I'm going to live right and dress right. Someday I won't have to take anything from anybody!"

Her mind skipped to her immediate problem on hand. "If I win this contest, I'll get a new dress and some new clothes. And I can get my hair done. Then I'll run away. But I'll need money." She considered it carefully. "I could get Mike to give me some dough," she thought, "but Mike won't have very much. I guess I'll have to figure out another way to get it. . . ."

She climbed the stairs to the high, little porch and let herself in the door. She could hear Maria moving around in the kitchen.

"Hello, Paw," she said, "aren't you working today?"

A tremendous figure of a man was hulked down over a sagging davenport. He lifted his head and regarded her bleakly. "Why in hell don't you stay home once in a while?" he asked. "Go on and help Maria."

"All right, Paw," she agreed meekly.

"All right!" he shouted in sudden anger. "Isa that what you tell alla boys chasing you . . . All right, Richard, all right, Victor, all right, Mr. Godalmighty!"

"You know I don't!"

"I don't know any sucha goddamned thing. All I know is you runa round . . . day and night . . . like any little bitch in heat. Now geta hell out and help Maria before I get sore!"

Krassy dropped her coat over a chair and walked out

into the kitchen where an old black iron range . . . stuffed with coal . . . was blazing angrily away. Maria in a sleazy kimono, and greasy felt bedroom slippers, was waiting patiently at a chipped and battered gray enamel sink. Water trickled slowly out of a tap into a large kettle she was holding.

"What're we having for supper?" asked Krassy.

"Spaghett," said Maria.

"Can't you cook anything besides spaghetti?" asked Krassy.

"Is good enough for peoples," said Maria.

"I'll be a son-of-a-bitch!" yelled her father from the couch, "ifa you're getting so damned fine for spaghetti you no have to eat!"

"I know it," said Krassy, "and I won't eat it much longer."

A week later, Krassy stopped at the *Stockyard Weekly News* to see Mike. Mike wasn't in, but Caesar Manola, Mike's father, was there. Caesar Manola was a worried man in his early forties. With an invalid wife, slowly dying of tuberculosis, he struggled to earn a living with his small weekly paper. The bloody stench of the stockyards district spelled poverty to Caesar Manola and most of the men living under its stinking mantle.

In one of the world's squalid districts, Manola wrote his pathetic news items concerning the nonentities of his neighborhood, sold advertisements to merchants with one foot constantly in bankruptcy, set type for his paper, and ran the rattling flatbed press in which it was printed. On Saturdays when the paper was distributed, small boys of black, coffee and cream, yellow, and white delivered it house to house for ten cents an hour.

Manola had seen little beauty in his life, less pleasure,

and no hope. He sat in his office typing bills to his advertisers. Krassy Almauniski walked up to the counter and asked for Mike.

"Mike isn't here," Caesar told her.

"Will he be back soon?"

"Fifteen or twenty minutes . . . want to wait for him?"

Krassy smiled at Caesar. "Not particularly. I just wondered how the votes are coming?"

"Are you entered in the contest?" he asked.

"Yes," she replied. "I'm Krassy Almauniski."

Caesar nodded. "I've seen your name. I think you are right up there. Come on in and sit down. Ask Mike when he gets back, he's counting the votes."

Krassy walked through the little swinging gate toward Caesar's desk. The big table was littered with galley proofs, library copies, and general debris. Krassy perched on the corner of Caesar's desk and smiled down at him. "I've heard a lot of nice things about you," she told him.

He smiled back. "Who from . . . Mike?"

"Oh no," she said, "I hardly know Mike. I've seen him around once or twice, that's all. I'm lots older than Mike. . . ." She paused, then continued, "I know I look young, but I'm really twenty-one." She gracefully swung her weight from one hip to the other.

Manola was suddenly conscious of the way her thigh swelled against his desk. He tried to push the thought away. "It's hard to tell a woman's age. The old ones try to look young, and the young ones try to look old. . . . You know, it's funny, though, I haven't seen you around."

"I graduated from high school four years ago," said

Krassy, "and I've been working in Michigan City until a couple weeks ago. I just came back."

"Ohhh," said Manola. He glanced up quickly, and in her vantage point above him he could see the soft sweep of the underpart of her leg.

"I'm surprised, though. . . ." Krassy continued.

"Surprised?" echoed Manola, forcibly moving his eyes away.

"Yes," said Krassy, "I'm surprised that the paper isn't offering a prize, too."

"The paper only sponsors the contest," Manola explained. "The different merchants give the prizes."

"I know that," replied Krassy, "but I think it would be swell if the paper gave a cash prize, too. It would make the whole contest seem so much more . . . important."

Manola shook his head. "No chance," he said. Krassy looking down on him thought he looked old and tired.

"Well," she said, "I must be running along. . . ."

"I'll tell Mike you were in," said Caesar.

"Don't bother," said Krassy, "he probably wouldn't know who you meant."

Caesar hesitated for a moment, then he asked, "Are you going to be around tonight?"

"I guess so, why?"

"If you want to stop back here around nine, I'll buy you a drink."

Krassy shook her head. "I don't think it looks good, me being in the contest and everything, stopping in your office so much."

"You could meet me someplace else," said Manola.

"Where?"

"How about Dixie's?"

Krassy had heard of Dixie's . . . a neighborhood bistro of local repute, but she had never been there. She turned his suggestion over in her mind, considering it carefully. As a rendezvous, she thought it might indicate that Manola didn't want to be seen with her publicly, because he was married. And as far as she was concerned, the suggestion of Dixie's pleased her because she had little fear of running into her own contemporaries.

"All right," she said, "I'll meet you at Dixie's at nine." She stretched herself down from the desk and walked to the door, feeling Manola's eyes following her. "See you now," she said and left the office.

After dinner, that night, she hurried to her room and changed into her good dress. Slipping on her overcoat, she stuffed a cheap costume necklace, rouge, and lipstick in her pocket. Beneath the coat, she hid a pair of high-heeled shoes. Then walking calmly downstairs, she made her way serenely to the living room door.

"Where you going?" asked Anton Almauniski.

"To a movie with some of the kids," she replied.

Almauniski eyed her suspiciously but could see nothing wrong. She was without make-up and wearing saddle shoes.

"All time you run around . . . going . . . going . . . going," he said. "Someday you be sorry."

"She go out with man," said Maria suddenly and with decision.

"You keep out of this," cried Krassy and turned on her in fury. "You don't talk enough English to know what the hell we're talking about!"

Almauniski rose from his chair and raised his fist. Krassy dodged around him and opened the door. "I'm going to a movie with some kids," she repeated. "I don't care whether you believe it or not!" She slammed the door and ran down the steps. On the sidewalk she continued running for a block, gradually slowing her pace as the distance lengthened from her home.

Three blocks farther on she stopped in an oil station and went into the women's toilet. She carefully washed her face and hands with warm water and dried them on paper towels. Taking out her rouge and lipstick, she did an expert job of make-up before the mirror bolted above the washbowl. She kicked off her saddle shoes and slipped into her high heels. Finally, she clasped the cheap brass necklace around her throat. "Nobody who didn't know me wouldn't guess I wasn't twenty-one," she told herself with pride.

Picking up her saddle shoes, she went to the front of the station. "Can I leave these shoes here tonight?" she asked the attendant. "I'll pick them up in the morning."

"Sure," said the attendant, "you can park your shoes with me any time you feel like it." He grinned broadly.

Krassy smiled back at him. "Thanks," she told him, "you're nice." She walked down to the corner and caught a streetcar. Ten blocks later, she got off in front of Dixie's. She was nearly half an hour early, so she started walking slowly up the block looking in the tired shop windows.

"Someday," she thought, "I'll walk into Saks and buy anything I want without even asking the price. I'll buy anything I want and nobody will have to give me the money. I'll have all the money I need!" She stopped in front of a secondhand dress shop and considered the clothes on wire hangers in the window. "And I'll know what to buy . . . and how to buy it," she added.

At nine o'clock Caesar Manola drove up to Dixie's in

a 1932 Pontiac. Originally a sedan, it had worked its
way down in the automobile world until only the front
half of the body remained. The rear of the body had
been sawed off, and reconverted into a small truck. Manola used it to haul papers, and as a pickup truck for
supplies in his business. He saw Krassy waiting for him
under the muddy red neon sign which alternately spelled
DIXIE'S and BEER.

"Waiting long?" he asked as he got out.

"No," lied Krassy, "I just got here." They entered the
tavern and stepped into a dimly lit room rank with the
sour smell of beer. A long bar ran down one entire side
of the room, and it was crowded with men and women
perching on stools. Back of the bar was a narrow,
frosted mirror, with bottles arranged in military rows on
glass shelves in front of it. An occasional orange-colored
bulb gave enough light for the bartenders to work by,
but kept the customers from easily reading the labels on
the bottles.

Manola led Krassy past the tiny tables which jammed
the center of the room, and worked his way toward the
back where booths, upholstered in imitation red leather,
hugged the walls. Finding a vacant one, he guided
Krassy into the booth, and sat down beside her. A weary
waitress slogged a wet cloth across the table top and
waited impatiently for their order. "What'll yuh have?"
she asked.

"I'll have a whisky Coke," said Krassy. On several
notable occasions, she had sipped a few swallows from
bottles of Coke spiked with whisky. She didn't like it,
but it was the only drink she was familiar with. She
ordered it now.

"You mean a Cuba Libre?" asked the waitress.

Krassy didn't know if she meant a Cuba Libre or not. "Yes," she said with dignity, "that'll do."

Caesar Manola ordered a double bourbon with plain water. When Krassy's drink arrived, she tasted it. "This is just a whisky Coke after all," she exclaimed, "with some lime in it!" Manola looked at her in surprise.

"Don't you drink?" he asked.

"Oh, sure," said Krassy. She didn't explain further.

By eleven o'clock, Manola was getting drunk. Krassy had finished two Cuba Libres and had managed to spill two others, but she, too, was feeling the liquor. "I can think all right," she told herself, "but it's getting hard to talk." Then she became conscious of Manola's hand on her knee. He wasn't squeezing; he wasn't exploring; his hand was resting there . . . waiting. Krassy snuggled her leg against his for a brief moment, then withdrew it. Under the table, his hand moved quickly up her leg and around her waist.

"I like you, Krassy," he said.

"I like you, too, Caesar," she said, "but . . ." Her voice trailed off.

"But what?" he wanted to know.

"You'll get sore if I tell you."

"I won't get sore," Manola promised solemnly.

"Well, I still don't know why you won't give a nice cash prize to the contest winner," Krassy said defiantly.

"If you win, maybe I will give a prize," said Manola.

"Oh, Caesar!" cried Krassy. "You will?"

"Maybe," he said. "Maybe I'd give a prize if you'd be nice to me."

Krassy caught her breath. "Don't say that, Caesar," she said, "it sounds like . . . well, you're trying to buy me."

"Perhaps I am," said Manola soberly. "I'm not kidding myself, Krassy. That's the only way I'd ever get you. I don't have any money. I'm nearly broke." He stopped and finished his drink before continuing. "But if you'd be my girl friend . . . I'd do damned near anything for you." His left arm tightened around her waist. Krassy held her breath and sat perfectly still. "How much of a cash prize do you think I should offer . . . just in case you won?" he asked. His fingers brushed lightly over her breast.

"One hundred dollars!" Krassy said with quick decision.

Manola withdrew his hand. Wearily he ordered another drink.

When they left Dixie's, Manola drove Krassy straight home, letting her off near the corner by her house. As Krassy climbed out of the ancient truck, Manola looked down at her and said, "I'll see what I can do about that prize." Krassy stood straight and beautiful in the light of the street lamp. She turned a serene face up toward Manola.

"You're sweet, Caesar," she said, "I'm sure you'll never regret it."

The following day Manola drove the old Pontiac into Luke's Honest Used-Car Lot. Luke, a dapper sleek man, with prominent front teeth, walked out of a small wooden shack which was located on the lot and served as his office. A number of sagging, motorized vehicles variously identifiable as 1928 Oaklands, Model A Fords, and assorted Chevies up to 1935 stood like tired, worn, worked-out nags at invisible hitching posts. The pride of the lot, a 1940 Buick stood glistening in glory, on a small, plank platform near the street. Luke tried to sell it during the day, and drove it for his personal use at night. Luke walked up to Caesar Manola and picked up the end of former conversations.

"Christ, Manola," he said, "I been thinking it over and I still can't do no better."

"Okay, Luke," said Manola, "I'll take the seventy-five bucks."

Luke ignored this sudden acceptance of his terms. "Hell, there ain't no calls for cars today. They're a drug on the market. You think 1938 was bad . . . let me tell you, Manola, this is a hell of a lot worse. I can't sell the ones I got. . . ."

Fear that Luke might not buy the car grabbed Manola in the stomach. "You offered seventy-five for it last week," he said.

"Sure," said Luke. "I know you and the Missus need the dough."

"Okay, okay," said Manola in relief.

"So I'll take it anyway . . . mostly to help you out." Luke looked piously at his dirty fingernails. "How is your old lady anyway?"

"About the same," said Manola.

"Hell, guy, with this dough you can have her lung collapsed and maybe that'll help her, huh?"

"Yes," said Manola.

"Those fat doctors are all sons-of-bitches," said Luke, "you'd think they was all little Jesus Christs in white coats. But they won't do nothing if you don't have some of that old dough to pass around regular . . . believe me!"

"Some of them are all right," said Manola.

"They told you cutting that lung out would help, huh?" asked Luke.

"They thought it'd help," hedged Manola carefully.

"Okay, so come in the office and I'll give you the dough," said Luke as he headed back toward the wooden shack. "Don't forget to bring your transfer paper and title with you," he called over his shoulder.

Caesar Manola climbed out of the old Pontiac and without a word followed Luke into his office. There, Luke paid him seventy-five dollars in fives and tens. Manola walked all the way back to his newspaper office.

On March 29, two days before the contest winner was to be announced in the paper, Mike arranged with Krassy to appear at the *Stockyard Weekly News* office for her official notification of winning the event. When Krassy entered the office, Mike met her at the door. Caesar Manola was seated at his desk.

"You're Mike Manola?" Krassy asked.

"Yeah," said Mike, "your face looks familiar." He winked at her and rolled his eyes toward his father seated behind him.

"I'm Krassy Almauniski," she replied. "I received a card that you wanted to see me."

"Oh, sure!" said Mike. "I want to be the first to congratulate you. You've been elected the winner of the *Weekly News* Beauty Contest." He kept a very straight face as he turned toward his father. "This is Krassy Almauniski, the winner of our contest," he said.

"How do you do, Miss Almauniski," said Caesar Manola. "Congratulations. I also got additional good news for you . . . the paper is offering a cash prize of a hundred dollars."

Mike Manola's mouth dropped open. He stared at his father in amazement. "A hundred bucks?" he asked.

"Yes," said the older Manola, "it's a good promotion for the paper!" He didn't look at Mike.

"Thank you, Mr. Manola," said Krassy, her heart singing with excitement, "I really don't know what to say. . . ."

Mike recovered sufficiently to turn to Krassy and resume business. "Miss Almauniski, we want to take a picture of you tomorrow, so this afternoon if you'll see the merchants who sponsored this contest, they'll give you your prizes. We got to take your picture tomorrow in time for our next edition."

Krassy left the *Weekly News* office triumphantly. "A hundred dollars," she told herself, "a hundred dollars . . . and new clothes. Soon I'll be out . . . I'll get away and never see the yards again!" She hurried to Solomon's Dress Shoppe, featuring dresses from $2.98 to $14.98, and lady's suits from $12.50 to $27.50. David Solomon regarded her sourly as she announced the reason for her visit.

"Maybe you should like a nice little house dress, yes?"

"No," said Krassy, "I want a suit."

"And I suppose for nothing you want I should give you my best $27.50 fitted suit which is an actual bargain if I was asking twice that much?"

"Yes," said Krassy.

Solomon was not impressed with such directness. Among his customers he was used to it. But half an hour later, Krassy walked from his shop with a new, black suit. Her only concession to Solomon's ranting, was that she would make such alterations as were necessary.

At Edna Mae's Thrifty Shoppers Mart, she finally selected a plain little hat, with a half-veil. It cost $2.65 and she selected it with the idea of adding as many years to her appearance as possible. Edna Mae, a large friendly woman, entered into Krassy's selections with warmth and as much good advice as it was possible for her to give concerning her shoddy merchandise. Krassy finally selected a $17.50 (the highest price range) beige coat, with black trimming around the pockets.

Quickly, Krassy picked out an imitation leather suitcase fitted with imitation ivory comb and brush, three cosmetic bottles, and a small round celluloid box for powder from Browser's Trunk and Leather Company. Wearing her new hat and coat, with her new suit packed in the suitcase, she stopped at the office of the Red-Top Taxi Company and received $5.00 worth of cab coupons. Using the phone in the Red-Top office, she arranged with the Deep Well Brewing Company to deliver the case of beer at her home.

Then she went to the Glamour Beauty Salon for her permanent and manicure. It was after six when she left the beauty shop, her hair stiff from the treatment, and hurried home.

Slowly she climbed the stairs and opened the door. Anton roared across the room at her, "It's time you got home, goddamnit!"

He and Maria were sitting in the living room, the case of beer in the middle of the floor. The case was nearly empty and the discarded bottles were littered around the room. Anton had stripped off his shirt, and his great chest and arms glistened under the light of the solitary bulb which hung on a wire from the center of the ceiling. He had loosened his belt and unbuttoned the front of his trousers.

Maria sat upright in the middle of the sagging davenport, her eyes flat and black behind half-closed lids. She was half out of the thin cotton dress which covered her widening body.

"I won the contest," said Krassy, "I've been collecting my prizes."

"You ain't good enough to win no prizes," said Anton. "You're lying!"

"She sleep with man," said Maria.

"You dirty dago," said Krassy. "What about you? You're not married to Paw!"

Maria made a high, whining sound and leaped from the davenport, with her hands outstretched before her. Krassy grasped an empty beer bottle at her feet and stood her ground. As Maria rushed by Anton he swung his huge fist, catching her in the side, and knocked her across the room. Maria smashed against the wall and crumpled slowly to the floor. Anton arose to his feet and shuffled toward Krassy.

"If you been out whoring I kill you," he said.

Krassy fled upstairs to her room. Anton sank unsteadily at the round oak table in the living room and rested his forehead against the edge. "Goddamn everything," he said in a choking voice.

The next afternoon Krassy didn't go to school. She returned home at noon, while Anton and Maria were both away, put on her new clothes and packed her few belongings in her new leather bag. Then in her high heels, she walked to the closest store and ordered a cab. On the way to the *Weekly News* office, she stopped at the beauty salon and asked permission to leave her suitcase. From the beauty salon she went to the newspaper office.

Caesar Manola was seated at his desk when she entered; no one else was in the office. "God, Krassy, you look beautiful!" he told her.

Krassy slowly pivoted around so he could admire her. "Do I look all right?" she asked.

"You look wonderful," Manola assured her.

"Where's Mike?" asked Krassy. "He said he wanted to take my picture for the paper."

Manola laughed. "I sent Mike down to the Loop on an errand," he said. "I told him I'd take your picture in case he didn't get back." Manola chuckled. "Today, where I sent him, I don't plan for him to get back," he added.

"No?"

"No," said Manola. "Today I plan to give you that hundred bucks!" He rose from his desk and picked up a small camera. "Come on outside. I'll take your picture now."

Krassy followed Manola out to the sidewalk. Squinting toward the sun, Manola posed her against the front of the building and took several shots. Then he took her arm and led her into the office again. He placed the camera on his desk, and picked up an envelope lying there.

"Here's your hundred dollars," he said.

Krassy took the envelope, avoiding his eyes, and put it in her purse. "Thanks, Caesar," she said, "thanks . . . a lot."

"Let's go upstairs," said Caesar.

"What's upstairs?" asked Krassy.

"I keep a room upstairs," he explained. "Sometimes I work here most of the night, so I sleep up there once in a while. Come on, Krassy. . . ." He took her hand and gently urged her toward the back of the shop.

Krassy permitted herself to be led in silence. She followed him back of the thin partition where the small flatbed press was standing. A narrow door opened to a steep flight of unfinished wooden steps ascending to a dark hall on the floor above. Following Manola up the stairs, she thought, "This can't be happening to me . . . this isn't true. I never really believed he'd give me a hundred dollars . . . I don't want him to touch me." She paused in the grimy hall while Caesar Manola opened the door to a room.

In the backwash of her panic, a cold voice of reason whispered softly, "Don't kid yourself . . . this is what you've been waiting for . . . you planned this . . . you *knew* it would happen. You've taken his money, now pay him off! Then you're free, Krassy! You'll be free of Maria and the old man, you'll be free of Caesar and Mike, and the Yards . . . and Hempstead . . . and . . ."

"Here we are," said Manola and stood aside to let her enter. Krassy stepped into a narrow little room containing an army cot covered with a khaki blanket. By the cot was an old kitchen chair . . . once painted red. A mirror, with distorting streaks, in a heavy wood frame, hung on the wall. Caesar walked across the bare floor and half lowered the shredded, rotting brown shade at the window. Then he turned to Krassy and put his arms around her.

"Sit here on the bed beside me," he told her and she followed his order mechanically. Quietly she lifted her hands to her head and removed the new hat. Caesar leaned over her and kissed her on the lips, the weight of his body gently forcing her down on the cot. Stretching on the cot, beside her, he placed his lips on her neck just beneath her ear.

"Listen to me, Krassy," he whispered, "listen to me for just a moment. Stay with me . . . be with me . . . never leave me. I love you, Krassy. I'd do anything to make you happy. I feel young again. For the first time in years . . . I have hope and ambition and dreams. The Yards aren't important any more. We'll go away . . . someplace . . . together. I can get a job. . . ." He paused for a second. "You do love me a little, don't you, Krassy?" he asked softly.

Krassy turned her head on the pillow and nodded silently. "Mother of God," she prayed to herself, "make him stop . . . make him keep quiet. Make him get it over with. . . ."

"Kiss me, Krassy," Manola urged. She felt his hands working at her blouse, gentle hands that didn't hurt. "You'd better take off your new suit," he whispered, "if you don't it'll get mussed." She was half conscious of his hands helping her to slide the jacket from around her shoulders, and she arched her back while he slipped her skirt down over her hips. The walls of the room pulsed and throbbed, moving in slowly around her, while the low ceiling moved higher and higher . . . pulling away . . . until it looked like something viewed through the small end of a telescope. Then the ceiling was blotted out by the shoulders and head of Manola.

She steeled her mind into a blankness, unfeeling and unseeing. She existed in an empty space for an eon of tortured time.

Then feeling Manola's body flung away from her, she was jerked back into consciousness, with a far screaming in her ears. In terror she raised her shoulders from the cot and saw Mike Manola standing over Caesar lying on the floor. Mike was kicking his father in the head.

"You bastard! You dirty, no-good-son-of-a-bitching-bastard!" Mike was screaming in a high, thin voice and tears were streaming down his face. "My girl . . . she's my girl. . . ." He choked on his sobs.

Caesar Manola grasped Mike's foot, and twisting it suddenly flung him against the cot where he half sprawled over Krassy. Caesar pulled himself to his feet as Mike charged at him, showering him wildly with blows. Caesar Manola swung a tremendous blow, in a wide looping arc, that landed solidly on his son's nose.

Krassy heard the bones crack . . . a sound like someone stepping on a matchbox.

Mike fell to the floor, blood pouring from his nose and mouth in a spurting, crimson stream. His screaming was stilled. While Caesar dropped to his knees by his son's side and tried to stop the red, gushing torrent, Krassy gathered together her clothes, and, unnoticed, quietly slipped away.

Downstairs, she dressed hurriedly in the pressroom, her mind cold, numb, and detached. When she finished dressing, she picked up her purse and walked to the Glamour Beauty Salon. There she recovered her suitcase. Then calling a Red-Top cab, she rode away. Krassy never returned to the Yards again.

A month later, Mrs. Manola died.

Two hours after she died, Caesar Manola committed suicide. Because of the Church, they weren't buried together.

A week after that, Mike Manola returned to Chicago and took possession of the *Stockyard Weekly News*.

THREE

P A R T   I

I went back down to the Loop, after talking
to Manola, determined to forget all about Krassy Almauniski. After all, nobody had seen her for ten years.
She'd probably left town, gotten married, or died.

And furthermore, what the hell difference did it make
to me?

At least that's what I kept telling myself. I wrote letters at the office, called on a few habitual deadbeats, and
pried out a few collections here and there. With the rest
of my time, I called on some new accounts and tried to
sell them the idea of letting the Clarence Moon Collection Agency handle their business. I lined up some new
business that way, and things were looking up a little
bit. During the day I was busier than the devil.

But at night it was different. I'd go to bed, and in an
hour or two I'd wake up and then I couldn't go back to

sleep. I'd try to squeeze all thoughts out of my mind
. . . with a sort of mental rubber squeegee . . . but I
could never quite do it. Little by little, I'd get around to
thinking about Krassy. First her face would start to
form, all indistinct and hazy, then it'd become clear and
beautiful and the next minute she'd be sitting in the
room with me.

I'd think up all the smart cracks I could think of, and
feed them into the conversation like a real comedian. I'd
hear her laugh chime out . . . and I was a hell of a big
guy, all right.

But it wasn't good enough. Because always in the
back of my mind was the question: "Where is she now?"
She could be anywhere in this world, or this continent,
or this country, or this state, or this county, or this
town. And if she was in Chicago? Well, there're over five
million persons in this area; somewhere in that milling
mess might be Krassy. After ten years, she'd be around
twenty-seven years old. That was all I knew.

But I've done a lot of skip-tracing. Enough to know
that most people follow a pretty definite pattern all their
life . . . even if they're taking a powder. So, I'd hunch
the pillow up high under my head, light a cigarette, and
lie there in the dark trying to figure out the next move
Krassy made when she left the Yards. At that time she
was around seventeen, had a new suitcase, a suit, coat,
and hat . . . and one hundred bucks. With that much
dope, it might just be possible to pick up the end of the
string . . . some place. But where?

That hundred bucks Krassy had was probably more
dough than she'd ever knew existed in the world. But
being broke all her life could do one of two things to
her. She'd either blow it fast or try to hang on to it, just

like a terrier. There was something about Krassy's picture that made me think maybe she'd hang on to it. So, if she was trying to hang on to it, she probably wouldn't have busted off for New York or Los Angeles or someplace in between. She'd probably stay here in Chicago . . . at least for a while.

But she couldn't live on a hundred bucks forever; so she'd have to get a job. What kind of a job? She hadn't any experience I knew of, so she'd have to end up clerking or waiting on tables. But then I remembered how beautiful she was, and I knew that she certainly must know it herself. At least to some extent. So why shouldn't she try to cash in on her good looks? Show business? Show business was obvious.

I felt pretty good that I'd followed the string that far. But the more I thought about it, the less satisfied I was to let it stand at that. Chicago isn't a good show business town. Damn few shows ever originate in Chicago. Most of them start in New York. She might have made the grade in one of the big nightclubs or hotels, but she'd have to know how to sing or dance even for that. I didn't know if Krassy could do either, but remembering that old termite trap where she'd lived . . . I doubted there was enough dough for dancing lessons. Before dropping the idea entirely, I decided I'd talk to Abe Blossom, a guy I knew. In the collection business, you don't make much dough, but you sure make plenty of contacts. Abe had been a theatrical booker for twenty-five years, and once I'd tried to collect some dough from him. It had been impossible. While I was trying to twist his arm, we'd sort of become friendly. I figured Abe might recognize her picture.

Abe's got an office in the Woods Building, and I went

in to see him. He's a square, stocky little guy who always dresses in gray. He wears light gray suits, with a gray, hand-painted tie, and gray suede shoes. He has a bright red face, tucked under a stiff mat of gray hair, and his cigars are big, long, and black.

"Greetings, Danny," he said. "Draw up a stump and let your muscles sag."

"Hi, Abe," I said, "how's business?"

Abe shrugged his shoulders. "All the joints where they got gambling, business is good and I can sell acts. All the joints where they ain't got gambling, I can't sell nothing. So they put the heat on the casinos, and nobody makes nothing including my acts of which I get ten percent . . . of nothing."

"That's tough," I said.

"Don't let it bother you, man," said Abe, "it's been going on for years."

"Look," I said, "maybe you can do me a favor. Have you ever seen this gal?" I pulled out the clipping with Krassy's picture and handed it to him.

Abe looked at it carefully and slowly whistled. "She's quite a dish," he said.

"Yeah," I agreed, "she is."

"What's her name?"

"Krassy Almauniski," I said, "but maybe she changed it."

"Jesus! With a handle like that she'd have to change it," Abe told me. "Is she in show business?"

"I don't know," I said. "I got a hunch maybe she was."

Abe handed the clipping back to me. "I don't know nobody by that name," he said, "and I don't ever remember seeing her around." That don't mean she wasn't around, but if Abe don't remember her . . . it means she sure as hell didn't make the grade around here.

I put the clipping back in my pocket. "Abe," I said, "if you were a babe with looks like that and didn't have any training in anything . . . and had to make a living . . . what'd you do?"

"I'd get in show business," Abe said promptly.

"We just got through hashing that over," I said. "What else would you do?"

Abe spit the soggy end of his cigar into a bright, brass spittoon by the side of his desk. "Maybe I'd go into modeling," he said. "A lot of dames with no talent but plenty of looks make a good living out of having their pictures taken. Maybe I'd try that."

I hadn't thought about Krassy being a model, but the more I kicked the idea around, the better I liked it. I thanked Abe and left.

First, I had some basic stuff that had to be done. I went to the main office of the telephone company, and went through all the old Chicago and suburban directories for the last ten years. Krassy had never been listed in any of them. Next I tried the gas and light companies. A clerk told me, in both places, she'd never been a subscriber to either service. The address on Clarence Moon's old data card had been her original home address, but it was obvious that Moon had contacted her someplace else. Where? I didn't know.

The merchandise which she'd originally charged was listed by items, but didn't give the merchant who'd sold it. I cussed old Moon for his sloppiness.

Finally, I went to the Retail Credit Bureau, and being in the collection business, they gave me all the help they could, which was nothing. They had no record of a Krassy Almauniski.

Then suddenly it made sense. What Abe said about her having to change her name was true. Krassy had changed her name. But, now, what the hell was it?

I didn't know her new name, but I'd give anybody eight, five, and even that her initials remained the same "K.A." For some damned reason, most people keep their same initials when they change their names. Maybe it's easier to remember, or maybe it's like the small boy who got a new boomerang for Christmas. He had a hell of a time throwing the old one away.

Looking for a gal with the initials "K.A." wasn't too much of a help, but it did help a little. At least I'd made up my mind I'd never find a girl by the name of Krassy Almauniski.

This much I had to go on: she was around 17, in 1940; she was blonde and beautiful; her initials were K.A.; and I had a picture of her. So with that dope, and my clipping, I started making the rounds of the model bureaus in Chicago. By comparing the present lists to the ones doing business ten years ago, I narrowed my calls down to around twenty-five.

The first seventeen were disappointing. I walked the pavements, climbed stairs, and rode in elevators. Most of the office girls in the bureaus had only been in their jobs a year or two. Checking the records of their models ten years back, with initials of "K.A.," didn't dig up anything.

But one other thing popped out of all this poking around. Krassy had never worked as a photographic model either in Chicago or any other major city. No one recognized her picture, which wouldn't be true if she'd appeared very much nationally in magazines and papers.

On my eighteenth call, though, I struck pay dirt. It was at Monica Morton's Model Bureau and School. Monica Morton was a distinguished looking dame in her middle forties, with solid-silver hair and a well-preserved figure. She went to some lengths to inform me that once, *some* years back, she'd been a Conover model. I stood around the desk in her reception room, and polished up a couple nice apples for her. She ended up by calling me Danny and digging into her files.

She came back with a couple glossy print photographs and a small index file card. "You're sure I'm not going to get this girl in trouble giving you this information?" she asked me.

"Naw, Miss Morton," I assured her, "you'll be doing her a favor." I repeated the old gag about the refund on the insurance policy.

She handed the photos and card to me. It was Krassy all right. But the card was made out for "Katherine Andrews." It gave her age as 20, height 5 feet 7 inches, bust 35, waist 24, hips 34; hair blond, eyes gray, home address Hannibal, Missouri; Chicago address on East Banks Street. Krassy had already started to hide herself in the city.

I looked at the photographs and caught my breath. That same lovely face, with the calm, serene eyes, looked back at me. The heavily braided hair had been replaced with a long, glistening page-boy that hung, gilded, to her shoulders. Her lips had that same quiet, proud smile that I'd learned by heart from the newspaper clipping.

"I'll be glad to pay you for one of these photos," I told Miss Morton.

"That's all right, Danny," she said, "we have an extra copy, so you can take one. We always take shots of our graduates and keep them in our reference files."

"When did you see Kras—I mean Katherine Andrews last?" I asked.

"Years, simply years ago," Monica Morton replied. "I don't think she's been back since she finished her course."

"She took a course from you, huh?"

"Oh, yes," said Miss Morton and glanced at a series of small symbols which had been written on the side of the card. "She took our most expensive modeling course. In those days it cost $250; today it costs twice that much."

"What do you teach?" I asked. "How to walk around?"

Monica Morton gave me a sympathetic smile. "Modeling as a successful career requires much more than that," and she took off into a well-rehearsed sales talk. I listened. And when she was through, I understood that Krassy had studied professional make-up, hair styling, voice modulation, diction, how to dress, social and professional etiquette, conversational English; how to use her hands and feet, how to walk and how to sit, and . . . as far as I could make out . . . even a little dramatic acting.

"Was she good at all this stuff?" I asked Monica Morton.

"As I remember her, she was an excellent student," she told me. "She was one of the most beautiful girls I've ever seen, and she photographed marvelously . . . simply marvelously. She was very serious and studied hard. We were all surprised when she graduated and then never followed through on her training."

"You mean she never worked as a model?"

"Exactly," replied Miss Morton. "After graduation, she simply never came back. She took the six-month course which requires ten hours a week. After she completed it, she simply disappeared. We wrote her several times when jobs came up, at her address at East Banks Street, but the letters were returned to us. I guess perhaps she left town."

When I left Miss Morton, I took Krassy's picture with me and grabbed a bus up Michigan Boulevard to East Banks Street. East Banks is a short, narrow little street on Chicago's Near North Side. It only runs a few short blocks in from the lake. Mostly it is filled with rooming houses which've been converted over from the old, original mansions which lined the street.

The house where Krassy had lived was on a corner. It was an old, brownstone house, four stories tall, with a high tower climbing up the front and sticking out a full story above the roof. The top of the tower had battlements like an old castle turret. Whoever had originally built the house spent a hell of a lot of dough on it. I've seen a lot of post office buildings which weren't as big as that house was.

I climbed the stairs and pushed a button by the side of the double front door. The doors were twice as high as I am, and the upper part of them was etched in frosted glass. The design whirled around into shocks of wheat, flying doves, and intertwining ribbons. One thing, though, you couldn't see through them.

The door was opened by a tall, horse-faced woman

with artificial-blond hair which needed a retouch job plenty bad. She was wearing a plain brown suit, and had heavy, horn-rimmed glasses. The frames had red brilliants set in deep. I asked for the landlady, and she told me I was talking to her.

Introducing myself, I pulled out a picture of Krassy and said I was trying to locate a Miss Katherine Andrews who'd lived there in 1940. The landlady said her name was Miss Dukes and would I please come in.

I walked into a tremendous hall which was practically bare. There was a clothes tree, umbrella rack, and old hand-carved table with a phone on it. The floor had all kinds of curlicue patterns made from blocks of different colored wood inlaid in it. In the middle of the floor was a small, round, nondescript rug. Miss Dukes led the way into the parlor which was another cozy room, slightly smaller than the Notre Dame gymnasium, with tall bay windows stretching from the floor to the ceiling. The room was furnished with creaking davenports, golden oak tables, and overstuffed chairs from the 1920's, and sported a fireplace. The fireplace was finished with little pink, glazed tiles . . . about the same color as a ready-made birthday cake. Over the fireplace was a big, blown-up photograph of Miss Dukes. It was good. Miss Dukes looked fifteen years younger, and those fifteen years made a lot of difference.

I gave Miss Dukes the old story about the insurance policy and she said yes, she'd known Katherine Andrews, who'd lived there for six or seven months in 1940.

"Did Miss Andrews leave a forwarding address when she left?" I asked.

"No," said Miss Dukes, "she didn't."

"You mean she just packed up and left?" I asked.

"Yes," replied the landlady, "she left one day with her suitcase."

"Did she owe you any dough?"

"No," said Miss Dukes, "she didn't."

"Do you have any idea why she might've left?"

"Yes, I do!" she said. Suddenly the bars were down and with fury in her voice she continued, "She probably knew her fiancé was going to be arrested. She didn't have the guts to stand by him!"

Her answer stopped me for a minute. So Krassy had been engaged! But if Krassy was engaged and in love with a guy, I couldn't believe she'd ever desert him. Particularly when the chips were down.

"Who was she engaged to?" I asked.

"A young man who lived here," Miss Dukes answered. "A fine young man. His name was Larry Buckham. He was a newspaper photographer and worked for the *Daily Register*. He took that picture of me . . . up there," she nodded at the huge blow-up above the mantel.

"Where did Miss Andrews work while she was here?" I asked.

"She didn't," answered Miss Dukes sourly. "Her folks lived in Minneapolis and sent her money."

Again the old cover-up. Krassy was filling in all her tracks. Why? "What happened to Buckham?"

"After he was arrested, the police held him for a day or two, and then let him go. He was fired from the paper."

"Didn't he come back for his stuff?"

"What stuff? The police took everything."

"Why'd they arrest him?"

"I'm sure I don't know," said Miss Dukes. I could tell from the sudden tightening of her mouth that she was through talking. Maybe she didn't want to talk any more, maybe she didn't know any more. Anyway, I got up and thanked her. She didn't walk to the door with me. She just sat on the faded old davenport and looked at her picture over the mantel. I let myself out.

The next day I went over to the *Daily Register* office. It was a lousy day, too. It was raining and the wet streets in the Loop splashed muddy water, all mixed with oil, every time a car went by. I felt depressed as hell and was just about ready to give up trying to trace Krassy. There didn't seem to be any percentage for me even if I did find her. But something, inside, kept urging me to find out about Larry Buckham and what happened to him. "Just find out about Buckham," I told myself, "then wipe your nose and keep it clean. Krassy doesn't mean a thing to you. She doesn't even know you're alive."

The picture editor, at the *Register*, was a guy named Bob Berry. He'd lost most of his hair, but what remained he carefully parted in the middle and brushed it out, fanlike, to cover the biggest possible area. The day I saw him, he'd been to a dentist. He had a little trouble talking because he was having two front teeth put in with a bridge. The dentist hadn't finished and all I could think of was that song about "all I want for Christmas is my two front teeth." So Berry whistled on his "w's" and nearly spit in my eye on his "p's." It turned out Berry had been working on the *Register* when Buckham was canned, although he hadn't been the picture editor then.

"Christ, fellow," he said, "that's a long time back. I remember Buckham all right, but I don't remember too much about the details. He was picked up by the larceny detail for something or other, and he made some kind of a settlement with them. They let him go, but the paper canned him. There weren't any stories on it that I remember."

"How's that?" I asked.

"I don't think he was booked, in the first place; and in the second place, it wasn't important. Hell, a hundred mugs a day get picked up for larceny around town. Buckham wasn't anybody important, so the papers probably played it down. They don't like to give publicity to a crooked newspaperman, anyway."

"What happened to Buckham after he left the paper?"

"I don't know. He left town. I know damned good and well he couldn't get a job on any other paper around here."

"Did you happen to ever meet Buckham's girl friend . . . a Katherine Andrews?"

"No." He paused for a moment and thought back. "He probably had a girl friend all right. I remember he was a good-looking son-of-a-bitch." Berry stopped. "Say, come to think of it . . . I think he did have a gal who was a stenographer or secretary or something."

All I said was, "Huh?"

"Yeah," said Berry dredging up the old memories, "come to think of it, I remember he did. It's like this: When the cops let him go, Larry beat it . . . wherever he went. All the photographers here have a desk." He pointed at two rows of them, with three desks in each row. "Buckham had a desk up near the window, while mine was in the back. He'd been on the staff when I was hired. Not that we were ever at our desks much, but I decided I'd move over to his old one. I cleaned it out and threw away the collection of crap in it. But there was one of those stiff-backed pads, with wide lines in it, ruled down the middle, like secretaries use to take dictation. It was filled with shorthand, and in the back of it were some diagrams . . . squares, and stuff. I was an eager beaver in those days and thought maybe I'd stumbled on something important. So I took it down to the business office and had one of the secretaries down there decipher it."

"What was in it?"

"Not a goddamned thing! It was full of quotations like 'One precious hour, set with sixty golden minutes' . . . a lot of stuff like that. The secretary said it looked like beginners' exercises."

"Did Buckham write it?"

"No," said Berry, "it was in a girl's writing, all right."

"What about the diagrams?"

"What about them? Nothing to 'em as far as I know. Just squares, and scribbles, and so forth. . . ."

"Was her name in it?"

"Christ! I don't remember," said Berry impatiently. His phone rang and he picked it up and started talking rapidly. I waited until he hung up and said, "Thanks. I'll be glad to buy you a drink."

"Never use the stuff except on holidays and holy days," he said.

"Incidentally," I said, putting on my hat, "was that all that was in the book . . . just shorthand exercises?"

"That's all. Except some scribbles in the back . . . diagrams . . . ticktacktoe, maybe . . . or something."

I left the *Register* and walked down Randolph Street in the rain. It was late afternoon and the drizzle had turned into a steady rain. It was getting dark, and the gray sky seemed so close overhead that you could reach up and poke a hole in the sprinkling system with your finger. Randolph glowed in a neon haze. I stopped in a bar, bought a drink, and tried to put some facts together.

At midnight, I was home, lying on my bed, smoking a cigarette and still trying to figure it out. Krassy had been going to school studying to be a model. She'd been engaged to Buckham. Yet Buckham was running around with a secretary. I couldn't imagine any guy being engaged to Krassy, and going around with another babe on the side. Maybe he'd gone with the secretary before he met Krassy? Maybe that's where he got the shorthand book?

But why, for Christ's sake, keep an old shorthand book knocking around in your desk for six or seven months, which was about the length of time he knew Krassy before he was arrested?

But on the other hand, suppose the book belonged to Krassy? If it did, it was important enough for Buckham to keep in his desk. Sentimental reasons, perhaps, but reasons good enough for him to do it.

That brought up another question: where did Krassy learn her shorthand? She might have picked it up in commercial classes in high school. Or maybe she was going to a secretarial school. It didn't sound logical . . . the secretarial school, I mean. Because that would mean she'd been going to two schools at the same time.

But my insides were pounding with excitement. Just the thought of picking up her trail, again, excited me. The idea of all the work involved in trailing her to the school wasn't so good. It would take time. A hell of a long time.

And I could be wrong so damned easily. I had no way

of knowing that notebook really belonged to Krassy. But I knew I wouldn't rest until I found out.

So the whole routine started all over again. I checked telephone directories, credit references, utility records, and even police records for Katherine Andrews. But this time it was tougher. I ran across a number of Katherine Andrews and it took a lot of sweat eliminating them and proving to myself they weren't Krassy. Finally, I ended up facing the prospect of making the rounds of the secretarial schools. There were literally hundreds of them. However, by checking back in the old directories, I eliminated about fifty percent of them to start with.

That still left too many so I had to do some more figuring. If Krassy was living on North Banks Street, and going to Monica Morton's in the Loop, it stood to reason that she'd try to go to a school located either on the Near North Side, or the downtown Loop area. She didn't have to, of course, but it'd be more convenient if she did.

By checking addresses, I again eliminated over half of the remaining schools. I still had plenty left; it would take me months to cover them. That meant I'd have to eliminate some more before I could get started; it wasn't too risky, eliminating them, because if I guessed wrong, I'd end up covering the ones I tossed out, anyway.

But if I guessed right, I'd save a hell of a lot of work. I knew that Krassy had left home with $100; she'd paid Monica Morton $250 for her modeling course, so Krassy would probably select as inexpensive a secretarial course as she could. Where she got the dough to pay Monica, or where she could dig up the dough for the secretarial school, I didn't know. But I thought I could gamble on the fact that Krassy was short of money and would buy pretty close on price.

By using the telephone, and pretending I was interested in taking a course, I picked out the schools which offered typing and shorthand at the cheapest prices. If they were the cheapest in the field today, they had also probably been the cheapest back in 1940.

Now while you can use the telephone to get general information, you sure as hell can't use it to start digging up information that's buried deep back in the years. I started hitting out on interviews with the different schools whenever I had time. It wasn't too easy, because in the meantime I tried to keep the Clarence Moon Collection Agency in business and continue to make some new business calls. But other than that, day and night I thought of Krassy and kept picking away at the ball of string trying to find its loose end.

About five or six weeks later, I was walking down East Ohio Street and I pulled out the list of secretarial schools I always carried. I'd make my regular business calls, then if I was near a school on my list, I'd stop in there, too. That way I kept cutting the list down all the time. There was a school called the Goodbody Business Institute, on my list, which was located on Ohio. I stopped in.

To reach Goodbody, you climbed two flights of stairs in a narrow building which was flanked by a stationery store on one side, and a small flower shop on the other. The first floor had a hardware store; the second floor was evidently converted apartments because I could smell soup cooking somewhere. Goodbody was located on the third floor, in the front of the building, at the top of the stairs. It was a large, dusty room, with a dozen desks in it, each desk supporting an old typewriter. Three of four girls were pounding away on typewriters, while an ancient phonograph played a military march. The girls were typing in time to the music. Just inside the door, I was stopped by a low railing which formed a small square cut off from the main room. Right on the other side of the railing, a grizzled veteran of the keys, with too much make-up, tired lines in her face, and brilliantly hennaed hair, was filing her nails. I asked for Mr. Goodbody, and she informed me she was Miss Goodbody. There wasn't, there hadn't been, and there never would be a Mr. Goodbody, she added.

She laid down her nail file and grinned at me. "That's good news," I said, "maybe I'll have a chance, then."

"Son," she said, "you're just thirty years too late! But come on in."

I went in and sat down at the desk beside her. I gave her the old story about paying the insurance premium and asked if she knew Katherine Andrews. By that time, I'd made so many calls and told the story so many times, I'd become careless. I damn near slipped up.

"No," she said, "I don't recall any Katherine Andrews. Wait a minute, though." She pulled out a big, black entry book marked 1940 and looked in it. "Nope," she said finally, "we never had a Katherine Andrews. We did have a Karen Allison, but that's not what you want."

"Okay and thanks," I said. I got up and started toward the door. Then it hit me what she'd said. Katherine Andrews . . . Karen Allison! The old psychological switch on initials! I turned back to Goodbody and pulled out the picture of Krassy. She took it and looked just once.

"Sure," she said, "that's the girl. Karen Allison."

I came back in and sat down. I could feel my hands shaking, so I didn't say anything for a minute. I lit a cigarette and offered her one which she took.

"Where'd she go when she left here?" I asked finally.

"She got a job some place and that's the last I know." Goodbody took a drag on the cigarette and rolled her eyes at the ceiling. "Let me think . . . you know she was a good kid. I never got to know her very well. She paid her tuition, worked hard, and minded her own business. And a gal like that, with her looks! Brother, she usually has a swarm of wolves hanging around a mile long." She seemed pleased with the description. "But I never saw any hanging around her."

"Where'd she go to work?"

"That's what I'm trying to remember. Don't get your water hot. Now let me see . . . oh, hell, I can't remember, but it was some advertising agency on Michigan Boulevard."

"Tell me what you do remember about it," I urged, "maybe I can locate her anyway. . . ."

"She'd done pretty well . . . developed into a good secretary. Not too slow, and not too fast either. She was a good steady hundred words a minute, as I remember. She'd made up her mind she was going to work in some ritzy advertising office. And I'll be darned if she didn't."

Miss Goodbody puffed on her cigarette and thought back. "One day she came in with a heavy piece of engraved stationery," she continued more slowly, "with a phony name at the top and a fancy Gold Coast address. But it had *my* telephone number on it. She wanted me to write her a personal recommendation that she'd been my private social secretary for five years."

"Did you write it?" I asked.

"Sure," she replied. "Then some man called and asked for 'Mrs. Gottrocks' and I said that was me. He wanted to know about Karen and I said she'd been with me for five years, was perfectly honest, and a good girl. He wanted to know why she'd left my employment and I told him I was leaving on a honeymoon with my third husband and didn't want a good-looking young girl around. He laughed and said he knew what I meant. I guess she got the job, because I never heard from her again."

"Can't you remember the name of the advertising agency?" I asked. I had visions of covering about four hundred agencies in Chicago.

"No," said Goodbody, "but I do remember it had a real long name."

"How long?"

"Plenty! It was something like . . . well like . . . Pard, Lard, Suffiled and Burp. . . ." She waved her hand.

"Are you kidding?"

"Sure, I'm kidding," she said, "but it was a long name and sort of ran together. It had four or five names in it."

"Will you help me look through the directory, now, and see if you can recognize it?"

"Sure," said Goodbody, and she got up and returned with a classified telephone directory. I turned to the section listing advertising agencies.

"You sure there weren't two or three names?" I asked.

"Nope," she replied, "there were at least four or five."

There were only a few with that many names in a firm, listed. Miss Goodbody quickly identified the company she meant. It was Jackson, Johnston, Fuller & Greene.

THREE

PART II

Krassy rode the Red-Top cab downtown to the
Loop. Each block carried her farther away from the
Yards . . . from Anton, Maria, Caesar, and Mike. It
took her farther away than the mere physical space involved; it took her away from a complete life, a way of
hopelessness, poverty, and despair. It took Krassy Almauniski away from the Yards forever, but it did not
take her away from herself.

Relaxing in the seat of the cab, Krassy dug a clipping
of rooms-for-rent from her purse. Several of them she
had marked with a pencil. Again scanning the list, she
asked the driver to continue through the Loop and let
her off on the corner of Division Street and Lake Shore
Drive. Krassy tore the coupons from her book and
handed them to the driver, and then, in a sudden gesture, handed him a quarter tip. The cabby eyed her

speculatively. "Thanks," he said and hesitated. Finally he added the word "Miss."

Krassy stood with her suitcase and looked around. From the Drake Hotel, on Oak Street, to the south, Lake Shore Drive swung in a tremendous and beautiful curve to North Avenue on the north. Majestic apartment buildings faced east to Lake Michigan, and their thousands of gleaming windows, like golden eyes in the sun, followed the streams of traffic surging past on the Inner Drive to where they merged and were engulfed in the roar of the mighty Outer Drive. This was the whitewashed face of Chicago. This was the Chicago Gold Coast. The street of fine broadcloths, silks, and furs. Nestling to its backside, nudging and nosing, is the Near North Side of Chicago . . . the heart and the strength of much that has brought past fame to the sprawling city.

Here, in a twilight fringe, are the countless small rooms, the studios, and tiny apartments in which have lived the painters, the musicians, and the writers who have alternately loved and hated their city. Here, too, at some time in their wanderings have lived the actors, the photographers, the radio people, the dancers, the singers, and the nightclub entertainers, the young college graduates, the newly-arrived-in-Chicago secretaries and stenographers. And here, mixing side by side, have been kept the mistresses of the mighty businessmen, the dice girls, the amateur whores, and the professional prostitutes.

Blocked by Lake Shore Drive and Lake Michigan to the east, the Near North Side extends only a few blocks west to Clark Street . . . where pretense ends. Once again the city becomes dirty, filthy, and vicious and tiny grubby stores elbow and squirm their way forward on small frontages in their constant search for customers. Bounded on the north by North Avenue, the Near North Side turns, trickles, and twists its way down to Chicago Avenue, and somewhere in a few blocks south loses its way in the maze of office buildings, stores, nightclubs, and cafés.

But safely within its boundaries no one asks questions, because no one really cares.

To Krassy it meant escape and safety. Picking up her suitcase, she slowly walked north on Lake Shore Drive to Banks Street, then she turned west looking for an address. It was a large, old brownstone house with a great tower in the front. She climbed the front steps and rang the bell by the side of the high, frosted glass doors. In a moment the door was opened and a tall, slender woman with light brown hair, and a thin face, stood facing her.

"You advertised you have a room for rent?" asked Krassy.

"Yes," replied the woman, "do you want to look at it?" Her eyes searched Krassy.

Krassy stepped inside and set her suitcase down in the reception hall. Motioning her to follow, the landlady led the way through the hall to a great, sweeping staircase which was carpeted with a narrow strip down its exact center. On the second floor the great stairway became a series of smaller steps to the third floor. From the third to the fourth floors, it was narrow and steep and wore no carpeting at all. Walking down the corridor, the landlady opened a door at the end of the dark hall. Outside the door was another tiny stairway.

"Where does that lead to?" asked Krassy pointing to the stairs.

"That goes up to the tower room," replied the woman.

"Does somebody live there?" asked Krassy.

"Yes," said the landlady. "It's been rented for five years."

Krassy followed her into a small room. It contained a large double bed, a dresser with mirror, one straight-backed chair with a faded tapestry seat. One corner of the room had been curtained off with elderly cretonne drapes. Back of the drapes a metal rod had been hung across the angle of the corner to serve as a clothes rack. A single window, long and narrow, faced on Banks Street. Heavy maroon plush drapes, remnants of another room's past glory, fell straight and stiff with grime from the top of the window to the floor.

But it was still the loveliest bedroom Krassy had ever seen. "Your ad says six dollars a week," said Krassy.

"Yes," said the woman. "I allow no cooking in the room," she added, "and there's a bathroom at the end of the hall."

"I'll take it," said Krassy. She opened her purse and took out a ten-dollar bill and two ones. "This is for two weeks."

"Who do I make out the receipt to?" asked the landlady.

"To Katherine . . . Andrews," said Krassy.

"Is your home in Chicago?"

"No," replied Krassy, "I'm from Minneapolis."

"Are you working here?"

"I'm going to work as soon as I find a job."

"My name is Miss Dukes," said the landlady. "I'll

give you two keys . . . one for the front door which is locked after eleven o'clock, and the other for your room. You don't drink?" she asked suddenly.

"No," said Krassy, "I don't drink."

"That's good," said Miss Dukes. "I run a nice place here and I don't permit any drinking in the rooms." She turned and went out, returning in a few minutes with Krassy's luggage. Krassy opened her suitcase and removed her two dresses. She hung them back of the cretonne curtain.

Her long, silk, man's-shirt-nightgown and a single change of lingerie she tucked into one corner of the big dresser drawer. The brush and combs and cosmetic bottles from her fitted bag she placed neatly on top of the dresser. Then she stretched out on the big bed. For a moment she was conscious of a peculiar, burning sensation within her loins. Momentarily she thought of Caesar Manola, then she flicked her mind to darkness and went to sleep.

For several weeks, Krassy kept carefully to herself, avoiding the other roomers and making her plans. Each morning she drank a cup of coffee and ate two doughnuts; each evening she ate a hamburger and drank a glass of milk. Carefully she watched her money, and walked from her boarding house to the Loop and back, on her trips looking for work. She had no intention of taking a job clerking or working in a restaurant. She wanted a job where she could meet "the right kind of a man." The "right kind" was nebulous in Krassy's mind other than he had a fine job, plenty of money, and he was polished and a gentleman. To meet this man, Krassy knew her only chance was through business, by working in an office and making a good impression. Krassy's life in the Yards had developed within her a shrewdness and cunning.

She had no illusions about a woman's place in a man's world. She was used to the idea of men drinking, lusting, squandering paychecks, mistreating their children, and beating their wives. Krassy knew that what she would get, she must get through a man.

"I'll get a million dollars," she told herself fiercely. "I'll get it and I'll keep it. But first I got to meet the guy who's got it." She knew that she didn't dress right, her English was incorrect, she was uncertain of "what was etiquette." But she also knew that she had that mysterious power of attracting men . . . of looking at a man and making him want her. In that power was her weapon . . . and her fortune.

But first she must get a job. Krassy scoured the secretarial schools until she found the Goodbody Business Institute which offered a course in typing and shorthand for one hundred dollars.

"That includes the use of the typewriters, paper, and music," explained Miss Goodbody. "It also includes me dictating to you for shorthand exercises." It was the cheapest course that Krassy could find, so she took it.

"Do I have to pay for it in advance?" asked Krassy.

"I never had a student that could yet," said Miss Goodbody. "But you can pay me twenty-five dollars a month; as a matter of fact, you *better* pay me twenty-five bucks a month . . . or no course."

Krassy enrolled with Miss Goodbody under the name of Karen Allison. She was sorry she'd told Miss Dukes her name was Katherine Andrews, but she hadn't had time to give much thought to a name when the landlady had asked her. She had realized Krassy Almauniski would never do; she must have a name that sounded good . . . *refined* like. In her room at night, she'd thought about it. Finally, she decided on Karen Allison. She kept the same initials, because it would be easier to remember until she became accustomed to it.

Krassy started going to Miss Goodbody four hours a day, to practice typing and shorthand. Grimly she sat hour after hour typing to the rhythm of a phonograph record, or sat taking dictation while Miss Goodbody read ancient letters aloud, or quoted from small volumes of adages, proverbs, and jingle poetry. At night she studied her shorthand book at home, trying to burn the symbols in her memory.

Then she met Larry Buckham.

As she was entering her room, a tall, slender young man was descending the narrow steps from the tower room, stuffing a folded newspaper into his jacket pocket. He stopped to stare at her for a long moment. In his hand was a camera with a flash unit. Krassy stood, hand on her door, face turned toward Buckham on the stairs. Suddenly, he raised the camera and the flash exploded in light before her eyes.

"Good Lord," he said, "do you live here?" He lowered his camera and started to remove the burned bulb from it.

"Yes," replied Krassy, "do you?"

"Right upstairs there . . . in the tower," he said. "Come on up . . . let me take some more shots of you."

"Some other time," said Krassy unlocking her door, "you were going out."

Buckham followed her into her room and sat down on the straight-backed chair, holding his camera on his lap. "It wasn't anything important," he said. "Each Thursday night I go down to a Camera Club meeting. I'd rather stay here and take your picture."

"Is photography your hobby?" asked Krassy.

"No," said Buckham, "it's my job. I work for the *Daily Register*. But I want to get out of the news business and get into commercial photography. There's more money . . . and more fun . . . in doing covers, advertisements, portraits, and things like that."

Krassy removed her coat and hat and hung them back of the cretonne curtains. "When are you going to start all this?" she asked.

"Just as soon as I get enough dough saved up. It takes a hell of a lot of money to open a studio. Cameras and equipment cost like the devil. . . . I've got some money now, but not enough. Say," he exclaimed, "have you ever done any professional modeling?"

"No," said Krassy.

"I know some photographers that could probably use you. I'll be glad to introduce you to them. You can pick up a lot of dough that way if you're any good."

"I'm not good," replied Krassy. "I don't know anything about it."

"It's easy," said Buckham. "Of course, you could go to a modeling school, but I wouldn't advise it. It costs too much money and they give you a lot of stuff you'd never use. You know. . . ." He waved his hand disparagingly.

"What do you mean?" asked Krassy.

"Oh, stuff like this," and Buckham unfolded a paper he had in his pocket and started turning the pages until he came to an advertisement. "Here's one from Monica Morton's Modeling School: Be Charming . . . Be

Beautiful . . . Be Lovely . . . Be A Cover Girl! Yat-tata, yattata, yattata. Get this: Feminine Charm Program! Figure Control, Posture and Walking, Voice and Diction, Style Coordination, Individual Make-up, Individual Hair Styling, Personality Development, Social Graces and Etiquette . . . and so forth and so on! That's a lot of malarky! All a photographer wants is something that photographs well."

Krassy had stopped in the middle of the room. Her head was tilted slightly to one side; her gray eyes were looking straight at Buckham, but she didn't see him. She was seeing something, perhaps, in a world where Larry Buckham and photographers didn't exist. "Maybe you're right," she said softly.

"Sure, I'm right," said Buckham. "Why waste all that dough? You know, I could teach you enough about modeling and posing for you to get by."

"All right," said Krassy suddenly, "I'll pose for you, but I won't pose for anybody else. I don't want to be a model."

Buckham was surprised by the intenseness of her answer, but he didn't argue with his good fortune. "Swell," he agreed, "come on up to the tower with me and I'll take a couple shots tonight." Krassy accompanied him up the stairs to the tower room.

It was a room about fifteen feet square, with windows on all four sides. Cream-colored drapes, operating on small tracks like a stage curtain, covered the walls as well as the windows. A large studio bed, which made up into a couch during the day, several easy chairs, a chest of drawers in black Chinese lacquer completed the room. Stacks of photographs, proofs, prints, and mats stood in all the corners.

"I've lived here about five years," Buckham explained, "and I sort of fixed this place up myself. I got in good with Dukes by taking her picture when I first moved in. I soft-soap her once in a while, and she's let me keep this room ever since." He pulled the drapes away from the windows on all sides of the room.

"It's like floating in your own private balloon up in the air," said Krassy.

"That's why I like it," he replied. "Incidentally, my name is Larry Buckham . . . I've been so busy talking I don't even know your name."

"My name is Katherine Andrews," said Krassy.

Buckham began setting up his reflectors and equipment. That night he took fourteen portrait shots of Krassy.

By the end of the week, Krassy was eating breakfast and having dinner with Larry Buckham each day. He'd tap on her door in the morning and they'd walk to State and Division. In a little restaurant there, they would eat and talk until Buckham was late starting for his office. In the evening, they'd meet for dinner at one of the many small cafés on the Near North Side. Krassy was careful to eat well and solidly, but never expensively. With Buckham paying the checks, she had cut her food bill to exactly nothing.

Buckham was a tall, sensitive man in his late twenties, highly emotional. He was filled with great enthusiasm which was countered by periods of bleak despair. A good craftsman, he had buried himself deeply in a world with no horizon other than photography. This love and devotion to his work, he transferred to Krassy. Within a month after meeting her, he proposed.

"Let's get married, Kathy," he said. "I've got a good

job . . . I'm making ninety bucks a week. That's plenty to live on. You can give up that secretarial school and we'll find an apartment to live in."

"But what about your studio?" she asked. "If you married me, it might be years before you could break away from your job."

"To hell with the studio!" said Larry. "I've saved up over three hundred dollars, and I've got about two thousand bucks already tied up in cameras and equipment. If we get married, it'll just take a little longer, that's all."

"All right," said Krassy, "we'll get married. Not right away, but we'll plan on it." Buckham took her in his arms and kissed her hungrily.

That night, after the rooming house was asleep, Buckham came to Krassy's room and stayed with her for the first time. He slipped silently down the stairs and gently scratched his fingers over her door, and when Krassy opened it for him, he tiptoed quietly in.

In the darkness of the room, and the privacy of her bed, Buckham buried his face in her breasts. "I love you, Kathy," he said. "You are everything in the world to me . . . you're good, and desirable, and my entire life. You *are* my entire life, Kathy, and if anything should ever happen . . . to break us up . . . I don't know what I'd do. . . ."

Krassy held him closely to her and gently ran her small tongue around the outline of his ear working his passion to a frenzy. Then she gave herself to him. "I don't like it . . . I don't like it," she told herself, "but maybe someday I will. . . ."

Nightly, Buckham slipped quietly down the narrow tower stairs to Krassy's room. During the day, he lived only to see her at night. And each night, he helplessly

watched for the gray dawn outside her window which
would send him back upstairs to his own room.

"Marry me now, Kathy," he'd plead.

And Krassy would reply to him firmly, "Not yet,
Larry, I've paid for my secretarial course and I want to
finish it. . . ."

"But why, Kathy? Why?"

"I know I'll never use it, but if we're married . . . I
wouldn't ever finish it. And I hate to ever leave anything
unfinished."

One night as he was lying with his head on her arm,
his face against her throat half buried in the long, golden
hair which fell to her waist, Krassy told him, "Larry, I'm
not going to let you make love to me any more . . .
until we're married."

"What?" exclaimed Buckham sitting up in the bed.

"It isn't right," said Krassy. "I don't feel right about
it. After we're married . . . then it will be all right."

"Don't you love me?"

"Yes, I love you, Larry. But I don't feel right about
this . . . I'm not that kind of a girl . . . I've never
done this before. . . ."

"Good God!" he said, "I'll marry you tomorrow. I
want to! How about it?"

"I don't think we should," said Krassy patiently. "I
don't think we should get married until we are all ready.
We should have a cute little apartment where we can
live, and we should have the furniture all paid for, and
everything nice."

"How long will that be?" asked Larry slowly.

"About six months, if we save our money and try
hard."

"You mean I can't make love to you . . . for six months?"

"Oh . . . maybe once in a while, Larry. But not every night."

The next day Larry gave Krassy three hundred dollars with which to buy furniture. Krassy found a small furniture store which offered a "complete living room suite for only $298." Carefully she memorized all the details in the window . . . an overstuffed davenport, overstuffed chair, two imitation walnut-finished end tables, a coffee table, a nine-by-twelve flowered rug, and a floor lamp. The furniture was cheap and shoddy, and Krassy knew it.

But Krassy didn't buy it.

Instead, she enrolled at Monica Morton's Model Bureau and School. She paid Monica Morton two hundred and fifty dollars, in cash, for the most expensive course she had. The remaining fifty dollars Krassy kept for her own needs. Her original hundred dollars had dwindled to less than fifteen.

That night, Krassy let Buckham into her room again. She described the living room set she had purchased in vivid, glowing terms, and drew little sketches of furniture arrangement and rooms for him, in the back of her secretarial notebook.

"They're keeping it for us," she said. "It's all paid for, and whenever we want it, they'll deliver it. I have the receipt and I'll put it away until we need it."

Larry kissed her. He was too happy to care what she did. But in the cold gray of the dawn, when he left her bed, he stopped for a moment and slipped the notebook, tenderly, in his pocket.

By September, Larry was impatient to be married. All

summer Krassy had received ten or fifteen dollars a week from him. "We need a lot of little things . . . mostly for the kitchen," she explained. "Dishes . . . and silver . . . and pots and pans. It all adds up, darling, but we must have them." Then receiving the money, she would stretch it out to cover her own expenses. She bought two inexpensive dresses at clearance sales, in conservative good taste, as Monica Morton had advised her.

During the day, she worked increasingly hard at Goodbody's and she developed a careful competence in typing and shorthand. She owed Miss Goodbody fifty dollars on her tuition, but she had made careful plans to pay it.

Listening to Buckham's talk in the evening about commercial photography which invariably ended with fabulous stories about advertising agencies, Krassy soon decided it was a world where she belonged. A world where art directors received $25,000 a year salary and copy chiefs $40,000; where account executives and vice-presidents had incomes ranging up to $100,000 a year on the big accounts. Some of the stories were true, some were false, some were hearsay, others were wishful thinking which had become part of the advertising legend.

At Monica Morton's, Krassy heard much the same stories. Legendary stories of girls who made their fortunes posing for national campaigns, and whose pictures were recognized in every home in the nation. If Krassy did not want to become a model, she at least wanted to become a part of the world of this Aladdin's Lamp and meet the men who rubbed it. She began to canvass the big Michigan Avenue agencies . . . looking them over, evaluating the stories about them, making up her mind.

Among the biggest, the most gaudy, and the most incredible was the firm of Jackson, Johnston, Fuller & Greene. This was the company, Krassy decided, she would work for.

By fall, Krassy had purchased all the theoretical living room furniture and kitchen equipment possible. Larry, in a sudden spurt of independence, had decided that his own bedroom furniture, in the tower room, was good enough for them to start. He was urging Krassy to set a definite date for their marriage.

"In a month, Larry," she promised. "We'll get married then and be together for always. But I do need some new clothes, and I've been trying to find some material to make them. I want to be married in a new dress. . . ."

"I'll buy you a new dress," said Buckham. "I'll buy you anything you want."

Krassy shook her head demurely. "That wouldn't be right, darling. After all we're not married yet . . . and it would be bad luck for you to buy my wedding dress. . . ."

"What difference does that make?" he demanded.

Krassy shrugged her shoulders. "None, probably," she admitted, "perhaps I'm just superstitious." Then suddenly her face brightened. "I know what we could do," she said, then she pursed her mouth sadly, "noooo . . . that wouldn't be right, either."

"What are you talking about?" asked Buckham.

"Well," said Krassy, "we could open a charge account at one of the big department stores. We could say I was your wife, and then when the bill for my dress comes next month, we'd already be married and it would be all right for you to pay it."

"That's a swell idea," he agreed. "I'll meet you to-morrow at noon and we'll open an account."

A few days later, Buckham received two charge-a-plates in the mail. One for Mr. L. A. Buckham, and one for Mrs. L. A. Buckham. He proudly gave the plate to Krassy. "Okay, honey," he said, "here's that wedding dress of yours."

Krassy was very busy. First, she bought a plain white, smartly tailored dress and a dramatic hat to go with it. They weren't expensive and she showed them to Larry. He was enthusiastic.

Then she rented a small, one-room apartment on East Delaware Street, registering as Karen Allison. The rent was $80 monthly, in a respectable building, and she paid a week's rent in advance when she took the apartment. "I'll pay you the balance by the end of the week," she told the manager, "when I move in."

Day by day, Krassy had made purchases at the department store; a set of matched, white leather luggage; a small gold wrist watch; a gold cigarette lighter; a portable radio; a traveling iron; an onyx and seed pearl dinner ring; a pair of fox furs. She was careful to select nothing too expensive, but the total came to nearly twelve hundred dollars. By pawning them, she received three hundred dollars in cash.

"But I need something for myself," she thought. She bought and charged two new suits, two matching pairs of shoes, a cocktail dress, and a smartly styled black coat. The clothing she carefully stored in her new apartment on East Delaware.

At Miss Dukes's, mail was delivered twice each day.

The postman left it in a heavy iron box on the front
steps, and Miss Dukes would carry it in to the wobbly,
round table in the hall. As the roomers returned home at
night, they'd stop at the table and sort through the mail.
On the first of the month, Krassy made a special effort
to be the first person to go through the mail, both morning and afternoon. On the third of October, a bill from
the department store arrived; it was addressed to Mr. L.
A. Buckham. Krassy quickly snatched it from the rest of
the mail and concealed it under her coat. Reaching the
safety of her own room, she tore open the envelope. It
was a statement for over twelve hundred dollars. She
carefully shredded it into small pieces and flushed them
down the bathroom stool. She kept flushing it until the
last small piece of soggy paper had disappeared.

That same day she called on a small printer located on
Grand Avenue, just east of the lower level off Michigan.
She arranged with him to print her a dozen letterheads
and envelopes on a heavy, expensive bond paper, social
correspondence size. The letterheads read:

> GERALDINE K. VAN DOREN
> 1444 LAKE SHORE DRIVE
> CHICAGO, ILLINOIS.

After additional consideration, she added the White-
hall exchange of Miss Goodbody. It was her home telephone number which Krassy had found listed in the
telephone directory.

The printer wanted to set the letterheads in type, but
Krassy insisted that a copper engraving be used. The
engraving, Krassy discovered, cost a great deal more
than type, but she was willing to pay for it.

The printer shook his head at her extravagance. "It won't cost you a couple dollars extra to print up a hundred letterheads," he said.

"But I only need a dozen," replied Krassy.

"You already got the cost of the copper plate," the printer argued, "and it don't cost hardly anything to run off the extra paper."

"A dozen will be more than I need," said Krassy.

The printer finally gave up in exasperation. Krassy only smiled to herself.

The morning of October fifteenth, Krassy failed to meet Larry for breakfast, and she left the rooming house considerably later than usual. It was a beautiful day with a light fall haze in the air. Two blocks away, the lake was rolling in long, slow swells, picking thoughtfully at the concrete breakwater. As Krassy stood for a moment on the steps of Miss Dukes's, she saw an elderly man, obese, with straggling white hair hanging beneath a pinched brown hat set squarely on the top of his head. He was turning up the walk, looking at the number of the house.

Something in his manner, or perhaps it was her own instinct, sounded a small note of warning to Krassy. The day was no longer beautiful, the haze in the sky turned the color of smoke from back of the Yards. She shivered and it wasn't from cold. As he passed her on the walk, she suddenly touched his arm and stopped him.

"If you're looking for someone in the house," she said, "I'm afraid there's no one home." She added "I'm the last one to leave this morning. . . ."

The old man turned impersonal eyes on her. They were rimmed in red and bloodshot. She could smell the raw, rank fumes of whisky . . . fresh on his breath this morning. Politely he lifted his hat, in a brief tilt, and replaced it securely on his head.

"I'm looking for Mr. or Mrs. Buckham," he said.

So soon! Krassy thought. She hesitated for only a moment. "I'm Mrs. Buckham," she said. "Can I help you?"

"I'm a credit investigator," the old man replied, "I just wanted to stop by and pick up a check for your account at the store."

"My husband isn't home," Krassy told him, "and I can't sign a check. He'll send you one tonight."

He shook his head. "I'm sorry then," he said, "because I must see your husband. I'll have to go down to the paper to see him."

Krassy thought quickly. Then tears welled in her eyes, and choking back a sob she said, "I know I can trust you . . . let's go some place where we can talk." Fumbling for her handkerchief, she turned her face away. "I'm going crazy," she moaned softly. "When I tell you . . . you'll understand."

The old man regarded her thoughtfully. "All right," he said finally, "where do you want to go?"

"Not in the house. If anyone should hear, I'd die of shame. Let's go down the street and get a cup of coffee. I'm so upset, I haven't been able to eat. . . ."

Silently, side by side, they walked down State Parkway to Division. Going into a chain drugstore, they seated themselves in a booth. Krassy ordered a cup of coffee, and the old man ordered nothing. "Well?" he asked.

"I don't know where to start. . . ." Krassy said helplessly.

"You know it's pretty serious," said the old man, "ordering things deliberately if you know you can't pay for them. Mr. Buckham, unfortunately, opened a new account in the middle of the month. If the store had realized how high the charges were, in proportion to his reported income, it'd never permitted that large a bill to run up."

"He's a beast!" cried Krassy. "Oh, I hope you get him!"

The old man looked surprised. "That's no way for a wife to talk about her husband."

"I'm not his wife!" Krassy dropped her eyes in shame. "I'm not and I never will be." She put both hands to her mouth to repress her sobs.

The old man shifted in his seat uneasily. "Maybe you better tell me what you're talking about. . . ." he suggested uncertainly.

Krassy opened her purse and removed a newspaper clipping. It was the story, with her picture, which had appeared in the *Stockyard Weekly News* concerning the beauty contest. Krassy had secured a copy of the paper and had kept the clipping. Now, in her hands, it became a deadly weapon. She handed the clipping to the old man and he slowly looked at the picture and read the story.

"That's me," said Krassy, "that was me just six months ago. After that picture appeared, Larry saw it. He came out to my house and asked me to pose for him. He's a newspaper photographer, too, you know?"

"Yes," said the old man, "at the *Daily Register*."

Krassy nodded. "He promised me that he could get me a lot of publicity . . . and I'd make a lot of money. I believed him." Krassy stopped and wiped her eyes. "I even came downtown to live.

"Next he told me he loved me . . . and I believed

that, too. He said we'd get married. Then . . . then
. . . after he'd gotten me all involved . . . and made
me live with him . . . he said he'd never marry me until
he had enough money to quit his newspaper job. . . ."

Krassy's slender hands quivered on the table top, and
the old man reached out and gently patted them. Krassy
drew a deep, sobbing breath.

"I didn't dare go home. My father would kill me for
being a . . . bad woman. I had no place to go . . . no
one to take care of me except Larry. I loved him Mr.
. . . Mr.?" she stopped her story in a question.

"Moon," the old man replied, "Clarence Moon."

"God, how I loved him, Mr. Moon!" she cried softly.
"Until he started to drink . . . then he became a beast.
One night he came home drunk. He told me he had an
idea how to get enough money to start his own studio. If
I helped him, he promised to marry me."

The words were tumbling out easily now, one after
another in a strong, damning thread. She rocked gently
from side to side. "He said he'd open a charge account
and get me a charge-a-plate. I was to go down and
charge things, then take them out and pawn them for
what I could get." Once again Krassy fumbled with her
purse and placed a thick roll of pawn tickets on the
table. Moon silently picked them up.

"I didn't want to, Mr. Moon . . . I pleaded with him
. . . I begged him not to. He just laughed . . . and
then, he struck me!" She lifted her fingers and gently felt
her lip. "He made out a list of things for me to buy, and
every day he was at me to get them. The days I didn't go
to the store, he'd get drunk and treat me filthy!"

"What about the woman's clothes you bought?"
asked Moon.

Krassy caught her breath. "He has another woman . . . he gave them to her . . . I know he gave them to her!" She spit the words. "But he made *me* buy them. . . ."

Moon nodded gravely. "How much money does Buckham have?" he asked.

"I don't know," replied Krassy wearily, "but he has two or three thousand dollars worth of cameras and photographic equipment."

"That will help," Moon said. He searched her beautiful, tear-stained face. The anguish and despair he saw there convinced him. Slowly he stood up from the table. "Maybe I shouldn't do this," he said. "Perhaps I'm just a sentimental old fool. I never married, so I never had a daughter. If I had, I hope that she might have looked like you . . . only have better sense. I'm going to have Buckham arrested on a larceny charge," he paused. "If I can't find you, I can't have you arrested, can I?" he added.

"No," said Krassy, "you can't. . . ."

"Well, suppose we just forget this talk we had and you disappear some place where I can't find you. Like going back home to your dad."

Krassy smiled with sudden hope. "Oh, yes . . . yes!" She, too, stood and standing on her toes kissed the old man on his forehead. "Thank you, Mr. Moon," she whispered, then turning she walked swiftly out the door.

For a moment Clarence Moon stood by the table. Reaching inside his coat pocket, he pulled out a small medicine bottle marked "cough syrup." He took a long drink from it. The smell indicated a high alcohol content. It might even have been straight alcohol.

Krassy hurried back to Miss Dukes's and packed her

suitcase. When she left, no one saw her go. She caught a cab and rode directly to her new apartment on East Delaware.

That afternoon the police arrested Larry Buckham. They didn't believe very much of what he tried to tell them. If it hadn't been for Miss Dukes, Buckham might have been sent up. Between the *Daily Register* and Miss Dukes, the police withdrew charges when Buckham sold all his photographic equipment and paid the store in full. The store was happy to drop proceedings, even if old man Moon did want the book thrown at Buckham.

Buckham was canned from the paper.

When he left town, he didn't have even a Brownie No. 2 Kodak to take with him.

FOUR

PART I

I didn't waste any time getting over to Jackson, Johnston, Fuller and Greene. I didn't go that same afternoon I talked to Goodbody, but I did go the next day. I was following Krassy now into places where it was going to be tougher to get people to talk. I knew I had to look better, and have a better story than the one I'd been using if I was ever going to get past the reception desk at the advertising agency.

After I left the business school, I went home and got out my blue suit and took it down to the corner and had it pressed. Then I went to see a young guy I knew who was working for an insurance company. I'd first met him a couple years before when I was taking some courses in night school; I was trying to make up for leaving school so early and lamming it away from home. And this guy, Cage, was in a couple of the classes, too. I liked him, and we used to go out and have a couple beers once in a while.

We talked about this and that for a couple minutes, then I said, "Look, pal, you got to give me some kind of an identification card . . . something that shows I'm working for your company."

"I can't do it, Danny," he said, "the company's strict as hell about that."

"You got to," I told him, "it's plenty important and I promise you won't get any feedback on it." I explained about just starting my own business. "I got a big collection to make," I lied, "and I been trying to trace a deadbeat. I lost him but I know where I can pick up the string again. I got to have some identification or I won't be able to get anybody to talk."

"There's nothing phony about this?" he asked.

"Naw," I said, "all I want is just some identification so I can ask some questions." We talked about it, back and forth, and finally my friend Cage agreed to get me a card. He was a nice guy and worked as a file clerk in the Northern Transcontinental Insurance Company office. He sneaked an employee's identification card out of the supply room and gave it to me to fill out. When I got through with it, it read:

THE NORTHERN TRANSCONTINENTAL INSURANCE COMPANY
Chicago, Illinois

Name of employee:	Daniel April
Position:	Claims adjuster
Years employed:	Nine
Height:	5'-11"
Weight:	175

Hair:	Black
Eyes:	Blue
Distinguishing marks:	None

Signed by: George M. Cage

Executive Vice-President

When Cage saw what I'd done, he nearly flipped, and for a moment, I thought I'd blown the whole deal. "For Christ's sake, Danny," he said. "I'll get kicked the hell out of here if anyone sees that."

"Nobody's going to see it," I told him. "Besides if any guy should call and check up on that card, he'll ask for whoever signed it. Right?"

Cage wasn't sure about that.

"This way, he'll talk to you and you can vouch for it," I added.

Cage still didn't like it. He didn't like it at all, but he agreed to let it ride, and back up my story if I needed him. We shook hands and I promised I'd meet him later and pop for drinks and something to eat.

That night, at my rooming house, I polished up my story a little, and thought about Krassy. I wondered what I'd do if I ran into her at the advertising agency. But after thinking it over I decided she probably wasn't there. Ten years in one job is a long time. She was probably married by now, had six kids, and was big and broad across the beam. It made me sick to think about it.

I took out the old newspaper clipping and the glossy print I'd gotten from Monica Morton and looked at them. She was lovely; and I'd lived with her in my mind so long that I felt I'd known her all those ten years. I got thinking what it'd be like to have a gal like that. Maybe she wouldn't want to live on what I could make. But that wasn't being fair to Krassy! Look at what she'd lived in at the Yards. She'd been engaged to some newspaper punk until he got himself in a jam. I didn't blame Krassy for busting her engagement. If a guy gets in trouble with the law once, he'll probably do it again. Krassy was too nice a gal to be married to a potential con. If she loved a man, what he had didn't make any difference; I knew she was that kind of a girl.

All night long I rolled and tossed, and in the morning I didn't bother to go to my office. I made myself wait over three cups of coffee until it was ten o'clock, then I went over to Jackson, Johnston, Fuller and Greene. The offices covered the twenty-ninth, thirtieth, and thirty-first floors in a big, plushy building on Michigan. The reception room was located on the twenty-ninth floor, and when I got off the elevator, I walked down the marble hall and through an Old English doorway. Inside, seated behind a neat little desk, was a burnished redhead. My newly pressed blue serge suit didn't fool her for a minute. She gave me the old one-two with her eyes and looked bored.

Her desk had six or eight telephones on it. Nothing else. Every couple of seconds, a phone would ring and she'd say, "Yes, Mr. Blunt. . . . You'll be back at eleven-thirty. Thank you." Or, "Yes, Mr. Harris. . . . No. No one called while you were out. I'll check you back in." She kept this up with hardly a pause, and then she'd scribble figures on a couple typewritten sheets that had long lists of names on them.

"How do you keep 'em all straight?" I asked her.

"I don't," she said briefly.

"I'll bet you do a pretty good job of it," I said and grinned.

She began to thaw a little. "I don't make many mistakes," she admitted.

"Do they all have to report to you?" I asked.

"Sort of," she said. "Everyone is required to report when they're out of their offices, or leave the building. That way, if something important comes up, we know where they are, or when they'll be back."

I agreed solemnly. "By the way," I said, "my name is Danny April. I thought I'd have to see the office manager, but you'll be able to help me even better."

"What do you want?" she asked.

"I'm trying to locate a Miss Karen Allison."

"Does she work here?"

My belly dropped. "She did work here," I said.

The redhead came right back. "I've been here three years, and there hasn't been a girl by that name since I started."

"Maybe I'll have to see the office manager after all," I said.

"Mr. Bard has charge of the office force," she said. "Did she work in the office . . . or was she on the creative staff?"

"What do you mean by creative staff?"

"Was she a copywriter, a radio writer, an artist? Did she work in production . . . printing, engravings?"

"Hell, I don't know," I said. "But I think maybe she worked in the office."

She started to get suspicious. "Are you a personal friend of hers or something?"

"No," I said, "but I want to do her a favor. I want to pay her some dough, and I can't find her." I handed her

my Northern Transcontinental Insurance card. She
glanced at it briefly. "Her aunt, Mrs. Joan Harmon Allison, from Minneapolis, died and left her as beneficiary
. . . a small insurance policy. But we've been unable to
locate Karen Allison. This was the last address we had
for her."

The redhead relaxed. "They're pretty strict around
here about giving out information," she said. "I'll see if
Mr. Bard will talk to you." She picked up a phone, jiggled a couple times and got the switchboard. In a moment she was talking to Mr. Bard and she explained
what I wanted. Then she turned back to me. "He'll see
you," she said. "His secretary will be out in just a moment."

I sat down on a long, leather davenport, and by the
time I'd reached the middle of an old copy of *Time*,
Bard's secretary came out of a little side door and motioned to me.

"This way please, Mr. April." I followed her down a
series of halls, with doors opening off like rabbit
hutches. Occasionally harassed-looking guys, with
bunches of paper in their hands, would bound out of the
doors and down the halls like their pants were on fire.

"Busy, huh?" I said to the secretary who was padding
along with a sure homing instinct.

"Not particularly," she replied. "They do that all the
time." Eventually we reached an office door, marked in
gold letters H. R. BARD. She opened the door and waved
me in. I walked into a fairly small office, containing a
double-sized desk, settee, two lounge chairs, a small
drum table with a brass lamp on it. All around the base
of the lamp, ivy and small cactus had been planted. On
the walls, in groups of six and eight, pictures in match-

ing frames were hung. The whole effect was to give you enough room to take a breath . . . if you stood sideways in the middle of the room.

Back of the desk, old man Bard was making a big show of reading some correspondence. I could hear his stomach rumbling halfway across the office . . . as if someone was blowing through straws in the bottom of a glass. After counting maybe to forty, he slowly raised his eyes and said, "Yes?"

I showed him my card and went through my explanations all over again. "What's the number of your office?" he asked. I gave him the insurance company's number which I'd memorized. "Then ask for Mr. Cage, he's the executive vice-president," I told him. Bard kept his eyes on me and started to reach for his phone. When he saw I didn't care if he called, he dropped his hand and said, "Well, I guess we don't need to bother about that. However, here at Jackson, Johnston, Fuller and Greene we're very careful about talking. You understand, don't you, that we serve some of the greatest corporations in America. We know their innermost thoughts and secrets; we have information which is strictly confidential. Besides, it has never been our policy. . . ."

"I'll give you eight, five, and even we got more dough at the Northern Transcontinental Insurance Company than you've got at Jackson, Johnston, Fuller and Greene," I cut in.

He sat and looked at me for a moment, his mouth still open for his next words.

"Besides," I continued, "all I want to know is if you got a girl working here named Karen Allison. It's got nothing to do with the color of next year's lawn mowers."

Bard started to laugh. "All right, April," he said, and then laughed some more. I thought the guy was a little touched. "We don't have Miss Allison with us any-more."

"She did work here?" I asked.

"Yes."

"How long?"

Bard thought it over. "I think she was with us for about three years," he said. "She started sometime in 1940 and it was late in the fall of 1943 . . . somewhere around there . . . that she left."

"Where did she go?"

"I don't know."

"What'd she do? I mean what kind of a job did she have?"

"She started out as our receptionist," he said. "Then she was promoted to personal secretary to Mr. Collins."

"Who's Mr. Collins?"

"Mr. Collins is vice-president of Jackson, Johnston, Fuller and Greene," he explained seriously and with some awe in his voice. "He's the account executive on the Joy Drug account . . . one of the largest advertisers in the world."

"Those the guys who make Joy Toothpaste and cold tablets . . . and that stuff?"

Mr. Bard winced slightly. "Yes," he said, "that *stuff* . . . and a lot more."

"Could you give me the last address you had for Miss Allison?" I asked him.

Bard pressed a buzzer, and in a moment the secretary who'd guided me to his inner sanctum popped back through the door. He told her what he wanted. She popped out. Bard and I sat and looked at each other without anything to say. Finally, his phone rang and he picked it up. Reaching for a pencil he scribbled an address on a memo pad. He hung up the phone, tore the sheet off the pad, and handed it to me. "That's the last address we had for Miss Allison," he said. "I'm afraid it won't do much good," he added, "it's seven years old."

I thanked him and stood up. Just as I reached the door, I turned and said, "Do you think it would be possible for me to see Mr. Collins? Maybe Miss Allison might've dropped a hint where she was going?"

"I'm sorry, April, but I think you're wasting your time trying to see Mr. Collins," Bard replied. "He's a very busy man . . . he hasn't time to see anyone . . . he hardly has time to see himself."

"Look, Mr. Bard," I said, "sure, Mr. Collins is busy. But suppose Miss Allison needs this money? Suppose she's sick . . . or out of a job? Even a big man like Mr. Collins wouldn't object to taking just one minute to help a young gal get a break."

"Perhaps not," said Bard and shrugged. "I don't think Collins ever took time to be human to anyone. Anyhow, I'll call and try to get you an appointment." He called the switchboard and asked for Collins' office; he successfully got past a secretary and was talking to Collins. He was no longer as impressive, nor as glib, as when he was talking to me. Bard talked to Collins with a hell of a lot more respect to his face, than he'd talked about Collins to me. He told Collins about me, and then said, "He wants to see you at your convenience, Mr. Collins, when you're not busy. I told him you probably wouldn't be able to see him." Collins said something and Bard hung up with a surprised look. "Collins said for you to go on up to his office," he told me. "Do you know where it is?"

"No," I said.

"It's on the thirty-first floor," he explained. "I'll have Miss Pierson show you up." He buzzed, and his secretary popped back in his office again. I followed her through the maze of corridors to the elevators. We caught one to the thirty-first floor. Here there was another, smaller reception room presided over by a blonde. She, too, was seated at a small desk, but it only had three telephones on it. Miss Pierson handed me over to her and gave her instructions concerning my delivery. As she left, she waved her hand at me. "If you can't find your way out, chum, just call Peerless Pierson, girl pathfinder." She caught a passing elevator and disappeared.

The blonde walked out from behind her desk and pointed down the long, broad hallway. "Mr. Collins' office is at the very end, to your right."

"Thanks," I said and walked in the direction she pointed. At the end of the hall was a heavy, walnut-paneled door with the name "Stacey H. Collins" lettered on it in a signature . . . a copy of Collins' own writing. I knocked on the door and entered a small office, knee-deep in carpeting, with an efficient-looking secretary seated at a desk. She was middle-aged, wore glasses, and was pounding hell out of a typewriter. She looked up from her work, and I told her who I was and that Collins was expecting me. She checked with Collins and said, "Mr. Collins will see you now." She got up from her desk and opened another door for me.

It opened into Collins' office. A huge, corner job with windows on two sides. Venetian blinds hung at the windows, and over the blinds were drapes. There was a big fireplace in the office, with a long settee in front of it flanked by end tables and lamps. Several groups of chairs, with cocktail tables, stood around in it, and in one corner was a big, walnut carved desk.

From this desk, you could look up the outer drive nearly as far north as the Edgewater Beach Hotel, and trace the shoreline of Lake Michigan as far as you could see. Off to one side of the desk, with the door slightly ajar, was a private shower and dressing room. Directly behind the desk was a small, cabinet bar with a freezing unit and ice cubes. It was one hell of a fine layout.

Collins was a fairly good-looking guy, somewhere in his middle forties. He was short, stocky, and his square face wore a smooth, emotionless expression. He had a good tan, which looked fine with his thick, black hair which was growing white around the temples. Nothing moved in his face . . . no emotion, no expression. Except for his eyes. He had bright, black eyes which looked hot and tired . . . and wary. They didn't go with his empty face at all.

I introduced myself, which he acknowledged with a nod, but he made no effort to get up and shake hands. I explained to him about the insurance payment for Karen Allison. Halfway through my spiel, he cut me off. "Bard told me all about it," he said. "What do you want to know from me?"

"I understand Miss Allison was your secretary for a while?"

"About two years," he replied.

"Well, Mr. Bard didn't know where she might have gone . . . and I thought maybe at some time she might have said something about her future plans to you."

"Not that I remember."

"Did she ever mention any place she'd like to live . . . or go for a vacation? Anything like that?"

Collins leaned back in his chair. He opened a box of cigarettes, selected one, and lit it with an expensive silver desk lighter. "It's been so long since she left that it's hard to remember," he said exhaling a deep breath of smoke.

"Did she write you after she left?"

"No," he said, "there was no reason she should."

"Did she say why she was leaving?"

His eyes burned at me hotly, but his face didn't change. The phone rang and he picked it up. He gave several short answers and hung up. He paused for a moment. "She said she was leaving town and that was all," he said finally.

That stopped me. Was this the end of the line? I tried to keep my face and voice steady. "She didn't say where?"

"No." He stopped for a moment and seemed to be listening. "Come to think of it," he went on slowly, "I have a feeling it might have been New York."

"Was she a good secretary?"

"Excellent."

"Didn't she ever use you for references?"

"Never."

I turned toward the door. "Thanks for your time, Mr. Collins," I said.

His voice didn't change; his face was expressionless. "I'm afraid I wasn't much help," he replied indifferently. His voice hung in the air for a few seconds and he reached for his pen on the desk and started signing some letters. Deliberately he laid his pen to one side and turned back toward me. "You know, April," he said, "I've often wondered what happened to Miss Allison. I hope you find her. If you do, I'd like to know."

"You would?" I asked.

"It isn't important," he shrugged, "but I'd be glad to make it worth your time . . . just for my own curiosity."

Leaving the building, I walked out to Michigan Boulevard feeling lower than hell. There was only one chance left. I pulled out the old address Bard had given me. It was in Oak Park. I caught a bus going down Michigan and transferred to an el. All the way out to Oak Park, I thought about Krassy. I thought about that bill Clarence Moon had marked paid; I thought about Katherine Andrews studying with Monica Morton and living at Miss Dukes's; I thought about Karen Allison studying with Miss Goodbody and working at Jackson, Johnston, Fuller and Greene, and living in Oak Park. Oak Park is a good Chicago suburb . . . and a long, long way from the Yards, in more ways than distance.

When I got off the el in Oak Park, I caught a cab; I didn't know my way around the suburb and I had no idea where Krassy's old address was. The cab pulled up in front of a good apartment building; it wasn't big, but it was good. It was four stories high, with three apartments to each floor . . . two in the front of the building, one in the rear. By the mailboxes were listed the names of the tenants, but there wasn't any "Karen Allison." In the basement there was a buzzer marked "Phillip Fromm, Supt."

I rang the button and waited.

In a few minutes there was a clicking at the heavy plate-glass door leading into the building from the

lobby. Opening the door, I went down a short flight of
stairs. At the foot of them, a door was open and an
elderly woman poked her head, nearsightedly, out of it.

"Is Mr. Fromm in?" I asked.

"No," she said. "He went downtown and won't be
back for a while, and if you're looking for an apartment
there ain't no vacancies."

"I'm not looking for an apartment," I told her, "I'm
trying to locate a former tenant who lived here by the
name of Allison."

"Nobody here by that name," she said.

"I know that," I said, "but maybe she left a forwarding address."

"How long ago was she here?" the woman asked.

"About seven years ago."

"We only been here a little over four years ourselves,"
she said.

"Who was superintendent before your husband?"

"I don't know," she said.

"Does your husband?"

"No."

It seemed hopeless. I was getting very tired, but I
made one final effort. "Who's the rental agent for this
building?"

"Bromberg and Spitz," she said, "downtown in the
Loop. They got offices downtown in the Loop," she repeated and closed the door.

That night I had dinner with Cage. We ate in a cafeteria. "Why so sad, junior?" he asked me. "Haven't you
located that guy you're after yet?"

"No," I said.

"Which reminds me," said Cage, "I want that card
back."

"I got to keep it," I said, "I'll give it back to you in a couple days. It looks like I'm washed up on this deal, but I got one more try to make tomorrow. I got to call on a real estate outfit by the name of Bromberg and Spitz."

Cage nearly choked on his coffee. "Jesus Christ," he said, "don't flash that card around that office! We do a lot of business with them."

"You do?" I asked.

"You're goddamned right we do," Cage replied. "I see letters from them every week in the files. We insure a lot of their stuff. It runs into big dough!"

"Who writes the letters from Bromberg and Spitz that you see?"

"Some big shot name of Keeley."

"Do you know him?"

"Hell, no. I don't know anybody over there. I just file letters they write to the insurance company." He slapped his cup down on the table. "Listen, Danny," he was alarmed, "don't go getting me in trouble."

"I won't, pal," I told him. We finished eating and I paid the check. Afterward we bowled, and I beat Cage three games, but I still paid for the games. Then I popped for a couple beers, and called it an evening. I went home and went to bed.

The next morning I called Bromberg and Spitz and asked to talk to Mr. Keeley. He answered the phone in a deep, booming voice.

"This is Parks at the Northern Transcontinental," I said.

"Yes, indeed," boomed Keeley, "and how are you, Mr. Parks?" He didn't know me from nothing, but the way he sounded I was an old Boola-Boola chum of his.

"I'm wondering if you could give us the name of the superintendent who had charge of your Oak Park Building in 1943?"

"Which building?" asked Keeley.

I gave him the address. "If he is still employed by you, could you please give us his present address, too?"

"Is anything wrong?"

"Not a thing," I told him cordially. "Just a routine matter regarding a lapsed policy. I hate to put you to any bother, but you can probably clear it up for us in a few minutes . . . otherwise, it might take us a long time."

"I understand. No bother at all, I assure you," said Keeley. "I'll have my secretary call you back."

"That'll be fine. Many thanks!" I said. I took a beat, but not too slow, because I didn't want him to hang up. "On second thought," I continued, "maybe I better call her back in half an hour or so. I'm just leaving the office . . . and I might be gone the rest of the day. Thanks just the same." I hung up. Fast. Because I didn't want him to suggest she could leave the information for me.

I fidgeted around my office for forty minutes, wrote a couple routine letters, made some other phone calls, and then called back to Bromberg and Spitz. I asked for Mr. Keeley's secretary and she got on the phone.

"Oh, yes, Mr. Parks," she said. "Mr. Keeley asked me to get some information for you. I have it right here. The superintendent you're referring to is Frank Royster. He was moved to another building in 1946."

"Is he still there?"

"Yes," the girl replied. "He has charge of the Lake Plaza Apartments, 6103 Sheridan Road."

"Thanks," I said and hung up.

I managed to keep busy the rest of the morning. At
noon I swallowed a sandwich and gulped a cup of coffee. Then I caught a Sheridan Road bus to 6100 north.
The Lake Plaza Apartments was another small, four-
story building, jammed in between a big building on the
corner and a large mansion to the north. I found Royster's name and punched his buzzer. A tall, lean guy
with an overhanging nose and a long, sharp jaw looked
at me from the other side of the locked lobby door. His
eyes were plenty unfriendly. I motioned for him to open
the door. Grudgingly, he did so.

"Are you Royster?" I asked him.

"Yes," he said.

"Mr. Keeley, at Bromberg and Spitz, sent me out to
talk with you personally," I said. I could see the name
Keeley meant plenty to him. He forced a smile on his
ugly face and opened the door wide.

"Come on down to my apartment," he invited. I followed him to the basement where he opened an apartment door. It was small, neat and clean, but there was a
"feel" around it of a bachelor's apartment. You can't
put your finger on it, but you can feel it.

"You're not married?" I asked.

"No," he said, "I never got around to it." He sat
down on the neat, overstuffed davenport and waved me
to a matching overstuffed chair. I offered him a cigarette; he took it, and I struck a light for both of us.

"It's important I get in touch with a Miss Karen Allison," I told him. "She's a beneficiary to a policy issued
by my company . . . the Northern Transcontinental.
She lived in the building at Oak Park while you were
there, I believe." I was watching him carefully.

"Yes," he said. He looked uncomfortable.

"Do you remember her?"

"Pretty well," he admitted. "She was a good-looking dame." He swallowed and his big Adam's apple jumped up and down.

"She moved in 1943, didn't she?"

Royster stared at the end of his cigarette and was obviously thinking back. "Yes," he said slowly, "it was in 1943 . . . sometime in the fall. I think she had an October lease."

"Did she say where she was going, or did she leave a forwarding address for her mail?"

"No," he said. "She didn't leave any word of any kind."

"Did she have a furnished apartment?"

"All those apartments were unfurnished," he said. "She didn't have no worries . . . she had plenty of furniture."

"Did she sell her furniture when she moved?"

"I don't think so."

"Then she must have moved it," I told him. "Do you remember the company that hauled it away?"

For a long time he was silent. He started to say something, then changed his mind. "No," he said finally, but he didn't look at me when he said it. "I don't remember the company."

I had a strong hunch he was lying. I jumped to my feet and jammed my hat on my head. "Goddamn it, Royster," I shouted, "you're lying! Just as sure as God made little green apples, for some reason you're lying . . . and I'm going to report it to Keeley. You're holding up a court process, and I hope Keeley kicks your ass out of this job!"

"Now . . . wait a minute, wait a minute!" said Royster. His face was mad, but he didn't let himself go. "I can't help it if I can't remember. . . ."

"I'll be a stuffed son-of-a-bitch if you can't remember," I told him. "You remember something all right!"

"Sit down," he said, "and let me think." I sat down and waited while he went through a routine of thinking . . . to save his face. Finally he said, "I don't remember the name of the company that sent the truck. . . ."

"So you *do* remember something," I said. "At least, now, you remember there was a truck!"

"Why, yes . . ." he said, "I remember a truck coming for it, now. But it wasn't any of the companies I was familiar with."

"What do you mean?" I asked.

"Well, when most people move they usually use a moving company that's pretty close to them. Or from the same general area, at least. It's cheaper. . . ."

"Then you didn't recognize it, huh? It wasn't from Oak Park?"

"No," he said, "it wasn't from Oak Park."

"If you remember well enough to know it wasn't from Oak Park, you got some idea what it looked like."

"I don't remember," he said.

"The hell you don't," I said. "I want you to tell me what that truck looked like. What color was it?" He didn't know.

"Listen, Royster," I told him, "I'll find that truck. I'll find it whether you tell me or not!"

"It was green," he said.

"If I find it and it isn't green . . . I'll not only have you fired . . . I'll work you over, myself . . . personally!"

"Hey, wait a minute," he said, "maybe it was blue!"

"So now it's blue? You sure it was blue?"

"Yes," he said.

"What was the name on it?"

"I don't remember that. If I did I'd tell you."

"What else do you remember about it?"

"Well, there was a wide white stripe, maybe a foot wide painted all around the top of the truck . . . just under the roof."

"Anything else?"

"No."

"You sure?"

"Yeah. . . ."

"Okay," I said. "I'm not going to bother to thank you. But, brother, if you been lying to me . . . you'll see me again." I walked out. He was still seated when I left.

The next day I started in on that old telephone. I got a list of all the moving companies from the 1943 classified telephone directory. There were between five and six hundred of them. I didn't know where to start, so I just started at the top of my list and worked my way down. I'd call a number and ask for the manager. When he got on the line, I'd say, "I'm with the Chicago Safety and Traffic Council. We're making a survey regarding the color of trucks and night driving. What colors are your trucks painted?" Right away the guy would tell me. My next question would be, "Have they always been painted that color?"

I found out that usually a company kept the same color year after year . . . sort of like a trademark. Most of them used red, orange, or yellow. I'd thank 'em and hang up. If they said their trucks were blue, I'd ask if they used any stripes of white on them. Some of them

did, but none painted a stripe of white right under the
roof.

Some of the companies had gone out of business, but
most of them were still kicking. When I called the Lima
Trucking Company, three weeks later, with my three-
hundred-and-sixty-seventh nickel, I found they painted
their trucks blue, with a white stripe under the roof.
They always had painted them that way as long as
they'd been in business.

The next day I went out to see them. They were located on the West Side and were an average-sized outfit.
The Lima Trucking Company offices were in a big stor-
age warehouse with the same name painted all along
one side. In the office, a thin anemic-looking guy in shirt
sleeves and vest came up to the counter to see what I
wanted. I showed him the card from Northern Transcontinental, and gave him the usual story of the insurance policy.

"Of course," I said, "I know it'll take a little work to
look up your records, but I'll be glad to pay you for your
time."

"Sure," he said, "what do you want to know?"

"See if you moved furniture for a girl named Karen
Allison from Oak Park, around the first of October in
1943?"

"It'll take a little time," the guy said.

"How long?"

"Maybe an hour. What was the Oak Park address?"

I gave it to him. "I'll walk up the street and get something to eat," I said. "I'll be back in an hour."

Fifteen pinball games later, I returned and he tossed
one in my face. "Nope," he said, "as far I can find out,
we didn't move any Karen Allison."

"You're sure?"

"Yes," he repeated.

"Did you move *any* dame from that address?"

"Sure. One named Candice Austin."

I fumbled the cigarette I was lighting. "In October, 1943?"

He cleared his throat. "Yes," he replied.

That was it! It couldn't be a coincidence. Krassy had changed her name again; this time she'd dropped the "K" initial but she'd retained the same sound with a "C."—Using "Austin" instead of "Allison" was running true to form. She'd probably taken it from Austin Boulevard in Oak Park.

"Where'd you move this Austin woman?" I asked.

"Some stuff we moved to Evanston, but most of it we brought down here and sold, from the warehouse," he said.

"Do you have the address in Evanston?"

"Sure," he said. He went back and picked up a big, canvas-bound ledger with pink sheets of flimsy paper; he started leafing through it. In a couple minutes he raised his head. "It was the Lake Towers Hotel in Evanston," he told me.

"Thanks," I said. I gave him five bucks.

FOUR

PART II

Krassy moved into the apartment on East Delaware. It was small, with a living room that held a hideaway bed, and a small sliding door which opened to a tiny pullman kitchen. But there was a large bathroom with a shower, and a large closet which was more than sufficient to hold her limited supply of clothing. But her wardrobe was growing. Including the dress and hat with which she had left the Yards the spring before, she had bought two new dresses during the summer, and the white dress and two suits which she had charged to Larry Buckham. She was so happy with her new clothes, her apartment, and her new freedom that she forgot Larry Buckham, Miss Dukes, and Clarence Moon.

She promptly called on Miss Goodbody, taking with her several sheets of the engraved stationery she had ordered made up. Miss Goodbody amiably agreed to write her a letter of recommendation.

"What do you want me to say?" she asked Krassy.

"Write to whom it may concern," said Krassy. "Just say I've been your social secretary for five years and I'm honest and trustworthy . . . and if anybody wants additional information to call you."

Miss Goodbody sat down at her desk, and dipped a blunt, stub-nosed pen in black ink. In a cramped, slightly illegible hand she wrote:

To Whom It May Concern:

Miss Karen Allison has been employed by me in the position of social secretary for the last five years. In that period of time, she has proved a fine employee in every way . . . capable, conscientious and dependable. It is with deep regret that I find it impossible to continue with her services. If any prospective employer should care to call me for additional information, I'll gladly give my complete recommendation concerning Miss Allison.

Sincerely,

"You want me to sign that Van Doren name?" she asked Krassy.

"Yes," Krassy told her. So Miss Goodbody added the signature of "Geraldine K. Van Doren."

"You won't forget that name if anyone calls you at home and asks for it?" Krassy was anxious.

"Of course not," said Miss Goodbody. "In the first place, no one hardly ever calls me, and then I'm not used to be called Missus," she laughed.

"And you'll give me a good send-off?"

"Don't worry, dear," Miss Goodbody replied. "When

I get through, they'll think you're Katherine Gibbs, herself."

With absolute composure, Krassy presented herself at the office of Jackson, Johnston, Fuller and Greene. With assurance in each step, she marched down the marble hall on the twenty-ninth floor. Dressed in a smart black suit, her blond hair burnished and shining, she matched the girl at the reception desk stare for stare.

"I'd like to see the office manager," Krassy told her.

The girl was the first to drop her eyes. "Do you have an appointment?"

"No," said Krassy, "I don't. But I'm looking for a job and I'd like to make an application."

"What kind of work do you do?" the girl asked.

"I'm a secretary," Krassy replied.

The girl looked surprised. "Oh," she said, "I mean you'll have to see Mr. Bard. He's in charge of hiring all the office help, with the exception of the people in the creative end."

"May I see Mr. Bard?" Krassy asked.

"Just a minute," the receptionist told her. She picked up one of the many phones on her desk, and asked the switchboard for Mr. Bard's office. "Hello, Mr. Bard," she said, "this is the twenty-ninth floor reception desk. There's a girl here looking for a secretarial job. Do you want to see her?" There was a slight, disapproving tone in her voice which Krassy resented. After a slight pause, the receptionist added, "Yes, Mr. Bard . . . I'll tell her."

Krassy knew that Mr. Bard was not going to see her. She reached out suddenly and picked the phone from the receptionist's hand. "Pardon me, Mr. Bard," she said, "I'm Karen Allison . . . Mrs. Van Doren's secretary."

"Mrs. Van Doren?" asked a man's voice on the other end of the wire. She could feel him struggling to attach significance to the name.

"Yes," said Krassy, "Mrs. Geraldine . . . K . . . Van Doren." She managed to put just enough importance in her inflection. Immediately, she felt the reaction from the other end.

"Oh, yes . . . certainly. Mrs. Van Doren," replied the man's voice in artificial recognition.

"I've been her social secretary for five years," said Krassy, "but she's leaving for Mexico and isn't taking me with her. She said that even if you couldn't give me a job, you knew so many people . . . that you might tell me who to see. . . ." Her voice trailed off helplessly.

"Why, certainly . . . certainly," said the man's voice. It sounded pleased and important . . . and now that no job was to be requested, it sounded relaxed. "I'm very busy today, but if you'll wait a few minutes I'll be glad to talk to you."

"Thank you," said Krassy, "I'll wait." She replaced the phone and met the receptionist's angry stare. "Thank you, too," said Krassy politely.

She crossed the reception room and seated herself on a long, modern divan with a red lacquered coffee table in front of it. Idly she leafed through a magazine. In a short time, a secretary appeared and escorted her through the numberless corridors to Mr. Bard's office.

"How do you do, Mr. Bard," she murmured, "I'm Karen Allison."

"Yes indeed, Miss Allison . . . won't you be seated?"

Krassy seated herself sedately and with her ankles neatly touching each other. She leaned forward in her chair and placed Geraldine K. Van Doren's letter on the desk. While Mr. Bard read it, Krassy made up her mind about him. She read him as easily as he read the letter.

"Hmmmm," he cleared his throat, "very nice, very nice. I'm trying to remember when I saw Mrs. Van Doren last. . . ." he said.

"I don't know, Mr. Bard," she replied. "Mrs. Van Doren has so many interests . . . it might have been either business or social."

Mr. Bard nodded his head in agreement, but his face remained slightly puzzled.

"The only job I've really had," said Krassy, "was with Mrs. Van Doren . . . and I hardly know where to start to look for another." She lowered her head and looked up at Mr. Bard from under her delicate brows.

"You do type, don't you?" asked Bard.

"Oh, yes! And I take dictation, too. I handled all of Mrs. Van Doren's correspondence . . . both social and business. It was very heavy, you know. . . ."

"Can you do a hundred words a minute?" asked Bard.

"Easily," replied Krassy with complete honesty.

"Really, Miss Allison, I wish I could help you. . . ." said Bard beginning to slide into his turndown. But Krassy headed him off.

"That's wonderful, Mr. Bard," she said with enthusiasm and smiled at him brightly. "I knew you'd help me. Already I feel at home in this beautiful office. . . ." Bard attempted to regain control of the conversation while Krassy continued breathlessly. "Everyone here seems so nice . . . it will be wonderful to work here . . . and I know you'll be the swell—the finest boss in the world!"

"We have no bosses here at Jackson, Johnston, Fuller and Greene," Bard pronounced sententiously, "we all work together. I always pride myself on not being a boss. . . ." He stopped suddenly and caught his tongue. He was trapped.

"You'll always be my boss," said Krassy in deep admiration, "and I'll always love it."

Mr. Bard was uncomfortable, but it was with difficulty he repressed the desire to throw out his chest and strut like a turkey around his desk. "We have a very large office force now," he said slowly, "I don't know just where we'll be able to work you in. . . ."

"Any place, Mr. Bard," Krassy assured him. "I'll be happy to do anything you want."

"Well," said Bard lamely, "see me tomorrow at nine o'clock."

"Thank you," said Krassy. For a moment she stood in his doorway and looked at him fondly. She smiled. Bard smiled back. "I'll see you tomorrow," she said.

"Yes," agreed Bard. After she was gone, Bard sat in his chair and wondered what he was going to do with her. "God!" he told himself in surprise, "I didn't *mean* to hire her." He decided to call Mrs. Van Doren . . . maybe there was still an out. After he had finished the call, Krassy was still hired.

Krassy became the receptionist on the twenty-ninth floor reception desk. Miss Brandywine, the receptionist of the previous day, was given two weeks' pay and . . . with deep regrets from Jackson, Johnston, Fuller and Greene . . . was informed her services were no longer needed. Krassy took over her desk and duties which consisted of checking all personnel, including executives, in and out of the office; maintaining contact with the thirtieth and thirty-first floors; and holding an impregnable line of defense against all salesmen who wanted to make appointments.

Krassy was viewed with suspicion and distrust by the other women employees. Miss Brandywine had been popular with her women co-workers and the story of Krassy "getting her job" soon became common office knowledge. Krassy ignored her current unpopularity and concentrated on her work. She was always pleasant . . . especially to Mr. Bard, who hurried past her desk each morning and seemed slightly embarrassed. After that first interview with Krassy, he never again saw her privately.

As Krassy became increasingly familiar with the office procedure of the advertising agency, she heard daily the magic name of Stacey H. Collins. Collins was vice-president of Jackson, Johnston, Fuller and Greene, and controlled the business and billing of the great Joy Drug empire. Collins had married the daughter of Hugh Stanton, president and chairman of the board of the drug company. The day he married Virginia Stanton he received the Joy Drug account. One week later, he became vice-president of Jackson, Johnston, Fuller and Greene. Collins, however, was not a remittance man; he had the background of fifteen years' experience in the advertising business. He was energetic, aggressive, and capable.

Collins was also ambitious.

Krassy was ambitious, too. She decided that Stacey Collins was a man worth knowing. To that end she made her plans, but she had patiently to await their maturing. Collins' office was on the thirty-first floor; he was seldom seen on the twenty-ninth. The first time Krassy saw him hurrying down the marble corridor, he swept past her without a glance. He was trailed by two harried copywriters and an art director. All were talking and arguing.

"He doesn't know I'm around," Krassy thought. "But he will!" she added to herself. Collins was a man with a square build and powerful body which controlled a tremendous driving power. He wasn't a tall man, but he wasn't short, either. Around five feet nine inches tall, he walked with a thrusting stride of assurance. Krassy quickly evaluated his black, fierce eyes; the stiff, dark hair; and his intense face. "I must think about this," Krassy told herself. And she did.

Four months later she stopped Mr. Bard as he passed her desk in the reception room. "May I see you for a moment, Mr. Bard?" she asked the office manager.

"Certainly, certainly. . . ." he replied. Bard stood for a second visibly hesitating about asking her to his office. Finally he asked, "What can I do for you, Miss Allison?"

"I understand Miss Moore, the receptionist up on thirty-one, is leaving," Krassy replied.

"Yes," said Bard, "she's getting married."

"If you haven't already arranged for a girl to take her place, I'd like to be transferred up to her desk," Krassy told him.

"Why?" asked Bard. "It doesn't pay any more salary than you're making down here." Krassy was earning $42.50 per week.

"That's all right," Krassy replied, "it isn't the money. The agency . . . and all the work that goes on . . . well, it fascinates me. I'd just like to know more about it. And then, maybe, some day I'll be more valuable to the company."

Bard beamed his approval. "I like to hear young people say that!" he said. "It proves they're thinking right. They have the right spirit. I'm sure you have a great future ahead of you, Miss Allison."

"Thank you," said Krassy demurely. "I . . . I hope you're right."

When Miss Moore left, the girls in the office all chipped in and bought her an automatic toaster which sat on a large, stained-walnut tray. The tray had a wonderful little device that neatly trimmed the crusts off the bread.

The coolness which had surrounded Krassy on the main reception desk did not follow her to the thirty-first floor. Here were half a dozen typists together with the personal secretaries of the officers, and account executives, of Jackson, Johnston, Fuller and Greene. Sandwiched between the twenty-ninth and thirty-first floors was the busy, rushing, hectic, bubbling, grouching, half-mad thirtieth floor which housed the "creative departments."

In neat little stalls, like blooded stallions, row upon row of copywriters pounded typewriters and squeezed dry their brains in an eternal search for new ideas to be used in their newspaper and magazine copy. In equally neat stalls, soured radio writers wrote repetitious commercials and grouched about "this whole goddamned business." Carefully protected from the public by glass partitions, a row of artists and layout men daily turned out artwork with the wonderful, mechanical precision of machines . . . only occasionally exploding into a heated uproar.

A mastermind, from the executive department, had conceived the brilliant idea of subscribing to a wired music service to relieve the dread monotony. He had read an article stating where such a music service had also increased the efficiency of the workers in an iron pipe manufacturing plant eighteen percent.

The service was installed in Jackson, Johnston, Fuller and Greene, and from 10:00 A.M. to 11:00 A.M. each morning, and from 2:00 P.M. until 4:00 P.M. each afternoon, the artists were fed a steady diet of phonograph records.

During the daily concerts, the artists made up new lyrics containing the largest selection of pornographic words possible. These they sang to the wired music accompaniment at the top of their voices.

At first, the copy chief, the radio director, and the art director had all protested . . . not only to each other, but to their individual staffs. When the art director called down one of his artists about it, the others left their boards and gathered around to listen.

"Look," explained the artist who had just succeeded in setting a new lyric about a revolutionary type whorehouse to the music of "Ah, Sweet Mystery of Life," "I'm drawing this dame here. Who am I drawing it for?"

"For Re-Newal Form Brassieres," replied the art director.

"Sure," agreed the artist, "and she's got to have a big set of knockers, right?"

"Well . . . right."

"Okay," said the artist, "a couple more songs like that and she'll have the biggest set of knockers you ever saw . . . and the client will be so hot he won't go home for a week!"

Gradually the copy and radio departments formed the habit of joining the art department on good rousing choruses, and the sound of the singing drifted up to the sanctimonious thirty-first floor. After a month, the wired music service was discontinued.

Krassy seldom ventured into the wilds of the thirtieth floor. The appraising eyes of the artists made her uncomfortable. The writers with practiced ease coined words, phrases, and double talk that made her feel unschooled, uneducated. She felt the great holes gaping in her unfinished education, but she carefully preserved a serene, untroubled face. A sense of security would follow her return to her desk on the quiet dignity of the thirty-first floor, after one of her few trips to the creative departments.

From the first day, at her new desk, Krassy had made it a point to greet Collins by name when he appeared in the morning. Coolly, efficiently she would say, "Good morning, Mr. Collins," then await a reply. The first morning Collins stopped in his stride and looked at her. "Good morning," he replied briefly and then hurried on. Krassy never varied the routine. Eventually, Collins asked her name, and after that he would reply, "Good morning, Miss Allison."

One afternoon, Mrs. Collins stopped in the office and asked Krassy to announce her. Virginia Collins was a tall, slender woman with an easy grace. She wasn't beautiful. Krassy thought she was hardly even attractive. She had a long, thin face, rather full lips, and brown eyes. Her eyebrows were natural and full, plucked only across her nose. Her light brown hair was cut short and waved casually around her face. She was wearing a cream-colored mink coat thrown carelessly over her shoulders, with the sleeves hanging empty at the sides. Under it, Krassy could see a knitted, sea green suit.

"So that's the Mrs. Collins?" Krassy watched her walk down the corridor and turn into her husband's office. "I don't think she's so much. . . ."

Krassy had been at Jackson, Johnston, Fuller and Greene a little over six months when she first saw Virginia Collins. In that time, she'd never gone out with any of the men that worked for the agency. All the executives were married; only in the creative departments were there single, unmarried men. At the Christmas party, which Krassy attended shortly after she'd started working at J. J. F. and G., she had met many of them. One by one they'd asked her to dinner in the months that followed. But Krassy was not interested. She wanted no entangling alliances; she desired complete freedom to work out her plans concerning Collins.

But as the months went by, Collins remained as unapproachable as the first morning Krassy had spoken to him. She became restless and worried . . . financially. The money she'd received from Buckham was nearly gone. She had stretched her small salary endlessly to pay her rent and keep her clothes together. Her meals, usually sandwiches and coffee, she ate in her apartment; at the office she missed lunch entirely. After some consideration, Krassy decided there was one copywriter with whom she might have an occasional dinner.

Tim O'Bannion was one of J. J. F. and G.'s senior copy men. His writing sparked many of their top campaigns. O'Bannion was an easy, insolent Irishman, cynical of each product and service of which he wrote. He wore mismatched slacks and jackets, usually with moccasin type shoes sporting heavy rubber soles. He consumed four packs of cigarettes a day, but drank only in moderation. At thirty years of age, O'Bannion made a salary of $18,000 a year, which he promptly spent on one woman after another. Meeting a new woman, he would stay with her just long enough to thoroughly explore her body, and pick her mind clean of ideas, thoughts, and inhibitions. As soon as he felt he completely knew her, he promptly lost interest.

O'Bannion and the girl always parted on the best of terms; sometimes he would call her up after a year, and she was usually glad to hear from him. O'Bannion had met Krassy at the Christmas party and been attracted by her. His invitations had been politely refused. He then started to drift by her desk on the twenty-ninth floor, from day to day, stopping to talk to her. When she moved to the thirty-first floor, Tim moved his calls with her.

"Ah, Karen," he would say,

> . . . Thy beauty is to me,
> Like those Nicean barks of yore,
> That gently o'er a perfumed sea. . . .

He would stop, stare at her, and suddenly ask: "Then what the hell did all those little boats do?"

Krassy, embarrassed and ill at ease with the poetry, would attempt to ignore the question, but O'Bannion would pin her down and delight in her squirming. "Now . . . now, Karen . . . or may I call you Miss Allison? This is the jackpot question. What did all those stinking little boats do? Go out and sink themselves?"

Krassy would be forced to admit she didn't know the quotation.

"Why, Karen," O'Bannion would rejoice, "I think

you're illiterate, I'm disappointed . . . I'm disillusioned . . . and for your information all those little boats

> The weary, way-worn wanderer bore,
> To his own native shore.

Krassy, angry at the closeness of O'Bannion's barbs, would busy herself with her phones. O'Bannion would wait patiently until she was finished.

"How about having dinner with me tonight, Karen?" He'd throw a leg over the edge of her desk and blow great clouds of smoke in the air, while waving aside her refusal. "Just think, Karen," he would say, "along with your dinner, I'll give you a free lecture on American poetry."

Or O'Bannion would suddenly appear at her desk and reach in his bulging jacket pocket. Carefully he would remove sheets of scrawled notes, short stubby ends of copy pencils, a cigarette lighter, a package of cigarettes, and a large bunch of keys. Finally, he'd present her with a bunch of slightly withered violets.

"I know they're not much, Karen," he would say seriously, "but after all it's the sentiment that counts. What does it matter that I removed them from the cemetery this morning?"

Krassy would watch him warily, not knowing if he was serious. Leaving the violets, O'Bannion would return to the thirtieth floor.

The night Krassy first had dinner with O'Bannion, he called for her at her apartment. She made him wait in the lobby. When she appeared, he made no mention of his long wait and suggested the Continental House, a restaurant famous for its food. O'Bannion appeared to be well known and the headwaiter welcomed him cordially. Throughout dinner Krassy found herself listening to O'Bannion in rapt attention as he talked well on many subjects. When he took her home, he dropped her outside her building door and made no effort to kiss her good night.

But the next day, he sent her a dozen roses. They were awaiting her when she returned from work.

O'Bannion continued, thereafter, to take her out to dinner several times each week. Seemingly oblivious to her charm, he made no physical advances and contented himself with talking. Holding forth on books, the world, politics, the theater, art, science, ballet, and philosophy, he held her curiosity. Gradually Krassy relaxed with him and found herself looking forward to his dinners. She was interested in the new world which he opened up for her in his conversations. She began to read some of the books he mentioned. Several times on Sunday, he took her to the art museum and pointed out masterpieces and artists' techniques, giving her resumés of their lives. Krassy absorbed it all.

One evening O'Bannion appeared at her apartment carrying a small, portable phonograph and several albums of records. In his coat pocket was a wrapped bottle of Grand Marnier. He gave the phonograph to Krassy and presented her with the albums. "I thought you'd like this," he told her, "I didn't think you had one." It was the first time he had been in her apartment and he glanced around.

Krassy piled records on the phonograph, and O'Bannion opened up the tiny kitchenette. Taking four glasses from the metal cupboard, he filled two of them with the liqueur and two with ice water. Then seating himself on the couch, he handed a set of the glasses to Krassy.

"Try it," he said.

"What is it?"

"Grand Marnier," he replied. "You'll like it."

Krassy cautiously sipped the liqueur, and she felt the sudden, sweet warmth of it slip quickly over her. "It's good," she agreed, "I've never tasted it before."

"There're a lot of things you missed," he told her, "and the chances are you'll go right on missing most of them. Oh, you'll probably get what you *think* you want. . . ." He stopped and shrugged. "Basically I'm just a sensualist. I like things I can feel, and taste and hear and enjoy. Nothing else is really important." He looked at her and picked up an album. "Maybe that's worse than being the way you are."

Krassy sipped her drink and stretched contentedly. "What albums did you bring?" she asked.

"Bach and Brahms," he said, "and a couple others . . . Sibelius, Monteverdi, and Couperin."

"Tell me about them," Krassy urged.

O'Bannion launched into a sweeping description. Sitting listening to the music, feeling the warmth of the liqueur within her, Krassy studied his face, his gestures, the play and rhythm of his words. She felt a restlessness building within her which was both new and strange. Occasionally his hands brushed her arms lightly and she found herself anticipating the next touch of his hands. "Why, I want him," Krassy told herself in surprise, "I want O'Bannion."

As he arose from the lounge to change the stack of records and pour more liqueur, she watched him move across the room to the tiny kitchenette. "All he does is talk," she thought. "He talks to me, and all he does is seduce me, rape me with words . . . he's drugging me with restlessness, and creating a desire that doesn't exist. It never will exist except in my own mind, and it's turning everything wrong and upside down. He wants me. I know he wants me . . . and all he has to do is reach out to me, but he never has. And now I want him. I want him worse than he wants me!"

O'Bannion returned to the lounge and sat down. His eyes touched hers briefly, and what he saw in them convinced him that he should reach out. With practiced ease he built her desire to a burning flame, then quenched it.

With her head on his shoulder, Krassy drew great sighing breaths. O'Bannion lit a cigarette. "Some day, Karen," he said, "you're going to be quite a woman." Krassy regarded his detachment with anger. But the restlessness and desire which had drained from her body, leaving only a drugged satiety in their place, were too strong to battle. She turned lazily on her side and put her arms around his neck.

"Do you love me?" she asked.

"I hope not," said O'Bannion.

"Why?" asked Krassy.

O'Bannion's sleepy blue eyes, wise in the loving of a score of mistresses, regarded her thoughtfully. "Probably I'm afraid of you, Karen," he replied. "Any man who gives himself up to your love is placing himself in a strange world. I don't know what you're looking for, my sweet . . . and I'm not sure that I want to be the guy who helps you find it."

Krassy slowly flexed her fingers, curled and uncurled her toes. Luxuriously she strained her body tense, then relaxed it as a spring would uncoil. "Am I so strange as all that?" she asked.

O'Bannion suddenly arose. "Yes," he said, "you're as strange as all that. . . . You are the most beautiful woman I've ever known. You're too beautiful to be real." He regarded her intently. "Ah, perhaps that's the rub," he continued. "You're not real."

Krassy leaned on one arm and looked up at him. "What do you mean by that?" she demanded sulkily.

O'Bannion hunched his shoulders, then slowly dropped them. "I can't tell you, Karen . . . I don't know myself. You look like a woman but you feel like a savage; you walk like a mannequin equipped with all the defense mechanisms of Freud. You listen . . . you seldom talk. What kind of a woman is that? And I keep wondering . . . why don't you talk? To hide your ignorance? I wish I knew. I don't know, Karen, really," he spread his hands gently from his sides, "but there's one thing I do know."

"What?"

"I want to see you again tomorrow night."

Krassy smiled to herself.

But Krassy smiled too quickly.

She took O'Bannion for her lover but she never succeeded in dominating him. O'Bannion spent several nights each week with her . . . taking her to the theater, opera, and ballet; he bought her books, and music albums, and presents . . . many of them expensive. But never once did he give her money, and never once did she find out with whom he spent the other nights of the week.

Krassy looked forward to the nights which he would spend with her, and she found herself building an emotional ebb and flow around their life together. Within her, however, there were certain demands which O'Bannion never completely filled. Physically, he lighted fires which burned and left her breathless, but emotionally he escaped her hunger for domination. And it was this domination, this feeling of power . . . in the moments of love when a man is subjugated to a woman's own desire and is helpless to find release without her consent . . . that Krassy wanted. She wanted to see O'Bannion squirm in his need and desire for her, but she never did.

"I don't love O'Bannion," she told herself repeatedly. "I need him, but I don't love him." What was more important, however, Krassy respected him. Through O'Bannion she found her way into the worlds of music and literature and art . . . all the things real and superficial . . . which she knew so little about. She learned to use his phrases, and lifted in part and in full his ideas, likes, and prejudices. She took them for her own, and the fact that they represented an ultimate and sophisticated appreciation, based on education, income, and opportunity, which she had never possessed bothered her not at all. Krassy, without knowing it, was adding a penthouse to a basement excavation without bothering to construct twenty solid floors in between.

O'Bannion's relationship with Krassy continued uninterrupted into the fall of 1941 . . . and then Krassy made her first contact with Stacey Collins.

The offices of Jackson, Johnston, Fuller and Greene closed promptly at 5:00 P.M. for the office force. The executive and creative departments continued until their work was finished. One late fall evening Krassy had lingered at her desk until 5:30. The phone rang from the main switchboard. The operator was trying desperately to locate Anne Russell, Stacey Collins' secretary. Collins was calling from Cleveland and Miss Russell had left the office for the day. Finally, Collins asked to talk to the receptionist on the thirty-first floor if she was in.

"Miss Allison," asked Collins, "are you sure that Miss Russell has left?"

"Yes, Mr. Collins," Krassy replied, "she left about half an hour ago. Is there anything I can do?"

Collins thought a minute. "This is very important," he said, "and I'd appreciate it if you'd follow through for me. I have a meeting with the Joy people first thing in the morning. It's damned important and concerns our entire budget and schedule for next year. Somewhere I've misplaced part of my papers . . . and I must have them. In my desk is a carbon copy of all the material bound in a dark blue cover. The book says "Proposals for Joy Drug, 1942." Please arrange to get that material to me by morning!"

"Yes, Mr. Collins," said Krassy, "I'll put it in the mail immediately. . . ."

"To hell with the mail!" snapped Collins. "It may not be delivered in time. The board meeting is at ten o'clock in the morning. I'll have to leave my hotel by nine o'clock. That material has to be here by then. Get in touch with Miss Russell when she gets home and have her bring it. Tell her to fly over! Do you understand?"

"Yes, sir," she replied. "What hotel are you staying at?"

He told her and hung up.

Krassy caught her breath. "This is it!" she thought. She went to Collins' office and found the blue notebook in his desk. Placing it carefully in front of her, she sat down in his leather chair and called the airline reservation office. She made a reservation for the late night flight to Cleveland.

Krassy never called Miss Anne Russell.

She hurried to the twenty-ninth floor and explained to Mr. Bard that Mr. Collins had requested her to bring the material to Cleveland. Waving Collins' authority in Bard's face, she quickly obtained money for tickets and expenses. Then with the notebook and the money, Krassy returned to her apartment. Quickly she packed her suitcase, and left before O'Bannion appeared. She had a date with him that night. Catching a cab to the Palmer House, she checked her bag and had dinner. After dinner she went to a show until it was time to meet the airport limousine.

Shortly after midnight, Krassy knocked on the door of Collins' room in Cleveland. Collins, who had spent the evening drinking at a club with clients, was getting ready for bed. Half drunk, he wrapped a robe around him and opened the door. Swaying, he stared stupidly for a moment. "Miss Allison," he finally said.

Apologetically Krassy stepped within his room. "I'm sorry, Mr. Collins," she explained, "but I couldn't locate Miss Russell, so I brought the material myself. I knew how important it was. . . ." She let the words trail away.

"Why . . . thank you," said Collins. He stood inside the door looking at Krassy, confused by both the liquor and circumstances. Krassy brushed past him, to the center of the room, and unwrapped the package she was carrying.

Handing the notebook to Collins she said, "I hope this is the right material."

Collins looked at it and nodded his head. "Yes, that's it."

With a smile of relief Krassy said, "I wonder if I could get something to eat? The dining room is closed downstairs, and I didn't have a chance to eat anything in Chicago before I caught the plane. . . ."

"Certainly," agreed Collins. "Where are you staying? Did you check in here?"

"I haven't yet," said Krassy. "I just arrived and came right over with your material."

"All right. I'll call room service and order you something," said Collins walking over to the phone. Beside the phone was a half-finished highball. He picked up the drink and downed it quickly. "It was nice of you to come," he said, "and after you've eaten, we'll get you a room here." He jiggled the telephone impatiently. "Hello? Room Service," he said, and proceeded to order Krassy a club sandwich and a pot of coffee. "Anything else?" he asked her. "They only have sandwiches and things like that this time of night."

"A sandwich will be fine," Krassy told him.

"If you don't mind, I'll have another drink while you eat," Collins said. He ordered up another bottle of soda. In a few minutes a waiter appeared with Krassy's food. After he had gone, Collins opened his suitcase and removed another bottle of Scotch.

"Here, let me do that for you," said Krassy taking the bottle from his hands. She poured a tremendous shot of Scotch in a glass, dropped in an ice cube, and splashed soda on top. She passed the glass to Collins who immediately took a drink. Krassy seated herself in a chair, and placed the sandwich and coffee on an end table by her side. She started eating her sandwich.

Collins sipped at his drink and watched her. "You are quite a person, Miss Allison," he finally said. "Tell me about yourself."

Krassy glanced up at him and smiled shyly. "I think you are a very amazing man, too, Mr. Collins," she replied, "I'd lots rather hear about you." She put her coffee cup down on the end table. "You know," she continued, "I've always admired you . . . so very much. Suppose you tell me about yourself. I know it would be a great deal more interesting."

Collins finished his drink, and walked unsteadily to the dresser to pour himself another. "What do you want to know?" he asked.

"For one thing," replied Krassy, "I've watched you day after day in the office. You're always busy . . . always rushing. Don't you ever get tired?"

"Yes," said Collins, "I get plenty tired. I get so goddamned tired I feel my brains turn to jelly. I get so fed up . . . with the rush and the push . . . and the details, I want to jump out the window. But I don't," he added.

"When you feel that way, then what do you do?"

"I go out and get drunk . . . like now," Collins told her. "I get rip-roaring, deadly, rotten drunk until I can't think any more. Then it takes a day or two to get over my hangover, and by that time I feel better."

"Maybe you'd better have another drink now," Krassy told him. "You're tired and disgusted about something, aren't you?"

"Yes," said Collins, "I'm plenty disgusted. Clients expect you to be a witch doctor. You always have to have a magic remedy, a magic idea to settle their ills. It's all their own goddamn fault most of the time . . . no foresight, no imagination. They fuss and fumble around and get one foot in the bucket, and can't get it out. Then they expect you to have some brilliant idea to pull them off the spot. . . ." He finished his drink and handed the glass to Krassy, unconscious of his action. She took the glass, arose from her chair, and mixed him another.

"They're always looking for a quick, easy way out," Collins continued. "They expect their advertising to make up for lousy sales coordination, expensive and wasteful manufacturing, stinking marketing and merchandising. Oh, what the hell!" He took another drink.

"Why do you do it?" asked Krassy.

He thought a moment. "Because I need the dough," he replied frankly. "It's the only way I can make all the money I want to make. Sure I beat my brains out, but they pay me for it . . . they pay me plenty!" Collins was getting very drunk now, but he continued to speak clearly. Only his eyes were blurred and unfocusing.

"I'll have a drink now, if I may," said Krassy. "If you'll finish yours, I'll mix us both a round. Then I must be going."

Collins finished his drink and handed his glass to Krassy. Once again, she poured it half full of Scotch and added a little ice and soda. For herself, she poured a few drops to cover the bottom of her glass, and filled it with water.

Collins took his drink without question and slumped down on the side of the bed. Krassy, primly, took her seat once again in the chair.

"What do you want out of life, Miss Allison?" Collins asked suddenly.

"Oh, I don't know," replied Krassy. "I've never

thought about it too much. A home and someone to love me . . . just like any other woman, I guess."

Collins nodded solemnly. "You'll get it," he told her heavily. "You're a very beautiful woman. A beautiful woman can get anything she wants out of life. . . ."

"Hurry and finish your drink, Mr. Collins," urged Krassy. "Then I must be going." Collins finished the whisky in his glass. Slowly, deliberately holding a steel control over each small motion, he placed the glass on the floor by the side of his bed. Straightening up, he held control for a moment longer, then with his feet over the side, he sank back until his head touched the covers. "Good night, Miss Allison. . . ." he said, and passed out.

Krassy sat quietly in her chair and waited for fifteen minutes. Then cautiously she arose and walked over to the bed by Collins. She placed her hand on the side of his face and shook it gently at first, then with increasing force. Collins remained unconscious. Easily, quietly, Krassy removed his shoes and socks, unwrapped the robe he was wearing and slipped it off. Then pulling down the covers, she rolled the snoring Collins between the sheets. Darkening the lights in the room, leaving only the light in the bath which peeked through a nearly closed door, Krassy undressed. She hung her clothes deliberately around the room. Wiping the lipstick from her mouth with her fingers, she smeared the crimson in streaks across Collins' face.

Naked, she climbed in bed beside him, and promptly went to sleep.

At 7:30 in the morning the phone rang, and Collins rolled from the bed, staggering in his sleep to answer it. The polite telephone voice informed him it was seven-thirty and he was being called as he had requested. Hanging up the phone, he dropped wearily in a chair, and for the first time saw Krassy. A cigarette in his mouth, a burning match in midair, he exclaimed, "I'll be goddamned!"

"Good morning, darling," sang Krassy and stretched her rounded arms above her head.

"I'll be goddamned!" he repeated and shook his head to clear it. "Did you stay here last night?" he asked foolishly.

"Don't you remember?" asked Krassy.

"I don't remember much of anything," Collins said and ran a limp hand through his hair. "After you ate . . . things are pretty hazy . . . I, uh, thought I went to sleep. Say! Didn't I pass out?" he asked anxiously.

"Not for a while you didn't," replied Krassy with only a touch of insinuation in her voice. Collins stared at her. "You know, Stacey," she continued, "this isn't a very pleasant 'morning after' welcome you're giving me. . . ."

"I'm sorry . . . I mean, I . . . oh, hell . . . what is your first name?" he asked.

"Karen."

"Honestly, Karen, I don't remember a thing. . . ." He took a deep drag on his cigarette. Krassy deliberately stretched again, carefully arranging that the sheet should casually pull away. The bleak morning light shimmered in silver along her body and turned to gold when it touched her hair. Collins stirred uneasily. "Did I . . . I mean, we did . . . uh, last night?" he asked.

Krassy laughed. "Maybe you've forgotten," she told him, "but I haven't!" She stood beside the bed and clutched her slip tightly to her body. "Order up some breakfast, darling, while I take a shower." She disappeared.

Sitting at a small, immaculately set table, heavy with linen and silver, Collins awaited her reappearance. When she returned, he drew up a bedroom chair for her and then reseated himself. Sipping a glass of tomato juice he regarded her seriously. "You know, Karen," he said, "I've laid myself open to a lot of trouble . . . if you want to make it."

"I don't know what you mean," Krassy replied.

"Well," he hesitated, "I've never . . . ever mixed business and pleasure before. It isn't good policy. Women at the office . . . or in my clients' businesses, I've left strictly alone. It always causes trouble. . . ."

Krassy bit deeply into a piece of toast, and sipped her coffee. "Really, Stacey," she said, "I'm free, white, and twenty-one . . . I wanted to stay last night, just as badly as you wanted me to stay. I haven't asked for anything . . . and I don't expect anything from you . . . or anyone else!" Her voice became low and husky. "I knew what I was doing . . . even if you didn't, evidently. I'm not sorry. I've always admired you . . . and last night I felt I was a very lucky girl." Her voice picked up determination. "But last night is all over . . . it's gone and past. Forget it completely if you like . . . and I'll forget it, too." She paused for a moment and glanced up at him. Then lowering her eyes she continued, "I'll catch the first train back to Chicago."

Collins' thoughts and emotions were confused. The thought of her, as he had seen her this morning standing beside the bed . . . he tried to shrug it away. And last night? He wished he could remember. Perhaps he was doing her an injustice; it made him uncomfortable.

"She's a gorgeous thing," he told himself, "and maybe she isn't playing me for a chump. Maybe she really does like me for myself. . . ."

Krassy didn't return to Chicago that day, or the next . . . or the next. Collins called Chicago and explained to Bard that he was keeping Miss Allison over to do some urgent secretarial work in connection with the board meeting. Krassy did, however, return to Jackson, Johnston, Fuller and Greene two days before Collins.

A week after Collins' return, Miss Anne Russell, Mr. Collins' secretary, was transferred to other duties on the twenty-ninth floor. Collins explained it to Bard. "Miss Allison is on her toes," he said. "She bailed me out of a tough spot in Cleveland. I need people like that around me."

"Very true, very true," agreed Mr. Bard, "but I understand that Miss Russell went directly home from the office. She was home all evening and never received your message." He shifted uneasily under Collins' deliberate stare. "Well. . . ." he concluded, "I admit, she might be alibiing . . ."

"It's not a question of alibis," returned Collins. "Miss Russell didn't deliver my material. Miss Allison did."

"Oh, yes," Bard agreed and cleared his throat. Damn my stomach, he thought, I wish it didn't rumble when I get nervous. "Miss Allison is a very fine employee."

After Krassy installed herself in her new office, one of her first callers was O'Bannion. He deliberately sniffed the air. "It's getting goddamned rarified up here, isn't it, baby?"

Krassy shifted uneasily. "It's a wonderful break for me," she told him.

O'Bannion sank his hands deep in his jacket pockets.

"You're not the only one who's getting a wonderful break," he observed.

"Stop it!" she told him angrily. "It's a fine position. I earned it . . . and I'm proud of it!"

"Look who's trying to kid O'Bannion," he told her quietly and walked out of the office.

Krassy saw Collins only one evening a week. Between his duties at the office, his trips out of town, and his appearances at home, Collins had little time for a mistress. O'Bannion continued to see Krassy several nights each week, drifting into her life and out of it in a quiet, thoughtful way. O'Bannion was still able to arouse her to heights of passion that Collins never touched. Krassy still wanted O'Bannion, still needed him. Occasionally she demanded his attentions in a peremptory manner. O'Bannion responded deliberately and detachedly.

Only once was the subject of Collins mentioned between them. Krassy, herself, brought it up. O'Bannion, who had failed to keep two consecutive dates with her, aroused her wrath and desire in equal parts. "You're still angry because I took that job with Mr. Collins," she accused him.

"I am?" he asked in surprise.

"Yes, you are!" stormed Krassy. "You hate Collins for being nice to me. You're jealous of him! But there isn't anything between us, darling . . . honestly." She slipped her arms around his neck and looked serenely in his eyes.

"I'm not jealous of Collins," he replied, "and I don't care whether you sleep with him or not."

"How can you say that! Tim, you know I couldn't sleep with two men . . . not at the same time! What do you think I am?"

"I don't know," O'Bannion replied.

Krassy drew back as if he'd struck her. "You don't?" she whispered.

"Look, Karen," O'Bannion told her, "I'm not criticizing you, I'm not judging you . . . and I'm not in love with you. There are probably two billion persons in the world right now. Each one wants something out of life, and I suppose each one has certain ideas on how to get it. If, for instance, you want to sleep . . . with an automatic water pump, like Collins, that's your business."

Krassy dropped the subject and never brought it up again. But she remembered O'Bannion's description of Collins and cursed him for it. Collins was like an automaton, she thought. Efficient, emotionless, pulsating with driving power and ambition, but incapable of lifting her to any heights of emotional response. Krassy by this time, however, had discovered an age-old, feminine secret. She hid her discontent with Collins, and forced herself into a display of emotion to please and satisfy him, and placate his masculine ego. The response she found natural to O'Bannion, she imitated and played back to Collins. Sometimes she thought O'Bannion knew this.

"Once I told you, you'd grow into quite a woman," he said with a cynical smile. "Baby, you're getting to the point where you can even fool yourself. That's quite a feat."

After several months, Collins became cautious about visiting Krassy in her apartment on East Delaware. "I'm too well known," he told her, "to get by much longer without getting myself in trouble . . . and you talked about. I think you'd better plan to move, where I won't be running into people I might know."

"Yes, dear," Krassy agreed. "Where would you suggest I moved?"

Collins, who lived with his wife in Winnetka . . . north of Chicago on the lake, thought it over. "How about Oak Park?" he suggested. "I don't know many people out there."

"I can't afford to pay much for an apartment," Krassy told him, "and I don't have any furniture."

"Don't worry about that," Collins assured her, "find a nice, quiet place. If you need furniture, I'll take care of it." Krassy did find a nice, quiet place in Oak Park. It was a small, dignified building on a tree-lined, residential street. She was pleased with herself . . . and pleased with Oak Park, a stolid, well-behaved, and stuffily respectable community.

Her apartment had a large living room, with a fireplace and a great picture window; a small, cozy dining room with French doors on two sides; two bedrooms and two baths; and a large, gleaming kitchen. One of the bedrooms she planned to remodel into a library and music room. The rent was $200 per month. Unfurnished.

When she told Collins about it, he gave her a check for a year's rent in advance. "Pay it yourself," he told her, "and keep the lease in your name. See about getting furniture for it." Krassy called on a smart decorator who had a small shop on Michigan Boulevard. His name was Cecil, and she told him what she wanted. Gently flapping his hands in the air, he ridiculed her conventional tastes. Krassy, who was impressed by his talk of moods, textures, fabrics, and balance, hastened to withdraw her own suggestions and left the matter of decorating and furnishing entirely in his hands.

Cecil finished with the apartment and Krassy was entranced with it. She had seen similar apartments only in the four-color reproductions of slick, home-furnishing magazines. When she received his bill, Krassy caught her breath, but Collins raised no objections. He gave her another check. "You know, Karen," he said casually, "you better plan how much you'll need to run your apartment each month. You can't do it on your salary."

Krassy admitted that she couldn't.

"Besides, you'll need new clothes occasionally," he added. "But I don't think we'll be going out very much," he concluded thoughtfully.

"I understand," said Krassy.

"I'm glad you do," Collins told her. "When I have the time to be with you, I want to relax . . . to unwind, and take it easy. I don't want nightclubbing, or entertaining . . . or anything else."

"But you want me?" asked Krassy.

"Yes, Karen, I want you," Collins told her and put his arms around her. The discussion ended with Krassy receiving $500 a month extra to run the apartment and buy her clothes.

"He'll just take it off his personal expense account," Krassy told herself. She rather liked the idea.

The night O'Bannion first saw the apartment, he whistled. "I admire your taste," he told her seriously. "I imagine it took a great deal of work."

"Yes," Krassy said, "I'm very proud of it." She wasn't sure if O'Bannion was being satirical.

"I couldn't have done better myself," he admitted, "but frankly it's a little too feminine for me." He dangled his wrists and smiled. Then Krassy knew he didn't believe her.

"When are you leaving dear old J. J. F. and G.?" he asked after a pause.

"I'm not leaving. Why?"

"Oh, I just thought you might be. . . ." O'Bannion was vague.

"I'm not leaving," Krassy repeated virtuously. "Why, with all this expense . . . I'll need every penny I can make to pay my rent and get the furniture paid for." Collins had suggested, once, that she might leave the agency, but Krassy vetoed the idea. She wanted to maintain at least a reasonable front of being respectably employed. And she didn't want to be pushed completely into the background of Collins' life. At the office, she could keep in touch with him and his activities.

O'Bannion cheerfully accepted her explanation, and said, "Christ, Karen, I'll swap jobs with you." But his trips to Oak Park became fewer. On the evenings they were together, he made no effort to establish their old intimacy. Stretching out in a chair, he would talk for an evening on any subject that crossed his mind. At midnight he would leave, pausing only to kiss Krassy briefly on her lips.

After he was gone, Krassy would roll and toss in her bed wanting O'Bannion, her body burning. But she knew, too, that the days of the old relationship were gone. For her own good, and for the protection of herself with Collins, O'Bannion must leave her life. No longer her lover, no longer sharing a secret from Collins, Krassy considered O'Bannion a potential source of danger to her security.

One evening she asked Collins: "Do you know Tim O'Bannion at the agency?"

"The copywriter?"

"Yes," said Krassy, "he's the one."

"What about him?"

"Well," said Krassy, "I met him last year at the Christmas party. Before I met you, he took me to the opera several times. I never particularly cared for him, but he . . . well, he kept pestering me, and I finally went out with him once or twice."

"Seriously?" asked Collins.

"Oh, no!" said Krassy, "but I guess he thought he was in love with me . . . or something. I haven't seen him for a long time but lately he's started coming up to your office . . . and bothering me again."

"What do you want me to do about it?" asked Collins.

"Well . . . couldn't you transfer him?"

"You mean, fire him? Don't you, Karen? I'll see what I can do about it," Collins promised.

Collins never had the opportunity to follow through on his promise. That was the night of December 6, 1941. On December 7, there was trouble in Hawaii. On December 8, Timothy O'Bannion enlisted with the United States Marines.

Krassy never heard of him again.

By December 14, 1943, two years later, much had happened in the world, but little had happened to Krassy. She was waiting in her apartment in Oak Park for Collins to appear for dinner. Her life with Collins had become static. With increased responsibilities, Collins was working later hours at the office; he was staying away from his home longer; and he now spent most of his leisure time with Krassy in Oak Park.

But the life was a secret and quiet one and Krassy was becoming bored. Collins was her only lover, and since

O'Bannion had left, Krassy had never wanted another man. Through careful saving of her allowance and her own salary from the office, Krassy had managed to build a small, but creditable savings account. That had been her only accomplishment.

That . . . and getting herself pregnant.

Krassy was pleased with the idea. Not that she intended to have the baby, but she was pleased with the weapon it gave her against Collins. That the weapon might be a two-edged knife which could cut both ways, she realized. However, it did steel her resolve to make a break with Collins.

She was waiting now to tell him. There was a knock at the door and Krassy opened it. The building superintendent, a man named Royster, was waiting there. "Good evening," he said, "I just wanted to tell you the wood for the fireplace finally came."

"That's nice," Krassy replied, "deliver it to me tomorrow."

"I can bring it up now," said Royster.

"No. Don't bother tonight."

"It wouldn't be any bother at all," he persisted.

Krassy looked at him with distaste. He was a tall, thin man with a sourly inquisitive face. She felt that Royster was too curious, too familiar with her. Deliberately she had kept apart from the other tenants in the building to prevent forming friendships which might lead to questions. Royster she had tried to keep at a distance, but she was uncomfortably aware of his probing. She felt that he knew about Stacey Collins, and although he treated her with an offhand respect, Royster never addressed her by name . . . never Miss Allison. And she resented his air of confederation.

"No," Krassy repeated, "deliver it tomorrow. I'm expecting guests now."

Royster slowly appraised her, making no effort to end the conversation. "What time tomorrow?"

Krassy started to close the door. "I'll let you know when I get home from the office. . . ."

Royster placed his hand on the door, stopping it short. Then he dropped his hand and turned at the footsteps in the hall. Collins was approaching. "All right," Royster said to Krassy, "I want to get it out of the basement." He walked away.

Krassy turned to Collins. "I can't stand that man!" she said.

"Who? The janitor?"

"Yes, Royster," she replied. "He gives me the shudders."

Collins walked in the apartment and removed his coat and hat. Krassy hung them neatly in the small, hall closet. "Are you tired tonight?" she asked him.

"Christ! I'm always tired," Collins replied. He rubbed his hand over the back of his neck, and gently kneaded the muscles. "I've got a hell of a headache."

"Sit down, darling," Krassy told him, "I'll get you a drink before we eat." Collins half sprawled on a long, low modern divan. Krassy went to the kitchen and poured two martinis from a shaker which she kept in the refrigerator. To one she added an olive, to the other a small onion. Returning to the living room, she handed the martini with the onion to Collins. "You'll feel better," she assured him.

Collins smiled and lifted the glass in her direction. "Well, here's cheers anyway," he replied. Krassy seated herself across from Collins, watching him warily. She waited for a few minutes, until he had finished his second drink and started his third, before she began to lead the conversation in the direction she wanted.

"I wonder where this will all end, Stacey?" she mused.

Collins paid little attention. "The war, you mean? Oh, it'll end pretty much like all wars . . . nothing accomplished, really . . . and nothing gained. . . ."

"No, I don't mean that," said Krassy. "I mean about us."

"I don't know," he replied. "Why, aren't you happy?"

"I feel like I'm living in a vacuum," said Krassy. "You and the apartment are my entire life. What life I have . . . I have to live secretly. It isn't good, Stacey."

Collins sensed an urgency in Krassy's conversation. It made him uncomfortable. "Well," he conceded slowly, "we don't go out much . . . maybe we should."

"No, it isn't that," replied Krassy. "It's a lot deeper than that . . . it's hard to explain." Krassy stopped a moment, marshaling her thoughts. She couldn't explain to Collins that she didn't care what people thought, because in her own devious way she did care. She cared a lot. She wanted a name, and security against ever returning to the Yards. She wanted independence from Collins whose word could turn her out of Jackson, Johnston, Fuller and Greene . . . and who could close the door of her apartment in her face.

As far as morals were concerned, Krassy believed it was a matter of opinion . . . her opinion. She believed in using her sex as other women used an education, or a trained talent, or social connections . . . or hard work. These things, too, she couldn't explain to Collins.

Krassy realized she was facing herself, and Collins, in

a showdown. She hadn't planned it this way, but suddenly the situation was there. She couldn't keep the vacuum airtight forever. Already, little cracks and breaks were letting enough oxygen in to start her breathing again. Collins must face her problem, too. He must decide. But already, Krassy sensed, Collins' decision had been made. He had made his decision years ago, but it was necessary that it be brought out and discussed.

"Well?" asked Collins.

Krassy, startled, looked up. "Oh," she said, "I was thinking. I've been thinking about it for several days . . . how to tell you. How to be diplomatic . . . if being diplomatic is important. And I guess maybe it is. . . ."

"What are you trying to tell me?"

"Bluntly, I'm pregnant."

Collins' face didn't change. He leaned slightly over the couch and set his martini glass on the cocktail table.

"Are you sure?" he asked.

"Entirely," replied Krassy. "I've been to the doctor and I've passed all my tests with flying colors." She smiled briefly.

Collins was silent. The silence hung between them as an invisible glass partition. Krassy could see through it to Collins. For a moment, she wasn't sure that her voice could reach him, and she felt she was sitting in a perfectly insulated soundproofed room. "Say something," she said and her voice sounded heavy in her ears.

"There isn't much to say," he replied.

"There's plenty you could say."

Collins evaded her eyes. "What?"

"You could say you were happy . . . and you'd marry me."

"I want another drink," he told Krassy. Rising from the divan he took his empty glass to the kitchen and poured a martini from the shaker. When he returned to the living room, Krassy hadn't moved. "I can't marry you, Karen," he told her. "You know that."

"I don't know it," Krassy said.

"But I'm already married. . . ."

"Men have been divorced before."

"If I divorced Virginia, old man Stanton would cut my throat."

"You don't love her," Krassy told him.

"Perhaps I don't, but she's good for me."

"Good for you!" snapped Krassy. "She's good only for the Joy account."

"That's what I mean," Collins said flatly.

Krassy turned cold eyes upon him. In them, Collins thought he could read her contempt, but he was in error. Krassy's instinct had told her she could never break Collins away from his wife and her connections. Now she was trying to decide how far she could go . . . how far to goad him . . . before forcing the inevitable showdown. She was eyeing him intently, cautiously measuring him as a wary adversary.

"There's more in life than money," Krassy said. "I'd hate to think you didn't have enough ability to get another job. After all, is Virginia just a meal ticket?"

"You know better than that." Collins' voice assumed a patient, reasoning tone. "Sure, I could get another job, but never one like I have now . . . and you like money and luxury just as much as I do. There are only a few advertising accounts which have the appropriation of Joy Drugs. It takes all kinds of politics to get those accounts . . . years of making contacts and pulling strings. . . ."

"Even marrying," said Krassy shortly.

Collins assumed a different tack. "Look, Karen, why get all steamed up about this? We've had two good years together . . . let's keep what we have. You can see a doctor, there're plenty of them. Have something done. . . ." He shrugged the sentence off, unfinished.

"I don't intend to have anything done," Krassy told him.

"Good God! Why not? Women have operations . . . like that . . . every day!"

"Because I want the baby!" Krassy told him.

Collins argued her decision, but Krassy remained firm in her defensible position. Finally Collins told her, "If you have the baby, you can't stay in Chicago."

"I know it," Krassy said, "I think I'll go to New York. No one knows me there, and I'll simply say I've been married and divorced."

"How will you live?"

"You'll give me enough to live on," Krassy told him flatly. Collins' face instantly became still and watchful. His black eyes searched her face intently. "Are you trying to blackmail me, Karen?" he asked softly.

"No," Krassy told him, "I won't do anything sneaky or undercover. I'll sue you right out in the open court!"

"That wouldn't be very smart," he replied.

"I know it," said Krassy, "but I'll do it, if there is no other way. You want to keep the Joy account, you don't want to keep the baby. All right! You keep your wife and your business, I'll take my freedom and my baby. But you, Stacey, are going to pay for it!"

They talked until late in the night. Collins wanted

Krassy to remain, to continue their life together. But the break had been made, and the breach was complete as far as Krassy was concerned. This was her opportunity to make a break on her own terms. She made the most of it. Finally, reluctantly, Collins agreed to give her forty thousand dollars in treasury bonds, five thousand dollars in cash, and all the clothes and furniture in the apartment.

Collins didn't stay in the apartment that night . . . or ever again. The next morning, at Jackson, Johnston, Fuller and Greene, Krassy handed in her resignation with two weeks' notice. The girls on the twenty-ninth and thirty-first floors bought her half a dozen pairs of black market nylons for a going-away present.

Krassy found a small apartment in Evanston at the Lake Towers. She rented it under the name of Candice Austin. Her own apartment, in Oak Park, she sublet with the approval of the rental agents. She decided to keep only enough of her furniture to use at the Lake Towers. The rest she sold.

The evening before she moved, she spent packing her clothes. Tired, she climbed into a steaming bath and stretched luxuriously in the soothing water. The tub filled with bubbles glistening in white and lavender and rose. Submerged to her chin, she scooped the water in long sweeps over her body. Suddenly she was conscious of a man's figure standing silently in the door.

It was Royster watching her with hungry eyes.

"How did you get in here?" she demanded, her voice cracking suddenly in fright.

"I got a passkey," he answered, never moving his eyes.

The fright was quickly overtaken by a wave of shaking anger. Stepping from the tub, Krassy walked past Royster who stepped aside as she passed. He followed her to the living room. Krassy walked to her small, walnut writing desk and picked up a pair of long, wicked scissors.

She turned on him quickly. "Get out!" she said. "Get out!" She held the scissors chest high and pointing out . . . as the boys in the Yards fight with spring knives.

"Now . . . don't be like that," Royster said. He took a step toward her.

"Get out!" she commanded, her voice high and intense with hate. "Get out . . . you goddamn, dirty, lousy, no good, son-of-a-bitching bastard! Get out . . . get out! Or I'll rip out your guts!"

Royster stepped back, his eyes wide and frightened. Krassy followed him, step by step across the living room, to the hallway, and to the door leading into the corridor, the scissors gleaming evilly in the subdued light. She slammed the door behind him, and put the night chain on the door. Outside, in the corridor, she could hear Royster. A deep breath whistled slowly from his throat. "You dirty slut," he said.

The next day, Royster watched a blue moving van, with a broad white stripe, haul Krassy's furniture away. He stayed in his apartment, watching from behind the curtains.

"The dirty slut!" he muttered to himself.

FIVE

P A R T   I

Now in telling about this, I hope I can make you see it the way I saw it. I know it's screwy for a guy to see a picture and start chasing a gal he's never met, particularly when he doesn't know what the percentage will be . . . even if he finds her. But something kept pushing and prodding me, and all I knew was that if Krassy Almauniski was still alive, I had to find her.

All those days and weeks and months when I was running down leads, I found myself thinking of her as my gal. She became just as real to me as if I was going to meet her for a date every night. I'd looked at her picture so many times, I could trace each feature with my eyes closed. But by this time, I could hardly tell what was real and what I was making up in my own mind. I'd find myself talking to her and holding conversations, and then I'd realize I was walking on my heels and I'd try to stop it. Then later on, I'd remember some of the things she'd said to me, or what I thought she had said, and I'd have a hell of a time convincing myself it wasn't real. The things I'd found out about Krassy . . . where she was born, and going to Mrs. Dukes' to live, and getting engaged to Buckham, and going to school at Goodbody . . . all made me respect her. A gal like that didn't have many breaks, and so she'd tried to make some for herself. Then she goes and gets herself a job with Jackson, Johnston, Fuller & Greene, and works her way up to being a big shot's secretary and having a nice apartment in Oak Park. It proved to me she had plenty on the ball.

That was enough for my mind to work on, and when I mixed it with all the things I thought of, and made up, and how crazy I was just for a sight of her, it all became confused and the lines blurred, and changed, and over-lapped. Just like I said, it was like trying to paint her picture in smoke. One minute she was real, and right here; and the next minute she was fading, and I couldn't stop her from disappearing completely.

Believe me, it was a hell of a situation.

I still had a living to make, so I had to do some work at the Clarence Moon Collection Agency, but I begrudged every moment I wasn't working at finding her. Even with the little work and time I put in the office, my business was growing and I was starting to make a little money. So one day when Bud Glasgow, who used to work with me at the old International Collections, got canned he came over to see me. Bud was a nice little guy who wore rimless glasses, and had worked for old man Crenshaw at International ten or twelve years. He didn't have too much ambition, but he could write blood-thirsty collection letters, and he was steady and dependable. So I told him he could come in with me on a percentage basis. I'd only be able to pay him twenty-five bucks a week, but I'd give him twenty percent of everything he collected. That would work out to a better deal than he'd had at International anyway, so he was glad to take it.

I left Bud in charge of the office, and writing letters, and covering the telephone, and I did the outside collections where it was necessary to get a little tough. I also kept on making a few calls to get new business. The rest of the time I spent trying to find Krassy.

After I got the address of the Lake Towers from the Lima Transfer Company, I didn't waste any time getting out there. I knew she'd had her furniture delivered under the name of Candice Austin, so I didn't have much doubt I'd pick up her trail again. But I was wrong.

The Lake Towers is a big white hotel, built in layers like a tremendous, frosted birthday cake, getting smaller at the top until finally there was nothing left but a big tower on it. It has a big, white, plaster lobby, with deep maroon carpeting and bright green chairs, with heavy plate-glass tables on little, black, iron legs.

I walked into the lobby and up to the desk clerk. I flashed my insurance adjuster's card and told him I was looking for a Miss Candice Austin who'd moved into the hotel in 1943, on the first of October. Without bothering to look up, he told me no one by that name was living there.

"Do you know all the guests in this joint by name?" I asked him.

"If they've been living here since 1943 I'd know them," he snapped.

I'd made him sore, but I'd been sure Krassy was still there and I was plenty disappointed.

"How long have you been here?" I asked him.

"Ever since the war was over in '45," he told me. I pulled out a picture of Krassy and showed it to him. "Do you ever remember seeing this gal?" I asked him.

"No," he said, "and believe me, if I'd seen her, I'd remember."

"I know she moved here in 1943," I told him. "Would you mind checking your records and verifying it for me?"

"Look, Mac," he said, "I don't have the time. Those files are seven years old. Christ! I wouldn't even know where to find them."

"I'd pay you," I told him.

"Naw," he said, "I wouldn't know where to begin."

"Is it okay if I ask around some of the boys here?"

"Sure, go ahead," he agreed, "but be careful the manager don't see you."

"How about me asking the manager myself?" I suggested.

"I wouldn't," he said. "He's a mean bastard. He wouldn't tell you anything, anyway. And if he saw you snooping around here, he'd throw you out."

I thought it over. Maybe the guy was right. Anyway, I could always ask around first, and if nothing happened, I could end up by talking to the manager. I went over to the elevators. There were six of them. I waited around for each one to hit the ground floor, then if there weren't any passengers for a few minutes, I'd show the elevator boy the photograph and ask if he'd ever heard of Candice Austin.

None of them had ever seen her or heard of her. They

were all young punks, anyhow, and none of them had been working at the hotel very long. Finally one of them said, "You might ask Syd; he's been around this place for years."

"Who's Syd?" I asked.

"He's the night clerk."

I gave the guy with the bright idea a buck and walked back to the desk. The day clerk I'd talked to was still on duty. I asked him what time Syd came on and he said at 8:30 P.M. It was shortly before dinnertime then, so I went out and had dinner in a cafeteria, in Evanston, and went to a show. When I got out, it was a little after nine, so I went back over to the Lake Towers again.

A round fat guy, somewhere in his middle fifties, was back of the desk. He had alert blue eyes, and wore a pair of front teeth well filled with gold. He was bald from the back of his collar straight up and over to his forehead. The hair on the sides of his head was thick, and he brushed it back. It gave a peculiar effect like the guy had parted his hair in the middle . . . with a part six inches wide. He had on a snappy blue suit, and a little light-blue leather flower in his lapel. I asked him if Syd was in.

"I'm Syd," he told me. So I wound up the old insurance routine again, flashed my card, and did my act about the lost beneficiary. By this time, I could do it with both hands behind my back. Syd listened intently. I was glad, because I had him pegged as a nosy guy with an overgrown curiosity. When I was all through, I showed him the picture. He looked at it carefully and handed it back.

"Never saw her," he said finally. "Never heard of her, either."

My belly dropped clear down to the floor. "You were here in 1943 weren't you?" I asked.

"Sure I was here in 1943," he replied. "I've been here since '39."

We just stood and looked at each other. I couldn't think of anything to say. Then suddenly he thought of something. "What month did you say she moved in?"

"In October," I said.

"Wait a minute," he answered. "I was gone for a while in 1943; that summer I caught pneumonia, and when I got better I went to Arizona for the rest of the year. I lost forty-five pounds. She might have been here while I was gone."

"How long were you away?"

He checked his memory briefly. "I left Chicago in August, and didn't return until January of 1944. The hotel here was short of help, and wanted me back . . . otherwise, I'd have stayed longer."

"It still doesn't make sense," I told him. "I know she moved in here the first of October with her furniture. Christ, in those days it was even tougher to get an apartment than it is now!"

"That's right. . . ." he agreed.

"Well, she just wouldn't move in here for three months would she? Look," I continued, "could you check your old registrations for October of '43 and find out *if* she moved out again? Maybe that'll give me some place to get started. I'll pay you for it."

"Sure," he said, "but you'll have to come back tomorrow. All those old records and transcripts are kept in the vault, and I won't have any time to go through them until late tonight. After 2:00 A.M. it is pretty dead around here, and I'll have plenty of time then."

I knew if I went home I wouldn't get any sleep. I'd stay awake all night wondering what Syd had found out about Krassy and then I'd have all day tomorrow to wait until he came back to work.

"That's great," I told him, "but if it's okay with you, I'd rather stick around and wait. It'll save me a trip back tomorrow night."

"It's all right with me," he said.

I thanked him, told him I'd be back, and left the hotel. The city of Evanston doesn't permit the sale of liquor and I had a hell of a long time to wait. I finally decided I'd go down to Howard Street. Howard Street is the dividing line between Chicago and Evanston. It's a wide-open little section and sells plenty of liquor and has shows and cheap nightclubs. I caught an el to Howard and got off. I found me a bar and went in and parked up next to it. I ordered a couple of quick shots, then slowed up, reversed my field, and started drinking beer. It was cheaper and I could kill time just as well. About 2:00 A.M. I slid off the stool and started back to Evanston.

Syd met me at the desk. "I was just going to look at the files now," he told me.

"Right," I said. I sat down in one of the bright green chairs, lit a cigarette, and tried to get comfortable. The lobby was deserted. Once in a while some man would come through the lobby from the street, and twice couples came through, a little high and usually laughing. But they all had their own keys and didn't stop at the desk. In maybe half or three-quarters of an hour, Syd appeared carrying a small metal box with file cards in it. On the front of the box was a label which said, "June-December, 1943."

He sat the box on the desk and opened the drawer.

Every so often there was a pink card which stuck out farther than the white ones. Each pink card carried a month typed on it. Under October, he pulled out the pink card . . . and twisted it up on its end like a flag. Then he started sorting through the white cards back of it.

Right up near the front was a card: "Austin, Candice, Miss. Apt. 1901."

"She checked in all right," he told me.

"When did she check out?"

He looked at the card a little puzzled. "That's funny," he told me.

"What's funny?"

"Miss Austin didn't check out, but evidently she gave up her apartment in December, because Mrs. Dana Waterbury moved in December 24, 1943."

"Couldn't Miss Austin have shared the apartment with Mrs. Waterbury?"

He shook his head and showed me the card. It was ruled down the center. There was a check-in date written on one side of the line which said, "October 1, 1943." Then just below it was: "Mrs. Dana Waterbury, December 24, 1943." "Why couldn't she?" I insisted.

"Because, it is a single apartment rented on a single-rate basis. In the second place, I remember Mrs. Waterbury . . . she lived here quite a while . . . three or four years. There was no one living in 1901 with her. She and her husband lived there until he went overseas."

"I thought you said it was a single-rate apartment?"

"It was," Syd said, "but during the war, the hotel didn't charge extra for service men on leave. Patriotism!" He laughed.

"Quite a gesture," I agreed. "You say you remember Mrs. Waterbury?"

"Sure."

"Did she look like that picture I showed you?"

"No," he said.

"When did Mrs. Waterbury leave?"

He looked at the card again. There was no check-out date on it. "She lived here long enough that it wasn't entered on this original card," he told me. "But as I remember it was in '46 or '47."

"Did Mrs. Waterbury leave a forwarding address?"

He shrugged. "If she did, we wouldn't have it now," he said, "it's been so long ago that all the mail stopped years ago."

"Who else around here might remember Miss Austin or Mrs. Waterbury?"

"I don't know," he said. "If the maid on that floor is still working here, she might remember. Or perhaps the housekeeper."

"How can I find out about the maid?"

"The housekeeper could tell you."

"What's her name?"

"The housekeeper? Mrs. Boos. She isn't here now, naturally, but she'll be on duty at eight o'clock in the morning."

"What time are you off work?"

"Eight o'clock."

"Would you mind introducing me to Mrs. Boos? It might help."

"Sure, I'll introduce you," he said. "You won't have any trouble getting her to talk; she's a regular old gossip."

I gave him ten bucks, which seemed all right with him.

I told him I'd see him at eight in the morning and walked out.

I didn't try to go back to Chicago again that night. I stayed in a small hotel, in Evanston, that soaked me plenty. In the morning I was back at the Lake Towers at eight o'clock. Syd was just coming off duty. He motioned me, and we rode an elevator to the third floor.

I followed him down the hall and around a couple turns. We landed up in a long, narrow room that had shelves built from the floor to the ceiling on all four sides . . . leaving only enough space for the door on one side, and a window on the other. In the middle of the room was an old-fashioned, high, roll-topped desk. A gray-haired, middle-aged woman was sitting at the desk. She was wearing a gray shirt-blouse, and a black skirt. Syd introduced us.

"Mrs. Boos," he said, "this is Danny April, a friend of mine. He works for an insurance company, and he wants some information about former tenants in 1901. I knew if anyone could help him, you could." Syd smiled ingratiatingly, and I tried to echo it.

"Certainly, certainly," she replied. "What do you want to know?" At this point, Syd bowed out, told me good-bye, and disappeared down the hall. I gave Mrs. Boos a quick run-down on my insurance story for Candice Austin.

"I wonder if you could tell me who the maid was that cleaned in 1901?" I asked her.

"I couldn't tell you," she replied, "it would be impossible. We rotate the maids on different floors constantly. There's no particular maid that is assigned definitely to a certain floor."

That was that. "You said you didn't remember Miss

Austin?" I told her. She nodded. "Well, would you mind taking a good look at this picture and telling me if you've ever seen the girl?" I handed her the glossy print of Krassy. Mrs. Boos took it in her hands and stared at it intently. Then she sort of turned it a little to one side, and peered at it under a different light.

Finally she said, "Why, yes, I know her. But when I knew her she had black hair and looked a great deal older."

"Who? Miss Austin?" I asked.

"No," she said. "That's Mrs. Waterbury."

"Are you sure?"

"Positive!" She folded her hands and dared me to doubt her.

"When she moved in here," I said slowly, putting the thing together in my mind, "her name was Candice Austin. It's on the card downstairs at the desk. She must have gotten married while she was living here, huh?"

"Probably," agreed Mrs. Boos, "but this is such a big hotel that tenants can live here quite awhile before I get to recognize them. I'm not in daily touch with them like the clerks and the rest of the downstairs staff. When I knew her she was already married. I had no way of knowing when or where she got married."

"Did you know her husband, Dana Waterbury?"

She shook her head. "No," she replied, "I never saw him. But he must've been killed in the war, because Mrs. Waterbury got married again and moved away."

"Oh, Christ!" I said to myself, "here we go again!" I took a deep drag on my cigarette, and kept talking. "Who'd she marry this time?"

"I don't know," said Mrs. Boos. "I remember reading something about it in the paper."

"Which paper? And when was this?"

"All I remember at the time there was a little announcement in the society section about her getting married. She was such a pretty woman," she added.

"You don't know the guy she married or where she moved?"

"I don't, Mr. April," she said. "It was long enough ago, that I just barely remember it. That's all."

I ground out my cigarette on the sole of my shoe. There was no ashtray on Mrs. Boos's desk, so I dropped the butt in my pocket. "You say she looked older than this picture . . . and had black hair. There's no chance you're making a mistake in identifying her?"

Mrs. Boos looked at me coldly. "I told you it was her," she stated distinctly, "and it is!"

I thanked her wearily and caught an el down to the Loop. I transferred back to my rooming house on a streetcar. Then I called Bud Glasgow at the office and told him I wasn't feeling so good and I wouldn't be in until afternoon. I felt plenty beat; I had a hangover from all the beer I'd had the night before, plus damn little sleep, plus a hell of a disappointment and letdown.

Krassy was married. Right now she was married and living some place with a husband. I felt the world had been wrapped up in a big slimy package and somebody had slapped me in the face with it. I took off my shoes and trousers, flopped down on my bed, and drifted off into a restless sleep. Around noon, I woke up, washed my face, and shaved. Then getting dressed, I went out and got some scrambled eggs and coffee, and by that time the world seemed a little brighter.

Not much, but a little.

I'd followed Krassy this far, and I might just as well

play the string out. If I didn't . . . I'd never forget her. All my life I'd keep remembering and wondering about her. And then another idea hit me. Maybe she wasn't married any longer! One husband had died; maybe the second one had, too. Or maybe she was divorced. What the hell! Maybe she wasn't happy and someday I could talk her into a divorce. All sorts of crazy ideas ran around in my mind, chasing each other, getting all tangled up, tripping over one another, and then starting all over again. I laughed. But as long as I had something to hope for, I was happy again.

There was still one lead I could follow. Mrs. Boos had read the announcement of Krassy's marriage in the paper. She didn't know which paper . . . or what year. I tried to tie the dates to make sense. The first desk clerk had been there since '46, and he didn't remember her. That might mean she'd been gone before he started work . . . or shortly afterward. Of course, with her black hair, he might not have recognized her picture when she was blonde. Hell! Syd hadn't recognized the blonde picture either as the brunette Mrs. Waterbury. It took Mrs. Boos with a woman's eye for features and make-up to do that! Syd had promised to get me the check-out date of Mrs. Waterbury, but he wouldn't have it until the next day. I decided not to waste any time; I wanted to get going right away.

And then a thought came to mind. "Why had Krassy dyed that beautiful blonde hair . . . black?" But I shoved it aside. It wasn't important.

I started for the offices of the *Chicago Daily Record*. The library, or "morgue," is located on the second floor. Most newspaper libraries look alike. Usually they are a big, square room, with high, green metal files running all around the walls. In the middle of the room are a couple of long, plain tables covered with scissors, paste pots, and brushes. The librarian is nearly always an old newspaperman who is put out to pasture in his old age taking care of the files. Indexed and cross-indexed . . . back and forth . . . is damned near every name you've ever heard of. Anyone who's ever had their name in the newspaper, once, is usually filed there. The librarian keeps the files up to date by clipping current items out of the paper, and filing them in big, square manila envelopes.

That was also the *Daily Record* library.

I asked a nice old guy, in shirt sleeves and a vest, if he had anything on a Mrs. Dana Waterbury. In about ten minutes he shows up with an envelope. "Nothing on Mrs. Dana Waterbury but I got something on her husband . . . Captain Dana Waterbury. Want that?"

"Sure," I told him. I glanced over a couple of old newspaper clippings. He'd been quite a war hero, a combat pilot, and had been killed over Germany in May, 1944. There was a brief mention in the obit that he was survived by a wife.

I gave the file back to the librarian, and as a matter of routine, asked him to check on the names of Karen Allison and Candice Austin. He did. He had nothing on them. I thanked him and left.

Next I went over to the *Evening Express*. Same kind of library, same kind of librarian. Clipping on Capt. Dana Waterbury, nothing on Mrs. Dana Waterbury. Karen Allison? Nothing. Candice Austin? Nothing. By this time it was getting late, but I figured I might squeeze in one more call at the *Daily Register*. The *Register* is a tabloid with a big night circulation in Chicago.

I hit paydirt.

The librarian had one small clipping under Mrs. Dana Waterbury. In its blatant style the clipping announced:

LOCAL MILLIONAIRE BANKER WEDS
SOCIALITE HERO'S WIDOW

> This morning in a quiet service, attended only by close friends, Howard Monroe Powers, prominent Chicago banker, married Mrs. Candice Waterbury, widow of Captain Dana Waterbury of Philadelphia. They were married by Cook County Judge Winfield L. Visolotti.

There was a little more to it, not much. The story appeared in the issue of January 17, 1946. I asked the librarian for a file on Powers. He brought it and it was bulky as hell. From the number of clippings I knew Powers was a big shot. Among them was a duplicate of the one I'd read about Krassy's marriage. After reading some of his clippings, I discovered Powers was president of the Lake Michigan National Bank and Trust Company; chairman of the board of the Chicago, Midwestern & Pacific Railroad, and served as a director of insurance companies, universities, hospitals . . . and so on.

It made me sick. It made my guts ache. What guy could buck competition like that? I was ready to give up. What the hell was the use? Then I discovered something.

In January, 1946, when Howard Monroe Powers married Krassy, he was sixty-five years old!

I added it up fast. Powers was now close to seventy.

He was still alive, because I hadn't seen a death notice in the clippings.

Krassy was twenty-seven or -eight.

Well, all right!

I still had hope.

FIVE

PART II

Once again Krassy was moving. And once again, reminiscent of a past moving day, Krassy had a stop to make at a beauty parlor. Relaxing in the cab, she directed the driver from Oak Park, to a hairdresser in the Loop. "A new name," she told herself, "a new life . . . and a new woman." The cab pulled out of the heavy stream of Michigan Boulevard, and glided smoothly to a stop before the flossy beauty salon. Krassy paid him off. He tipped his cap, and watched her cross the crowded sidewalk; he waited until she had disappeared within the doors before driving off.

In a small reception room, hung with soft, gray drapes, Krassy announced herself. "I'm Candice Austin," she said, "I have an appointment with Leon."

"Yes, Miss Austin," murmured the girl, "this way, please." Krassy followed her down a long, narrow hall, honeycombed with small cubicles . . . each filled with a patient woman. Women sitting under driers, women in curlers, women holding heads over shampoo basins, women having hair combed, women having hair cut, women having hair touched up. Before one of these empty little spaces the receptionist stopped and turned to Krassy.

"Please be seated," she said. "Leon will see you immediately." Krassy entered the cubbyhole, removed her coat and hat, and sat down. In a few minutes, a slender dapper man, wearing a white surgeon's smock buttoned completely up the neck, made his appearance.

"I would like to do something about my hair," Krassy told him.

"So?"

"I would like to make it black."

"Black?" asked Leon. He fingered the gilded silver hair, and gently rolled it between his fingers. "Most women would give a great deal to have hair like yours," he said softly.

"But you can do it all right?" insisted Krassy.

"Oh, yes . . . I can do it easily," Leon replied. "If that is what you want."

"That is what I want . . . to make it black. Raven black."

Leon shrugged and started to work.

Four hours later, Candice Austin registered in the Lake Towers Hotel. The room clerk waited in silence as the tall, black-haired woman, with the grave eyes and fragile, gentle face was assigned to apartment 1901. His eyes were impressed.

Krassy liked the Lake Towers; she liked the pretentious white building, the swinging glass doors, the rococo plaster mirrors and hanging chandeliers. She liked the uniformed doorman and bellboys and elevator men . . . the obsequious service. Possibly for the first time in her life, she felt free to relax for a while . . . free of the old fears in the temporary security of Collins' settlement.

Her apartment was small. It consisted of a living room, bedroom, and bath, with a combination kitchen and dinette. Her furniture from Oak Park she rearranged many times. When she was finally satisfied, she viewed her new home with approval . . . it was quiet and relaxed, with a casual dignity.

There was one more detail to attend to.

Krassy went to see a doctor. This particular man of medicine specialized in performing abortions. While maintaining an ethical practice, he performed his specialty on the chosen few having the right introductions and the right bank accounts. The success of this practice could be somewhat evaluated on the basis of a large and expensive home which he maintained, a three-car garage . . . filled, an extravagant wife, and memberships in many exclusive clubs.

Attached to his waiting room were two general examination rooms, and a small, clinically clean operating room complete with table, sterilizing cabinets, and instruments. The doctor, a short, fat man with ruddy cheeks, thick black hair with a gray streak, and large horn-rimmed glasses, was vaguely interviewing Krassy. He had a small card which he pretended to be filling out.

"And how long have you been pregnant, Mrs. . . ." he glanced down at the card and cleared his throat, "Mrs. Augman?"

"Two months," replied Krassy.

"And your husband?" He cocked his head, "I mean . . . is your husband living with you?"

"He was," said Krassy, "but he's just gone into the service."

"Are you working?" the doctor asked.

"Oh, yes . . ." said Krassy. "That's what worries me, doctor. I must continue to work . . . and if I'm pregnant, I can't."

"Hmmmm," said the doctor clearing his throat again. "You have no family to help you?"

"Oh . . . no," said Krassy. "And neither has my husband. They can't help me at all. Doctor, I must be able to keep on working. I . . . we . . . well, we haven't the money to support a baby, now."

The doctor gravely nodded his agreement. "You're sure you're only two months gone?" he asked.

"Oh, yes!" Krassy was definite.

"Well . . . let me make an examination," he suggested and waved his hand generally toward the small operating room. Krassy arose, gathered her gloves and handbag firmly, and marched in.

Half an hour later, Krassy was resting on the small couch in the doctor's waiting room. The nurse asked her if she felt all right, and Krassy said she did.

"Go right home, now," the nurse told her. "And stay off your feet tonight and tomorrow. You'll be all right."

Krassy arose gingerly to her feet. She felt perfectly normal. She left the doctor's office, leaving behind the tiny fetus and four hundred dollars.

October in Evanston is a month of beauty. Krassy loved to walk the lake front streets, with the high arching trees turning from green to amber and vermilion and purple. Often she would wander the campus of the university filled with girls dressed in careless sweaters and skirts, and young men in uniforms wearing no insignia . . . studying in desperate uneasiness, awaiting their service assignments.

But best of all, Krassy liked the lake. She liked the great stones piled and half buried along the beach which held off the wrath of the lake. The rocks, like mailed hands, protected the soft-skinned land against the gnawing of the waves. Under the clear, October skies, the water stretched away and across the horizon. Some days, the lake shimmered with a metallic sheen, and it would stir and seethe in mighty constraint, throwing small, deadly waves in a constant probing of the great stones and delicate sandy beach.

Occasionally, the day would be hazy, and the sky would fill with ghostly smoke, and then the lake would roar and shake its mighty fists in anger. Whitecaps would ride the waves with skillful ease, to throw themselves against the shore and break into spray that cast a million miniature rainbows. Krassy would sit and hug her knees and sometimes feel a restlessness build within her which throbbed to the restless tempo of the lake. Uneasily she would arouse herself, and walk back to her apartment . . . vaguely dissatisfied.

In November, Krassy enrolled her services at the Servicemen's Canteen. Three nights a week she worked as hostess, serving sandwiches, coffee, and doughnuts . . . and occasionally as a dancing partner. She listened to boys from Iowa, Colorado, and Arizona; to boys from Maine, New York, and Florida; to homesick boys and sophisticates. In a way the tragedy and comedy of GI brown and blue didn't touch her. From eight until twelve on Monday, Wednesday, and Friday she saw them come and go . . . bodies without faces from cities, farms, and states which were only names. Krassy listened to their stories and their conversation without really hearing or caring. The Canteen was a sedative, a drug . . . in a period of marking time. Something was going to happen. Krassy was sure of it! But what it was, she didn't know. She had time . . . days or weeks or months. She was waiting.

She was careful, however, to avoid all the downtown Chicago shops and restaurants and clubs. Collins, and her life with him, was rapidly slipping into the past. Each week she became more detached from it, but she was careful to avoid any place where Collins might appear. Or where she might be recognized.

On the night of December 17, 1943, she met Dana Waterbury. Not at the Canteen, but at the Officers' Club, where she and several other hostesses from the Canteen had been invited as extra guests.

In her usual preoccupation, she was only half listening to the young officer with whom she was dancing. When the music stopped, she realized he had asked her a question.

"I'm sorry," she said, "but the music . . . I didn't hear what you said?"

"I asked you," he replied distinctly, "what your name is?"

"It's Candice Austin," she said. "Why?"

"Because I think I'm going to marry you," he replied.

Krassy laughed. "Don't forget, Captain," she said, "I've heard that before . . . in the Canteen."

"Possibly," he agreed, "but this time it's different. This time . . . I mean it!"

"And what is your name?" she asked. "I always prefer to known a man's name before I marry him."

"Say! You're not already married?" he asked anxiously.

"No. But you haven't told me your name yet."

"It's Waterbury. I come from Philadelphia."

The music started again and couples began dancing. Waterbury looked down into Krassy's quiet, serene face. "Come on back to my table," he urged her. "Come on back, and let's have a drink . . . and catch up on all our conversation." He guided her back to a small table, where two other officers were sitting. He made the introductions around the table and pulled out her chair. "You'll excuse us, please," he said to the others, "but Candice and I have several things to talk over." They laughed and stood up. "You'll excuse us, Waterbury," one of them replied, "if we do our drinking at the bar."

"You weren't very polite to your friends," Krassy said.

"I'm too busy to be polite right now," Waterbury said, "but I think they understand. . . ." He signaled for a waiter, and continued. "Where do you live?"

She told him, and then asked, "How long are you going to be in Chicago?"

"For a little while, at least," he said. "I'm here on a bond-selling tour. Those other chaps," he motioned toward the two men at the bar, "and myself were brought back from Europe . . . especially for the big event." He laughed softly. "Perhaps the brass figured we should get a break before our number comes around again." He became sober, and nodded toward his friends. "Both those fellows have nearly doubled their missions."

"And you?"

"Yes," he said, "I have, too."

Krassy swirled the drink around in her glass. "What did you do before the war?" she asked.

"Not much," said Waterbury. "I lived in Philadelphia. I went to Princeton and was graduated from there; I didn't study very hard. In the summers, my family moved up to Cape Cod, and most of the time I sailed. Have you ever been to the Cape in the summer?" he asked.

"Yes," said Krassy, "quite often."

"Did you like it?" he asked eagerly.

"I loved it," Krassy replied.

"Do you like sailing?"

"Oh, yes!"

"Where did you learn to sail? Here on the lake?"

"Have you ever been to Berkeley?" she asked cautiously.

"No," he said. "I've been to San Francisco many times, but I never got across the bay. Why?"

"Because Berkeley was my home . . . when I was a little girl," she explained. "My father used to take me sailing there." She asked slowly, "Is your father still alive?"

"Very much so," replied Waterbury. "Right now he's in Washington. He's in the shipping business."

"Is that what you'll do after the war?" she asked.

"Probably," Waterbury agreed. "All my family have been doing it since William Penn hired the family skiff," he smiled.

Krassy smiled with him. "And the rest of your family . . . your mother? Do you have any brothers and sisters?"

"Yes. Mother is alive . . . and I have one sister . . . two years younger than myself. Hey! I seem to be answering all the questions!"

"Isn't that all right?" asked Krassy.

"Not at all!" he said. "I have several thousand to ask you. Such as why you're so beautiful . . . and why haven't you been married before now? Are all the men in Chicago blind?"

"No," said Krassy, "they're not blind." She paused to take a cigarette from Waterbury, and waited until he lit it for her. "As a matter of fact," she continued, "I just moved to Chicago a few months ago."

"Where was your home?" asked Waterbury.

"Originally it was in Berkeley," she said. "Then both my parents were killed in an accident . . . when I was quite young. Since then . . . I've spent most of my time in school . . . and just traveling around."

"No other relatives?"

"No," replied Krassy. "A few distant ones, but no close ones."

"That's rugged," said Waterbury sympathetically.

"Not too rugged," said Krassy bravely, "fortunately my parents left me enough money . . . that I don't have to worry. But it is lonesome . . . sometimes." She looked at her watch. "It's getting late," she added. "I should be leaving."

"I'll drive you home," Waterbury suggested. "We have a car at our disposal on the tour."

"I'd love it," said Krassy.

Waterbury went up to Krassy's apartment with her. She mixed him a drink, and seated him in Collins' favorite easy chair. Then she scrambled eggs and made coffee. They ate it off the coffee table in the living room. Waterbury stretched out his long legs, lit a cigarette, and jammed his hands in his pockets. "I like it here," he announced.

"That's nice," said Krassy.

"I wish I didn't have to leave," he said. His face was expressionless and his eyes steadily watched the ceiling.

"I wish you didn't, either," said Krassy. "But you must, you know."

"I may have so little time . . . that I'd like to spend it all with you," he said.

Krassy shook her head. Waterbury arose from his chair and crossed over to the lounge; he seated himself beside her and put his arms around her. He kissed her, and Krassy returned his kiss with simulated passion.

"Don't make me leave. Not tonight!" His voice was urgent.

Krassy gently disengaged his arms. Taking his face between her two hands, she looked directly in his eyes. "You want to make love to me, is that it?"

"Yes," Waterbury replied levelly.

"No," said Krassy. She stood behind the couch and held her arms behind her back. "I want to wait until I'm sure," she told him softly.

"I'm sure," he said. "Aren't you?"

"I don't know . . . not really. But I'm going to wait until I *am* sure." No persuasion from Waterbury could change her mind. He returned to the club that night.

One week later, on December 24, Krassy married Dana Waterbury.

Waterbury, with his Air Corps connections, managed to secure priorities and seat reservations, and they flew to Philadelphia to spend Christmas with his family.

The Waterburys lived in an old, square, red brick

house with a white-columned, rotunda porch, located in
a quiet, dignified residential section by-passed by busier
sections of the city. Massive green shutters hung at the
windows, and the heavy, slate roof was neatly painted.
The house sat well back from the street, and a narrow
flagstone path wound its way to the door. The path was
flanked on both sides by a hedge trimmed with military
precision. Several great trees, now hung with snow,
stood silently, and on guard, between the house and the
street.

Dana Waterbury dropped his luggage on the porch
and thundered the heavy brass knocker on the door. It
was opened by an elderly maid, neatly dressed in a black
uniform with a small white apron.

"Merry Christmas, Ruby!" he shouted.

"Why . . . Merry Christmas! Dana, Mr. Waterbury,
I mean," she cried happily. Then catching sight of
Krassy, she smilingly stood aside.

"Candice, darling," Dana said, putting his arm
around her and pulling her inside the door, "here we
are. And this is Ruby. Ruby, this is my wife . . . Mrs.
Waterbury."

Ruby permitted her mouth to open in momentary surprise, quickly she recovered. "Merry Christmas, Mrs.
Waterbury," she said. "And congratulations!" She
turned to Dana in confusion. "I mean congratulations to
you . . . Mr. Dana."

Dana laughed. "Where is everyone? I want to show
them a real Christmas present!" A tall, slender girl raced
from an adjoining room. He turned in time to catch her
as she flung herself in his arms.

"Dana! It's Dana!" she cried, wrapping her arms

around his neck, hugging and kissing him enthusiastically.

"Wait a minute," he protested happily, "break it up. I have a brand-new wife here to show you. . . ."

Krassy faced the tall girl, with shoulder-length hair. "Wife?" Chris asked. "Wife!" She turned to Dana in amazement, then smiled at Krassy. "Why, Dana . . . you lucky man! Where did you ever find such a raving beauty!" She held out her hand to Krassy warmly. "Dana is such a dope sometimes . . . I've always been afraid he'd marry a hag or something. . . ." She looked at her brother fondly. "Anyway, I'm Chris . . . welcome, congratulations, and Merry Christmas!"

Krassy smiled back at her. "Thanks," she said, "but I think I'm the lucky one." She hugged Dana's arm affectionately.

Dana put his arms about both girls and squeezed them. "It's okay . . . and Roger . . . as long as you both think I'm wonderful," he grinned. Mr. and Mrs. Waterbury, Dana's parents, descended the wide, turning staircase.

Chris catching sight of them called, "They're married . . . isn't it wonderful?"

"Dana!" His mother stopped momentarily.

"Well, well, well. . . ." Mr. Waterbury said softly.

Reaching the foot of the stairs, they hurried toward the couple. "Congratulations," said Mr. Waterbury cordially to his son, "and now do I get to kiss the bride?"

The Waterburys had a guest for Christmas dinner. A tall, white-haired man, with a tired face, deeply lined, he was an old friend and business associate of the elder Waterbury. A widower, spending Christmas in Philadelphia, his name was Howard Monroe Powers.

Seated at the big, white-linened table, in the spacious old dining room, Krassy accepted a plate filled with turkey, chestnut dressing, mashed potatoes and sweet potatoes, and cranberry sauce. Salads and side dishes surrounded her. "Where is Maria?" she asked herself. "My God! Whatever made me think of that?" Suddenly her hands were shaking and cold. She placed them in her lap and held them quiet. "No," she thought, "I won't think of her . . . or anybody else. Now I'm right. This is where I belong." She picked up the heavy, sterling silver fork, with an indistinct crest worn smooth, and started eating. "Merry Christmas, to me . . . from Krassy," she thought.

"How long are you going to be home, dear?" Dana's mother asked him.

"I could only wangle a forty-eight-hour leave," he replied.

"Are you returning to Chicago?" asked his father.

"Yes," said Dana.

"Then where?" asked Mrs. Waterbury.

"I don't know. As soon as this bond tour is completed, I'll probably get shipped back over."

"Where will you live, Candice?" asked Chris.

"I think I'll stay in Chicago . . . at least for a while," replied Krassy. "I have a comfortable little apartment and know a few persons there . . . now."

"Why don't you come and live with us?" asked the elder Waterbury.

"I'd love to . . . later, perhaps," Krassy evaded.

"Don't worry, Charles," Powers pompously told the older Waterbury, "as long as she's in Chicago, I'll keep an eye on her." He turned to Krassy and continued: "As a matter of fact, if there's anything you ever want, while Dana's gone . . . you just ask me."

Krassy lowered her eyes. "I'll remember," she promised.

"Uncle Howard means it," said Chris. "Why, he has so much money that it's a terrible shame!"

Powers laughed in amusement. "When you were little, you didn't think so. I remember the time your dad wouldn't give you a horse."

"Oh, yes!" Chris was delighted. "But you did. And it made father angry."

Charles Waterbury protested: "I thought you were too small to have a horse . . . that's all."

"The moral of this is," Dana told Krassy, "if I'm gone and you should ever need a horse . . . see Uncle Howard."

"She'll do no such thing," said Dana's mother, seriously. "Your father can buy all the horses anyone needs." And Krassy joined the laughter.

The next day, Krassy and Dana flew back to Chicago. The day they were married, Dana had moved his luggage into her apartment, so they settled comfortably at the Lake Towers. Occasionally, Dana would be away for two or three days at a time, attending bond rallies in Detroit, Cleveland, Indianapolis, St. Louis, Kansas City, Minneapolis, and Milwaukee. He would return to Chicago, after such a trip, tired and exhausted.

"This is a war of money and material," he told Krassy, once, holding up a drink and rattling it, listening to the tinkle of the ice. "Sometimes I feel like a damned fool being held up on display. 'Look,' " he mimicked, " 'here's Captain Waterbury. Captain Waterbury has knocked down twenty Nazi planes . . . Captain Waterbury is here, today, to ask *you* to buy more bonds . . . MORE bonds!' " He leaned over in his chair and held his head in his hands, then straightened again. "The truth of the matter is that Captain Waterbury doesn't give a goddamn whether anyone ever buys a war bond. All Captain Waterbury is worrying about, these days, is when his orders will come sending him back to Europe . . . to get his ass shot off!"

January slipped into February, and February into March. In March, Waterbury's orders arrived. "It looks like the tour is over," he told Krassy. The night before Dana left, he took Krassy to dinner at the Yar.

The once quiet, dignified restaurant was a hustling, voice-filled, clattering place. In a corner, at a small table, Dana ordered an elaborate meal, and a magnum of champagne. "We're not leaving here," he told Krassy, "until we kill that bottle . . . and its nearest relative. When I walk out of here, I'm going to be very drunk and very happy. And you, too, my sweet."

The gypsy orchestra played, and Waterbury morosely filled and drained his glass . . . time after time. When the food was finally served, he occasionally picked at it. Krassy was silent, answering only his direct questions.

Now that he was leaving, Krassy was sorry. Her sorrow was not a personal thing . . . either for him or herself. She would miss him . . . not that she was in love with him, for she had never deluded herself with the illusion . . . but once again she would return to being lonely. He had given her the protection of his name, and clothed her in a new, and solid, respectability. She didn't try to look ahead . . . after the war . . . when she must pick up the threads of her life with him again.

Krassy had felt safe and secure with him. His assur-

ance, and easy, good humor had been amusing; his love
for her had been sincere and in it she had the satisfaction
of stability. Behind him he would leave a loss of com-
panionship.

They left the Yar and returned to her apartment. Dana
was drunk . . . and not happy. Silently he undressed,
showered, and slipped naked into bed. Krassy loitered in
the bath. Eventually, she turned out the light and slipped
into bed beside him. Waterbury pulled her to him, hungrily, and later he lay beside her, his head resting on her
outstretched arm; his face partly pressed against the side
of her breast.

Krassy found herself thinking of the other nights he
had held her in his arms and made love to her. They had
not been unpleasant, she thought. Yet never once had
she been completely aroused by him, or swept up and
away by his passion. She had found she could simulate
ardor . . . convincingly and realistically. In it, she
found a certain physical satisfaction that in no way
touched her emotions.

Now, she flexed her body in relaxation. "We haven't
talked about so many things," he said suddenly. "Tonight I could spend telling you how much I love you, but
instead of that . . . there are some other things I have
to say. . . ."

"Perhaps some things are best left unsaid," replied
Krassy.

"No," said Waterbury, "this concerns such everyday
things as money. Yesterday, I went down to see Uncle
Howard and his attorney. I want to tell you how things
are . . . just in case something should happen to me."

Krassy became very quiet.

"I've arranged to send you three hundred dollars a

month," he continued, "from my overseas pay. I've changed my government insurance over to you . . . and the money my grandmother left me."

"That isn't necessary," murmured Krassy. "I have plenty."

"It isn't a great deal," Dana continued. "When my grandmother died, she left Chris and me twenty thousand dollars each. That's all the money I have in my own name." He paused a moment. "Just in case . . . anything did happen to me . . . and you needed more, why Dad would take care of you. He has plenty, I guess."

Krassy didn't say anything. She stroked his head until he fell asleep.

In the morning, Dana Waterbury left. His absence made little difference in Krassy's life, although several events occurred as a result of her marrying him. First, in April, she received a check for $300. Then in May, she received a second check, and later in the same month the news that Captain Dana Waterbury had been killed over Germany. As a result she collected $10,000 worth of government insurance, $20,000 from Dana's grandmother's estate, and a bonus. The bonus was a personal life insurance policy for $7,500 which Dana had forgotten to mention.

Howard Monroe Powers was of great help to Krassy in her collection activities. Powers' own high-priced attorney handled everything, with a minimum of effort, worry, and detail for Krassy.

As president of the Lake Michigan National Bank & Trust Company, Powers' office was a place of majesty and awe. Krassy enjoyed the respect and hushed reverence with which she was received and ushered into the presence of Powers. Usually he was seated at his tremendous desk, with leather fittings, and plate-glass letter holders. Directly behind him was a high, arched window of a single pane of glass, inset with a stained glass shield. The shield was shining amber, with a crimson bar dividing it in half. Below the bar was a brown acorn; above the bar, a green oak tree. Curling around the shield was a ribbon with the motto: TRUST BUILDS OAKS FROM ACORNS. Krassy thought it very impressive, although the first time she read it, she thought it said, TRUSS BUILDS OAKS FROM ACORNS. She knew that couldn't be correct, so she read it a second time . . . correctly.

Powers would rise from his seat and sweep gallantly around his desk to hold both of Krassy's hands. As her visits increased he increased, proportionately, the period of his hand-holding. One afternoon, he exclaimed, "Candice, my dear, you must have *known* I was thinking about you!"

"You were?" she asked.

"Yes," he said. "For months now you've been staying in . . . not going anywhere. It isn't right. You're still young and have nearly all your life before you."

"I . . . I don't think it's right to go out. Not yet, anyway," she said. She opened her purse, took out a small, dainty handkerchief, and touched the sides of her eyes gently.

"Of course you're right . . . in a way, that is, my dear," Powers hastened to reply. He patted her hand fondly. "But there are limits to everything. Perhaps it wouldn't be right to go . . . well, drinking and cavorting around nightclubs . . . but who could find fault with your going to the opera?"

Krassy lifted her eyes questioningly.

"Yes," he said, "that would be perfectly all right. I have a season's box, you know . . . and tonight is *La Boheme*. I'll take you. . . ." He paused for a moment before continuing with a forced little laugh. "After all I am old enough to be your father. Ha."

"And my grandfather, too," Krassy thought. However, she hurried to ask him, "You're sure it's all right? It isn't disrespectful to Dana?"

"Of course not, of course not!" Powers reassured her heartily. "And we'll even go further tonight. Suppose we plan to have dinner at my club this evening?"

"I think I'd like that," replied Krassy.

"It's settled then! I'll send a car around for you," Powers smiled and patted her hands again.

In Krassy's apartment was a small calendar in a tiny leather case. The drawings were done by an artist famous for his type of beautiful women with exaggeratedly long legs, tiny wasp waists, tremendous busts, and sensual eyes. Each month, Krassy carefully removed the last picture and deposited it in the drawer of her writing desk.

The calendar had belonged to Waterbury and, in his leaving, he had forgotten to pack it. In December, the last drawing was exposed and Krassy realized that Waterbury had been dead for over six months. With sudden impulse, Krassy opened the drawer of her desk and took out the old drawings. She picked up the small, leather calendar case, too, and carried pictures and case to the kitchen. She threw them away. She didn't feel badly about it; it wasn't an act of sadness. Rather, she felt a sudden swelling of relief. A part of her life had come to an end again, just as the calendar had come to the end of its printed time.

At first Krassy had received occasional letters from Chris and several letters from Dana's mother. She had written polite little notes in reply. Eventually the correspondence had trickled off, and now the only news she received of them was through Howard Powers.

Powers soon began to escort her constantly . . . to plays, concerts, and opera. In the half year since Dana's death, Powers' avuncular attitude had gradually changed.

With calculation Krassy had helped him change it. Powers was careful not to extend his interest obviously or beyond a point where it could be withdrawn without losing either his dignity or self-respect. He still patted her hands, and had progressed to the point of holding them in the theater. On rare occasions, he casually rested his arm over the seat in his car, permitting it to gently touch her shoulders. Krassy did nothing to stop his growing sense of possession. She took each opportunity to ask him about her clothes, and in return complimented him on his appearance, his new suits, his choice of plays and music.

She also permitted him to invest small sums of her money in stocks and bonds. Invariably they returned a profit to her. On one such occasion, she bought Powers a solid gold cigarette lighter, and presented it to him. "You are the smartest man I've ever known," she told him and kissed him playfully. Powers seemed to return her kiss in the same spirit, but Krassy easily sensed the emotion he attempted to conceal.

"You are quite the nicest girl I've ever known," Powers replied gallantly. "Now I shall have to do something extra nice for you."

The year of 1944 flowed smoothly into 1945 and by

that summer Powers was completely infatuated with Krassy. This was the situation Krassy had long been considering and had contributed her earnest efforts to promote. Just how far it would progress, and how it would ultimately end, was something that Krassy had not yet decided.

Powers was a well-preserved man in his late sixties. His wife had died some twenty years before . . . and without bearing him children. Although he was a man of great personal wealth, he lived a lonely life, with few acquaintances, and only a handful of personal friends. On his wife's death, he had sold his great town house and, later, his farms in Lake Forest. Living alternately between his downtown club and his apartment on Lake Shore Drive, he spent little money on his personal life.

His one exception was the *Lorelei*, a beautiful fifty-six-foot schooner, with diesel auxiliary. During the war, it had been laid up, but to Krassy's delight, Powers refitted it, and completely manning it, planned a month's cruise to Mackinac Island and down the Great Lakes to Buffalo.

Krassy loved the long, sweeping lines of the *Lorelei*, and she would lie for hours aft, watching the creamy wake trailing behind in the blue waters of the lake. Or twisting on her back, she would shade her eyes with her arm and trace the towering masts above the mahogany deck and watch the spreading white acres of canvas against the sky. Sometimes Powers and the captain would let her take the wheel, and with her legs braced wide apart, she would hold the great, brassbound wheel and feel the *Lorelei* like a live thing under her hands.

But at night, she would stretch restlessly in the berth of her small private cabin, and think to herself, "This can be mine . . . this . . . and this . . . and this," enumerating in her mind the fortune and influence of Howard Monroe Powers. Powers could give her the financial security she had always sought; protection against the filthy little house in the Yards, a golden barrier between her and cheap, imitation silk dresses in bargain basements, and lingerie bought from the crowded counters of five-and-ten-cent stores.

On some nights, the creaking stays on deck would arouse her from sleep and hearing them, for a wild half instant, she would remember the sound of the bed in her father's house, and she would wait to hear the soft slap-slap of Maria's feet on the floor.

She knew she could marry Powers, and she believed it was what she wanted. However, instinctively, she hesitated to take this final step. There was no other man in her life; carefully, deliberately she had withdrawn from any associations after Waterbury's death. His name had given her a respectability unhesitatingly accepted by Powers and his friends. Krassy was careful not to jeopardize this invaluable asset, and she kept it blameless and shining. It was her key to unlock Powers' millions . . . if she could force herself to marry him.

There was another alternative, and Krassy debated it often. "I can have an affair with him," she thought, "but he's so stuffy and respectable it might cause trouble. One of these days his conscience would start bothering him, and that would be the end of it." If this was true, Krassy felt she would lose her most powerful weapon . . . Powers' respect for her. She also considered the same type of pressure she had used against Collins; she might permit herself an affair with Powers and then confront him with her pregnancy. But although this had been successful in reaching a settlement with Collins, Krassy convinced herself it would not succeed with Powers. The situations, behind the two men, were entirely different. Collins had been married and at the financial mercy of his wife. Powers was free. And it was more than probable that if Powers fathered a child, at his age, he would demand the right to maintain contact with it; even to the point of adopting the child.

Krassy turned the subject over continually in her mind, and spent long hours considering it. Weighing her experience and instinct against the character of Powers, as she knew him, Krassy reached the reluctant conclusion that she must marry him. The thought of physical contact with him brought her a feeling of revulsion. "But he's nearly seventy," she thought, "he probably won't live very much longer. Maybe only a year or two. And besides, a man at that age oughtn't to be too hard to handle. He probably won't want to make love very often anyway."

In the bright sunlight of the deck, Krassy watched Powers standing stripped to the waist, wearing a pair of white duck trousers and white canvas sailing shoes with heavy rubber soles. She measured the slackness of his arms, and the sinking flatness of his chest. And although his skin was deeply tanned, he looked old. The loose, stringlike muscles of the flesh beneath his chin, the myriad tiny lines etching his eyes, forehead, and the corners of his mouth undeniably announced his age. Powers wore his age with distinction, it was true, holding his lean body erect. And with his silver-white hair, and quiet command, he demanded respect.

"But not love," Krassy thought, "nor even desire." The dry heat of his palms as he stroked her hands and arms brought an uncomfortable awareness to her. His occasional, fleeting kisses from pale lips were unpleasant. "But he *is* an old man," Krassy repeated, again and again. "I can stand it for a few years. And then? Then Mrs. Howard Monroe Powers with more money than she can ever spend! Whatever you want . . . yours! . . . for the rest of your life."

Beating her way down from Mackinac, the *Lorelei* on her return trip brought Krassy within twenty-four hours of Chicago. The last night out, Krassy had dinner with Powers in his master's cabin. The steward cleared away the meal while Krassy and Powers sipped their after-dinner brandy. Suddenly Krassy emptied her brandy into the coffee cup and smiled up at Powers.

"I feel I should drink gallons and gallons of brandy tonight," she said. "I'm blue. . . ."

"Why, my dear?" asked Powers.

"Oh . . . this lovely trip . . . the beautiful, beautiful *Lorelei*," she paused momentarily. "I wish it would go on forever," she added.

"Every trip must end sometime," Powers told her sententiously.

"Unless you're the Flying Dutchman," said Krassy.

"And you wouldn't like that. . . ."

"No, of course not. I was just fooling. But honestly . . . I've had a wonderful time, Howard. And," she hesitated and shyly dropped her eyes, "I'll miss not seeing *you*."

"But you'll see me," he protested.

"Oh, certainly . . . but not *every* day . . . not like this. Do you think it's forward of me to say that, Howard?"

"Not at all . . . no! I'm very proud."

"Somehow I've come to depend entirely on you," she told him softly. "All the nicest things in my life are connected with you . . . dinners, and plays . . . and seeing people. . . ."

"I hoped you'd say that sometime, Candice," Powers replied.

"Well . . . it's the truth! I look forward to seeing you, Howard. I'm always happiest when I'm with you."

"Sometimes I've thought I took up too much of your time," Powers said slowly. "Perhaps you'd rather be . . ." he swallowed, ". . . with younger men."

"Younger men!" Krassy scoffed. "I've had enough of younger men . . . they're egotistical and crude and cruel, Howard. They're not like you . . . kind, gentle, and sympathetic."

Powers beamed his approval. "But I'm getting . . . a little older," as an afterthought.

"I don't think you're old!" Krassy replied with candor. "I think you're the most interesting man I've ever known. You're handsome . . . oh, yes, Howard, I've seen other women look at you. . . ." Powers glanced hastily in the bullseye mirror on the cabin wall. "And you are so . . . well, so distinguished. . . ."

"You mean that, Candice?" asked Powers.

"I've never meant anything more . . . ever!"

There was a long moment's pause. Powers studied the few drops of brandy in the bottom of his glass. Finally he said slowly, "Candice . . . you've brought me happiness, too. Doing the things you liked has been fun. But because of Dana . . . and his father . . . I don't know what to say. . . ."

"Forget Dana!" Krassy urged. "Forget the Waterburys. Dana is gone . . . he'll never walk back into my life. I've nearly forgotten him already, Howard. *You* made me forget him!"

"Then," said Powers drawing a deep breath, "I'd like to go on making you forget him. . . ."

"Why, Howard, what a lovely proposal!" laughed Krassy as Powers suddenly stopped.

Powers looked at her in surprise; then he replied firmly, "Yes, I guess it is." Krassy shoved back her chair from the table and slipped around to Powers' lap. Sitting on his knees, she wrapped her arms around his neck.

"Darling!" she whispered, and gently nuzzled his ear, "my dear, darling Howard. . . ."

Powers kissed her fully on the lips. "When shall we be married?" he asked.

"Not right away," Krassy said hurriedly, "let's be engaged for a while first. It will be so wonderful being engaged to you. We'll have a wonderful time . . . and then we'll get married. Just like saving the dessert for the last."

He laughed and hugged her tightly.

The next morning the *Lorelei* made Chicago. That same day, Powers bought Krassy an eight-carat diamond engagement ring. There was no formal announcement of their engagement.

But Powers insisted they must write the Waterburys. Krassy attempted to argue him out of the idea, but eventually wrote Chris at his insistence. Powers, himself, wrote a long, facetious letter to Charles Waterbury, concerning their engagement. Chris did not reply to Krassy, although Powers received a brief, four-line note from Charles offering conventionalized congratulations. After that, Krassy and Powers didn't mention the Waterburys again.

Krassy continued to see Powers each night for dinner, and accompanied him often to the opera that fall and winter. Occasionally she invited him to dinner at her apartment. Powers seemingly was content to leave Krassy to her own activities, and he made no intrusions on her privacy.

The engagement brought no new, or overt, overtones into their relationship; Powers' air of possessiveness neither increased nor decreased. Eventually, Krassy's distaste of physical contact with him became dormant as he made no further demands on her. Powers wanted Krassy to marry him before Thanksgiving, but she postponed it to Christmas, and then again until after New Year's.

Finally Krassy married Howard Monroe Powers on January 17, 1946. They were married by County Judge Visolotti in his chambers. It was a quiet wedding attended by Krassy, Powers, the judge, and two professional witnesses. Immediately after the ceremony, and before the papers became aware of the importance of the story, the couple left for a honeymoon in Mexico City.

The honeymoon was not without incident. Powers' possessiveness became immediately apparent. With a vigor and potency surprising to Krassy, he took her for his wife. His demands were intense and unyielding, and from their first night together Krassy fought desperately to hide her revulsion. Each night, with Powers asleep by her side, she struggled to control the trembling of her body, and the gagging hysteria in her throat. Holding her eyes closed, Krassy would force her mind to scan a black velvet curtain. "The curtain is black," she told herself, "and I am getting sleepy." She would repeat it over and over again. Sometimes it would be broad daylight before the black curtain dissolved before her eyes and she fell asleep.

By 1949, Krassy no longer used the black curtain to go to sleep.

Instead, she used a handful of phenobarbitals.

SIX

Finding Powers' address was as easy as finding
a bump on the end of your own nose. I just looked it up
in the phone book and there it was . . . a big, coopera-
tive-owned apartment building on Lake Shore Drive. I
went to look at the building, and I hung around across
the street for a few minutes . . . on the outside chance
Krassy might come out and I'd get a chance to see her.
After a couple minutes I left, as I didn't want to make
myself conspicuous hanging around.

That night, in my room, I thought things over.
"Danny, my boy," I told myself, "you've found her, but
what the hell do you do now?"

I couldn't walk up to her and say, "Look, I know you.
You don't know me . . . you never even heard of me.

But I've traced you all the way from the stockyards, kid, and I think you're terrific!" I had to use finesse.

Finally I got an idea. It wasn't too good, but it was the only thing I could think of. I got a small blue pocket notebook and a hand-clocker—one of those gadgets you hold in your hand and press a little button. It clocks up a bunch of numbers. I went back to Krassy's apartment house, and stood down by the corner. As each car would go by, I'd clock it off on the counter. Then every hour, I'd enter the time and the number of cars that went by. Once a kid came up and asked me what I was doing and I told him I was taking a traffic survey. No one else even bothered to ask me.

Around eleven-thirty, I saw a tall, black-haired woman come out of the apartment, and get into a cab. There was a cab stand right across the street from the apartment. Halfway down the street, where I was standing, I couldn't be sure if it was Krassy or not. After she left, I hung around for another hour.

The next day, at about the same time again, this same woman came out of the building. This time I was down closer to the corner and I could see her better. There was no doubt about it.

It was Krassy.

She looked thinner than I thought she would look, and her hat had a short veil which covered her eyes so I didn't really get too good a look. She got in a cab and drove off. I had a hunch, then, that she probably left the building around the same time every day. I didn't think it was smart to try to follow her in a cab from the stand across the street. It was possible that I'd get a cabby who might know her. So the next day, I picked up a cab downtown, and drove up Lake Shore Drive at eleven-thirty. The cabby turned around past the apartment building, and pulled over to the curb. We waited. In a few minutes, Krassy came out, walked across the street, and got in a taxi. They started off toward the Loop and I told my jockey to follow them.

We tailed the cab down Michigan, and when it got over the bridge, it turned right to Wabash and started down under the el tracks. South of Monroe, it pulled up in front of an office building and Krassy got out. I gave my driver a bill and followed her into the lobby. She walked over to an elevator and got on it. The elevator was pretty well filled, but several other people were still trying to get on, so I managed to squeeze in, too. She never noticed me.

On the third floor, she got off and walked down to the end of the hall without turning around. At the very end, was a heavy walnut door without a number or a name. She knocked at the door, waited a minute, and the door opened. She walked inside, and I was standing staring at the door.

There didn't seem to be much to do about it, so I went down to the opposite end of the corridor and lighted myself a smoke. I stood there and smoked it, and tried to figure what the deal was. The elevator stopped again, and two guys got off. They went through the same motions as Krassy, and disappeared behind the door. In a few minutes, another dame showed up, then another man, then two men, then two dames. They all went the same place as Krassy.

But by that time I had it figured. It's a bookie joint; a private club bookie layout. I didn't have a chance of crashing it, and I didn't want to. I was not ready to meet

Krassy yet, and I didn't want her to know I was tailing her.

But one thing I did know, Krassy was playing the horses. Not that she couldn't afford it. With dough like old man Powers' you can play 'em, buy 'em, and sell 'em. About one o'clock the door opened and Krassy came back down the hall. I turned my back toward her as she got on the elevator. As soon as the door slammed shut, I beat it down the stairs and reached the lobby as Krassy was walking out the door to the sidewalk. She cut over to Michigan, then turned south and headed toward the Congress Hotel. She went through the hotel lobby to the restaurant. I hung around outside, and walked by the door once in a while. She sat at a table alone and drank three double martinis. After three double martinis, which is a hell of a jolt in the middle of the day, she ordered a light luncheon. She didn't act like she was expecting anyone . . . and no one joined her.

She played around with the food on her plate, took a few bites, and then paid her check. When she left, she took a cab back to her apartment building. I called it a day and checked back to the office for a little work.

I tried to piece the thing together. I couldn't understand Krassy going down every day to play the horses when she could place bets over the phone. Unless, of course, old man Powers didn't want her to gamble. Being a banker, he might consider it bad form to have a wife shoveling dough away . . . but then he could afford it. I eventually decided that Krassy was either bored or fed up, and was playing the horses because she didn't have anything else to do. The fact that she was drinking plenty martinis in the middle of the day made me pretty certain she was unhappy . . . or sore at old man Powers.

But I still hadn't answered my big problem. How was I going to meet her? And what reason would she have to continue to see me afterward? I had plenty of time to try to figure something out, so I didn't try to rush it. It had to be right.

The next week, I stayed away from Krassy's building entirely. Then one morning, I couldn't stay away any longer, and I found myself walking toward it. A block away, I turned west off the Drive, and passed Astor Street. Halfway between Astor and North State, there's a big, old graystone house which has been cut up into small, expensive apartments. Back of the main house, by the alley, is a small coach house. Pulled up in the driveway, between the main house and coach house, was a long, blue station wagon trimmed in light wood. However, there was no doorway on the side of the coach house which faced the main building. There was a small recessed door which opened from the coach house into the alley, and another main door which opened from the side of the coach house facing the street.

A young guy, about my age, was loading the back end of the station wagon with luggage. The luggage was all expensive-looking with that deep, rich sheen which costs plenty. As I walked by, a cleaning truck drove up and stopped. The driver got out and walked up to this young guy carrying a couple of newly cleaned suits. The guy laid down some of his luggage and turned around and gave the driver hell. "Look," he said, "I told you to have those suits back here yesterday. Now I'm all packed and I'll be damned if I'm going to repack just for them!"

The driver said something which I didn't hear, then

the young guy pointed toward the coach house and said, "All right! Take them inside and leave 'em." The driver stepped inside the door from the alley, and in a minute came out again without the suits.

"I'm sorry about those suits, Mr. Homer," he said, politely, "anyway, have a good trip."

"Sure," said Homer. He closed up the back end of the station wagon, locked it, and walked around to the front of the car.

"When will you be back?" asked the driver.

Homer checked the lock on the front and side doors of the coach house, and then climbed in his car. "Not until May . . . or later," said Homer and stepped on the starter. "I'll call you when I get back," he added.

"Thanks," said the driver. "Have a good time."

Homer waved a hand at him and drove off. I walked on thinking to myself that some guys have it lucky. Here's this guy in the blue station wagon going to Florida, or Arizona, or California, or some place for six months. However, I didn't think about it too much at the time, and it sort of slipped out of my mind. That night, though, it came back.

I propped myself up in bed, and shook a cigarette loose from the pack, and went back to wondering how I was going to meet Krassy. Suddenly the memory of Homer flashed back in my mind. Then the idea struck me.

I went back to Homer's coach house a couple times. There were never any signs of life around it. The front of it, which faced the back of the main building, was a completely blank wall. There were windows on both ends of the coach house . . . the sides running parallel to the street . . . but you couldn't see them from the main building. The main door, at the top of two short steps, opened from the sidewalk into the coach house. Next to the door was a mailbox and the name—Edward A. Homer. There was also the small, recessed door, which I'd seen before, that opened off the alley.

At the office, I sat down and addressed a couple of envelopes to myself . . . writing very lightly in pencil. Inside the envelopes I stuffed some sheets of blank paper, sealed the flaps, and mailed them. The next morning the envelopes were delivered back to my office, postmarked and canceled. I erased my name and address with a gum eraser, and typed in Mr. Edward A. Homer with the address of the coach house. I figured Homer had left a change of address with the Post Office, and I needed some personal identification for what I had to do next.

Walking down Clark Street, I came to a dinky little hole-in-the-wall shop. Outside was a sign which said, KEYS MADE—50¢. I went in. A bleary-eyed old guy was sitting on a straight-backed chair, behind a counter about the size of a card table. On the wall back of him was a board with a number of nails sticking out of it. Hanging from the nails were a lot of blank keys.

"I want to get a key made," I told him.

"A duplicate?"

"No," I said. "I been out of town a couple days and I lost my keys. Now I can't get in my apartment. I want you to come up and make one."

"You got any identification?" he asked.

"Sure," I told him, and threw the letters I'd addressed to Homer on the counter. "Want more?" I started to fumble at my pocket like I was looking for my driver's license.

"Naw," said the old man, "that's okay." He picked a

handful of blank keys off the wall, gathered several small hand tools, and stuffed them in his pocket. He locked the store behind him, and we grabbed a cab to the coach house, as I didn't want him to get a chance to ask questions. When we got there, he started to walk up to the front door.

"No! Not that door . . . I left a chain on it. Better try the one on the side," I said and pointed toward the alley. I didn't want anyone to see him fooling with the front door. The old guy shrugged his shoulders and walked around the corner and down to the recessed door. I leaned up against the wall beside him and smoked . . . keeping an eye cocked for cars going through the alley. But none came past.

While the old guy worked, he kept up a mumbling conversation about locks, and once he tried halfheartedly to sell me a new lock for the door. He finally found a blank key that fit. He rubbed it with a piece of carbon paper and put it back in the lock. Then he pulled it out and inspected it for a minute or two. Finally, he took a tool from his pocket and started gouging out nicks and cuts on the blank. Every few minutes he'd rub it with carbon paper, put the key in the lock, and try it. Finally, the key turned in the lock and the door swung open.

"That's great," I told him and put my foot in the door. "How much do I owe you?"

"Three bucks," he said.

"Hell!" I said, picking the key out of the lock and putting it in my pocket, "your sign said fifty cents!"

"Fifty cents for the key," he explained, "and two fifty for making the call."

I paid him off, and as soon as he turned away, I stepped inside the door of Homer's coach house. The side door opened into a short, dark hall that led to the kitchen. The kitchen was gleaming in white enamel and chrome. At one end of it was a small dinette table painted a jet black, with four light, bleached wood chairs. Each chair had a Chinese red seat. A heavy, woven grass partition, like a corded rug with Chinese scenes, dropped from the ceiling and could be raised or lowered. When it was lowered, it completely separated the dinette section from the kitchen.

Opening off the kitchen was the living room, which was big, covering the rest of the downstairs of the coach house. The floor was carpeted wall to wall in a deep, brilliant green. Modern furniture, upholstered in watermelon red, was grouped around the center of the room, and faced a tremendous fireplace. End tables and coffee tables were painted black. So was the fireplace, except it had gold designs on it. Above the fireplace was a huge plate-glass mirror, set flush against the wall and extending from the mantel to the ceiling. The walls of the room were deep, dusky gray. Groups of pictures, in narrow black frames, with big white mats hung on the walls. The windows, facing the street, contained venetian blinds, and one big set of drapes hung from the ceiling to the floor. The drapes ran on a track like a stage curtain, and were completely drawn covering the entire end of the room and the three individual windows in it. The drapes were the same green as the carpeting.

Believe me, it was one hell of a fine room.

A small staircase ran from the living room upstairs to the second floor. Here, there was a bath with a plate-glass shower stall, a bedroom with an oversized bed, and another room. This extra room was about the same size as the bedroom and had been fixed up as a study.

There was a carved desk, a small divan, two easy chairs, a big combination radio-phonograph, and a small television set. The walls were lined with bookcases and record cabinets.

I walked back downstairs and out to the kitchen. Hanging on the back of the kitchen door were the suits the cleaner had left nearly a week before. I switched on the light and it worked. Trying the tap in the sink, I found the water was working, too. But the telephone had been disconnected in the living room.

That afternoon, I called the telephone company, gave my name as Edward A. Homer, and told them I wanted the phone connected again. "However, I want a private number now . . . and I don't want it listed under Information," I said. The phone was reconnected the following day and I had my private number.

Then I was ready to meet Krassy.

Nobody can look too far ahead to plan things. I knew I couldn't introduce myself to her as Danny April, a small-time collection agent; also I was smart enough to know that I couldn't keep up a big front forever. But I figured that after she got to know me, maybe when the time came for me to tell her who I was, it wouldn't make too much difference.

Using Homer's apartment, I decided I had to use his name, too. I didn't dare take his name off the door, and I couldn't afford any slip-up. I tried on one of Homer's suits and it fit me pretty well; and I selected a tie from dozens hanging on the back of his bedroom door. When I was all dressed up, I walked over two blocks to Lake Shore Drive, turned left, and walked another block north to the building where Krassy lived. A doorman, in a deep maroon military coat, opened the door for me.

"What floor is Mr. Powers' apartment?" I asked him.

"Twenty-third," he replied. "Is he expecting you?"

"Yes," I said. "Why?"

"Mr. Powers isn't home now," he told me.

"That's all right," I said. "I'll see Mrs. Powers instead." I walked by him and stepped quickly in the elevator, before he had a chance to ask my name and phone up to announce me. "Twenty-three," I told the elevator boy.

The elevator glided to a smooth stop, and I stepped off into a small, private foyer complete with a marble bench and a tiny fountain. A single, heavy door with a tremendous brass knocker opened off the foyer. I walked over and started to lift the knocker before I saw a small button set in the right side of the door. I rang it. In a few minutes, a butler opened the door. He had a heavy, white face with oversized bags under his eyes. His gray hair was parted on one side, and combed back along the sides of his head. He cocked an eye at me and wished me good day.

"I'd like to see Mrs. Powers," I told him.

"Is Mrs. Powers expecting you?" he asked.

"No," I said, "but I think she'd like to see me. Here just a minute," I tore out a leaf of my notebook and scribbled on it, "One horse player to another." I folded it over a couple times and handed it to the butler. "Please give this to Mrs. Powers," I told him, "and tell her it's Mr. Edward A. Homer to see her."

He closed the door softly in my face, and left me standing in the foyer. I crossed over to the fountain and discovered there were live goldfish swimming around in it.

In a few minutes I heard the door open behind me,

and a quiet, husky voice asked, "You wanted to see me?" I turned around.

It was Krassy.

For a minute my mind went blank, I couldn't say anything. She was as beautiful as I'd ever dreamed; she was the loveliest woman I'd seen in my life. But she looked older than I'd expected . . . older and tired. Her face held a tiredness behind its serenity I can't explain. Maybe it was her eyes; at first you didn't realize how intense they were; they seemed to be looking, and trying *not* to see at the same time. Glistening black hair fell to her shoulders and framed her face with soft dignity. Looking up at me from under her delicate brows, she stood waiting for my answer. I'd forgotten her question when she asked me again.

"Yes," I said, "I wanted to see you. My name is . . . Homer."

She nodded her head without speaking.

"Well . . . I've seen you around once in a while," I said. "That is . . . down at the club."

"Club?" she asked.

"Down at the bookie's."

"Oh."

"You see, it's like this, Mrs. Powers," I stumbled on. "I'm sort of in the business myself. I make a small book, too . . . and well . . . I just live around the corner, and I thought maybe it'd be more convenient to place your bets with me."

She just stood and looked at me; listening intently and sizing me up.

"You know . . . not having to go downtown," I said, "and having other people see you. . . ."

"What difference does it make if people see me?"

"Why, nothing . . . I suppose," I said, "except maybe Mr. Powers doesn't approve of it . . . or something."

"Possibly," she said and regarded me thoughtfully. It made me sort of uneasy. I couldn't tell what she was thinking; then it was as if she'd made up her mind about something and reached a decision. Suddenly she smiled and everything was okay again. "All right," she agreed, "I'll give you a try." She paused. "After all I've always believed in helping the small . . . businessman." She smiled, and her eyes lost that intense look, and she seemed to relax.

I pulled out my notebook and scribbled down my address and telephone number—Homer's, that is—and handed the slip to her. "You can either place your bets in person or phone 'em in," I told her.

I walked over to the elevator and rang for it. She turned and opened the big door to the apartment. I glanced back, and she had stopped in the doorway, and was looking at me. Then with a brief wave of her fingers, she closed it behind her.

Leaving the building, I was walking on layers of foam rubber and my legs had small steel springs that made me bounce in a way I'd never bounced before. I felt good . . . I felt swell . . . I felt terrific! I'd met Krassy and gotten away with it. She'd accepted my story and the way was open . . . wide open . . . to see her again. And to keep seeing her. She was as lovely as I'd imagined. She was one hell of a woman!

And then I started worrying, too. I had no way of knowing when she'd call me. I had to be at Homer's apartment to answer the phone. If she called a couple times, and there was no answer, she'd probably blow the whole thing off. That meant I had to stick around Homer's most of the day; at night it didn't matter. She'd never call at night, anyway.

The next day, I let myself in Homer's apartment at nine o'clock in the morning. I hung around until six that night without hearing from her. It was agony cooped up in that apartment waiting for the phone to ring . . . but it never did. I stretched out on the lounge and tried to nap, but my mind was buzzing and I couldn't sleep. In the afternoon, I began to get hungry and there wasn't anything to eat in the place. I decided I'd have to put in a supply of food. That night, I returned to my room, depressed as hell.

The following day the phone rang around eleven o'clock in the morning. My heart jumped to my throat and I had trouble talking around it to answer the phone. But it was only the telephone company. They were checking the phone and wanted to know how I liked the service. I told them swell. Krassy didn't call that day, either.

By the next, I'd given up hope. I figured she'd just listened to my story, and brushed me off politely. Then the door bell rang. I peeked out from behind the blinds, and she was standing by the front door. I hurried to open it, and she walked into the living room and glanced at it casually. "I thought I'd drop around to see how you were doing, Mr. Homer," she said.

"I'm glad you did," I told her.

"You don't seem to have much of a crowd here," she said.

"No. Most of my customers call me to place their bets. I got to be careful," I explained. "If a lot of people were seen coming and going from here, somebody would report it to the cops and I'd get closed up."

She nodded her head gravely. "Well, I won't bother you again," she assured me.

"I don't mean *you* . . . Mrs. Powers," I said hurriedly. "I want you to come whenever you want to. I was just . . . explaining . . . why there isn't a crowd of people here. Look," I said to change the subject, "I was just going to have a drink . . . can I get you one? Scotch, martini, brandy?" I'd discovered that the real Homer had laid in a good supply of liquor. He kept it in a big enamel cabinet under the kitchen sink.

"That would be nice. I'll have a martini . . . very dry," she replied. I went out to the kitchen and mixed a shaker of them. When I returned, she'd taken off her fur coat, and was sitting idly in her chair. I gave her the drink. She tasted it. "Good," she told me. We sat and talked about horses, and she told me about her boat called the *Lorelei*. After her second martini, she opened her purse and handed me twenty dollars.

"Put it on Rocket Lady, in the sixth today at Santa Anita," she said. "To win." I jotted it down in my notebook. "What are the odds?" she asked.

That threw me. Then I started ad-libbing. "I'll call my partner," I told her, "he handles that end of it. I only work the front." I picked up the phone and dialed the number of a small bookie joint, located in the back end of a meat market just around the corner from my rooming house. A little guy by the name of Sam operates it for the syndicate. I used to see him around and, once in a while on Saturday nights, I'd run into him and we'd buy a few drinks. I hadn't talked to him in months, and I was sweating plenty. If he didn't recognize my voice, or wouldn't give me odds without me identifying myself, I was sunk.

"Hello, Sam?" I asked. "What're the odds on Rocket Lady, in the sixth at Santa Anita?"

"Who's this?" Sam asked suspiciously.

"Look 'em up then," I said, "I can't wait until *April*!"

"April?" He sounded confused. "What about April? . . . Oh, sure! April! Danny April?"

"That's right," I said, sighing in relief.

"She pays six to two," he told me.

"Okay," I told him, "I'll call you back." I hung up the phone and turned to Krassy. "Six to two," I told her.

"All right," she said. She stood up and I helped her with her coat. Gathering up her purse and gloves she started for the front door.

"Look, Mrs. Powers," I said politely, "do you mind going out the side?" She stopped and turned around. "For your sake . . . you know. That's why I have this arrangement. You can enter or leave by the side, and no one can see you from the street."

"No," she smiled, "I don't mind at all, Mr. Homer. As a matter of fact, I think it is a very good idea. . . ."

As soon as she'd gone, I called Sam back and placed Krassy's bet.

"That's a lot of dough for you, ain't it, Danny?" he asked.

"Sure," I agreed, "but I got my own business now."

"You must be doing pretty good now, huh?" said Sam.

"Not bad," I told him. "Say, Sam, I'll get this dough to you before the race this afternoon. But I got one question to ask you. How good is my credit?"

"Well," said Sam slowly, "it's like this, Danny. When

a guy don't need money, his credit is good. Far as I
know, you always been a level guy. Why?"

"It's like this," I said. "I'm awful damned busy these
days. Sometimes I don't get around to my office for a
couple days, so what I want to know is if I place a bet on
the phone, you'll cover it for me?"

"Sure . . . within reason," said Sam.

"When I'm around I'll drop the dough off," I said.
"But regardless I square my account with you the first of
each month?"

"Look, Danny," said Sam, "you and I been friends. I
don't like to see no guy, who's a friend of mine, get in
trouble. Sure, I can give you credit if you want it, but
Danny . . . remember *I* don't do the collecting. The
syndicate has guys . . . *special* . . . for that."

"Yeah, I know," I told him.

"Okay, just so you understand," he said.

After that my life began to assume a crazy sort of
pattern. In the beginning, I didn't see Krassy every day.
Sometimes she'd call me two or three days in a row and
place her bet by phone; then she'd drop by in person,
and stop for a drink, maybe a couple days in succession.
However, the times of her phone call and the times of
her visits were regular; they always fell between the
hours of eleven in the morning and one in the afternoon.
Partly because of the hours the tracks were open, and
partly because of her own personal life, I guess. Mostly,
she would place just one or two bets a day . . . all of
them to win. Her bets were anywhere from twenty to
fifty bucks. I'd pass them on to Sam.

After I hadn't seen her for a few days, she'd appear in
person and give me the money for the bets I'd covered
on the phone for her. When she left, I'd hike over and

give the dough to Sam. On her occasional wins, Sam would give me the dough, and I'd pay her off. She lost pretty regularly, and the amount would run from six hundred to maybe a thousand dollars a month. She didn't seem to mind.

There was one thing, though, that bothered me. Most horse players have it in their blood. They run a fever. But Krassy wasn't like that. She didn't seem to be particularly interested in either winning or losing. The amounts she lost, she could easily afford, I guess. But when she won, she didn't seem to get much of a kick out of it either. Another thing, most players spend a lot of time doping out weights, track conditions, jocks, and past performances. A real gambler knows each blade of grass inside the track anyplace the horses are running. But Krassy didn't. She picked a horse she liked for one reason or another . . . and bet it to win.

Her phone calls became fewer, and her personal appearances more regular. I kept playing it straight. I never made a pass at her, or got out of line in anything I said. I always called her Mrs. Powers, although by this time she was calling me Eddie.

So I got in the habit of going to the office early, then getting up to Homer's apartment at eleven o'clock and staying there through one. After Krassy would leave, I'd go back downtown and work the rest of the day. My own business kept shaping up better and better, and I even hired another guy named Henry Spindel to help out on personal collections. Spindel and Bud Glasgow had no idea where I went when I'd leave for the coach house. I'd never mentioned it to them, and I'd never mentioned Krassy, either. I figured it was none of their business.

Eventually, Krassy stopped at the coach house every

day, around noon. I'd always have a shaker of martinis mixed and we'd sit and talk. One day she mentioned something about music and I told her about the phonograph and room full of albums upstairs. She wanted to see what records I had, so we went up and she browsed through them. Finally, she pulled some out and I put the records on the machine. It was all longhair stuff, but she liked it. She sat curled up on the divan, sipping her martini and listening to the music. After a while, she said, "Eddie, you constantly amaze me."

"I do?" I asked.

"Yes," she said, "I'd never dream you liked this kind of music. Tell me about yourself."

"What's there to tell?" I said.

"Is Chicago your home?"

"No," I replied. "New York . . . New York City. I was born and raised there." I figured I was safe in telling her that, because as far as I knew, she wasn't too familiar with New York. And I thought telling her I was from New York might impress her.

"Did you go to college?" she asked me.

I was beginning to like the idea of impressing her. I decided that Edward Homer, with this apartment, this kind of music, born in New York . . . had to go to college! So I said, "Sure. But I only went two years . . . to Columbia." Columbia was the only college I could think of around New York, and I knew a little bit about their football teams.

"Oh," she said. "But you don't speak like . . . well, like a New Yorker."

"You mean my English is lousy?" I asked. "Check that off to evil companions. After all you don't need a degree to talk to horses."

She smiled again. "What about your family?"

"Oh, my folks still live in New York," I told her.

"What does your mother think about your gambling?"

"She doesn't know," I said, "she thinks I work for a broker."

Krassy watched the olive bobble around in her glass. Her face was thoughtful. In a little while she left.

Another afternoon, she appeared later than usual and downed a couple drinks quickly. She said, "Eddie, tell me, do you have a girl?"

"No," I told her.

"I should think you'd have a lot of them," she said. "You're a nice-looking fellow . . . with plenty of money."

"I always been pretty busy," I said.

"I never thought men were ever too busy to have girls."

"Not that so much," I told her, "but why play around and waste a lot of time and dough on a dame that doesn't mean anything?"

"Haven't you ever met a girl who did mean something?"

"Yes," I replied.

"Who was she? Tell me about her?"

"If I did, you wouldn't like it, maybe," I said looking her squarely in the eyes.

She lowered her head slowly. "You might try it and find out," she replied softly. But all of a sudden my nerve left me; I was too scared, too afraid I'd say or do the wrong thing. I let it go by.

At Christmastime I had a few bucks in the bank. Not much, but the Clarence Moon Collection Agency had been making a little dough so I gave Glasgow and Spindel fifty bucks apiece, and took the three hundred and fifty bucks I had left. I went down to Jacobson's Loan Shop on North Clark Street and bought a little necklace of pearls . . . a choker of real ones which had been left in pawn. The pearls weren't very big, and neither was the choker, but they were the real stuff. Then I got a black velvet box and put the pearls in it. I took it to a gift wrapping place, and they wrapped it in blue paper and pasted on silver stars. On my way back to the coach house, I stopped and bought a Christmas tree. One that was small enough to sit on the table, and a couple strings of electric lights.

I set it up in the living room and strung on the lights, and wrote a note which read: "Merry Christmas to Mrs. Powers." I put the card on top of the box of pearls and placed it under the tree. The next day when Krassy came over, she saw the tree on the table.

"What a lovely tree, Eddie!"

"You like it?"

"You know, I really believe you're a sentimentalist!" She walked over to the tree, and saw the package under it. She picked it up, then turned. "Is this for me?" she asked.

I told her it was.

"Let me open it now! I love presents! I can't wait to see what it is!" She turned the box over and over in her hands, as happy as a kid.

"Okay," I agreed.

Quickly she tore the wrappings from the box and opened it. Lifting the pearls in her hands, she walked to the mirror and clasped them around her neck. "They're lovely, Eddie!" she exclaimed, "Oh! I love them!" Then returning to the tree, she picked up the card and sort of motioned with it. "I want you to do me a favor," she told me.

"Anything you say," I said.

She held up the card. "Don't keep calling me 'Mrs. Powers,'" she said, "I want you to call me Candice."

"All right, Candice."

She crossed over to me, stood on her toes, and put her arms around my neck and kissed me. "That's for my lovely Christmas present," she said. Her eyes were close to mine, and I could see straight down into them . . . like I was looking into real deep water, where the depth becomes so great that it seems to move and swell without the slightest ripple. I kissed her back. I kissed her hard for all the months I'd dreamed of her, and walked the streets trying to find her, and for all the love I had inside me . . . for her.

Then she was crying and pushing me away. "Oh, Eddie," she cried, "Eddie . . . Eddie . . . Eddie. . . ."

I took my arms from around her and stepped back. "Maybe I shouldn't have done that," I said.

"I wanted you to," she told me. "I've wanted you to do that since nearly the first day I met you."

"Then why are you crying?"

"I don't know . . . just being silly, I suppose," she told me. "And I *am* married. What do you think of a married woman, Eddie, who lets another man kiss her like that?"

"If it's you and me . . . I think it's great," I said.

"Eddie," she said softly, "before we go any further . . . before we get too deeply involved with what we think and what we want, I want to tell you something."

"There's nothing you got to tell me," I said.

"Mix us up some more martinis," she said, "and let's go up to the study and play some music . . . and talk."

"Okay." I went out and mixed up another shaker, and then we went upstairs. Krassy selected some Bach and put it on the phonograph. She leaned back on the divan and I sat down beside her, placing the shaker on the floor.

"Why do you think I married Howard Powers?" she asked me.

"I don't know," I said.

"It wasn't because I loved him," she said. "I've never loved Howard . . . ever! Did you know I'd been married once before?"

I hesitated; then I decided I'd better say no. "No," I told her, "I didn't know."

"Well I have been," she said. "I was married to a wonderful, fine man . . . Dana Waterbury. He was killed in the war. I loved him, Eddie . . . I adored the very sight of him. He was sweet, and good. Dana was the first lover I ever had, and he was my husband." Her voice caught in her throat, and tears filled her eyes. "When he was killed, Eddie, my world came to an end. There was nothing more to live for. There were no men . . . there was no *man*, who could ever take his place. The idea of belonging to . . . or loving . . . another man was unthinkable!"

The way she said it hurt me like hell. "He was a very lucky guy," I finally managed to say.

"I was also a very lucky girl," she told me softly. "Howard was an old friend of the family's. Dana's family had known him for years . . . he was 'Uncle Howard.' After Dana's death, Howard was good to me. He helped me over my loss . . . my lonesomeness and despair. But Howard was an old man, old enough to be my own grandfather. He never talked about love to me . . . Eddie. He just wanted to help and protect me. Finally he asked me to marry him, and I did."

"Why?" I asked. I poured out another drink.

"Because I *didn't* love him! Can you understand that, Eddie? I thought it would be like . . . well, a father and daughter. Nothing . . . nothing too intimate about it. We both could be happy, and have company . . . and not be lonesome any more. I thought Howard was too old to fall in love."

"So?"

"So, at first it was like that. And then Howard started getting possessive and jealous. He started making love to me. . . . I couldn't stand it, Eddie. I hated it! I tried to make him leave me alone, but he demanded me . . . as his wife. It's incest!"

She was shuddering and crying at the same time. I put my arms around her and held her close. I hated Powers so much my guts hurt.

"He wants to know where I go . . . what I do. That's why I bet with you, Eddie . . . just to put something over on him. It's just a tiny, little victory of my own, Eddie. And Howard detests drinking! I never drank before, but now I like it. Now I can go home, with my brain nice and fuzzy, and go to sleep for a while. And forget how unhappy I am!" Her eyes stared at the floor, hot, burning, and half crazy with hurt.

I took her chin in my hand and tilted her face toward me. And kissed her. "Why don't you leave the old bastard?" I asked.

"I'm going to, Eddie . . . I really am. But I don't know where to go . . . or what to do. I don't have any money of my own, and there's no place to go . . . nor anyone to help me."

"I'll help you," I said.

"Eddie, do you know what you're saying? Howard has millions. He has power and connections! He could break you like . . . a stick."

"To hell with him," I told her.

"Do you really love me?" she asked.

"Yes," I replied.

"Are you sure?"

"Sure, I'm sure! How about you?"

"Don't be silly, darling," she said. "I love you . . . or I wouldn't be here. Which reminds me . . ." she exclaimed sitting up, "I must go to buy you a Christmas present. A wonderful, gorgeous, gigantic present!"

"Wait a minute," I told her, pulling her back down beside me. "There's nothing you can buy with Powers' money that I'd like. Besides, I'd rather have you here for a few more minutes than anything else in the world!"

"You would? Oh, I love to hear you say that!" She slipped around on the lounge and put her arm around my neck; her lips were on mine . . . suddenly demanding. I smoothed my hands down the side of her body and to her hips, and pulled her to me.

"Look," I whispered, "there's nothing I want except you."

She kissed me hungrily without answering.

"You know what I mean?"

"Yes," she was breathless.

I stood up from the lounge and took her hand. Without a word she followed me to the bedroom.

SEVEN

The next few months dissolved in a rosy glow.
I saw Krassy every day, except on Saturdays and Sundays. She explained that Powers was home on the week ends, and she couldn't slip away. I would mope around the coach house, eating my heart out, and loathing the thought that Krassy was with him. And always I'd wonder what the answer was going to be. I wanted Krassy to run away from him . . . to get a divorce . . . to go with me somewhere . . . anywhere! Yet I hadn't told her the truth about me; who I was . . . just plain Danny April with a cheap, little collection agency. I'd become so tangled up in my own lies, that now I was afraid to tell her the truth. On the other hand, she was still playing the role of Candice Waterbury Powers, and somehow I had the feeling I must never let her know

that I knew her real identity; that if I did, it would change our whole relationship.

I was still Eddie Homer, man about town, gambler, and bookmaker. Within the near future, the real Eddie Homer would return; the thought of him walking in on Krassy and me gave me nightmares. Yet like a guy with a skinful of snow, I couldn't face realities; fact and fiction . . . what were lies and what was truth . . . were so mixed up in both Krassy's life and my own that I kept postponing making a decision. I couldn't bear to make a move that would keep me from seeing Krassy.

One afternoon Krassy appeared, her eyes bright within deep shadows, and I thought her face was swollen.

"Eddie, darling," she asked, "what are we going to do?"

"I've told you," I said. "Leave Powers and come away with me."

"We've gone all over that . . . before. I'm afraid of him, Eddie . . . for you as well as me."

I kissed her eyes, and held her to me. I could feel her body shaking.

"Don't worry about me," I told her, "we'll do whatever you want to."

"You know, Eddie, there is something . . . oh, this will sound silly . . . but it would make me very happy."

"What?"

"You could call me about dinnertime . . . just to say hello. Dinner is the hardest time of all, my darling. I think of you, and our lovely afternoon together, and then I must sit down and face Howard. . . ."

"But what about you getting a call? Wouldn't that make him sore?"

"I get a lot of calls . . . from many different people. He'd never know. And if I couldn't answer, I'd just not take your call . . . but you'd understand. And I'd know you were thinking about me. . . ."

My heart sang, and I held her as tightly as I could. "Sure, baby," I said, "I'll call you. I'll call you every night. I'll say I'm John something-or-other . . . what name shall I use?"

"Your own will be all right," she said. "Howard doesn't know who you are, if he should hear it . . . and I'd love to hear it. Over and over, again."

"All right."

"And remember, darling, if I can't answer it . . . if Howard is too near . . . you won't be angry?"

"I'll never be angry with you," I told her.

And so I called her each evening at six. I'd phone her apartment and the butler would answer. Usually he'd take my name and report back that Mrs. Powers was not at home. I'd hang up with a sick, bad taste in my mouth, hating the butler, hating Powers. Sometimes, though, Krassy would answer the phone herself, and we'd hold a short, whispered conversation and she'd tell me she loved me. Then I'd hang up and the world was a beautiful place for a lucky guy named Danny April.

In the afternoons, Krassy would come to the coach house, but she didn't bother to place bets very often anymore. Mostly we'd sit around and drink martinis, and listen to the music, and make love. I moved the big automatic phonograph into the bedroom, and we'd lie on the Hollywood bed, with all the window drapes tightly drawn. The room would be cozy, and dark and warm. I'd prop myself up on an elbow and in the darkness I could faintly see the sweep of her body against the whiteness of the bedclothes. On the pillow, like a deeper shadow, her black hair spread like a mantilla around her head. Sometimes I'd place my fingers under her chin, and trace them lightly down her body, over her stomach and the roundness of her hips. She would be perfectly still, perfectly motionless like a carved ivory statue. Then she would catch her breath, and murmur softly to herself.

Once she said to me, "Darling, do you have much money?"

"No," I told her. "Not a lot . . . not like Powers."

"I don't mean that," she smiled. "I mean do you have enough money to buy me presents?"

"Once in a while," I told her.

"No! I mean each day! Can't you buy a twenty-five-cent present for your mistress?"

"Don't say that!" I didn't like the sound of it.

She laughed aloud. "I think you're embarrassed, Eddie," she teased. "But I am your mistress, aren't I?"

"I'm nuts about you," I said.

"Then you must buy me a present. A new present each day! And you must never spend more than a quarter for it."

"What's the idea?" I asked.

"Just because I love to get presents," she explained. She leaned over and kissed me. "I've always liked presents . . . and best I love to open them. So now I have you, I insist it is my right to have a present *every* day. Not a big present! And you can't spend over twenty-five cents for it. Remember!"

It amused me. I thought it was a very funny idea.

"Sure," I told her, "I'll get you plenty of two-bit presents."

"You must wrap them nicely," she added warningly, "and be sure you put in nice cards." The game soon became a habit, a ritual. Each day, I'd buy her a little present from somewhere. A bunch of daisies or an egg beater. Sometimes, it would be a ball and jacks, a sack of marbles, a pocketbook edition of a novel, or a string of blue beads . . . or any one of a thousand things on sale in the dime store. I'd wrap it up in gift wrappings, and put in a card appropriate to the gift.

With the blue beads, I wrote on the card: "Wear these sapphires at your lovely throat . . . adoringly, Eddie." With the novel, I enclosed a card saying, "This proves my point . . . see what'll happen if you don't leave Powers! Eddie." And so on, and so on. There were maybe twenty-five or thirty others. All of 'em were silly, and Krassy loved them. She'd pretend to hold her breath, and opening the package she'd exclaim on its wrapping. Then in surprise she'd laugh and hold up her present. "It's lovely, darling," she'd say joyfully and push the hair back from her face. "It's just what I need!" Then she'd kiss me, and read the note, and laugh some more.

It was a wonderful life all right. My life was revolving around Krassy. At night, I still slept in my old rooming house because I was afraid that lights would be seen in the coach house. In the morning, I'd get up and go down to the collection agency, and work until ten-thirty. Then I'd go up to the coach house, around eleven, and wait for Krassy. She'd come over and stay with me until one-thirty or two. Then, after she went home, I'd go back downtown and work the rest of the day. At six, I'd call her from a downtown phone, then have dinner, and either go back to the office . . . or I'd go home. Glasgow and Spindel were busy; the outfit was making money; I had Krassy; and I was damned happy.

And then there was the week end that Krassy told me Powers was going out of town.

"Just think, darling," she told me excitedly, "we'll have a wonderful three days all to ourselves!"

"Where's he going?" I asked.

"To Washington," she said, and pushed it aside. "Business . . . politics . . . I don't know."

"What would you like to do?"

Her face lighted up with anticipation. "Let's do something wonderful . . . something crazy, and lovely!" She stopped and thought. "I know! Let's go away some place . . . away from Chicago. Where no one knows us . . . and we can be together."

Her excitement was gripping me, too. "That sounds great!"

"Howard is leaving late Friday night. So we won't plan to leave Friday. I'll let the servants go for the week end, and you can pick me up about noon on Saturday."

"I don't have a car," I reminded her.

"That's all right," she said. "I have one . . . we'll take it, and drive up to Wisconsin. Maybe we can find a little lodge with a big, stone fireplace, and pine trees . . . and a lake. . . ."

"Sure, baby," I agreed, "sure!"

"Pack an overnight bag with warm clothes. You pick me up about noon. Don't bother to ring the bell, because if I'm in the back . . . I won't hear it. I'll leave the door unlocked, and you walk in. If I'm not around, I'll be back in my room packing."

"You make that apartment of yours sound like the Union Station," I said.

"It is," she said. "It is worse than Union Station . . . it's cold and gloomy and stuffy. It's everything I hate! Just think, darling, I'll be away from it for three wonderful days!"

The next day was Friday, and Krassy came over as usual and we finished up our plans. I got some maps of Wisconsin and we looked them over and found a small winter lodge. That night, I couldn't sleep. Saturday morning, I got up early and shaved; I packed a small suitcase with a couple woolen shirts, a pair of heavy slacks, and some warm socks.

Promptly at noon, I stood in front of Krassy's building carrying my luggage. On thinking it over, I decided it would be better if I didn't go into the building with the suitcase. It might look funny or something. So I walked across the street to the cab stand, and made a deal with the last cabby in the line-up to keep an eye on it for me. I told him I'd be back in about ten minutes and gave him a buck.

As I walked in the building, the doorman stopped me.

"Who did you want to see?" he asked.

"I want to see Mrs. Powers," I said.

"I'm sorry. Mrs. Powers isn't at home," he told me.

"I know she's home," I said, "and she's expecting me."

"Mrs. Powers isn't at home," he repeated. For a minute I was stopped, then I remembered that with Howard, and the servants gone, the doorman probably thought Krassy wasn't home either.

"Okay," I said, "so we won't argue. Just call up on your house phone and announce me."

"I'm sorry," he repeated flatly, "but Mrs. Powers isn't at home."

I started to get sore. At that point, I should have gone outside and telephoned her, and had her call the doorman and tell him off. But I was getting more burned by the second, so I shoved him to one side. He grabbed my arm.

"Take your hands off me," I said, "or I'll bust your goddamned face in!" He dropped his hands, quickly, and looked around. "Call Mrs. Powers and tell her I'm on my way up. The name is Homer." I got in the elevator where the operator had been watching with his mouth half open. "Any argument from you, Bud," I told him, "and you'll get it, too."

He didn't say a word. The doors slid shut, and we shot up to the twenty-third floor. I stepped out into the same private foyer. The elevator slammed its doors behind me and dropped down to the main lobby. I walked around the little fishpond, over to the door and started to ring the bell, then remembering Krassy's instructions I put my hand on the knob and turned it. The door swung open and I walked inside . . . to find myself face to face with the butler.

"What are you doing here?" he asked.

I was confused . . . caught off balance. I was still sore about the doorman, and I was surprised to find the butler in the apartment. Automatically I told him it was none of his business, but before I could say anything else I heard Krassy's voice saying, "It's all right, Robbins. I'll handle this." Robbins gave a tight bow, and walked down the hallway and disappeared inside a door.

Krassy put her fingers to her lips, and motioned for me to follow her. She turned toward a high, arched doorway leading into a tremendous, high-ceiling living room. Three short steps dropped from the hall into the room. It was quite dark. Drapes were partly drawn over the two-story windows. On one side of the room was a huge fireplace . . . big enough to barbecue a cow in.

Krassy was wearing a suit, with a small hat, and had on black gloves. She was carrying a large purse.

"What's the trouble, dear?" asked a man's voice. With a start, I realized a man was sitting, slumped deeply, in a chair before the fireplace. His back was toward us, and I could see only the top of his silver-white hair above the chair.

"Nothing, Howard," Krassy replied walking toward him. It was Howard Monroe Powers sitting there. He didn't turn around and Krassy walked up behind him . . . still talking soothingly. My mind was frozen in surprise as I followed behind her.

"Was it that Homer fellow again?" he asked.

"Now, don't worry, Howard," Krassy said softly, "it's all taken care of. . . ." She was behind him now, and she stretched out her hand and patted his head. Then removing her hand, she opened her purse and stepped back.

With one, smooth motion she produced a revolver, placed it at the back of his head, and pulled the trigger.

There was a single shot.

And part of Powers' head seemed to fly across the room.

EIGHT

Krassy whirled toward me and shoved the gun into my hands. I stood there, holding the gun, frozen to the spot. She turned quickly and ran toward the archway leading to the hall. Then I realized she was screaming.

"My God! My God! He's shot Howard!" she cried hysterically. The old gray-haired butler suddenly appeared in the archway and looked at me in horror. "Call the police!" she screamed to him. "He'll kill us all! He's mad . . . crazy mad!"

The butler disappeared, and I stared at the quiet figure in the chair. The hair was the bright color of catsup now . . . like a bottle had been emptied over the top, and was draining with slow inevitability down the upholstery. Then I became conscious that several other people had entered the room. Down at the far end, standing in a little huddled group, were a maid, a cook in a white apron, and a chauffeur.

I knew I had to get out fast. My mind started to work again, as the first shock of surprise and horror began to wear off. Back of me, Krassy was still screaming. I knew the butler had phoned the cops and they'd arrive soon. I began running toward the group of servants. Somewhere, in their direction, was the kitchen . . . a back door . . . maybe service stairs. The maid and cook darted away shrieking in fright. The chauffeur stood his ground for only a moment, then he turned and ducked through a large door behind him. At a dead run, I followed at his heels through a big, formal dining room; he raced ahead of me through a tremendous butler's pantry and into the kitchen. He was struggling to open the back door when I caught up to him. Like a cornered animal, his eyes wild with terror, he turned on me and lunged. I swung my arm in a wide haymaker and hit him on the side of the head with the barrel of the gun. He dropped to the floor, in front of the door, his eyes rolled back, his mouth open. I had to drag him back from the door, and step over him, to wrench it open. Dimly, I heard a new sound . . . a growing, screeching crescendo. The wail of police sirens.

I burst out into the back hall. For a second I hesitated, looking around, then I punched the button to the automatic service elevator. A red light went on, and indicated the elevator was coming up from the first floor.

Then I realized the sirens were still. The cops had arrived. By now they were probably in the building, and would be on their way up. I turned and ran back to the kitchen. Opening a drawer in an enameled table, I grabbed a silver knife, and a big metal meat cleaver. I rushed back to the hall, and the red light button showed the elevator had now reached the eighteenth floor. I turned and raced up the service stairs to the next floor above. The twenty-fourth. I heard the elevator stop below me at the twenty-third. With my ears at the sliding doors, I listened but could hear nobody in it.

I slipped the silver knife between the catch on the elevator doors, bending the knife nearly double levering it back. Then holding the narrow crack ajar, I slid the blade of the meat cleaver into the crack and jimmied the door all the way back. Holding the door open, I looked down directly on the top of the service elevator. It was about two feet below me. I held the door open, sat on the floor, and put the knife, cleaver, and gun in my pockets. Then releasing the door, I dropped down on the top of the elevator below me. Immediately the door clanged shut. It was dark in the elevator shaft, and it was cold. The wind roared up and down it like a wind tunnel. The top of the elevator was like a big wooden box, and I sat down on it, and wrapped my arms and legs around the heavy metal cable.

Suddenly the door, in the elevator below me, opened and it was filled with cops. "He didn't use this elevator," one of them said, "or it wouldn't be at this floor."

"The bastard probably used the service stairs!"

"Up or down?"

"How the hell do I know? I hope it was down. If it was, we'll get him when he tries to get out the back."

The elevator began to drop to the ground, me riding on top of it. That was around noon . . . twelve-thirty, probably. I didn't think to look at the time. The rest of the afternoon, I rode the elevator up and down while they searched the building, the apartments, stairways, and even the little elevator shed housing the machinery on top of the roof.

By six o'clock that night, the cops were convinced I'd managed to escape from the building. From their conversations which I overheard, I learned that Powers' body had been removed, that Krassy had made her statements, and there was a dragnet out over the city for me. At dinnertime, the cops left, leaving a harness cop on the back exit, to prevent me from re-entering the building . . . in case I came back. He would be relieved at midnight.

By nine o'clock, the service elevator had practically stopped running. It was stationed at the first floor, and no one used it. I heard the cop pull up a chair and seat himself just within the back entrance of the building . . . close to the elevator and somewhere to the right. After a while, I heard the rustling of paper, and knew he was settling down to read.

Reaching in my pocket, I pulled out a cigarette lighter. It was windy in the shaft and hard to keep the flame going. By its flickering light, I examined the top of the elevator and discovered a small trapdoor which was used to make repairs, and which opened into the inside of the cage. The door pulled back on hinges, and I gently eased it open. It didn't squeak, and I pulled it all the way back, so it was lying flat on the roof of the elevator.

Stretching out on my stomach, I reached an arm inside the trap. I could touch the light bulb which was fastened to the ceiling of the cage. The bulb was hot, and it felt good to my fingers which were cramped and frozen. For a couple minutes, I warmed my hands until my fingers had feeling again. Then I loosened the bulb

and plunged the inside of the elevator into darkness.
Slowly I stood up on my feet, and raised and lowered
them until circulation returned.

Once in a while the cop would clear his throat, or
move around in his chair. I could hear him. I decided to
risk smoking a cigarette. Not that the cop could see it,
but maybe he could smell the smoke. My nerves were
jumping and I needed one bad. So while my feet were
coming back to life, I lit a cigarette and blew the smoke
over my head . . . hoping the draft would suck it up
the shaft.

Finally, my feet were alive, I could feel with my hands,
and my cigarette was finished. I moved directly to the
edge of the trapdoor, and squatted down on my
haunches. The inside of the elevator was pitch black
compared to the lighter blackness of the shaft. Reaching
in my pocket, I pulled out a handful of change. I selected
a coin with my fingers, and dropped it through the trap-
door.

In the silence it rang like a bell.

I could sense the cop listening. Then I heard the rustle
of his paper again. I dropped another coin through the
trap. This time, I heard the chair squeak, and I knew the
cop was standing up listening. His heavy, slow footsteps
approached the elevator. Outside the door he was listening. I tensed myself, and dropped another coin. It felt big
. . . like a half-dollar . . . and it chimed on the floor
of the elevator.

The inside of the elevator flooded with light as the cop
flung the door back and light poured in from the hall.
He had pulled his gun, and he peered suspiciously inside. The darkness of the elevator stopped him for a
minute. He stepped back, and let the door close. I could

hear him walk back to his chair and pick it up. Then he returned, opened the door, and kept it propped open with the chair. He stood in the doorway and looked around the elevator. His eyes caught the flash of the half-dollar on the floor.

He stepped inside the elevator and bent over to pick it up. I could see his shoulders beneath me, under the trap-door.

I launched myself through the trap.

Feet first!

I landed on the cop square in the middle of his back, and it slammed him face down on the floor of the elevator. I rolled over to one side, freeing my right hand, and slugged him with the revolver. He went out fast.

I stepped into the hallway and made for the back exit, and in the light I realized I looked like hell. I was covered with grease and oil. Outside the building, I cut straight to the alley without being seen. Halfway down the alley, where it was good and dark, I paused by a pile of dirty snow, left over from a storm weeks ago, and tried to wash off my face and hands, and dried them on my handkerchief. I did the best I could, and felt I was a little cleaner; I put the handkerchief back in my pocket and headed toward North Avenue.

Run! Grab a cab! Swipe a car! Christ! I managed to keep a grip on my panic; a small remaining bit of reason told me I couldn't take a chance. A running man is suspicious; a cab driver has a memory; a stolen car can have an accident. So I walked. On North Avenue, I cut over to Clark Street, and started south toward my old rooming house. On Clark, I began to feel better. No one would give much attention to my dirty, battered look.

Too many other people on that street look the same way.

I passed a small hamburger stand, and realized I was hungry. A guy and his girl were seated at the counter, and an old bum was gumming a cup of coffee. I went in and ordered a bowl of chili, a hamburger, and coffee. I made myself eat the food slow.

At the corner, I caught a streetcar and rode it down to Superior. There I got off, and cut over to my rooming house, stopping only to buy a couple papers.

No one was in the hall when I got home. I went up to my room, stripped off my clothes, and walked down the hall to the bath. I took a long one, but the water was cold.

So far everything was okay.

But as soon as I got in bed, I started to shiver. I shook like I had the D.T.'s. I couldn't stop it. Up to now, I'd been so damned scared I'd no time to think. Now it hit me! Like a club! I started to climb out of bed . . . then I realized I didn't have any place to go. I'd come home . . . to the only place I knew. It was as good as any.

Back in bed, I started getting sick. I staggered to the bathroom and vomited. It didn't help any, I still felt sick. And then I began to think of Krassy! Why? Why had she done it? Why had she framed me? I rolled and tossed, and my body was hot, and my mouth was burning, I started sweating and the sheets became wet, and they wrapped all around me. Time passed in a funny, sticky, hot way, and then I remembered something else. I couldn't think very good anymore, but I remembered I still had the gun which shot Powers. I had to get rid of it; I had to. . . . Thoughts would jump complete in my mind . . . then they would just sort of fade out. Where would I hide the gun? Blank. Cops would be watching trash dumps and sewers. Blank. I had to get rid of it fast. Blank. It kept up like that.

Somehow I got some clothes on and I walked over to Chicago Avenue. Out of nowhere, part of the night I'd been to Evanston and drank on Howard Street came back. I caught an el and got off on Howard. I walked north and toward the lake. Somewhere, in that direction, was a cemetery. I found it. The main gate was locked, so I walked around the high wall, until I found a place protected from the street. I was stumbling, and my arms didn't work too well, and I had a hell of a time hauling myself over the wall. It was dark, and there wasn't any moon, and maybe after twenty minutes I came to a grave which was still covered with fresh earth.

I got down on my hands and knees and started digging a small hole. I was careful to pull out each handful of dirt and place it beside me where I could find it. I clawed my fingers raw and bleeding, on the cold, half-frozen ground, digging a hole into which I could stretch my arm. I stuffed the revolver in the whole length of my arm, and then the knife and cleaver. I filled the hole up with the same earth I'd removed, and was careful to do the neatest job I could with it. When I was through, I went around scooping up some handfuls of dirty snow and plastering them over the hole. When the snow melted, it would leave no trace of my digging.

I got back to my room all right. But I discovered I'd been up all night without socks or a shirt. And I hadn't worn an overcoat, either. I got back in bed.

That was the last thing I remember for two weeks.

Distinctly, that is. Time and day and night and things like that didn't exist. I had pneumonia. The next day, when I didn't show at the office, Glasgow came up to look for me. He had me taken to the hospital. All that time I don't know what happened. A couple times . . . I think . . . maybe I came out a little, because in the layers of my fuzziness a little idea kept skipping around. It wasn't an idea, exactly, it was more like a memory which kept trying to tell me something.

Then when I started getting better, and could lie there in the hospital, and think a little bit, it hit me! The idea. I asked Glasgow to go to my room and bring me the newspapers I'd bought the night I escaped the cops.

The story of the killing was splashed all over the front pages, complete with pictures of Powers and Krassy. Krassy was wearing the black suit and hat she'd had on in the apartment. The veil on the hat covered her eyes and the upper part of her face, and she held her head turned partly away. It wasn't a good picture, and you couldn't tell much about her looks, except you knew she must be a damned good-looking woman.

One headline read: GAMBLER KILLS MILLIONAIRE BANKER!

The other sheet, a tabloid, said: GAMBLER PLAYBOY SHOOTS BANKER BEFORE PLEADING WIFE'S EYES!

Both of the stories followed pretty much the same pattern. One of them read:

> Edward Homer, notorious Chicago gambler, today forced his way into the home of Howard Monroe Powers, banker and philanthropist, and shot him to death before the eyes of his wife. Mrs. Powers, who had been molested lately by Homer's attentions, had left word that the gambler should not be admitted to the Powers' apartment. She was leaving to go downtown, when Homer threatened his way past the doorman, and

broke into the apartment shortly after noon today. Forcing his way past Herbert Robbins, the Powers' butler, Homer went to the living room to confront the well-known banker.

According to Mrs. Powers, who was present, but helpless, Homer approached Mr. Powers and said, "I've been waiting to give you this," then pulling a gun he shot the banker in the head as he attempted to rise from his chair.

Mrs. Powers rushed from the room calling to the butler for help. Robbins immediately notified the police who hurried to the scene of the killing. Homer made his escape from the apartment, by the back entrance, after brutally attacking Arthur Buehler, the Powers' chauffeur, who heroically attempted to capture the killer.

There was more of the same with statements from the doorman who said he'd been given explicit instructions by Mrs. Powers to keep me out, but that I'd jammed a gun in his ribs and forced him to let me by. The elevator operator told how I'd threatened to slug him.

Robbins, the butler, maintained I had "either managed to pick the lock on the door, which was always bolted, or used a skeleton key" to get in. He told about meeting me face to face in the hallway, and my face "was a furious red with a very angry look." He also stated he'd seen me in the living room, holding the smoking gun still pointed at Powers.

Buehler, the chauffeur, gave a blow-by-blow description in which he and I fought in the kitchen, and I'd saved myself from certain capture only by shoving the gun against his head, then batting him with it.

The thing had sure shaped up. God what a beautiful frame! Krassy had pulled the old mousetrap play to perfection. I didn't have a chance! I told Glasgow that I wanted to catch up with everything that had happened since I'd been sick, and would he mind getting me back copies of the papers I'd missed. He got them all right.

The killing continued to be big news and there were lots of pictures of Powers . . . old ones and mostly biographical; and there were pictures of Robbins, Buehler, the doorman, and even a so-called "composite sketch" of Homer drawn by a police artist from the descriptions given to him. It looked as much like me as an aardvark. Even my own mother wouldn't have recognized me from the drawing. But Krassy! Krassy was cagey! Her doctors refused to permit her to be photographed, and the only available picture was the one taken the day of the killing, the one with the black hat and veil, in which she looked like any one of a thousand other women, and not at all like Krassy Almauniski, Katherine Andrews, Karen Allison, Candice Austin, or Mrs. Dana Waterbury.

Her lack of pictures, however, didn't affect the continuing flow of details concerning the crime. Mrs. Powers told how she'd gone to my apartment once to ask me to stop molesting her. There were pictures of Homer's coach house, and a description of the "luxuriously furnished bookie rooms." The cops had fingerprinted the joint, and had found a number of prints which they couldn't identify.

Krassy also told how I'd attempted to shower her with expensive gifts . . . which she'd promptly returned to me. As evidence, she showed the cops the notes that came with them: "Wear these sapphires at your lovely throat . . . adoringly, Eddie," . . . and all the others, too.

And Robbins, innocently, backed her up on her story. He told how I called her every night around dinnertime and how "madame refused to speak to the fellow."

Mrs. Powers repeated her story over and over again. She had her witnesses . . . plenty of them. Robbins, the maid, cook, chauffeur. She told about meeting me one day at the race track . . . and how I'd forced my attentions on her. She'd never gone out with me . . . never seen me alone, except when she had called at the coach house to plead with me to leave her alone. And at that meeting, so she stated, there were numerous other persons present who were making bets. These persons, however, never came forward to substantiate her story.

Then the cab driver, the one I'd left my suitcase with, decided he needed a little publicity, so he came forward with the suitcase, and told how I'd left it with him the day of the killing. The cops looked over the heavy clothing and decided I'd planned my getaway to Canada. They started looking in that direction.

That brought the situation pretty much up to date. The nurse walked in my room and said, "You'll be able to leave tomorrow, the doctor says, Mr. April."

And that was the answer. I was Danny April. I wasn't Eddie Homer! Hell! There was no such guy as the Eddie Homer the cops were looking for. Eventually, the cops would find the real Eddie Homer . . . but it wasn't *me* . . . it wasn't the same guy. I'd never been picked up by the cops, so I knew they couldn't match fingerprints back to Danny April. But there was something else! I *never* could . . . *as long as I lived* . . . afford to get picked up by the cops, *or* fingerprinted for any other purpose. If I did, inevitably the prints would be matched.

And I was glad I'd loved Krassy the way I did. Because I had loved her so much, it had saved my life! I'd wanted her so badly, that I'd built up a person who was real to her. A person called Eddie Homer. She believed it . . . and she was hanging a frame on the guy who'd loved her so much he had lived a complete lie himself.

Eddie Homer, the gambler, the bookie; Eddie Homer who lived in the coach house, and loved Bach, who was born in New York, and went to Columbia; Eddie Homer whose mistress she'd been . . . didn't exist! He didn't exist anywhere in the world.

Except in her imagination.

The cops were going crazy trying to find him. He had no criminal record. He'd disappeared into thin air.

After I got out of the hospital, nothing new developed for a week. I went to the office each day; saw Glasgow and Spindel and read the papers. Then there was real news.

Eddie Homer had been found!

The real Edward A. Homer had been picked up, blue station wagon and all. He'd driven up to the coach house . . . and straight into the arms of the cops.

But it wasn't the *right* Mr. Homer! Mrs. Powers couldn't identify him . . . neither could the other witnesses. And Mr. Homer was mad as hell and threatened to sue everyone for libel. He proved conclusively, and with the aid of twenty reputable witnesses, that he'd been in Miami, Florida, the day . . . the hour . . . and the minute . . . of the killing. He'd never met Mrs. Powers, and from his remarks, you got the impression he wasn't sorry, either. Then the old guy from the key shop stepped into the picture. He told about making a key for the coach house, but he couldn't identify the real Edward Homer as the guy he'd made the key for. All he could remember was he'd made a key for another guy. It was all pretty damn confusing.

But there was no doubt the original Edward A. Homer was innocent, and he proved he'd lived in the coach house for three years . . . and had never run or operated a bookie joint. There or any place else.

It was a fine mess, all right! The cops were helpless. They kept trying to add up the situation, and finally decided that possibly Mrs. Powers, herself, might also be a little *confused*. But Mrs. Powers' undoubted sincerity concerning "an Eddie Homer" at this point had become an obsession and was unshakable. Her obvious sincerity, plus about thirty million dollars, plus the best legal counsel in the country, convinced the cops.

The inquest found that Howard Monroe Powers was wilfully shot to death by an unknown person operating under an alias. Other aliases and true name unknown. It recommended that such person be found and turned over to the due process of law of the State of Illinois, County Cook.

But they never found him. Me, that is. And Mrs. Powers, unable to overcome her grief, has moved to France. The Riviera.

I'm just Danny April, owner of the Clarence Moon Collection Agency. And I get along pretty good. Except at night. Then I see the beautiful figure of a woman, on the bed beside me; her hair black as death and floating around her head like a mantilla. She doesn't have any face. It is smoky-like, and when I go to kiss it, it dissolves away and there's nothing there. Instead, I hear a faint, high scream of a siren wailing, and the doors break down and the cops are there. They're arresting me and they take me down to the station. They fingerprint me. Then a big cop looks up and laughs in my face and says, "Welcome, Danny April, we've been waiting for you." And they take all the change out of my pockets, and when they count it they call the electric company.

And they say: "We've got another customer for you." They drop the coins in a meter-box, and somewhere a dynamo starts whirring, and the lights start to flicker, and a low moaning starts up in all the cell blocks. And then the cops say real polite: "Won't you please come in and be seated?"

THE TOOTH
AND THE
NAIL

PROLOGUE

His name was Lew; his second name is unimportant, except for one instance, which I shall tell you about later; and he had been known as Lew Austrian, Lewison Clark, and Patrick Paris. Actually, however, he'd been born Luis Montana, which is Spanish, and later Americanized it to Lewis Mountain—which means the same. His name, in itself, was peculiar in a way, because his family have been Americans for many generations and by the time he was born were not Spanish at all. But the old names remained, and that's why he ended up with a name such as Luis Montana.

And, furthermore, he wasn't born in California, or Texas, or Arizona or New Mexico—or any of the border states where you'd expect to find the descendants of the Spaniards. He was born in Iowa which is approximately in the center of the United States and where you may expect to find anyone. He was born on a farm, a good one with rolling acres of rich soil; it had been his grandfather's farm, and after his grandfather died his father owned it.

When he was alive, he was a magician—a maker of miracles, a prestidigitator, an illusionist like Harry Houdini or Thurston. He had been a good magician, but because he died too soon he never became really famous like the others I've mentioned. However, he accomplished something that neither of these men ever attempted.

First, he avenged murder.

Secondly, he committed murder.

Thirdly, he was murdered in the attempt.

ONE

The Judge of the Court of General Sessions, County of New York, smoothed down his black robe, deliberately arranged the papers before him, and nodded to the assistant district attorney. The attorney arose from the prosecution's table and walked a few feet toward the jury box. In the somber austere room, with high ceilings, he was the center of attention and he paused confidently, for a moment, before he began the opening statement for the prosecution. As he turned slightly, his eyes swept the table where the defendant was seated beside the counsel for the defense, and the eyes of the jury followed his glance. In that exact instant, with the jurymen's eyes on the prisoner, he began speaking. He spoke fluently and well, in an easy conversational voice, pacing slowly and deliberately before the jury box which seated nine men and three women.

The assistant district attorney was named Franklin Cannon. A man of middle age, of middling stature and undeterminable colored hair, he was a deliberate and unemotional man attempting to fulfill the obligations of his office. He disliked histrionics and prepared his cases carefully—presenting his logic, facts, and evidence to a jury with an honesty and sincerity that often was severely damaging to his opponents. Cannon appreciated the importance of the opening of a trial; at such a time, the jury often formed lasting impressions of both the prosecution and defense to which it clung with bias throughout the entire trial.

Cannon, talking now, was conscious of the scrutiny of the jury's eyes. As he continued to talk in generalities, he felt the eyes probing his face, examining his clothes, observing his gestures; a dozen pairs of ears weighing the sound of his voice, sifting his words. With the minutes going by, he could sense the easing of tension among the jurymen, the visible disappearing of aloofness as each became accustomed to his appearance and the sound of his voice. It had been Cannon's experience that all new juries are uneasy at the opening of a trial, and he was content to spend the additional time and words to build this first rapport between them. One by one, they would come to think . . . "He reminds me of Cousin Joe, the way he talks" or "he looks a little like Bob Elton out in the engineering department" or simply "Cannon talks like a pretty reasonable man."

Whichever it was the jury thought—the familiar comparison or the sudden acceptance of him as a person— whenever the decisions were made the barrier would suddenly go down and then the prosecution would get on with the business of sending a man to the chair.

Abruptly, Cannon stopped and walked slowly toward the jury box. Pausing, he seemed to be searching in his mind. Slowly, almost kindly, he said, "You must remember that the man accused here is not bound to prove his innocence . . . it is the obligation of the state, my obligation . . . too, to prove his guilt."

The chief counsel for the defense arose from his chair and stood beside the table. "Your honor," he said, "would you instruct the jury that what the counselor has just said is a matter of law. It has nothing to do with his own particular magnanimity."

Cannon turned and, in turning, seemed to bow to his opponent. "Certainly, it is a matter of law," he replied courteously.

The eyes of the jury were fixed on the defense attorney, partly hostile, partly surprised by the sudden intervention. Cannon, sensing the jury's sympathy for himself—which might quickly be dissipated when the defense made its presentation—turned now to the serious business before him.

"In many respects this is both an unusual case, and a very interesting one." Cannon's voice had assumed a grave note. "The defendant is accused of murder. The fact that he is so charged is the reason he is here, but it does not necessarily mean that he committed a murder. The State of New York will attempt to prove that he did kill a man known to him as Isham Reddick . . . an employee working for him as a valet and chauffeur.

"We will attempt to prove the accused had a motive, and the opportunity." Cannon turned and walked to his table, pausing for a moment to pick up a sheaf of papers

—through which he riffled. The silver-painted radiators, in the silent courtroom, released small puffs of steam. The rows of oak benches, the limply hanging flag, the green roller shades at the windows, the silent specters of other trials of other men, waited patiently.

Cannon was finished with his notes, and he replaced the papers and returned to a position a few feet from the jury box. "Undoubtedly each of you has heard the expression . . . circumstantial evidence. And most probably you have heard it referred to in a rather derogatory way. . . . It's not uncommon to hear a criminal, after conviction, maintain complete innocence and insist that all the evidence was circumstantial."

The attorney smiled, and a number of the jurors returned it. "There are very few cases, particularly of murder, where the facts and evidence are not at least partly circumstantial. Possibly only in a case where there are eyewitnesses to the very act itself, where the witnesses can identify both the victim and the accused, do you find a case without some circumstantial evidence. . . ."

The counsel for the defense interrupted. "Objection," he said. "This is a matter for argument, and is theoretical to the point that it can neither be proved nor disproved."

Cannon faced the judge. "If it please, your honor," he replied calmly, "I feel this matter of evidence . . . particularly of circumstantial evidence . . . is of the utmost importance to the jury . . . and must be completely understood." Turning to the attorney for the defense, he smiled, "I'm sure the counselor is planning to refer to it himself."

"Gentlemen," said the judge, "on points of law concerning evidence I will instruct the jury!"

Cannon nodded politely and returned to address the jury. "It is the obligation of both myself . . . and my associate," he turned and indicated Deputy Assistant Attorney Rickers, "to prove the *corpus delicti* in this case. In a homicide this term refers to the death of the person alleged to have been killed. Occasionally, newspaper feature writers," Cannon glanced with a quiet smile toward the press bench, "contribute to the myth that without a body, there is no conviction. This is not exactly the truth, although it makes excellent reading on a dull Sunday afternoon. What they mean to say, undoubtedly, is that without *evidence* of a body, there can be no conviction. But, ladies and gentlemen of the jury, that is something entirely different! In several no-table cases, which I can quote, verdicts of guilty have been found without the actual physical presence of a *corpus delicti*, although the evidence of a *corpus delicti* was proved beyond a reasonable doubt.

"In most jurisdictions, only direct evidence will avail to prove the fact of death, although circumstantial evidence may, of course, be resorted to in order to show that the death was produced through a criminal agency. Now, with these points in mind let us return to the night of November twenty-second of last year."

The jury was listening intently. "It is the contention of the state," Cannon continued, "that on that date, sometime preceding midnight, the defendant killed a man named Isham Reddick. Reddick was employed in his household, an establishment located on East Eighty-ninth Street, here in the City of New York. Evidence will be introduced to show that Reddick had become a thorn-in-the-side of the defendant, that Isham Reddick was blackmailing him, and the defendant had on at least

one occasion . . . and probably on others . . . paid
Reddick a substantial sum of money. On the night of
November twenty-second, there was a meeting between
the defendant and Isham Reddick ending in vio-
lence. . . ."

"Objection," stated the counsel for the defense. "That
is a conclusion."

"What are you attempting to establish, Mr. Cannon?" asked the judge.

"I'm attempting to outline the position of the case for
the state, and to indicate what we will later prove."

"Continue, Mr. Cannon," said the judge, "although I
shall point out to the jury that at this time there is no
evidence yet introduced to substantiate in any way what
you are saying."

"Thank you," said the counsel for the defense. Returning to his seat beside the defendant, he continued to
watch Cannon warily.

Cannon resumed, cautiously, the threading of his
speech. He wanted no interruptions at this point. The
afternoon shadows were filling the corners of the bleak,
forlorn room and he glanced at the watch on his wrist.
A little longer, and it would be time to adjourn until the
following day. It would give the jury an entire evening to
consider his remarks before the opposition took up its
defense. "Sometime during the night of November
twenty-second," Cannon continued, "and into the early
morning hours of the twenty-third, the body of Isham
Reddick was dismembered and destroyed in an attempt
to remove all evidence of the crime! And, in the possibility of detection or discovery, to circumvent conviction
and punishment for the crime! Fortunately for justice,
however, all traces of the crime were not removed. All

evidence of the body was not destroyed beyond recovery
. . . and other indisputable proofs of the crime were
preserved by the early appearance of the authorities.

"This evidence will be presented to you. You will ap-
praise it, weigh it, consider it. After you have heard the
entire case, after you have seen the evidence with your
own eyes, if you believe beyond any reasonable doubt
that the accused is guilty . . . it is then your duty, your
obligation . . . to return to this court your verdict at-
testing it." For a moment he stood silently, then added,
"Thank you."

The judge, glancing at the old-fashioned Western
Union clock on the wall, gaveled his desk once, and adjourned the court until the next morning. The court
stood respectfully while he walked to his chambers.

Two

It all began on the day I met Tally Shaw.
Meeting her, with due apologies to the poets, was not
the same as listening to a nightingale sing in a garden, or
finding a spring of cool water after thirsting for days in a
desert. But the fact that she was, that day, a complete
stranger both to me and to New York, standing on Seventh Avenue arguing with a cab driver, put into motion
all the events that were to happen later. And, if one
believes in inevitability, then it was inevitable that I
acted the way I did. A cab had stopped in front of the
hotel where I was living and its passenger did not have
enough money to pay her cab fare. The cabby was ada-
mant about keeping her luggage, and the girl was pleading with him, desperately, to let her have one small bag.

The Delafield—a small, not quite shabby hotel—

which receives most of its business from show people, does not have a doorman, or the girl might have borrowed the money from him. As I pushed past them to go into the lobby, I heard the girl say, "It's ridiculous! I only owe you a dollar!"

"I can't help that," replied the driver, "I'll hold the luggage and you can have it when you pay me the buck."

"I don't know how it happened . . . I had the money, I don't know where it went. . . ." She rummaged through her handbag urgently. "It might've fallen out when I had lunch. I remember I had it then. At the station just before I took the train. . . ."

I stood in the center of the doorway, holding open the door, listening to the argument. Urged on by my curiosity, I stepped back to the sidewalk letting the door close, still following the conversation. "Look, lady," the cabby protested indifferently, "maybe you did, maybe you didn't. I keep the suitcases till you pay me or . . . I'll call a cop."

The girl was frightened. "No, don't do that! Keep one of them . . . keep the hatbox. Is that all right with you? I'll just take the little handbag."

He shook his head. "Nope! I keep both of them!"

"But I must have at least one . . . or I can't get in the hotel. They won't let me register without paying in advance. . . ."

"I keep both of 'em." The cabby's voice was final.

I discovered I was standing by the girl's side and, to my surprise, I heard myself saying, "If the lady will permit me, I'll pay the bill." The cabby swung his small suspicious eyes at me, and the girl turned wonderingly. "How much does she owe you?" I asked him.

He replied, "A buck."

"Here it is . . . and give the lady her luggage." He placed a large tan hatbox and a small leather satchel on the sidewalk. Circling around to the driver's seat, he slipped behind the wheel and drove away. The girl remained silent. "Well," I told her, "you now have your choice . . . either say 'thank you,' or I'll take the luggage."

"It was nice of you," she gave me an embarrassed smile. "Thank you very much."

"Lost all your money, huh?" I asked.

"Yes." She regarded her purse, misery in her eyes.

"Any idea where you lost it?"

"It must've been at the station . . . in Philadelphia." Her words began to tumble out. "I stopped in the station for a sandwich. Then I was on the train. I didn't look again until I reached the hotel. I didn't hire a porter . . . or buy anything else. . . ."

"Can you wire back for more?" She shook her head hopelessly. "Anyway," I said, "there's no sense standing out here on the curb. Come on, I'll buy you a cup of coffee while you decide what to do." The Delafield has a small luncheon counter, which is open twenty-four hours a day, and I headed for it. Picking up her luggage, I received a surprise. The hatbox was neither any heavier or lighter than you might expect, but the small leather satchel could not have weighed more if it had been filled with fire plugs. "Don't you find this a little heavy to carry around?" I asked politely.

She agreed, rather nervously. "Yes . . . but it's good exercise," and then smiling, she shrugged it off.

We climbed on stools and she ordered a cup of tea. The counter was nearly vacant although it was invisibly festooned with the ghosts of generations of cream cheese and jelly sandwiches. "Just as a beginning," I asked the girl, "do you know anyone in town you can phone . . . any friends or relatives?"

"No. I'm a complete stranger."

"Where'd you come from?"

"Philadelphia . . ."

"The answer is easy," I told her. "I'll lend you five dollars and you can go back. Catch a train tonight . . . they leave practically all the time."

"I can't do it," her voice was very low.

"The five bucks? You can send it back sometime."

"I didn't mean that. I . . . just . . . can't go back to Philadelphia." Turning, she faced me, her eyes wide and set with determination.

"Why not?"

She didn't reply. Abruptly I realized I was wrong. What made her eyes so wide was not determination, but fear! I said, "All right, let's change the subject. Tell me about yourself; I'm not the Traveler's Aid Society, but I'll do until it comes along. . . ."

It was then she told me her name was Tally Shaw. She had no family; her last relative, an elderly uncle, had died the preceding week. She had taken what little money was left and come to New York. And here she was—no money, no friends, no job. As I listened, I watched her and realized it was an extremely pleasant pastime. While she talked, she held her eyes to the bottom of the teacup—as if attempting to read the leaves. Occasionally she turned the cup slowly, around and around, in her fingers. There was an unconscious grace in the movement, her head arching on a slender neck, her profile lovely. She did not, however, possess what could be called a striking beauty although that was an asset in itself. Her charm depended on a shyness, a quietness—a blending of softness and repose.

Highlights danced on her hair. The regularity of her delicate features was contradicted by her mouth—warm, and a shade too wide—and high prominent cheekbones which lightly brushed an enigmatic expression . . . a gentle touch of the Oriental . . . across her face.

"What had you planned to do here in New York, before you lost your money?" I asked.

"I really didn't have any plans," she shrugged. "I would have to find a job . . . of course."

"Have you ever had a job?"

"Well . . . sort of . . . before Uncle Will died."

"Can you do typing . . . take shorthand?"

"No . . . not without studying."

"Do you have any repressed desires? Can you sing . . . dance? Ever want to be an actress?"

She set the teacup firmly on the counter and smiled. "I can't sing a note," she replied. "I like to dance . . . you know, just ordinary dancing to an orchestra. And I don't know a thing about acting. Do you?"

"No," I assured her, "I know very little about it either. Although through the force of economic necessity or the problems of seasonal employment, when I've had to . . . I've sung in the chorus of *The Student Prince,* danced a mean waltz in *The Merry Widow*, done speaking parts up to, and including, five lines in summer stock." I lit a cigarette and added, "Tally, I've also sold tickets in a carnival, worked clown alley in the circus, and been a dealer in Nevada. . . ."

"Oh," she regarded me gravely, looking a little puzzled, "you're an actor!"

"Only through necessity," I told her, "and not through choice. Through choice, if I have anything to say about it, I'm a magician."

"Can you do tricks?"

"Certainly. And someday you should catch me at them."

For the first time she really laughed. Momentarily, she seemed to have forgotten her problems. "I love magicians!" she exclaimed. "All my life I've loved to watch magicians and clowns."

"I agree with you," I said, "except personally I don't like clowns."

"You're just being jealous!" She looked at me carefully and then said marveling, as if just then she had seen me for the first time, "you said your name was Lew. What is your real name?"

"Lew Mountain. Lately, I've been working under the name of Patrick Paris . . . or Professor Paris."

"Are you working in a show now?"

"I'm working in the floor show of a nightclub. Which brings up another subject. I don't have too much money. As a magician I know it's unkind to my profession to admit we can't make it materialize from the air. So with that thought in mind, I hurry on to what I can do. By waving my hand in the air, thus . . ." I faked a pass and palmed the key of my hotel room, "I can make available to you . . . tonight . . . all the secrets, all the mysteries and joys, the romance and glamour of the . . . Taj Mahal!" I held up the hotel key.

"What's that?" she asked.

"It's the key to a warm bath, a rather hard bed, four waterproof walls, and a doubtful ceiling and floor. It is the key to my room . . . number 302, situated in the

Hotel Delafield . . . where we are now." She had been watching with a smile, but the smile disappeared. "Wait a minute!" I told her hurriedly. "Don't leap at the wrong idea. You must have a place to stay tonight . . . perhaps for a few days. I rent my room by the month. You stay here, and I'll find a place to bunk for a couple of nights. Which reminds me! I know a fellow who has an apartment right near here. Why . . . for years now . . . he's been flooding me with weekend invitations."

The smile tentatively reappeared. "Oh," she said. Then brightening, "Will it be all right with the hotel?"

"Not entirely," I told her. "The management would far prefer that I pay the double rate . . . and we live in sin. They're not moralists, you see, they're realists. But a little palm salve to the maid and the bell captain . . . and you could stay forever." Rising from the stool, I picked up her luggage. "Come on," I said, "I'll get you moved in now." She arose and followed me to the back of the luncheonette where a door opened into the hotel. I placed her luggage on the floor, and poked my head into the lobby. Max, the bell captain, was leaning against the newsstand and reading the magazines. With the sure instinct of a man smelling a fast buck, he raised his head as soon as my eyes hit him. Immediately he put aside his reading and sauntered over to me. I stepped back within the lunchroom and he followed me.

"This is an old aunt of mine from Montreal," I told him, nodding to Tally. "She's here for the mud and the baths, you know. Because of the shortage of rooms in all the spas, she'll have to use mine for a few days."

"She's pretty well preserved," he observed, after eyeing her carefully.

"Yes, isn't she? It's the water that does it. Now, can

you get her stuff up to 302 without the desk knowing it, and charging for a double?"

"I can get Yankee Stadium through the lobby without the desk knowing it," he assured me.

"Okay," I agreed, handing him a bill. "Here's your take for the luggage. I'll see you upstairs."

Max picked up the hatbox, and nearly dislocated his shoulder on the small leather satchel. "Jees, lady," he said, "what you got in here, a troop of midgets?"

Tally blushed and attempted to take the bag away from him. "I'll carry it," she said. "It's awfully heavy. . . ."

Max squinted his eyes. "You don't look like a lady wrestler," he said shrugging off her hands. "I've carried plenty drunks that weighed more'n this." He seemed literally to vanish into the lobby.

Room 302 was located on the back of the building facing away from Seventh Avenue. It was a medium-sized room finished in plaid wallpaper, with all the wood trimming of the doors and windows painted white. The elderly furniture had been modernized to the extent of a coat of black enamel paint; this included the bed, dresser, straight-backed chair, and a small telephone stand. The handles and knobs had been removed from the furniture and replaced by small, round circles of wood also painted black. The lamps, which harked back to the roaring twenties, retained their old bases, although supporting new shades of a particularly hideous elongated modern design. Only the prints on the walls remained unchanged. They would remain hotel pictures until the day the termites chewed them free from their frames.

Tally surveyed the montage calmly. "The nicest thing

you can say about the room," I told her, "is that it's paid up to the end of the month." Surprisingly enough, she patted my hand.

"You don't know how lovely it looks to me," she replied.

"If that's the way you feel about it, I might as well show you the entire layout. Not that you'd get lost finding out for yourself, but this way you won't have to waste time walking. Here is the bath. It doesn't lead anywhere. This is the closet; but don't make the mistake of trying to get in it and turn around. I did that one night and missed a show." By the bed, I lifted the tufted chenille spread up from the floor and pulled out a wooden footlocker. "This," I explained, "is the kitchen. You are not supposed to cook in the rooms, but it's all right if the management can't get in the door while you're doing it." I unlocked the footlocker and handed her the key. "Keep it locked whenever you're not using the stuff. The maid knows . . . they always know . . . but tomorrow morning give her this dollar and she won't say anything."

From the locker I removed an electric hot plate, a nest of plastic picnic dishes, cups and a few pieces of silver together with several aluminum pans, a coffeepot, and a small, flat, iron griddle. "There!" I exclaimed, "All the conveniences of dining in! I keep coffee, sugar, and canned soup under lock and key; and the cream outside the window."

Tally nodded. "Utilitarian . . . to say the least. I don't imagine you often have large dinner parties."

"Just during the height of the season," I said modestly, "and then never more than . . . oh . . . well . . . myself."

She put the utensils back in the locker and shoved it under the bed. "I know I'm imposing on you terribly," she said soberly.

"Not at all," I replied, keeping it light, playing it flippantly. "I always expect people to drop in."

Rising to her feet, she smiled. Inexplicably, her face was dusted with a sweet and inscrutable expression. "I'll find something real soon."

"Take your time, kid," I told her. "Be choosy . . . start at the top if you can. Then you can always work down." Taking my hat, I stepped out into the hall. "I'll see you in the morning," I said, "around noon. And you can make me a cup of coffee."

"I'll be up before then," she said.

"Yes, but I won't," I told her. Walking down the street, deciding who was in town, and where I could find a place to sleep, I recited aloud:

> Meet me by moonlight alone,
>   And then I will tell you a tale.
> Must be told by the moonlight alone
>   In the grove at the end of the vale.

I felt very good.

Three

Charles Denman, chief counsel for the defense, was a dark sardonic man with a lean alert face. Standing near a window in the courtroom, his figure was silhouetted against the light and in the air behind him dust motes stirred sluggishly. Denman had been addressing the jury all morning, undermining the opening speech made by the district attorney on the day before. "Usually," he said, "this is the time when the defense states what it hopes to prove . . . even while I again remind you that neither the indictment of the defendant nor the prosecutor's statement are proof . . . but I believe that we will delay revealing our defense," his voice dropped to a confidential level, "because, frankly, I don't believe the prosecution has found soundness or merit in its case.

At this time, theirs is the burden of proof, and there let it remain.

"You are going to be asked to listen to quite a story . . . in which someone . . . has supposedly been killed. There is no corpse of the murdered person, there is no motive, and there were no witnesses. From this skein of gossamer fabrications you will be asked to decide . . . beyond all reasonable doubt . . . that murder has been committed. Except that this is a learned court, and an innocent person's life is on trial here, I would say that the entire story is so . . . unbelievable, as to be unworthy of a half-hour television play." An answering smile came from the jury box. "However," Denman continued, "we will do what we can, as we go along, to show you the inconsistencies, the doubtfulness of the charges. I'm sure that you will need little help to notice the lack of proof supporting the charges which will be introduced."

Turning, he nodded in the direction of Cannon. "Yesterday, my respected colleague, Mr. Cannon, said . . . and I quote him . . ." Denman walked deliberately to the table and selected a sheet of paper; carefully, he put on a pair of heavy, tortoise-shell-rimmed glasses. Holding the sheet before him, he read clearly, "You must remember that the man accused here is not bound to prove his innocence. It is the obligation of the state to prove his guilt." Denman replaced the paper on the table and removed his glasses. "Of course, Mr. Cannon also admitted many other things, too." Denman swung around and returned casually to the jury box. "I didn't read the entire statement, because I believe you will agree it was rather wordy."

Denman's face was now extremely earnest. "I ask you

to remember, however, the seriousness of that statement. Saying it is one thing . . . doing it, another. When evidence and exhibits are introduced into this case . . . and undoubtedly they will be introduced very impressively . . . ask yourselves what it proves. Please say to yourself, 'What does this mean?' Is it evidence of fact? Does it actually mean anything when reviewed in the light of the entire case? Many persons who were innocent have been convicted by circumstantial evidence . . ."

Cannon was on his feet, interrupting. "Objection, your honor!"

"Objection sustained!" the court ruled. The judge instructed the jury, "You must overlook the last remark of the counsel for the defense."

Denman smiled to himself. Although the judge might advise the jurors to overlook the remark, some of them might remember it. Denman had been working hard, turning the opening sympathy of the jury away from the district attorney and attempting to win it for himself. He was beginning to tire with the advancing hours of the day. This case was one which he regarded uncertainly. As an attorney he believed it was his duty to defend the guilty as well as the innocent. To an extent circumscribed only by his own cynicism, he was dedicated to his profession. He fought for the rights of the defendants, protected their rights as defined by the law, and sometimes even financed the costs of their defense. He did this not out of friendship, and certainly not for financial gain, but for the satisfaction he derived in fighting for an equality before the law. Sometimes he felt more sympathy for the men he believed to be guilty. The client, in his present case, had maintained his innocence.

Denman's clients seldom lied to him, and if he was convinced they were lying, he refused to represent them. But with this man, he could not be sure. Denman was not sure that he knew the entire story; what he did know of it fascinated him.

"There is very little more that I want to add now," he continued, "except to remind you that my client has pleaded 'not guilty.' That means he *is not* guilty . . . until such a time as the charges are irrefutably proven. And, ladies and gentlemen, that time will never come! I ask of you, beg of you, to keep your sense of appraisement, maintain your feelings of skepticism, and keep your mind open until both sides have been heard." Denman stood before the jurors silently for a moment, then nodded gently, turned, and retired to the defense table.

The judge recessed the court.

Denman's assistant, a young man with protruding blue eyes and a crew cut, helped him arrange his folders in a briefcase. "I thought it went very well," he remarked to his superior. Denman glanced up to watch his client being escorted from the courtroom between two officers.

"Well enough, I suppose," he replied to the younger man. "No one can tell for sure . . . until it's too late."

The reporters opened the little gate in the low wooden railing and approached Denman. "I suppose I can quote you as being optimistic, counselor?" one of them asked.

"What else?" asked Denman smiling.

FOUR

Of course on the morning after I met Tally, I returned to the Delafield around noon, and she opened the door. She was completely dressed . . . in the same dress of the day before. Probably, it was the only dress she had. Or at least, it was the only one she had with her. Her hair was combed; she had her make-up on and she looked beautiful. The hot plate and coffeepot had already been set up, on top of the dresser, so we sat down and had breakfast—which included a sack of doughnuts I had brought along. I sat on the chair, balancing a cup, and tried to make conversation. "Have you been up long?"

"Oh, yes," she replied. "Hours . . ."

"Well, I suppose it's fine if you can wake up in time. How'd you sleep?"

"Lovely! How did you?"

This was real sparkling dialogue, but I liked it. Just sitting and talking to her, it was the tops. "Great," I told her. "I slept with a guy's dog all night. He has this mutt, which always sleeps on the extra bed; whenever anyone sleeps in it, the dog won't give it up. With some persuasion, however, the dog will share it. He shared it with me, but he insisted on the pillow."

She laughed, and in the morning it sounded as bright as the sunlight. "Did you work last night?"

"Sure. All three shows."

"Is it fun?"

"Not particularly," I told her. And then I realized it was just a pose . . . it was fun. It wasn't difficult to remember when I thought it was the greatest thing in life. So I started telling her about it. . . .

Our house, on the farm, had been a great, square, frame one. Across the front had been a porch narrow in depth but stretching the entire width. It had a series of plain, undistinguished wooden posts . . . or pillars . . . placed every eight feet which supported a railing. In the summers, my father and mother kept a couple of rocking chairs on it, and would sit there in the evenings after dark. Although the house was three stories high, it had a perfectly flat metal roof . . . painted a faded red. Surmounting the roof was a glass-enclosed cupola . . . about six feet square. On top of the cupola was a long elaborate lightning rod . . . pointing up to the Iowa skies. The cupola could be entered only by a ladder which projected through an opening in the ceiling of a room on the third floor. No one ever entered it as it was usually occupied by mud hornets, yellow jackets, and pigeons. Why it was ever built, or even conceived—this misplaced captain's walk in the middle of the prairies, I'll never know. The house had been built by some forgotten pioneer, long before the Civil War, and had been purchased many years later by my grandfather. Like most farm houses, it always needed another coat of paint.

In the front yard were great oak trees, standing in grass which seemed to spring from the ground a foot high, and never grew any higher. From the branch of one of the trees my father hung a rope with a worn-out automobile tire for a swing. But I don't remember ever using it; perhaps because I had no brothers or sisters to play with me, and it seems senseless to swing by one's self. Back, and away, from the house were all the farm buildings—the barn, the equipment sheds, corn crib, silo, and chicken house. Growing up with the animals, they had little attraction for me, and no novelty. Early enough, my first duties were gathering eggs and helping my mother feed the chickens; by slow degrees I graduated to the milk house, and then to milking . . . and later to the fields.

It is easy to give the impression that I was worked too young . . . and too hard. That isn't true. My life was the same as many farm boys and, I believe, it was better than most. Always we had a hired man to help with the chores, and my mother usually had a farm girl to help her in the house. Our farm was prosperous, and our way of life was good. But a farm, I think, is a lonely place unless it is truly part of your life. Unfortunately, although I lived on one, it was never part of mine. After dark, the land seems to expand, to push all things away, farther and farther, until the farm on which you live is an island. The rest of the world is far away; in the distance are the highways, but they do not lead to you. Across the miles a light gleams in the window of another house, but that light is part of a different island and has nothing to do with you. The tree frogs start hesitantly, always slowly, playing a chirping dissonance which gradually grows and swells in confidence and volume as if a conductor were leading; then lowering, it gently falls away following God-knows-what theme, until on cue it swells and crashes again. Sometimes the pigeons in the cupola mourn restlessly in the early translucent darkness, and the fireflies come out searching the night with their pinpoints of light for something which they never find. Unless it is death in the cold morning dew.

When I was nine, just shortly before my tenth birthday, I saw a magic set displayed in the mail order catalog which was delivered to us each spring and fall. For hours I read the description, read and reread it again until I could repeat it word for word. I wanted that set more than anything in the world. Until that moment, gripped in the fever of my newfound desire, I realized I had never really wanted anything before in my life!

My mother was helpless, before the intensity of my pleadings, to deny me the gift for my birthday, although I imagine the cost far exceeded what she had planned to spend. Together we sat down at the round kitchen table and filled out the order, and I addressed and stamped the envelope. That night I could hardly sleep for excitement, and in the morning I was waiting when the RFD mailman drove up in his model T Ford. With the letter safely on its way, I drew a deep—and contented—breath.

There has never been a day like the day the magic set arrived. Never again will the sunshine be as bright, nor the sky as blue, nor the world as beautiful. It arrived in a large, flat, black box made of cardboard; on the cover was a Mephistophelean magician with patent-leather black hair, and long curving sideburns. He was dressed in evening clothes and was pulling a placid rabbit out of a silk hat. Within the box was an instruction book, and the simple equipment necessary to make a quarter disappear in a glass of water, change a penny into a dime, and make silk handkerchiefs appear from eggs; there were large cardboard dice, glass wands, paper that changed colors . . . the enchantment of all the world of make-believe and illusion. In my lap, in the black cardboard box, I held the secrets of the cabala, the mysteries of alchemy, the key to the Unholy Sabbath; a fellow of Paracelsus, a familiar of Cagaster, a student of the Egyptians.

From that day on, I was never very far away from the set. As I grew older I spent my allowance, and then my youthful wages, on more complex equipment. I practiced in my room at every opportunity; in the barn and in the fields, I carried odd cards and silver coins to palm until my hands and fingers worked independently of my brain.

My first public appearance, as a magician, took place in the town of Fairfax—about seven miles from our farm. We drove each Sunday to the Unitarian Church, in Fairfax. On the occasion of a church dinner, I offered my services for the after dinner program. Somewhat cautiously the minister accepted. His acceptance was based partly on the fact that my father had been a member of the congregation for over twenty years, as well as the fact that there was little new talent to offer. The talents of the congregation had been seen on many occasions, by the same jaundiced audience. That evening I shared the bill with a fifteen-minute slide travelogue of the Falkland Islands—located off the southern end of South America and notable only for their dreariness; a piano concert by Mrs. Randy Fuller, a widow who gave music lessons; and a brother and sister duet by the Ostander kids.

I literally brought the house down . . . or rather the church. I'll never forget the feeling as I stood in front of the small audience and listened to the applause of family friends, neighbors, and fellow church members. To me, it sounded thundering. Driving home that night, my father congratulated me and gave me ten dollars. I pocketed it . . . for professional services.

The summer I finished high school I was seventeen. My parents had discussed sending me to the agricultural college at Ames that fall. I didn't seem to care about this one way or the other. I was neither pleased nor displeased. When fall came, if they wanted me to go, I'd go. That was the way it was. In July, though, a carnival played the Fourth at Oneida, our county seat town—about ten miles the other side of Fairfax.

My mother wasn't feeling well, that week, and so my parents were not planning to go. A family named Murray, on the next farm, was going to drive over to Oneida and they offered to let me ride along. In those days we had movies although they were silent, and on the farm my father had erected a high antenna, and we had a huge, twelve-tube super-heterodyne radio. So movies and radio weren't novelties, but I had never seen a play in a theater or been to a circus or carnival. There were no towns with theaters where vaudeville or shows played within a hundred miles, and it was seldom that a carnival came within a reasonable driving distance.

The Murrays and I arrived at the carnival grounds after dark. Strings of orange, blue, green, and red lights swung in the velvet realm of night. Silhouetted against a great golden moon, a Ferris wheel churned slowly in its orbit, and a merry-go-round piped and trilled—the horses prancing and the lions racing. The smell of candy floss, of buttered popcorn, the frying hot dogs, the roasting peanuts, hot tamales and chili, the sawdust and hay trampled into the ground arose and hung, clinging in successive layers, in the quiet air of the prairie night. My senses were assaulted—by sight, by sound, by smell. In that first moment I was lost. I was drunk with an excitement, with an exhilaration which I had never known before.

Quickly I separated myself from the Murrays. Guided by knowledge which I could not identify, I walked straight to a small red trailer, parked to one side of the midway. A middle-aged man, with bushy sandy hair and heavily veined nose, was seated on the steps. He was coatless in the summer heat, his shirt open at a hairy throat and sleeves rolled high on his freckled arms. "Are you the owner?" I asked.

He turned his heavy eyes slowly to look at me, to acknowledge my presence. He grunted—it might be either an affirmation or a denial.

"I want a job," I told him earnestly. "I want to work for you. I'll do anything . . ."

"I don't need anything done," he replied.

"I'm good with stock," I told him. My ears buzzed with sound and excitement.

"Go on home, son."

My hands had been thrust in my pockets, and now in my embarrassment I found a silver dollar in my hand, and I removed it from the trousers. Passing my hand before his eyes, I made the silver appear and disappear at will; it ran up my arm, stopped, rolled down to palm, and faded into the air. In the background I could hear the grind of the talkers pitching for the hanky panks and string games, the fish pond, fortune wheel, and milk bottle games. The rides—dipper, scooter, and baby whip—crashed and clanked mechanically in the night. The jig show with its three-piece combo blasted loose-jointed music to mark the beginning of a new bally. And through it all, the fun house, the monkey drome, wild life and torture shows; the rattle of the shooting gallery, the penny pitch, the cork gallery, lead gallery, and scales —all the world was throbbing and contracting and calling as I manipulated my coin before the man with the red-veined nose. Abruptly he rose to his feet, standing on the top step of the trailer towering above me. "You ain't bad, kid," he said slowly. "You said you wanted to work?"

"Yes . . . yes . . . sir!" I stammered in my eagerness.

The man shouted a name into the noise and confusion of the night. "Hey, Hym!" Immediately a figure materialized beside the trailer; a heavily muscled man, with thick bullish neck, and terribly scarred ears. "Hym, take a look at the kid. He's good." He motioned me to resume my palming.

Hym watched me from mean speculative eyes. "Yeah," he agreed. "Nice clean yokel face. He could do all right selling." He turned to the man in the trailer.

"You talked with him?" The man with the red nose shook his head. "Okay," said Hym, "I'll talk to him."

We walked silently to the chow-top—the cooking tent —and sat at a planked dirty table. Hym rested his arms on the boards, and regarded me cautiously. "You live near here?" he asked.

"No," I replied, lying . . . not knowing why, except caution seemed to demand it. "I come from a town in Minnesota—about three hundred miles from here."

Hym grunted, pleased with the information. "Got any folks who might come after you?"

"No," I replied, resolutely shutting my parents from my mind.

He nodded, "Okay, kid. Here's the pitch. I'm putting you on as a ticket-seller. I start you at the girl-show 'cause the admission there is thirt' cents. That gives odd change outa dollar. Some mark hands you a buck, you give 'im a ticket and change for fort'-five cents. I got hustlers keeping the line movin' so's the mark don't geta chance to count change till too late." Reaching in his pocket, he withdrew a handful of silver. "Like this, see. I'll show you. Make like I've already handed you your ticket—here, I shove it in your left mitt. Why the left mitt? Because the suckers, most of 'em, keep their change in their right pockets. I got a reason . . . I'll show you later. Now you hold out your right mitt for your change. I count it for you . . . Outa one dollar, sir, thirt' cents, thirt'-five, fort'-five, fifty, seventy-five . . . and *oneee* dollar. T'anks, kindly."

I found myself nodding instinctively to his counting; in my hand was a heap of pennies, nickels, and dimes. "Okay," said Hym with a wicked grin, "count it yourself, kid." I did—there was fifty cents in it. There should have been seventy. Hym continued with his lecture, "So this mark is standing there with a handful of change, before he can count it, you say real loud: 'Move along, friend . . . keep movin'! Please don't stand there blockin' all your neighbors. The show's just startin' and they wanta get in, too! Keep movin'!' Then one of my boys in the line gives a shove, and the line moves along. The mark puts the change in his pocket, with his right hand. He don't have to change over from the left, so he never can be sure. And that's it. Got it?"

I found, suddenly, I was unable to say the words . . . to agree. Miserably I looked at him, and his eyes were fixed on me in a hard, expectant stare. As if reading my mind, he shrugged and lurched awkwardly to his feet. From a distance, I heard my voice saying, in mingled shame and excitement, "Yes . . . I've got it!"

"All right," said Hym. "You get your meals free in the chow-top, and you can find your own place to sleep in any of the sleeping-tops. You get paid ten bucks a week." He waited for my protest, and when it didn't come, his savage face relaxed. "Insida week, kid, you'll be stealing three times that much from me." He walked to the opening of the tent, pausing for a moment to add, "Never shortchange on a mark who gives you half a buck or less; on a big bill there ain't no limit to what you can grab. Don't let your fingers get too goddamned sticky and try to steal me blind." Shrugging his shoulders, he raised his palms in a little forgiving gesture, "Take a little . . . give a little, okay. But don't forget, kid, I got mine coming, too." He walked out into the noise of the night.

FIVE

"The witness will please take the stand," the clerk announced. Cannon approached the witness chair and asked conversationally, "What is your name?"

"Daniel F. Mikleson."

"You are a member of the New York City police department?"

"Yes, sir. I'm a lieutenant, attached to the Homicide East squad."

"Do you remember what happened to you on the morning of November twenty-third of last year?"

"Yes, sir." Shifting his weight in the chair, assuming a more comfortable position, the lieutenant explained that he had been sent to examine the premises of a brownstone house located on East Eighty-ninth Street.

"Was it in answer to an anonymous phone call?"

"Yes, sir. On the telephone. A man called from the public phone booth on the Eastside subway station . . . the stop at East Eighty-sixth Street."

"Did you talk to him?" Cannon added, "And if you did, what did he say?"

"I talked to him. He said, 'There have been awful smells coming out of the chimney at that house. I think there's been a murder committed.'"

Cannon glanced thoughtfully at the accused, then turned his attention back to the witness. "And after the call, you proceeded to the premises. Did anyone accompany you?"

"Yes. Another detective named James Lowery."

"What happened when you arrived at the premises?"

"It's a large brownstone house, a private residence. There's a heavy plate glass door, in the front, which is protected by iron scrollwork. We rang the bell and pounded on the door for some time. . . ."

"How long?"

"Ten minutes. The bell was working because I could hear it ringing in the back of the house."

"What time was this?"

"When we first arrived, we parked the squad car in front of the house and I looked at my watch. It was 10:28 in the morning."

"Thank you. Now after ringing the bell, and pounding on the door for ten minutes, what did you do?"

"We couldn't be sure that the call wasn't the work of a crank, or just a neighbor being nasty. I had just about decided to check back to the desk, when the door was opened by a man."

"How was he dressed?"

"He was wearing underclothes, although he had a dressing robe around him."

"How did he look? Was he shaved? Did he have his hair combed?"

"No, sir. He was not shaved, and his hair was mussed."

"Do you see that same man here in the courtroom?"

"Yes, I do." The lieutenant looked steadily at the defendant. "He is seated over there."

"Please go over and place your hand on his arm." The officer walked stiffly to where the accused was seated, touched his arm briefly, and returned to the witness stand. "Now," resumed Cannon, "what did the defendant say when he opened the door?"

"He acted very astonished. He . . ."

"Objection!" Denman's voice remarked.

The judge agreed. "Sustained," he ruled.

"All right," Cannon was unruffled, "after he opened the door, what happened next?"

"Nothing . . . for a minute or two," replied Mikleson. "He was silent. I showed him my credentials and he asked what I wanted. I told him it had been reported there had been a murder on the premises, and it was my job to look around."

"What did he say, then?"

"Nothing. He was acting peculiarly and . . ."

"Objection!" Denman's voice was curt.

"Sustained!" ruled the court.

"Was he shaking his head?" asked Cannon.

"Yes. He was moving it slowly from one side to the other. I had to repeat what I said before. Finally, he asked me if I had a warrant. I replied I didn't have one, but I could get it if he insisted. I told him I'd leave Detective Lowery to wait for me, and I'd come back with one.''

"Then what did the defendant say?"

"He said to me: 'You might as well come in, now.' "
Step by step, Cannon led the witness through a description of the house. Mikleson identified photographs of the defendant's bedroom, and the adjoining bath, as ones having been taken in his presence by the photographic detail. Cannon offered them into evidence and they were marked as exhibits.

"I'll return to the photographs later . . . with the court's permission," explained Cannon, "but at this time I would like to continue with my present line of examination." There was no objection from Denman and the prosecuting attorney continued. "Tell me, when you reached the basement of the house what did you find?"

"There was a large furnace room, together with laundry and bathrooms." Mikleson added, "Also there were some other . . ."

"Let's concentrate on the furnace room, please. Where is it located in regard to the front and back of the house?"

"It is at the back of the house."

"Are there any windows in it?"

"Yes, sir. Two. Both are rather small and located high up in the walls . . . just about exactly at ground level."

"In other words, it is extremely difficult to see into it from the outside?" Cannon asked.

"Yes," replied Mikleson. "It is nearly impossible to see into it, from outdoors, unless you bend double to look in."

"Was there anything unusual in the furnace room?"

"The house requires a very large furnace . . . it's a big place. That day was a warm one, but there was a real, blistering fire going. . . ."

"One moment, please," Cannon interrupted. "With the court's permission, and opposing counsel's consent, I would like to introduce the official weather reports for the dates of November twenty-second and twenty-third of last year. I have secured them from the weather bureau's official records, and can introduce an expert witness if necessary."

"I'll waive the introduction," said Denman, indifferently.

"Proceed then, Mr. Cannon," directed the judge.

"During the warm spell last fall," said Cannon, "the official temperatures for November twenty-second were a low of 68 degrees, and a high of 74 degrees; on November twenty-third a low of 71 degrees, a high of 76 degrees." He held up a card and passed it to the jury. "All right, Mr. Mikleson, continue please."

The detective returned to his testimony. "The furnace was extremely hot . . . so hot I couldn't put my hand on it."

"You attempted to place your hand on it?"

"Yes, sir. To test it. On the outside, the furnace was covered with thick insulation, but even through the insulation it was too hot to touch."

"Did that seem unusual to you?"

"Yes, it did. Because of the weather . . . it was so warm that hardly any heat was needed at all. Also, it is very bad on a furnace to get it that hot; ruins them. Then I looked around the furnace room and saw that it had recently been scrubbed."

"How recently?"

"Very recently. Although the room was very hot, in one corner of the room there was still a small pool of moisture on the floor."

"Can you describe the floor?"

"It was a hard-surfaced floor composed of large, square, concrete blocks. Where the blocks fitted together, there were small cracks."

"What else did you notice about the room?"

"From the marks on the floor and the wall, there were indications a large wooden workbench, recently, had been in the furnace room."

"But it was no longer there?"

"No, sir. It was not."

"Just a moment," Denman interrupted. "I'm objecting to that. In the history of that house . . . nearly seventy-five years old, there have probably been many benches in the furnace room. And they're no longer there! I'm sure the counselor is being . . . ah . . . overzealous in attempting to read an unsubstantiated interpretation into the workbench."

"It is entirely relevant, your honor," Cannon turned to the judge. "I can prove the bench had been in the furnace room, up until the night of the murder . . . and the evidence is important."

"Continue," ruled the judge, "on the condition that all reference will be stricken if it's not proved later."

"With the overheated furnace, the water on the floor, and the missing bench, you decided to investigate further. What did you find?" Cannon asked Mikleson.

"In the furnace room?"

"Yes. Just the furnace room."

Mikleson moistened his lips with his tongue, turning slightly away from the direct view of the defense table.

"Well," he said slowly, "on the floor, by the outside of the furnace there's a small area where the concrete is chipped away . . . about like a small saucer. Part of this shallow hole runs under the outer shell of the furnace a few inches. . . ."

"Is this a picture of the indentation . . . or hole?" asked Cannon exhibiting a photograph.

"Yes," said Mikleson. Cannon offered the photograph into evidence and asked Mikleson to continue. "The cracked space," the officer resumed, "is a little distance away from the door of the furnace; to one side of it. The floor slopes slightly in that direction, too. In that small cavity in the floor, nearly hidden from sight, I found part of a human finger!"

Cannon exhibited a medical vial with a glass stopper. Within, floating in clear formaldehyde, was a section of finger approximately two joints in length. "Is this the finger you found?"

Deliberately, Mikleson identified it. "Yes, I cut a V-shaped notch in the fingernail. That's the nail!" It was offered into evidence.

"After you discovered the finger, Mr. Mikleson, what did you do?"

"I hurried upstairs to where Detective Lowery had been waiting with the defendant and called headquarters. I asked them to report my finding to the medical examiner's office . . . and to send down the laboratory and photographic details."

"Thank you, Lieutenant. That will be all," said Cannon. Then turning to the counsel for the defense, he asked, "Do you wish to examine, Mr. Denman?"

"Yes," Denman said rising. He glanced at a sheet of paper, covered with notes, which he held in his hand,

and leisurely approached Mikleson. "About this mysterious phone call you received . . . it came to you direct?"

"No, it came to precinct and was transferred to me."

"You don't know who it was, but you are sure it was
a man?"

"Yes, sir. I could tell it was a man."

"Was it a deep voice?"

"No. It was . . . ordinary."

"It wasn't a bass or a deep baritone. It was in between
a tenor and a baritone?"

"That's right."

"Isn't it true that some women have contralto
voices?"

"Yes, so I've heard."

"Now, over a telephone a woman's voice . . . a deep
contralto voice . . . can sound very similar to a man's
tenor voice. Particularly, if a woman deliberately attempted to disguise her voice. Now I submit to you,
Lieutenant, this point: You cannot say . . . positively!
. . . that it was not a woman calling, who might be
attempting to disguise her voice!"

"Well . . . it's . . ."

"Answer yes or no, please!"

"No-o-o, sir," replied Mikleson hesitantly. "I can't
say positively it wasn't . . . but I don't think . . ."

"No opinions, please, Lieutenant! I just want facts.
Let's get back to this mysterious phone call coming from
an unknown person . . . and you don't know whether
it's a man or a woman, who's trying to stir up some
trouble. What did this person say?"

"The person said: 'There have been awful smells coming out of the chimney at that house. I think there's been

a murder committed.' " Mikleson under continued examination gave the address, approximate time of the call, and the efforts to trace the call back to the public phone booth.

"All right," Denman said finally. "Tell me, is it the usual procedure of the Homicide Squad to run around the city following leads reported by such unreliable methods?"

"Yes, sir!" Mikleson suddenly became emphatic. "Many times we receive information . . . and tips . . . from strange sources." His statement made a definite impression on the jury.

Denman attempted to turn the point aside. "I should imagine it must keep you busy chasing down leads furnished by cranks, crackpots, and mysterious strangers . . . with personal feuds to settle. Then is it true, Lieutenant, that the Homicide Squad personally investigates all the trash and refuse burned in all the incinerators in this city?"

"It does if the incinerators got bodies in them!" Mikleson retorted grimly.

With a sigh, Denman returned to his examination of the witness.

SIX

There was about Tally an inward assurance, a calm acceptance of life which, after my own years of wandering and instability, appealed to me deeply. For several weeks she tried unsuccessfully to find work. It would take her months, possibly much longer, to build the contacts by which she could make a living from modeling or to find a job as a receptionist; or any other of the better paying jobs that she might possibly do. There remained only the unskilled jobs, the ill-paid ones, the ones offering drabness and monotony.

At the club, the Martinique, where I was working, the first show went on at nine-thirty each night. Consequently, I arrived at the club before nine o'clock to get in my costume, check my props, and put on my make-up. But regularly each evening, I would meet Tally at the

Delafield and we'd have dinner together in one of the inexpensive grab-joints along Eighth Avenue, and then wander over to Broadway. Sometimes we'd just walk along with the crowds, pausing to gander the lobby displays in the theaters and motion picture houses. At night the narrow grubby shops are dazzling in green, lavender, and rose neons; recordings blare over loudspeakers, from doorways of cut-rate record shops, blasting noise into the street; tiny turtles with hand-painted shells crawl aimlessly over each other in an endless attempt to escape from display windows; windows are crowded with plaster faces of a suffering Jesus whose melancholy eyes search one out in any corner of a room; litters of playing cards with naked, overdeveloped women on the backs. In some of the tiny shops busy merchants stitch personal initials on wild, absurd, top banana caps the width of manhole covers; in others one can buy natural-looking rubber dog turds available for practical jokers, at popular prices, brass replicas of the Statue of Liberty, equipped with thermometers, barometers, but not speedometers, rayon ties with one's birth date and individual sign of the zodiac, Spanish shawls, switch-blade knives, *moiré* photographs of women which can be manipulated to swing their hips and breasts back and forth, souvenir bracelets of New York City, wrist watches selling for $2.75 with a lifetime guarantee from the unknown (and unlocatable) manufacturer, shoddy Oriental rugs that would drive an Arab to tear up his Koran.

There are penny arcades with machines on which to practice torpedoing an enemy ship; machines to test the strength of one's grip; peep machines to watch a cloudy film of a striptease. There are stands selling orange juice, papaya juice, coconut milk, and mint-flavored grape juice; hamburger and hot dog stands. There are ball-rooms where a roll of tickets permits a choice of dancing with strange, tired, and bored hostesses. There are spots to buy marijuana cigarettes, and other drugs.

The crowds push, shove, and parade—promenading to a beat and pulse which comes with the night and flees with the morning. It is a street of dreams, all right; and most of them bad!

In the evenings, after dinner, we walked hand in hand —talking, laughing, exploring. When it came time for me to leave for the club, I'd take Tally back to the hotel, leaving with a promise to see her in the morning. One night, while we were looking over the pictures in the lobby of a movie, I realized that Tally might have a chance to get on with the circus—the Big One—which had just opened its season in New York. "I have an idea," I told her. "How'd you like a job with the circus? The pay for a show girl isn't bad—and you don't have to have any experience—just have to be beautiful. You get nearly nine months' work, room, and board. How about it? Tomorrow we'll go over to the Garden and catch the matinee . . . and see about it."

"Were you ever with the circus, Lew?" she asked.

"Sure," I told her. "I was with it for two seasons. That was before the war. I was real young then . . . and it seems a long time ago."

Tally tucked her hand over my arm. "The circus . . . what's it like?" We started back toward the hotel, walking slowly through the crowds, sometimes stepping into the street, dodging through the human stream.

"Of course," I said, "when you say the 'Big One' . . . you mean just one circus . . . because there's only one

Big One. It opens its season here, every year, in Madison Square Garden. It's a tough stand . . . all cramped together. Later on when it moves out, it plays under the tops . . . seventy-five thousand yards of canvas. It travels about fifteen thousand miles a year, and when it gets back to Florida in December it's really beat up. You know you've had it."

"Is it really as hard as all that?"

"Sure," I told her. And I remembered it . . . the kid, the wise guy, the sharpie from the carney getting on with the Big One. After what I'd had in the carnival years, I thought I'd never had it so good. The Big One was luxury compared to what the carney had been. "But you learn to take it. In rain storms, cloudbursts, hurricanes —everything the weatherman can throw at you. Dust storms, sand storms, the old thermometer at 110 degrees doesn't mean anything. You play four hundred performances in a little over two hundred days, while you're standing, performing, and striking the show in eighty towns scattered over twenty-five states."

"But how can they do it?"

"Well, the Big One travels in its own train. The train has four sections. You sleep in it, and eat in it. With all the equipment and personnel . . . and animals . . . the show covers eighteen acres when it makes a stand and pitches its tents."

"If . . . I . . . should get the job, you wouldn't consider coming along with me?" she asked.

"No," I told her. "I'd like to . . . it'd be fun. But I've spent too long now trying to build up my own act. If I ever went back, I'd have to return to clown alley, and behind that clown make-up, no one would ever hear of me again. There're perhaps fifteen hundred people

working in the Big One, and of them all—none is so lost
as a clown."

We were back to the hotel, now, and I had to hurry.
"Tomorrow we'll go over to see it," I said. She looked at
me and nodded, but not too happily, I thought.

The next day we stood in the great passageway, behind the arena, hugging the wall closely. Before us a
great line was forming, broken here and there—leaving
gaps—which filled, formed, and pressed together. Tally's
eyes swept the confusing swirl of color before her—
beautifully groomed horses with riders holding giant
gilded candelabra; animated vegetables walking on red-
hosed legs; the mighty bulls—the towering elephants
carrying howdahs, the envy of Eastern potentates; tall,
stately, lovely show girls dressed as calendar months,
each surrounded by pages, courtiers, and grotesque little
dwarfs; giraffes—tall, stumbling, and ungainly with tremendous satin bows on unbelievable necks; zebras
hitched to clown wagons; tiered, pillared, rococo floats
dusted in gold and silver, sprinkled with stars, draped
with velvets and silks; space ships of plastic and chrome,
spouting sparks and rocketing colored fire, crowded
with interplanetary men; a phalanx of ancient Romans
with plumed helmets, golden breastplates, and short
broad swords; dancing girls in brief white buckskins and
sombreros, with ivory sixshooters; tigers pacing restlessly in crimson and gold cages; monkeys dressed as
tiny men; trained pigs, scrubbed pink and white as hospital nurses; acrobats in leopard skins and silken tights;
Persian houris from the tales of Scheherazade, accompanied by Ifrits, jinni, and mamelukes; and they continued
to form into line.

Mother Goose characters with gigantic, carnival

heads—Bo-Peep and Little Jack Horner; Boy Blue with a tremendous horn, Old Mother Hubbard and the Knave of Hearts; chariots and broughams; coronation coaches and buckboards; Atlas carrying a huge globe on his shoulders; and clowns. Clowns.

Clowns in all sizes, costumes, and colors; laughing, crying, strutting, jumping; driving miniature cars; riding make-believe animals. Incredible, delightful clowns!

For a moment Tally closed her eyes to the confusion, and when she opened them a clown was standing by her side watching her. His head came to a point and perched on the top was a tiny hat, precisely creased with a gigantic pheasant feather in its band. Great, pendulous, red lips drooped in dejection, while the eyes—swooping upward in broad, painted, black lines—regarded her with perpetual and overwhelming surprise. "Go on, you dig me?" the clown's voice croaked.

She laughed without embarrassment. "I'm sorry. You surprised me, that's all."

"This is Hammy Nolan," I told her. "I've known him since we were in the alley together. Ham, this is a friend of mine . . . Tally Shaw."

"Hi, kid," Ham acknowledged the introduction in his normal voice.

"How are things going?" I asked.

"So, so," the clown replied. "Same as usual . . . too early in the season to tell, though. Nothing ever changes very much in this business."

"Ham, Tally here needs a job. Is Seaton still the program director for the show?"

"Yeah, still is."

"Do you think he needs any girls?"

Nolan shook his head slowly. A huge ruffled collar

encircled his neck, and his ballooning costume magnified his size. "Now's not the time to ask him, Lew. The First-of-May'ers haven't cleared out yet."

Tally glanced at me, puzzled. I explained. "He means the people who join the circus in the south, and stay with it when it comes north. They leave around the first of May when the show takes to the road. They're called First-of-May'ers."

"Wait another three or four weeks," Nolan advised.

"I guess you're right," I agreed.

Ham regarded Tally. Behind the grease mask, it was impossible to tell what he was thinking. When he finally spoke, however, his words left no doubt. "A good-looking gal, Lew. Are you still doing that magic act?"

"Yes."

"She'd sure dress up your own act. Why don't you use her yourself?"

For years I had performed as a single, and the idea of giving the act more flash with a girl hadn't occurred to me. My bookings were getting better; I was working pretty steadily now; and my agent had been getting more money for the act. "That's an idea," I said. Turning to Tally, I asked, "How about it? Do you want to work with me?"

"I'd like to . . . if you want me," she replied quietly.

That was the way I got a partner. After that day in the circus, I spent each afternoon . . . all afternoon . . . rehearsing Tally. I worked out special bits of business so she would have an opportunity to remain on stage. Basically my act was built around three major illusions—catching a live goldfish in the air with a miniature fishing pole; pouring milk out of a pitcher and having it vanish in midair as I poured it; and a rope that crawled from a basket, and then stood on end like a cobra. Also, and this was very important, between each of the major illusions, I had a number of shorter tricks which I worked . . . one after another . . . very quickly.

By careful timing, and prearranged moves, to catch the audience's eyes for a split second, Tally permitted me to work free of the crowd's observation. Through this misdirection, my act was better, faster, and could be more complicated.

We arranged for a costume to be designed and made for her. It was a white, sequined leotard, as form fitting as a one-piece bathing suit; and with it she wore full-length black hose and black gloves. The first time I saw her in it, she took my breath away. She was stunning!

I added the traditional black evening cape to my own evening clothes—but this cape had a difference. It was made in such a manner that I could change the color of the lining from crimson to purple to yellow, by opening and closing it. But it was Tally who immediately put new color and new life into the routine.

After we were married, I moved back into the Delafield. I had been there only a few days, when belatedly I realized something was missing. It was the small leather grip, the very heavy one which Tally had owned. "Hey, doll," I said, "where's all the luggage?"

"What luggage?" At the moment she was digging out the coffee maker from under the bed.

"You know what luggage," I replied.

"Why . . . my hat box is in the closet, dear."

"Yes, but where's that little leather grip . . . the one you had weighted down with uranium or something?"

"Oh, that." She replied casually, not looking up from the floor where she was kneeling. "I got rid of it."

"Why?"

"It wasn't worth keeping."

"What was in it?"

"Nothing. Just some old stuff."

I don't know why I thought it was important; perhaps it was because she only had two suitcases in the world . . . and now she only had one. "Don't you have any other clothes stored away somewhere?" I asked.

"No." She arose from the floor, tossing the hair from her eyes, and dusting her hands. "You took me for better or worse. No, I have only the clothes that are here." Smiling, she leaned over to kiss me. "You knew I wasn't an heiress; do you want to divorce me?"

"I'll keep you," I told her, "and even occasionally buy you a bargain basement dress." She busied herself making coffee, and I didn't say any more about it. But I couldn't help wondering about that heavy case. Someday, I knew she would tell me about it; in the meantime, I couldn't stop speculating over a few things: why she had left home in such a hurry; why she had no strings anywhere; and why she hadn't brought more clothes?

I didn't pretend to know very much about women, but I still had enough sense to doubt that any woman . . . if she had a choice . . . ever leaves home with just the dress on her back, and a few pieces of lingerie.

SEVEN

Cannon was involved in the examination of Harold Lafosky, a member of the laboratory squad, who was a witness for the prosecution. Lafosky testified that he had arrived on the premises together with officers Meyers and Cane. They had examined carefully the furnace room, first; and later the rest of the basement. Finally, they had completed the examination of the upper stories of the brownstone.

"Now," said Cannon, "I am going to show you several objects. I want you to identify them if you can. First, do you recognize this?" He opened a flat, cardboard box and extracted a small, charred, nearly flat piece of metal. The lump of lead was stained darkly by fire.

"Yes." Lafosky identified it, "I found that bullet underneath the furnace, within the ash receptacle."

Cannon handed him the bullet. "Please tell me how you can identify it without question."

Lafosky turned the bullet over in his fingers, and looked at it closely. "I scratched it with my initials, using a knife." He returned it to Cannon.

Cannon offered the bullet into evidence; the clerk accepted it and marked it as an exhibit. Cannon returned to his witness and extended another very small box, not more than two inches square. "Open it, please, and tell me what you see inside."

Lafosky opened the box. "I see a tooth, here."

"Have you seen it before?"

"Yes, sir." Lafosky continued, giving the location of the brownstone, the time, and the date he had found the tooth.

"Where, at what time and place, did you discover the tooth?" asked Cannon.

"The same place as the bullet . . ."

"The same place as the bullet? Please be more specific, Mr. Lafosky."

"Underneath the firebox of the furnace, in the ash receptacle."

"Can you further identify it, without question, as being the same tooth you found?"

"Yes, sir. You'll notice the tooth is badly burned and stained by smoke. It was impossible to mark it with a pen or pencil. Consequently, I placed a small mark . . . like a 'plus' sign . . . on it, using red nail polish."

"Do you now see that same mark?"

"Yes, sir. I do."

"You are certain it is the same mark?"

"I am certain of it."

"I also submit this into evidence," remarked Cannon handing the box to the clerk, and then picking up a heavy, brown Manila envelope. "Please observe this envelope closely. Have you ever seen it before?"

"Yes. I have my name, Harold Lafosky, written across the flap of the envelope, together with the date of November twenty-third of last year."

"What is inside the envelope?"

"A small amount of ashes."

"Where did you find these ashes?"

"Underneath the firebox of the furnace, in the ash receptacle."

"The same place where you found the tooth, and the bullet, is it not?" asked Cannon.

"Yes. The same."

"All right. Now about the ashes. Was there a large amount in the ash receptacle?"

"A fair amount, sir, although not a great deal. Enough to cover the floor of the ash receptacle. But the ash receptacle, itself, had been thoroughly cleaned out before."

"Cleaned out by you?"

"Cleaned out before the police got there."

"If it had been cleaned out before the police arrived, how do you account for the presence of the bullet and tooth?"

"Objection," Denman addressed the judge. "That answer will be simply a guess on the part of the witness."

Before the judge could rule, Cannon rephrased the question. "Let me ask you this: is it not possible that the tooth and the bullet had been in the body of the fire, in the coals of the furnace, and fell through the grate after the furnace had been cleaned?"

"Yes." Lafosky nodded.

"You then placed a sample of the ashes in this envelope, sealed it, and signed it with your name?"

"That is correct. I scooped up some of the ashes with the envelope, sealed it, and signed it."

"Thank you," said Cannon. He offered the envelope into evidence. Lafosky was excused, and Herman Meyers was called to the witness stand.

Meyers, in answer to Cannon's questions, identified himself as a member of the police department who had accompanied Lafosky and been present during the examination of the basement furnace room. "While Mr. Lafosky was examining the furnace, what were you doing, Mr. Meyers?"

"I was looking over the rest of the room." Meyers, a big man with beefy shoulders and an angry red face, seemed impatient with the questioning. "I was giving it a going over."

"Did you find anything?"

"Of course I found something." Meyers, as many police officers do, felt that time spent in a courtroom was time wasted.

"Objection!" Denman regarded Meyers with interest. A witness with a quick temper was always an undependable witness. "This witness is prejudicing his remarks."

"Please just answer my questions, Mr. Meyers," Cannon said smoothly. "That way we won't give Mr. Denman an opportunity to interrupt us." Meyers shot a belligerent glance at Denman and nodded. "Now tell me what you found when you examined the furnace room."

"I found a trash box."

"The trash box was full?"

"That is correct. It was filled with odds and ends of junk. All kinds."

Cannon carefully unwrapped a roll of oiled paper. The package was about twelve inches long, and when it was opened exposed a length of bone, badly charred and so smoked that it resembled a length of black stick. Attached to it was a paper tag. "Do you recognize this?" He handed the roll of paper, wrapped around the bone, to Meyers, who examined it reluctantly. The witness identified it, and Cannon asked, "Where did you find it?"

"In this trash box I was telling you about."

"The trash box in the furnace room?"

"That's the one."

"What is this you found?"

"It's a piece of bone."

"After you found it, what did you do?" Cannon asked.

"I tied this tag on it, and signed my name and the date."

Offering the bone into evidence, Cannon continued. "Mr. Meyers, did you find anything else of interest?"

"Yes, sir."

Cannon handed him a small piece of two-by-four wood and a tatter of canvas—both badly burned. "Were these what you found?"

"Yes." Meyers identified both by his personal markings and the exhibits were handed over to the clerk. Meyers was then released from the stand, and Arthur Cane was sworn in. Cane testified that he, too, had been present with Lafosky and Meyers and had examined the rest of the basement, as well as some parts of the house.

"In examining the basement, what did you find?" asked Cannon.

"Well, sir," replied Cane, "there's a downstairs bathroom with a shower . . ."

"Just a moment," interrupted Cannon, "before we discuss that, did you also examine the furnace room?"

"Yes, sir."

"What did you find?"

"I took some scrapings of dirt from between the cracks in the concrete floor. I put the scrapings into a glass vial, and on the vial I pasted a gummed sticker. I then wrote my name and date on the label."

"Is this the label? And is this the vial?"

"That is right."

"I notice the word 'furnace' marked on it also." Cannon held it so the witness could see it. "Did you write that?"

"Yes, I wrote 'furnace' on the label."

"Why?"

"The label is small, and I didn't have too much room to write on. I wrote the word 'furnace' to identify the scrapings in that vial as having been found in the furnace room."

"Very well. Now, referring back to the bathroom in the basement, which you mentioned, can you describe the room to me?"

"It's a small room, eight by ten feet in size. There's a toilet, a wash bowl, and a shower stall. The floor of the room and the floor of the shower were still very damp, with small pools of water."

"What did you do next?"

"I disconnected the trap in the drain below the wash basin, and from it collected some residue . . . such as is usually found in such places. This residue I also put in a glass vial, pasted a label on it, and signed my name and the date. On this second label, however, I added the word 'bath-b.' This was to identify the vial as containing material found in the bathroom located in the basement of the house."

"Is this the vial?" Cane identified it, and Cannon submitted both vials into evidence. "Then," Cannon continued, "you examined other rooms in the basement. What did you find?"

"In the laundry room was a metal locker, or work box, which contained the usual household type of hand tools."

"Please describe them."

"There was a hammer, a hatchet, pliers, nippers, two saws, screwdrivers, a small soldering iron, and several packages of nails."

"Is this the hatchet you found?" Cannon handed the sizable, claw-type hatchet to Cane; the witness examined the initials which he had marked on the tool and identified it. "And now one final identification, Mr. Cane. This white envelope, containing a number of hairs, has your name and the date of November twenty-third marked on it. Can you identify this envelope, and state where you found the hairs?"

"The hairs are from a brush owned by Isham Reddick, a chauffeur living at that address. The brush was found in Reddick's room, located in the servants' quarters on the top floor. I removed the hairs from Reddick's brush, placed them in the envelope, sealed it, and marked it with my name and the date."

"Thank you. That will be all," concluded Cannon. Denman arose for cross-examination, recalling

Lafosky to the stand. Denman concentrated on Lafosky's damaging evidence of the tooth while ignoring his other testimony—for the moment. The tooth, which could be held for positive identification, was extremely dangerous evidence and Denman was anxious to minimize its importance. He referred to the notes he had taken. "All teeth look pretty much the same, don't they, Mr. Lafosky?"

"Not to a dentist, they don't."

"Are you a dentist, Mr. Lafosky?"

"No."

Denman regarded the witness as if he were examining a specimen. "Suppose you just constrain yourself to answering my questions. Mr. Lafosky, if I showed you . . . say . . . a hundred individual teeth, selected just one, and then asked you if it was the same one—many months later, you couldn't be positive, could you?"

"If I marked it, I could," Lafosky replied guardedly.

"Well, possibly, but did you write your name on this tooth you swear you found last year?"

"No. I—"

"No is correct, Mr. Lafosky. Did you write or scratch your initials on it?"

"How could I? It—"

"Yes or no, please. That's simple enough. Just reply yes or no."

"Yes or no," replied Lafosky grinning.

"Very amusing, Mr. Lafosky," remarked Denman, his lip curling derisively. "I see that in addition to not being a dentist, you also are not a comedian. You are rapidly proving a great number of things you are not. I grant you seem to have a certain parrot-like ability to repeat things. Perhaps you picked this ability up, in the same manner a parrot does—by coaching!"

"Your honor, I object!" said Cannon. "The counsel for the defense is demeaning the witness unnecessarily."

The judge replied calmly. "I feel the witness is not entirely blameless. However, Mr. Cannon, the court instructs Mr. Denman to continue his examination."

Denman, satisfied with the exchange, eyed Lafosky coldly. "As I understand it, you marked a tooth you found with nail polish? Is that correct?"

Lafosky squirmed uneasily. "Yes."

"Why did you select nail polish?"

"Well, it sticks to enamel."

"Interesting, very interesting. I suppose you have a particular shade you prefer to use?"

"No. Any shade will do."

"Do you carry a bottle around with you," asked Denman, "for the purpose of marking such teeth as you may find?"

Lafosky reddened. "No," he replied, "I found the bottle in the house . . . in the maid's room."

"You found it in the house. What was the name and make of it?"

The witness glanced at Cannon, but received no help. "I don't remember," he replied slowly to Denman's question.

"What was the name of the color on the label?"

"I don't know . . . just red I guess."

"No guessing now, Mr. Lafosky." Denman's voice was gently chiding. "Any of the ladies present today can tell you that no nail polish is just red. Each has a different name . . . well, for instance . . . Frosty Pinky or Sunset Memories . . . Reddy Freddy . . ." The spectators in the courtroom began to laugh. The judge quickly rapped the room back to order. "Tell me," Denman continued relentlessly, "why did you mark it with a 'plus' sign?"

"It was a simple, easy sign to make," Lafosky replied walking into the trap.

"True . . . true," murmured Denman. "There are only two signs more simple; one is a 'minus' sign which is only half as complicated as a plus sign; the other is a simple period. Now isn't it true, Mr. Lafosky, that you really don't know, but are only guessing, that this is the same tooth. You certainly can't recognize the tooth; you can't remember the kind of nail polish or its color; and all you did was to make a mark which can be duplicated exactly by any boy or girl who ever finished first grade?"

"I'm positive it's the same tooth," replied Lafosky stubbornly.

Denman needled him gently. "I am reminded about the old saying, that only fools are positive, Mr. Lafosky."

"Your honor!" Cannon objected angrily.

"Strike the last remark of the attorney for the defense," the judge directed. He turned to the jury. "Forget what Mr. Denman has just said. In points of law it is necessary for witnesses to give as positive evidence as possible."

Denman bowed politely. "Your pardon," he said suavely, "I thought the witness was only attempting to prove something again."

"Objection!" Cannon shouted.

The judge nodded, and rapped for attention. "No more remarks, please, Mr. Denman." Behind his set face, he was unsmiling.

Denman dismissed Lafosky; he had done what he could to make the witness out a fool. Of the lasting effect on the jury, he couldn't be sure. Denman shrugged to himself, checked his notes, and then called Meyers back to the stand.

EIGHT

Tally and I were doing three shows a night at the Martinique. This wasn't unusual; most clubs have that many shows, and some of the sucker traps do four and even as many as five. The early show starts sometime around nine-thirty; there's another shortly before midnight; and the last one is around one-thirty. It's rather an upside-down way of living, because by the time you get to bed it's nearly morning. You get up around noon, or early afternoon, and this gives you just the hours before dinner; in those few hours you try to do all the things that other people do during the course of their regular days.

What is important about living this way, though, is the perspective through which you look at things. The hours that count, the important hours are the ones of darkness, the hours of the night. Daylight means only the opportunity to get your laundry, or rehearse your act, or give your agent a call. At night when the lights are turned on, your life lights up with them. What I'm saying, perhaps, is that your life is like a nightclub, itself. If, for any reason, you've ever had occasion to stop at a nightclub during the day, you'll find it a dreary desolate spot. The rooms and halls are silent and deserted except for a few porters and cleaning women—and they are working, inevitably, under a bleak solitary work light. The chairs are piled on top of the bare tables, and the tables are pulled out from the walls so the cleaners can get behind them. The carpets look shabby, the pictures and mirrors seem in terrible taste, and the walls need painting. And over everything, penetrating each room, each piece of furniture and fixture, is the smell of flat souring beer. Out in the kitchen the steward is ordering groceries; and behind the bar, the liquor steward is checking, too. In the office, a bookkeeper makes entries from the day before. It looks like a restaurant which is going out of business.

But at night, it's different. The subdued lights glow warmly throughout the club; the orchestra plays, filling the rooms with music; the tables are draped with white linens; while the bartenders rattle cocktail shakers like ice-filled maracas. It's a different world.

After a while, this world becomes the real one.

Between shows there is very little to do. With not enough time to go very far, or do very much, the performers, as a rule, after taking off their costumes to keep them fresh, sit around backstage talking, or playing gin rummy. Some read magazines and newspapers, write letters, or make long telephone calls.

Tally and I shared a small dressing room. It was scarcely more than a large closet, with two straight back chairs, and a lighted make-up table. After the first show, we'd change into our street clothes and go for a walk; between the second and third shows, we'd wait in the dressing room.

And talk.

Each night, in one way or another, she told me a little about herself . . . how her parents had been killed in an auto accident when she was a very small child, and she had gone to live with a great uncle and aunt. The aunt had died eight years later. "Then there was just Uncle Will and me," she explained. "Even then he was an elderly man, but somehow I never thought of him as such. He was big and solid, and nearly completely bald . . . so bald, in fact, that it looked like his head had been shaved. He didn't talk much, and was uncomplaining; he was generous . . . and impractical, too."

As she talked I tried to see her in relation to this man who had raised her, tried to imagine her as she was then. "Impractical?" I asked. "What did he do?"

"He was an engraver," she replied, "but he was really more than that. He was an artist. A real one. See . . ." She unsnapped a small bracelet from her wrist, and opened a tiny locket attached to it. "This is me . . . an engraving Uncle Will did of me on my fourteenth birthday." She handed the locket to me, and I tilted the flat golden surface against the light. Suddenly the face of a young girl was smiling into mine. The miniature details of the features, the featherlike tracery of the lines were exquisite. There was nothing to be said. Nodding, silently, I snapped it shut and handed it back to her. She continued, "He always wanted to be an engraver . . . a great one, in the tradition of Dürer. As a young man, he went to Europe to study there. Engraving as an art was beginning to die out; when he returned to this country, he married and in order to earn a living . . . he became a photoengraver."

"Is that what he did then . . . the rest of his life?"

"Yes." Her voice was tied by sympathy to the past. "He always had a job . . . and made good money. He kept an engraving bench and tools at home, and once in a while he'd start a steel engraving or an etching at home. When he had finished it, he'd pound it up or destroy it. Or he'd give it to anyone who said he liked it. . . ."

On another night, in the dressing room, Tally was brushing the long velvet gloves which belonged to her costume. She performed the simple job with a concentration that reminded me of a woman doing housework. There was an incongruity between the homey action and the sleek sophistication of her half-naked costume that touched me. I thought of her growing up in her uncle's household. "Tell me," I said, "more about the house where you lived . . . the place where Uncle Will kept his engraver's bench."

Momentarily, she continued the brushing. The gloves achieving a satisfactory state of perfection, she hung them over a clothes hanger. Casually, she crossed the small dressing room, regarding me indifferently, then with a sudden laugh, she plumped herself down on my lap. Our double weight caused the aging chair to creak and groan, and it could be heard through the thin partition. In the next dressing room, a little dancer called, "Hey! You're not supposed to do that on company time!" Tally blushed, and hurriedly attempted to rise.

Catching her around the waist, I held her quiet. "Don't bother to deny it, hon," I told her laughing. "Let them think what they like!" The dancer clapped loudly in return.

Tally slipped her arm around my shoulder. Lighting a cigarette, I passed it to her. "Go on," I said, "ignore the interruptions."

"Well," she replied, "we lived in Philadelphia on a little street . . . but it could just as well have been the same street in Cincinnati or Chicago."

"Were you ever in Cincinnati or Chicago?" I asked, grinning.

She shook her head, smiling back at me. "No. But our street looked like so many other streets in Philadelphia that I know there must be streets like it all over the country. . . ."

"Sure, hon."

"It was one of those streets of row houses . . . you know, they continue for a solid block on both sides of the street, and are exactly the same. But, while each block is exactly the same, no two blocks are alike. I mean," she sorted her words carefully, "the houses on our block were a little different than the row houses in the next block . . . and that was a little different from the next one . . . and so on. Do you understand?"

"Yes," I replied, "I follow you."

"In our row all the houses were two stories, but not including the basement, naturally. The houses all used the same adjoining walls, and were built directly up to the sidewalk. There were six little cement steps up to the porch. I know the number of steps because I used to play on them. I'd bounce a ball up the steps, hopping on my left leg and counting; then I'd hop on my right leg, bouncing the ball down the steps again. All the little girls in our row did the same.

"Every house had a small wooden porch, painted white and each porch had two wooden pillars. On the second floor, there was a green bay window. Ohhh, and there's something else! Everyone in our block was very proud that the windows *all* had marble sills. It wasn't really marble, but it was stone and looked a little like it. So we called it marble."

"Honey," I told her, "this may come as a terrible shock, but only in Philadelphia do you find row houses like that."

"Really?" she frowned, and leaning over the dressing table she snuffed out her cigarette.

"The bedrooms were built exactly over the dining room and living room . . . it wasn't very pretentious. A workingman's home . . ."

"With you in it, doll," I said, kissing the back of her neck, "it was a mansion."

"No," she replied gravely, "it was really a small house. In the winter, Uncle Will glassed in the downstairs porch. We used to store our galoshes and umbrellas there. When Auntie was alive, she always wanted to find another house . . . but we never did." She sighed, "It feels funny, talking about them this way."

One night, I was seated reading the paper in the dressing room, the chair tilted against the wall, my feet propped on the make-up table. There was a story in it concerning a con man who had been picked up for working the old sealed envelope switch. Briefly, it's this: the sharper hustles up a sucker, and gets the mark to put up some money . . . for one reason or another. The sharper gives him security to hold . . . usually government bonds, which he puts into an envelope and seals in front of the mark. Later when the sucker begins to wise up, he opens the envelope and discovers it's stuffed with newspaper. The con man had simply switched the envelopes and taken off with the loot. It's surprising, though, how the racket goes on forever.

I read the story aloud to Tally, and when I had finished, I chuckled. Surprisingly, she didn't join me. "No one ever pulled that on Uncle Will," she said, "but I guess it's the only one they missed."

"You mean the old man was a mark?" I asked.

"No, not that. He was always open to a hard luck story, and he was always an optimist; between the two, he was nearly always broke. All during the years he was working, he made a good salary but we never had any money. Oh, the rent was paid," she shook her head, "and the grocery bill, and we had enough to wear—but it was always just being able to make it. Uncle Will would lend money to anyone who asked him. And he was forever buying things . . . things that would make a fortune overnight . . . and never did! He bought land during the last bubble in the thirties and lost it; he speculated in funeral lots in cemeteries which were never developed; he put money in the stock of a rear-motor automobile and not even one car was ever made." She shook the memories away, wearily. "He invested in South American government securities at a big discount, and they were later canceled by a new government. Everything he did . . . went wrong."

Tears welled up suddenly in her eyes; mascara trickled down her face streaking her make-up. "The poor old man," she said. "Uncle Will was . . . he thought everybody was honest . . . like himself. Even when he was old and sick . . . and childish . . . he still believed in miracles."

"Take it easy, kid," I told her. "You may not know it, but that mascara running looks like the marble face of Venus cracking up." I handed her my handkerchief, and she wiped her eyes. "There, that's better," I added. "Now, what was all that hollering about?"

She managed a smile. "I was being foolish. It wasn't anything. It's still so soon after Uncle Will's death . . . I feel bad whenever I think about him." She stood before the dressing table, and began repairing her make-up. "It's funny," she said, "about the only two men in my life . . ."

"Wait a minute," I said. "Is this going to be a confession? If it is, don't expect me to reciprocate with my boyish confidences unless my lawyer and agent are present."

"Don't be silly." She caught her hair in a velvet bow, and turned to face me. She smiled, "I'm sure you've been very trustworthy. Anyway, you interrupted me at exactly the wrong word. I was saying that the only two men in my life, who I have loved, are you and Uncle Will. And you are both so different. Uncle Will was . . . a . . ."

"A real blue-nosed Philadelphia square," I said.

"Don't be jealous, please!" Her eyes twinkled, and I grinned. "No," she continued, "he lived in a wonderful world all by himself. While you . . . wise guy . . . know all the answers, don't you?" Standing on her toes, she locked her arms around my neck, and kissed me on the mouth. Then holding her head to one side, she asked, "Well, don't you?"

"You're not just whistling up a breeze, kid," I agreed

solemnly. "Furthermore, I think the quality of lipstick has degenerated since I was a youth."

She refused to rise to my chaffing, and looked into my face, her eyes very near to mine. I realized, belatedly, she was serious. "I love you, darling," she said softly, "and I'm so glad you're in love with me." Gently, she loosened her arms, and taking a step back, looked at me. "But I'd hate to be the person you really hated, Lew."

"Wait a minute!" I said, trying to laugh it off. "Where'd this conversation come from? I don't hate anyone. I love the world. I'm a do-gooder! I beat a drum . . ."

"Yes, dear." Tally turned, smiling sweetly and slipped into her coat. "I'm going out to get a candy bar. May I bring you one?" she asked, banteringly.

"No," I replied, "bring me an oyster instead. One with a pearl in it."

And so, for a while, that was the way it was. It was a life held tightly within itself, in the night; a dressing room where we waited until the show went on, and the orchestra played our cue. The applause from the tables; the paychecks on Friday. Sometimes we walked the early morning streets back to the hotel, stopping for pre-dawn coffee and rolls with the truck drivers, milk men, and cops. It was Broadway when the night has gone and the lights have vanished, but day has not yet arrived. The sidewalks are bare and lonely; the hour is bleak and unlovely; but it's wonderful if you're walking along with the gal you love.

Then it's not bare or lonely at all.

NINE

The man in the witness chair was Deputy Chief
Medical Examiner Howard M. Eggleston. Dressed in a
neat charcoal gray suit, with a lighter gray and maroon
striped tie, he answered questions precisely and with authority. Cannon asked, "How long have you been in the
medical examiner's office, Dr. Eggleston?"

"Seven years."

"In that period of time how many autopsies have you
performed?"

"Each year?"

"Yes, each year."

"Well, between two hundred and two hundred and
fifty . . . the number is not the same each year."

"Yes, I understand that. But is it fair to say that in

seven years you have performed between fourteen hundred and seventeen hundred and fifty autopsies?"

"That would be correct, sir."

"Dr. Eggleston, you would consider that figure a conservative estimate? If it were necessary, you could get the exact number as a matter of record from your files?"

"The number would fall between the two extremes of the figures you mentioned. It can be substantiated by the official records."

"Thank you, Doctor. Now in those seven years, as a result of your duties, you have examined a great number of bodies . . . literally running into the hundreds. You have examined both men and women, children, too, of many ages and races?"

"That is correct. Under the law, an examination is required in all cases of homicide, accidental, unnatural, and suspicious deaths."

"You have made identification of bodies with members missing, such as head, arms, legs?"

"In some cases, yes."

"And in cases where bodies have been so badly decomposed as to make features and fingerprints unrecognizable?"

"Yes."

Denman arose. "This is very interesting," he addressed the judge, "but what is the counselor attempting to prove?"

Cannon, in turn, addressed the bench. "As the counselor for the defense knows very well, I am establishing the background of the witness for expert testimony."

Denman, who had no desire for the extreme efficiency of the medical-legal activities of the medical examiner's office to be too well established with the jury, snapped,

"The defense will grant Dr. Eggleston to be an expert," and sat down.

Cannon returned to his witness. "Now, Dr. Eggleston, I have a number of exhibits. As I introduce them to the court, I will ask you to identify them. First, this hatchet identified by Mr. Cane; have you examined it in your laboratory?"

"I have."

"What did you find?"

"At the point of the V where the claws on the hatchet come together, there were traces of blood and broken sections of hair."

"Could you identify the blood as human blood?"

"Yes, sir. It was human blood known as type O."

"Was it possible to identify the hair?"

"The hair was identified as coming from a human head."

"Thank you. Now here is an envelope, also identified by Mr. Cane, which contains several hairs taken from the hair brush of Isham Reddick. Have you examined these hairs?"

"Yes, sir," replied Eggleston. "The hairs in the envelope are identical with the hairs found on the hatchet."

The jury, as a body, leaned forward, its eyes fastened on Eggleston. "You mean that without a question, without a doubt, the hairs from the hatchet and the hairs from the brush are identical?"

"That is right."

"Will you please show us how you reached that conclusion?" A projector and a small screen were set up, and cross sections of the hairs, greatly enlarged, were demonstrated to the court. Eggleston in a dry definite voice pointed out the duplication of cellular construction and points of identification. When he had concluded, Cannon resumed his examination. "Here is a piece of canvas, identified by Harold Lafosky. Have you examined it?"

"Yes, sir."

"What did you find?"

"The canvas had been burned by fire, and contained traces of paint, and stains of blood." Eggleston paused, then added, "It was human blood."

"Could you identify the type?"

"Yes. It was type O."

"Here is a vial with a label containing the name of Detective Cane, and bearing the word 'furnace'—identifying it as having come from the furnace room. What did you find in this vial?"

"Scrapings, such as are found in the cracks and on the floors in furnace rooms . . . dirt, soot, coal dust, wood and fiber splinters, traces of oil and turpentine. Also, traces of human blood."

"Could you identify the blood by type?"

"I could. It was type O."

Picking up the second vial, Cannon offered it to Eggleston. This vial contained the sediment taken from the water trap beneath the wash basin in the basement. Cannon asked Eggleston what it, too, contained. "Dirt, fatty particles such as are used in soap bases, lye, both natural and synthetic bristles from brushes, and traces of human blood."

"You identified the blood by type, Doctor?"

"I did. It was type O."

"Again, Dr. Eggleston," continued Cannon, "I have an envelope . . . a large, heavy Manila one. This envelope was identified by Mr. Lafosky. It contains a sampling of ashes gathered from the ash receptacle beneath the firebox of the furnace. You have examined the contents. Will you tell the court what your analysis showed?"

The deputy chief medical examiner withdrew a slip of paper from his pocket, referred to it briefly, and then recited a long list of chemical properties, in a flat unaccented voice. When he had finished, Cannon turned to the jury and said, "I'll ask the witness to reword his statement." He smiled briefly, "I couldn't understand a word he said." The jury nodded in grim agreement.

"Well," resumed Eggleston, "in addition to coal ash, wood ash, certain residues of vegetable origin . . ."

"Such as what, Doctor?"

"Cotton, linen. There was also evidence of protein origin . . ."

Cannon interrupted him. Very slowly, pronouncing each word distinctly, he asked, "Does that mean the possibility of human flesh . . . or rather, what might at one time have been human flesh?"

"That is correct."

There was a long moment of complete silence in the courtroom. Cannon stretched it to the breaking point, then coughing gently, broke the spell, and proceeded with his introduction of evidence. "Now, Doctor, another important point of identification." The prosecuting attorney unrolled the sheath of oiled paper. Within was the length of blackened charred bone, attached with a tag bearing the name of Detective Meyers. "Can you tell me if you have examined this," said Cannon, "and if you have, please tell me your findings."

"I have examined it," Eggleston stated. "It is a length of bone medically termed the *tibia*."

"In layman's language, Dr. Eggleston, that would be called the shin bone?"

"Yes."

"What more can you tell the court about it?"

"It is of human origin and belonged to an adult male."

"Could you determine the height of such a male?"

"Yes, within certain limits. The male was between five feet ten and six feet tall."

"How could you determine this, Doctor?"

Eggleston launched into a detailed discussion based on the measurements and proportions of the human body. Cannon put a question to the medical examiner. "Is it not possible that a deformity in the bone structure might affect other portions of the body?" Eggleston agreed that such a deformity was possible, but that where it existed, it could also be detected by additional research. "That possibility does not exist in this situation, then?" asked Cannon.

"No," replied Eggleston, "the bone was from a normally developed male."

"Thank you. And now, one final identification." Cannon presented the vial of formaldehyde containing the section of finger. Eggleston had examined it, and stated that it was a well-preserved section of a human finger, consisting of that portion between the middle joint and the tip of the finger. It was from the third finger of the right hand. "Can you tell the court how it had been severed from the hand?" asked Cannon.

"By a sharp instrument."

"Can you identify the instrument beyond being a sharp one?"

"No."

"Is it not true that a sharp instrument such as a hatchet might have done it?"

"It could have been done by a hatchet."

"Thank you, Doctor, that will be all." Cannon turned to Denman. "Your witness, Counselor."

"I will reserve the privilege to cross-examine the witness later," Denman replied without rising from his seat.

Cannon then called Officer Charles L. Risko to the stand. When Risko had taken his oath, Cannon asked him, "You are employed in the Bureau of Identification, of the Police Department, City of New York. Is that correct?"

"Yes, sir. That is correct."

"Your job is to keep a record of fingerprints taken by the police department, make comparisons, and identifications where possible?"

"Yes, sir."

"How long have you been doing such work?"

"For eleven years."

"You were given this section of finger?" Cannon held up the vial for Risko's identification.

"That's right. It was turned over to me by the Homicide Squad, and I proceeded to raise a print from it."

"It was a good clear print? One that could be examined with accuracy?"

"Yes, sir. It was. I secured a very satisfactory print."

"Then what did you do with it?"

"I processed the print for identification."

"What do you mean by that?"

"I sent it through the regular channels for identification," explained Risko. "First, through our own files here in New York."

"Was the print identified?"

"Yes, sir. Immediately. We had the prints of one Isham Reddick taken on his application for a license to drive a cab."

"Will you show us how this identification was made?"

A copy of the print made by Risko from the severed finger and a copy of the corresponding finger taken from the application were projected on the screen. Risko pointed out the identical characteristics of both prints, some thirty-four in number, which made a positive identification. He was then excused, again without cross-examination by Denman, and Cannon called Lincoln M. Means to the stand.

"You are employed in the Bureau of Licenses, Police Department, City of New York, Mr. Means?"

"I am."

"You have with you the original application made out by one Isham Reddick when he applied for a license to drive a cab?"

"Yes, sir."

"Will you please read the information regarding Isham Reddick's physical appearance that you have?"

Reading from the original application form, Means recited aloud: "Sex . . . male; age . . . 36; eyes . . . blue; hair . . . dark brown; weight . . . 175 pounds; height . . . 5 feet 11 inches . . ."

"Just a moment, Mr. Means. Will you please read again, his height as indicated on your record?"

"Yes, sir. Five feet eleven inches."

"That was written in Reddick's own hand?"

"It was written by the man who signed himself Isham Reddick."

At this point, Denman objected to the identification of

the application as being in Reddick's handwriting. He was sustained in his objection, by the court. Means was excused from the stand, while Alvin G. Hartney, a handwriting expert, was put on the stand by the prosecution. A positive identification was made by the expert witness regarding the writing on the application based on other writing found in Reddick's room. Means was then returned to the stand.

"Once again, Mr. Means, in Reddick's own writing taken from the license application, please read what he wrote as his height."

"Five feet eleven inches," Means read.

"He did not write six feet, or six feet one?"

"No, sir."

"Nor did he write five feet nine?"

"No, sir."

"It was five feet eleven inches?"

"That is what he wrote."

"That will be all." Again, Denman waved the witness aside, reserving the right to cross-examine later. Obviously, he was waiting for Cannon to complete his web of identification. Beside Denman, the accused sat, head partly bowed, hands folded on the table.

The next witness taking the stand was Stanley Boss, a doctor of dentistry. He identified himself as practicing in the City of New York, and had been located in his present offices for nearly ten years. Cannon then began examining him concerning the tooth found and identified by Detective Lafosky. "Can you say if you have ever seen this tooth before?" he asked Boss.

"Yes, sir. I am very familiar with it."

"Will you please tell the court how you can identify it?"

The dentist, a small, slender man with an undistinguished face, adjusted his rimless glasses nervously. Clearing his voice, he began, "Well . . . last year, a patient called . . ."

Cannon interrupted smoothly. "Please give us an exact date, if you are able . . ."

"Yes. Yes, I can. I looked it up in my files. It was the day, to a week, before the patient came in. He came in September nineteenth, so when he called it was September twelfth."

"Thank you, please continue."

"Well," Boss cleared his throat anew. "I received this call for an appointment. It was from a new patient . . . never heard of the man before. Said his name was Isham Reddick. I asked him how he happened to call me, and he said he'd looked me up in the classified book. I told him I was busy . . . filled with appointments for a week. He said he'd like to come the first opportunity, so I made an appointment for him on September nineteenth."

"He showed up for the appointment?"

"Yes. Right on time. My wife, Mrs. Boss, acts as my nurse. She took all the personal information concerning him. Including blood type in case of surgery. It was . . ."

"Objection!" snapped Denman.

"Sustained," agreed the court.

"We'll call Mrs. Boss, later," said Cannon, "please continue, Dr. Boss."

"Mr. Reddick complained that his three back molars had been paining him. I took X-rays, but could find bad caries in none of his teeth. There seemed to be no reason for his distress. The patient, however, had a tooth missing from the front of his mouth and it greatly affected his appearance. We discussed the possibility of replacing it. He told me it would depend on how much it cost, and I made him a very reasonable . . . actually a very low . . . price to put in a removable bridge, and he accepted it."

"Doctor, will you please point to the identical tooth in your own mouth comparable to the position of the missing tooth in the mouth of Isham Reddick."

Boss parted his lips widely, in a grimace, and pointed to the first tooth in the front left side of his mouth. He held the pose for a moment, then withdrew his finger and closed his lips.

"You then proceeded to make the tooth for Isham Reddick?"

"Yes, sir. I made it myself."

"You made it to exact measurements?"

"That is right, to very small and accurate measurements. I keep a complete record of all work done, measurements . . . and degree of coloring."

"There are degrees of coloring? How many?"

"There are as many degrees in the coloring of teeth as there are degrees in the coloring of skin. False teeth, particularly when placed next to a patient's own teeth, must be very carefully shaded to match."

"So, Dr. Boss, when you saw this tooth which has been offered in evidence here, you could identify it as the same one you had made for Isham Reddick?"

"Yes, sir. It is the identical tooth."

"Will you please tell the court how you happened to identify the tooth. Did the police come to see you?"

"I read about it in the paper. What first struck my eye was that it was practically in the same neighborhood.

Then when I read the name . . . Isham Reddick . . . I remembered he had been a patient of mine. The papers said a tooth had been recovered; I didn't know if it was the one I'd made or not. But I also had a complete chart of his teeth, as a matter of regular routine, and a set of X-rays. In the case of an identification, I might be of some service."

"That was very commendable of you, Doctor. So, you then notified the police that you would help?"

"Yes, sir. I felt it was my duty," Boss replied complacently.

Mrs. Boss next was called to the stand and testified that a blood-type record was made for reference in case of extractions and dental surgery.

"What type blood did Mr. Reddick have?"

"According to my record, it was type O."

"Did he tell you that himself?"

"No," the nurse replied. "He didn't know, or at least he didn't remember. I took a small sample and then sent it to the lab for typing. The laboratory returned the report on it, and I entered it on his card."

TEN

To paraphrase a line of Porgy's, "happiness is
a sometime thing." The feeling of happiness is difficult
to recall—after any length of time—perhaps because it is
transient . . . intangible . . . effervescent. Often it is
misidentified as contentment—which, I believe, is a
compromise between being happy and being miserable.
Later, when one looks back into the months and years,
it is impossible to recapture clearly the moments of complete happiness; but it is quite easy to remember long
periods of time when contentment prevailed.

I know, however, that those months of our marriage
in New York, when we were working at the Martinique,
were happy ones. Our world consisted of two rooms—a
hotel room with plaid wallpaper and a tiny bare dressing room. The two rooms were connected by a great

long street which sometimes was lighted by neon, sometimes by the gray light of morning—just beginning to soften the black lines of night—as we returned from one room to another.

Tally recognized what we had at that time better than I. Perhaps that was why she didn't want to give it up, although actually there was no choice for us. Only a few days before we closed at the Martinique, I hurried back to the hotel with a new contract for five weeks at the Lark Club in Philadelphia. As I explained to Tally about it, she listened quietly. Seated on the bed, she nervously twisted the gold wedding ring on her hand, and all emotion was carefully screened from her face. When I had finished describing the contract, she said, "Lew, I . . . wish you wouldn't take it." Her voice was so low as to be barely audible.

"Listen, honey," I said, "you've been away from Philadelphia nearly three months. That's long enough to start getting over your uncle. You ought to be able to go back now."

Shaking her head, slowly, she refused to meet my eyes. Then it came to me that beneath the impassive face she was struggling with other emotions . . . ones which I couldn't identify. Swallowing several times, Tally said, "It . . . isn't Uncle Will." She examined her hands, her head lowered. "Do I have to go with you?" she asked softly.

I lit a cigarette. "Sure, doll," I told her, keeping my conversation light. "The manager in the club at Philly said, 'I don't give a damn about that magician, but be sure the doll gets here.'"

But she couldn't smile. She replied, more to herself than to me, and her words were thoughts, wondered aloud. "Why did it have to be back there . . . why couldn't it have been Chicago or Los Angeles, or some-place else?"

"In this business," I said, "you take the jobs as they come. In a way, we're lucky. We don't have to lay-over for a while."

Tally arose from the bed, wandering about the room —stopping by the dresser, repositioning her hair brush, going to the window, glancing out through the glass, returning to the chair, pausing; and all the time think-ing, but what she was thinking—I didn't know. Finally she asked, "Couldn't you go, Lew, and leave me here?"

"Not very well," I told her. "They bought the act as it is—not as a single."

"I guess there's a reason for it happening this way," she said, her voice resigned.

The following week we closed in New York and be-gan packing for Philadelphia. I had my old wardrobe trunk, and Tally had begun to accumulate a few things herself. The hatbox no longer could hold all her clothes. Proudly, she bought a set of matched luggage. Two of the cases were standard size, and a third was quite small, a small overnight case. When I returned to the Delafield after being out all day, making last-minute business calls, arranging for the trunk to go ahead, and finishing up all the other details, we checked out of the hotel. Max helped us into a cab. "See you around," he said. And so, Tally carrying her small case, we left for Phila-delphia.

In Philadelphia many of the nightclubs are concen-trated along Locust Street . . . and Thirteenth. Some of them are good, some of them bad. The Lark Club was small, new, and in the process of attempting to establish a policy of entertainment—struggling between smartness and sophistication, and dullness and vulgarity. When we arrived it was mixing the lot. On the bill, a comedian named Lemmie Hall performed with the subtlety of a sex offender out on bail, doing imitations with the aid of a hat, and introducing the rest of the acts. There was an attractive gal singer, with a good voice; a line of dancers called the Five Lovely Larks . . . a nondescript collection of chorines with tight secretive faces, skinny legs, and rented costumes; and Tally and me.

The interior of the Lark Club was small, and the walls were hung with dark velours; the tables, chairs, and bar were made of modern light woods. Customers sat shoulder to shoulder, jammed into the room, and the dance floor was no larger than a waiter's tray. The performers worked from the floor, and the show was backed by seven musicians wearing red coats. The leader played a violin, and the guitarist played a guitar, but, unfortunately, both instruments were electric. Occasionally, the two musicians would accidentally mix their volume controls and the feedback over the mike resembled the disemboweling of banshees.

The Lark's main claim to fame was a larger-than-life marble statue standing in a prominent position near the center of the room. It was a sculpture of a nude man kissing a naked woman. The white marble was illuminated by small spot lights at the base, and against the black velours of the background, a viewer received the impression that Aphrodite and boy friend had been toying in a flour bin.

We had been playing the Lark Club for a week, when the phone call came. Tally and I were staying at the Hotel McAndrews, which is another show business hotel. It is located on one of the incredibly narrow side streets, near the nightclub district, and is at least fifty years old. However, the McAndrews has been kept in good condition and is comfortable, although old fashioned. Except for the lobby, that is. This has been redecorated with fluorescent lighting, chrome furniture, imitation leather, and tubular accessories, plus a coat of salmon pink paint on the ceiling. The lobby is L shaped with the registration desk and two elevators on the vertical side of the L; on the other side, a stairway leads to the floors above, and a doorway opens into the Highland Bar & Grill. Inside the bar, there are two doors each leading to a different street, as the Highland is located on the corner of the building.

Our room was on the top floor, on a corner, facing the front of the building. The corridors, in the McAndrews, are dimly lighted, and the walls are painted a dark chocolate brown to the height of a shoulder with a continuation of a slightly lighter brown to the ceilings. Ancient red carpeting covers the floors, and even during the brightest daylight hours, the halls have a dark and archaic appearance. The rooms, however, are very comfortable.

In ours we had a large double bed, a television set which played one hour for each quarter deposited in the coin slot, several comfortable, faded, overstuffed chairs, and two large reading lamps. Connecting was an old-fashioned, linoleum-floored bathroom, with a high tub resting on metal, clawed feet. With two extremely large closets at our command, Tally set up our electric plate in one of them and we used it for a small kitchen.

When the day arrived . . . the one with the phone call . . . we were sleeping late. The phone rang, and I let it ring for several minutes hoping that Tally would answer it. But when she made no effort to do so, I pulled myself together, sufficiently, to reach out an arm and take it off the receiver. Putting it to my ear, I said, "Yes . . . what is it?"

A peculiar quality of silence on the other end aroused me to complete consciousness. Instantly I was awake, listening intently, although there was nothing to hear. "Hello! Hello!" I paused and jiggled the receiver. "Hello?"

After a long moment, over the line a voice said thinly, "I'll pay you twenty-five grand for 'em."

"Who is this?" I asked. "You'll pay twenty-five grand for what?"

"You know," replied the voice, and hung up.

Slowly I returned the phone to its cradle. Swinging my legs over the side of the bed, I reached for my cigarettes on the bedside table. Thinking it over, I decided someone was trying to kid me. Someone I knew . . . possibly someone in the show was attempting to pull a gag. I shrugged the idea away, and now wide awake began making some coffee. While the water was boiling, Tally awakened and sat up in bed. "Boy, are you a lousy maid," I told her. "Do you want a cup?"

"Oh, yes, please." Stretching her arms in the air, she shook her head, her hair fanning over her pillow as she leaned back. Taking the cup to her, I sat beside her on the bed. "Did I hear the phone ring?" she asked sipping the coffee.

"Those sure weren't the Bells of St. Mary's," I told her.

"Who was it?" she asked drowsily, not really caring.

"A voice. A mysterious voice . . . and if I sound corny I can't help it."

"Stop fooling, darling," she replied. "Who was it, a wrong number?"

"I wouldn't be surprised if it was Lemmie Hall. Probably his idea of humor . . ."

"What did he say?"

"Whoever it was said in a disguised voice, 'I'll pay you twenty-five grand for them.'"

"What!" Tally sat upright in bed, spilling her coffee. Leaping to my feet, I took the cup from her trembling hands. Her face was gray with fear, and she was unable to speak.

"Doll!" I placed the cup on the table, and gathered her hands into mine. "Tally! What is it? What's wrong . . . tell me!"

She pulled her hands free, and throwing her arms around my neck buried her face against my chest. We sat like that for a long time, not saying anything . . . just holding each other. Finally, she said, "Lew, I don't know . . . I don't know what to do. . . ."

"What is it, Tally? Tell me, and whatever it is, we'll figure out what to do." I lit a cigarette, and pressing her back against the pillows, placed it between her lips.

"I don't know where to start," she said slowly. "I don't even know exactly when it started . . . there was this man. We called him Greenleaf."

"Who was he?"

"I don't know . . . really, I don't."

"Did you ever meet him? What did he look like?"

"I never met him. I only talked to him a few times on the phone. . . ."

She began trembling, and I patted her shoulder. "All

right, doll," I said, "you talked to him on the phone. About what?"

"About the plates . . . the counterfeit engravings Uncle Will was making . . ."

"You did what?" I stared at her, not believing her words. Her mouth quivered, and I said more softly, "Look, perhaps you'd better tell me in your own words . . . right from the beginning." Walking over to the dresser, I got her a clean handkerchief. She wiped her eyes, and attempted a smile.

"Once," she said, "I think I tried to tell you how Uncle Will was . . . he believed everyone. All his life, he was generous and sweet . . . and wonderful. And everyone took advantage of him, with crazy ideas and plans to make money. When he was an old man he didn't have anything left.

"The company he'd worked for all those years was sold and the new owners let him go because they thought he was too old. At first, he just couldn't believe it. He'd sit around the house all day and pretend to read the want ads, and write letters to different companies, but . . . of course . . . nothing happened. After a long time, he just had to believe it. When he finally did face it, it broke his heart and his spirit, too. He was just an old man, too old to work, too useless to be worth his pay."

Hugging her arms around her body, she sorted through the memories of the past. "His mind . . . I don't mean he went crazy or anything like that. He simply refused to live in the world the way it was. Little by little, I could see him changing . . . oh, unimportant things at first. He began to stop shaving . . . skipping days, and then a week; he stopped wearing ties; his shoe laces would break, and he'd just tie them further down the shoe.

"He had always liked to eat, but he ate less and less— and refused meat and potatoes, and sometimes I'd find stacks of old, stale slices of bread hidden in his room. Like a kid . . . you know how kids hoard food to have enough to run away from home? It reminded me of that; he was turning back into a child . . . talking and thinking like a small boy."

"How'd you get along?" I asked.

"Well . . . naturally . . . I had to get a job. Uncle Will had a very small old-age pension, but it didn't begin to be enough. I worked extra as a cashier in a store downtown, and on Saturdays and Sundays I handled the cash register for Mr. Doremus. He owned the drugstore in our neighborhood, and we had traded with him all my life. Working like that, I was away from home a lot and that left Uncle Will alone . . . which wasn't good, but it couldn't be helped. He was able to take care of himself; he wasn't helpless or anything like that. After a while, when I came home he'd be away. He'd walk downtown, and back, which was a long ways. On nice days he'd sit in Washington Square, in the little park, which is right in the middle of the printing and publishing district. He probably hoped to see some of his old friends." Nearly inaudibly, she added, "I thought it was good for him. It gave him something to do."

"Sure," I consoled her, "he liked to go back to the printing district, the same as an old railroad man hangs around a station."

"That's what I thought, too," Tally continued. "Then one day Uncle Will came home . . . happy, walking on air. He was very secretive, all puffed up with importance like a kid. He let drop the fact he was going to get a job. Although he wouldn't tell me anything more about it, he hinted that it had something to do with the government. Very secret! I thought possibly he was making it up.

"For several weeks, he talked about a very important man he'd met. They would meet downtown and talk together in the square. And then one day, Uncle Will came home with a check; it was made out to cash and signed by a man named Greenleaf."

"How much was the check for?"

"For thirty-five dollars. At first, I didn't believe the check would be good. Uncle Will was very happy; he told me that Greenleaf was backing him and was going to lend him thirty-five dollars every week until he landed a big job. We needed the money so desperately that I decided to cash the check. Then I held the money . . . without spending it . . . in case the check was returned. But it wasn't returned; it was good. After that, each Friday Uncle Will gave me the check, and I endorsed it and had it cashed."

"Weren't you suspicious?"

"At first I was," she agreed, "but then . . . oh, I don't know. For once someone was giving Uncle Will money instead of taking it, and we needed the money . . . so badly. Uncle Will started working in his little shop down in the basement; he'd work down there all day long . . . and sometimes at night. He kept the workshop padlocked, and never let me in. When I asked him what he was doing, he'd evade the subject and tell me not to worry . . . he was going to take care of everything! Lew, I want you to know that . . . well, it sounds funny, but he was like a kid with a big secret. I didn't have the heart to hurt him . . . so I left him alone. I knew he was still a wonderful engraver, and I believed . . . honestly and truly . . . that he was just making some gadget for Greenleaf."

"And all this time you never met Greenleaf?"

"No. Several times, he called on the phone to talk to Uncle Will, and I'd answer the phone if he was in the basement."

Tally had regained complete control of herself now, talking slowly—sometimes hesitantly—and I poured her more coffee. She straightened against the pillows and held the cup firmly, occasionally sipping from it, while she went on. "One night Greenleaf called. Uncle Will picked up the phone and I could hear his part of the conversation. He'd finished whatever it was he'd been doing, and was now anxious to get his big, new job. I gathered Greenleaf told him it would take days; he wanted Uncle Will to come right downtown. Unpredictably Uncle Will became childishly stubborn . . . and shouted he would take them, himself, to Washington. He began arguing and I was surprised to see him crying. Large tears rolled down his face, and he was shaking so badly that he couldn't remain standing. He sank down on a chair by the phone. Just before he hung up, I can remember he said, 'Nobody can have them, until I get my job!'

"Then he tottered to the kitchen and sat beside the table. He put his arms on it, holding his head, and he sat there, babbling and half crying. I was terribly worried that he might have a stroke or a heart attack. I tried to calm him, and after a while he told me what had happened."

Will Shaw had met Greenleaf one day in Washington Square. The meeting was quite by accident, but they had continued to meet after that and became acquaintances. The old man had told his newly found listener that once he had been a master engraver. Greenleaf, in turn, confided that he was a personal friend of the head of the Bureau of Printing and Engraving in Washington, D.C. Greenleaf promised to speak to his friend regarding a job for the old man. Will Shaw, in the dimming memories of his mind, recalled that the Bureau was always looking for expert engravers . . . and once, in his youth, he had turned down an opportunity to work in it. Immediately, he took new hope.

Several weeks later, however, Greenleaf relayed the information from Washington that Will Shaw was too old; sympathetically, and confidentially, Greenleaf told the old man that his friend in Washington didn't believe that Shaw could do the work well enough. The spirits of Will Shaw plummeted to new depths of despair. Greenleaf eventually suggested a solution—one which the old man was in no condition to weigh or consider, but which he grasped eagerly. Will Shaw was to make a duplicate set of plates; he was to make them so expertly that they would be indistinguishable from the original engravings. Greenleaf would take the plates to Washington and show them to his friend. When the Bureau was unable to tell the duplicate plates from their own, the proof would be before its eyes, and the job would be given to the old man. Greenleaf had been careful in his discussion with Will Shaw not to mention the word "counterfeit," and now Shaw wishfully pushed the old knowledge from his head . . . the regulations concerning the reproduction of government money . . . and permitted himself to be persuaded by Greenleaf. Greenleaf because of his familiarity with the Bureau in Wash-

ington, Shaw vaguely believed, could safely waive rules
and regulations.

In his enthusiasm to help Will Shaw, Greenleaf gener-
ously offered to advance money to the old man on
which to live while he worked on the engravings.
Kindly, Greenleaf cautioned the old engraver against the
danger of hurrying the work—pointing out that all their
plans would be ruined unless the plates were absolutely
perfect. Will Shaw, to secure the job, must take all the
time he needed to do the work; when finally he was
hired on a good salary in Washington, he could repay
the loan to Greenleaf.

"The old man must have been pretty far gone to fall
for it," I said. "It was an obvious confidence setup from
the very beginning. Will Shaw met Greenleaf . . . accidentally . . . like a chicken meets a chicken-hawk."

"Uncle Will was possessed with just one idea . . . to
get a job. Lew," her voice pleading, "you must remember that the old man wasn't . . . right . . . any
more. . . ."

"All right," I agreed. "He was sick and senile. Then
what happened?"

"When I finally understood, I made Uncle Will give
me the key, and I went downstairs to his workshop.
Inside, on his engraver's bench, were complete plates for
five-, ten-, and twenty-dollar bills. I knew the government would consider them counterfeit plates, and I was
also sure that Greenleaf intended to use them, himself.
Something told me that I had to get them out of the
house at once. It was still pretty early in the evening, so I
put them in that little leather bag I had with a lock, and
took them over to Doremus' drugstore. Everyone working there had a clothes locker, to keep coats and uni-

forms in, and I put my bag in my own locker, and turned the combination. I was worried sick, and I sat at the fountain and had a Coke.

"I tried to decide what to do. Right here in Philadelphia there's a U.S. mint . . . it's a big, brownish brick building and I've seen it many times. I made up my mind that in the morning, I'd take the plates there and give them to someone in authority. And then I decided that I wouldn't, because they might think Uncle Will was dangerous . . . and send him to an institution. I thought about just mailing them to the mint, anonymously, but I was afraid to do that, too, because I've read about how the F.B.I. can trace things through the mail. I'd been there at Doremus' for over an hour, and the more I thought about it, the more confused I became. Finally, I decided that the next day, I'd just take the plates over to the Delaware River Bridge and throw them in the water.

"When I got home, the house was very quiet. Uncle Will wasn't around. I went into the kitchen where I'd left him, and then looked upstairs in his room. Back in the kitchen again, I noticed that the door leading downstairs to the basement wasn't tightly closed, and a light was on. Immediately I thought that Uncle Will had gone down to his workroom. Opening the door to call . . . I saw him. He was lying at the foot of the stairs on the concrete floor."

"Dead?" I asked, but there was no question in my voice.

"Yes." She paused, then continued quietly. "I don't remember too much about the rest of that night. I called the doctor, and he notified the police. As far as the police were concerned, it was just a routine investigation of an accidental death."

"Wasn't it accidental?"

"At first I thought it was," she said. "I knew Uncle Will had been terribly upset. In that condition, he might have fallen or stumbled down the stairs . . . even had a stroke . . . and broken his neck."

"You didn't tell the cops about the plates . . . or Greenleaf?"

"No. There was no trace of Uncle Will's plates and I thought it was better not to bring them up. The police were very nice and hardly talked to me at all. The doctor gave me a sedative, and one of the neighbor's girls stayed with me all night. By the next day, when the police returned to talk to me I'd had a chance to think it over. I definitely decided not to say anything about the plates or Greenleaf. I just told them about Uncle Will growing old and ill."

"What made you change your mind about his death not being an accident?" I asked.

"Well, after the police left the second time, I had a chance to look around the house. I was sure someone had been there and had searched it. Not obviously . . . with things thrown around or drawers pulled out . . . signs like that because then the police would have noticed it. But when you've lived in a house a long time, it becomes a habit for things always to be in certain places . . . the broom always stands in the right-hand corner of the closet, or the way you arrange laundry in your dresser. Little things like that had been changed. Nothing was missing, only it seemed to me that someone had been looking all through it. And the one time it could have happened was the night Uncle Will died, because I'd been there ever since."

"Didn't the cops search the house?" I asked.

"No, not like that," she replied. "They looked around the rooms . . . but not in the same way."

"Okay," I said. "Then what?"

"It frightened me because I didn't know what it meant, and I didn't know what to do about it either. A girl I'd worked with at the drugstore agreed to stay with me until after Uncle Will was buried . . . which was two days later. After the funeral, she stayed with me that night . . . and then returned home. The following day, the phone rang—and it was Greenleaf."

"Could you identify Greenleaf's voice right now if you heard it?" I asked.

She thought a moment. "No, I'm not sure that I could . . . although, as I remember, it sounded sort of affected."

"Affected? Was there something distinctive about it?"

She considered my question for a moment. "Not really . . . I guess. He was an Easterner, I think."

"Did it sound like Philadelphia . . . New York . . . Boston?"

"No. More broad than those." She shrugged helplessly. "It was just . . . different. Anyway, on the phone he said that he wanted the engravings, the ones Uncle Will had made. I told him that I didn't know what he was talking about and he laughed. That made me angry, and I said if I ever found them that I was going to turn them over to the government and tell how he had fooled Uncle Will into making them. He laughed again and told me to remember all the checks I'd signed. After that, everything was quiet for a moment, and I thought he had hung up. Suddenly he said, and he sounded cold and threatening, 'I'll pay you for the plates . . . or perhaps you might prefer another accident in the family.' "

"And that was all?"

"Yes . . . just about. But as he was hanging up he said something else that didn't make sense. It sounded like 'loon who ought to.'"

"Loon who ought to?" I repeated it. "Are you sure that's what he said?"

"Yes," she said, positive, "that's the way it sounded although it sort of ran together, and wasn't as clear as that. But he said 'loon who ought to' and then he hung up the phone."

I said, not too surely, "I suppose he might have turned his head away from the phone for a moment and you heard only part of the sentence . . . about being a loon who ought to take advantage of his offer. Or something like that . . ." In my own ears it sounded weak. Too weak and out of character for the man. "Anyway," I added, "it's not important now. What happened next?"

"I was really frightened," she said, "Uncle Will's death, then the house being searched, my lying to the police, and this threat of Greenleaf's about . . . an . . . accident. I wanted to get away, to run away from everything, so I packed my hatbox . . . just as fast as I could . . . and hurried from the house. At Doremus' I picked up the grip with the plates, from my locker, and took the first train to New York."

"The rest I know," I told her. "You met a tall wealthy man with talent and married him . . . the dream goal of all red-blooded women!"

A smile warmed her strained face. "Exactly, darling!" she agreed. Bending forward she kissed me on the lips, the coffee cup rattling between us.

"Incidentally," I said casually, "you got rid of the plates in New York."

"Oh, no," she replied, "they're in that new little bag in the closet."

"Jesus Christ!" I leaped from the bed, slammed open the door of the closet and withdrew the small heavy bag. Opening it, I saw a magnificent set of deep-etched steel, counterfeit plates. Staring at the beautiful phonies, I could feel the cold sweat of fear break across my forehead.

ELEVEN

Denman had recalled Deputy Chief Medical
Examiner Eggleston for cross-examination. The counsel
for the defense concealed his worries well. Cannon had
succeeded, Denman believed, in establishing the fact of a
body in his case, identifying the body of the man who,
when alive, had been known as Isham Reddick. Although there were still loose ends in the prosecution's
case to be tied up to make the case more solid, Denman
had few doubts that Cannon would make every effort to
tie them. Now, however, the defense could see the
course the prosecution would follow and it was necessary to counter the testimony which had impressed the
jury.

"Dr. Eggleston," Denman began quietly, "you have
identified blood discovered on a hatchet, a piece of can-

vas, and two vials of scrapings, as containing evidences of human blood; is that right?"

"Yes, sir."

"The counselor for the prosecution has established that you are an expert medical witness, and we certainly have no desire to question that."

"Thank you," Eggleston replied dryly.

"Now the traces of blood which you found, you have identified as a type known as O, is that correct?"

"That is correct. It was type O."

"As an expert medical witness, Dr. Eggleston, will you please tell the court how many known types of blood there are?"

"There are four types."

"Only four types?" Denman's voice expressed surprise. "You mean, Doctor, that in all the millions . . . even billions . . . of persons on this earth, they have only four types of blood among them?"

"Yes," replied Eggleston stiffly, "that's true."

"And everyone falls in one of the four types? Think of that!" Denman mused the point silently for a moment. "Well, now, Doctor, suppose you tell us what the four types are, if you will?"

Eggleston repeated clearly and distinctly, "There are four classifications of human blood. These are types O, A, B, and AB."

"What is the most uncommon type, Doctor?"

"Type AB."

"And the most common?"

"Type O."

"Very interesting. Type O, what? The most common type . . . there are literally hundreds of millions of people who have that type of blood? Is that correct?"

Eggleston cleared his throat. "Yes."

Denman turned and looked at the jury casually, then refaced his witness. "Among the twelve men and women in the jury box, the mathematical probability is that some of them have blood of O type?"

"Objection!" stated Cannon. "That calls for a conclusion."

Denman drawled, "Your honor, I don't think it calls for much of a conclusion that the jury has blood in its veins."

Cannon flushed. The judge, however, ruled in Cannon's favor. "Rephrase your question, please," the bench directed Denman.

The counselor for the defense shrugged and returned to the witness. "Dr. Eggleston," he said, "you definitely identified the type of blood found on the various objects as O. Can you, as a medical scientist, definitely identify that blood as having been the blood of Isham Reddick?"

"No, sir," the witness replied, glancing toward Cannon.

"Then all you have done is classified into generalities," Denman said depreciatingly.

"I identified it as belonging to the same type of blood as Isham Reddick's."

"But you can't prove it was Isham Reddick's blood?"

"No, sir."

Denman turned contemptuously away from the witness and faced the jury, although his words were still addressed to Eggleston. "In other words, you have proved nothing?"

"That is not true!" Eggleston replied firmly.

Denman faced around savagely. "Well then, Doctor, what did you prove?"

"That it was not impossible for the blood to have belonged to Isham Reddick." Eggleston regarded Denman steadily.

Immediately, Denman shifted his attack. "I hope you can be more specific about the mysterious ashes you analyzed, Doctor. For a moment I wish to refresh your memory concerning the testimony you gave Mr. Cannon." Denman reading from a sheet of paper, quoted:

A: There was evidence of protein origin.
Q: Does that mean the possibility of flesh . . . what might at one time have been human flesh?
A: That is correct.

Denman paused and regarded Eggleston. "Do you remember saying that?" he asked.

"Yes, sir," replied Eggleston.

"Will you tell the court what you meant by the term 'protein origin'?"

"It means having a high protein content . . . predominantly protein."

"And what is protein, Doctor?"

"In biochemistry it means any of a class of naturally occurring complex combinations of amino acids . . . ah, let's see . . . containing carbon, hydrogen, nitrogen, oxygen, and usually sulfur, which are essential constituents of all living cells."

Denman pondered his next question carefully. Finally, he asked, "Aren't proteins found in vegetable as well as animal substances?"

"Yes," replied Eggleston.

"Ah," Denman smiled, "then the ash containing a high protein content could have come from vegetable substances?"

"No," replied Eggleston. "Chemically the dif . . ."

"Please just answer my question!" Denman interrupted the witness, and paused to weigh his situation. It was an extremely dangerous one. Deciding to return to safer ground, he said, "Now just a minute ago, Doctor, you finished telling the court what was meant by protein, didn't you?"

"Yes. I gave you a biochemistry definition."

Denman shook his head in reproof. "I asked you . . ." he turned to face the judge, "will the court please instruct the recording clerk to read back the next question which I put at that time. Also, the answer of the witness." The bench so instructed, and the clerk read aloud:

Q: Aren't proteins found in vegetables as well as animal substances?

A: Yes.

"Now," continued Denman addressing Eggleston, "you heard what the clerk has just read. I'll reword the question once more. Proteins are also found in vegetable substances? Is that correct?"

"Yes," replied Eggleston. He was surprised to find himself so quickly on the defensive.

"All right," said Denman with the air of a man who has just exposed a fraud, "we'll leave the subject of vegetable protein." Walking slowly to the exhibit table, he picked up the roll of oil skin, and turning held it up without unrolling it. "Dr. Eggleston," he said, "I'm not going to impose on the sensibilities of those present today by opening this exhibit again. You have already identified it once, so you know what I am talking about. You know what it is?"

"Yes. It's a bone called the tibia."

"A human bone?"

"Yes. A human bone."

"You are positive of that?"

"Yes, sir."

"It couldn't be the bone of one of the primates?"

"Yes, sir. It could!" Eggleston replied acidly. "Man is a primate."

Behind him, Denman could hear Cannon's soft laugh, but he gave no indication of his irritation. "Naturally, Doctor," he smiled blandly, "I'm sure we've all studied high-school biology. What I was going to ask before you anticipated my question . . . incidentally," he turned to the judge, "will the court please instruct the witness to stop anticipating my questions?"

"Your honor," said Cannon rising, "I distinctly heard the counselor ask a question to which the witness made an intelligent reply. I feel that Mr. Denman is unfairly taking advantage of the witness." As he sat down, his eyes met Denman's and passed on happily. The court instructed the witness to content himself with answering only the question put to him.

"All right," said Denman, returning to the witness with dignity, "I will begin my question again. It couldn't be the bone of one of the primates other than man . . . apes, monkeys, or lemurs? Naturally, I do not include marmosets because of their size."

"It couldn't be an ape, monkey, or lemur," Eggleston told him grimly.

"Without any question of a doubt it is human?"

"Yes, it is human."

"Now, Doctor, you testified that this so-called leg

bone . . . the shin . . . was from the leg of a normal, adult male. Which leg is it from?"

"From the left."

"You testified in some detail that the man was not less than five feet ten in height, and not more than six feet. Is that right?"

"That is correct, sir."

"When you examined the bone, what was its condition?"

"It was badly burned and charred."

"Was the entire length of bone you identified as the tibia present when you examined it?"

"I don't quite understand your question, sir."

"I'll put it this way. Was the bone entirely complete, was it present in its normal size and length except for being burned and charred?"

"No, sir."

"The fire then had consumed part of it . . . made it shorter than it normally was?"

"Yes," Eggleston agreed, "the ends had been destroyed."

"Yet, from this damaged, incomplete bone you insist that the man could not have been less than five feet ten?"

"That is correct."

"You will take an oath that under no possible circumstances this man could have been five feet nine and three quarter inches?"

Eggleston twisted uneasily in his chair. No man, under the circumstances, could ethically have been positive of the quarter-inch variance. "I doubt it," he said.

"I'm not asking you to doubt anything," Denman replied, pressing his advantage. "I'm asking you this: Is it entirely beyond all medical possibility that the man could have been five feet nine and three quarter inches?"

"It's against all probability."

"I didn't say probability," Denman corrected him quickly. "I said possibility!"

"Well," agreed Eggleston reluctantly, "there's a possibility. . . ."

"Thank you!" Deliberately Denman began his attack on the other extreme of height, and after considerable maneuvering finally drew an admission from the medical examiner that the man might possibly have been slightly over six feet tall.

Standing beside Eggleston, although really addressing the jury with his remarks, Denman dismissed the witness. "Thank you, Dr. Eggleston. Actually this irregular piece of bone, which you have identified as not coming from an ape, monkey, or lemur, is in a badly burned condition, incomplete in material form, and you insist it came from man. It came from the left leg of a man who originally was not less than five feet ten and not more than six feet in height. This same unknown man, in the last few minutes, has shrunk in height, and at the same time gained in altitude. I'm sure if we had time, the Doctor and I could finally agree both on a midget and a circus giant."

Eggleston stood wearily, visibly relieved to leave the stand. At the last moment, Denman casually called him back, a trick the attorney had found effective with tired witnesses. Denman quickly drew forth the admission, from Eggleston, that the bullet found in the furnace had not contained evidence of blood. Skillfully, the defense attorney prevented the medical examiner from testifying that the extreme heat of the fire, which melted the bullet out of shape, could also have destroyed blood and flesh segments which might have originally clung to it. Cannon tersely whispered to his assistant to make a note to recall Eggleston later and to solicit this information.

Lincoln Means followed Eggleston to the stand for cross-examination. Adding the minutes on the clock to himself, Denman decided that he might be able to finish two, possibly three more witnesses before the court adjourned for the day. When the jury was locked up for the night, his cross-examination would be the last testimony for the jurors to remember. Pressing the palms of his hands against the seams of his trousers, Denman began his questioning. After reidentifying Means as an employee in the Bureau of Licenses, he asked, "If I were applying for a license and told you that I was six feet tall, would you measure me?"

"No," replied Means.

"Why not?"

"Well . . . we don't have a scale for that purpose. It isn't necessary; there's no reason to lie about your height."

"Would there be another reason?"

"You look like you're six feet tall. I'd believe you."

"If I'd said I was five feet two, though, you wouldn't believe me?" Denman asked.

"No, sir. That's obviously wrong."

"Now suppose I said I was one hundred and eighty-six pounds. Would you believe that?"

Means looked at him critically. "You're a big man, I'd say you probably weighed around one hundred and ninety-five pounds."

"Now for the moment, you believe I am six feet tall,

and weigh one hundred and ninety-five pounds. Is that correct, Mr. Means?"

"Yes, sir."

"Six feet tall, one hundred and ninety-five pounds," Denman repeated the figures softly while he removed his billfold and took out his driver's license. Holding it up, he read, "Six feet one and a half inches, weight one hundred and seventy pounds." He faced the witness again, "We disagree by one and a half inches, and twenty-five pounds. That's quite a discrepancy."

The judge addressed the counsel. "How long ago was that license taken out, Mr. Denman?"

"A little over a year ago," Denman replied, "and I assure the court there has been no substantial change in my weight since then."

"Thank you," replied the judge. "You may proceed."

"Mr. Means," continued Denman, "what is your own weight?"

"About a hundred and sixty pounds."

"About . . . you say? When did you last weigh yourself? On accurate scales . . . say, in a doctor's office?"

Means thought back. "Couple, three years ago . . . for an insurance examination."

"And your height?"

"Five seven and a half."

"With or without your shoes?"

"Without my shoes."

"And when was this?"

"At the same insurance examination."

"When I was examined for insurance," Denman said, "and when I was measured for height, my doctor didn't ask me to remove my shoes. He simply compensated half an inch for them."

"Well," replied Means uneasily, "maybe mine did, too."

"Don't be concerned," Denman's voice was friendly, "I'm not attempting to trap you. I'm simply proving that the human memory is not infallible. Most persons only weigh themselves occasionally, and then on unreliable scales, or if they do have factual figures—it is possible that the figures have changed or are out of date. Right now, Mr. Means, you honestly don't know if you are five feet seven, seven and a half, or eight; also it is probable that you weigh one hundred fifty, fifty-five, sixty, or sixty-five pounds." Denman paused, then asked politely, "Is that correct?"

"Yes, I suppose so."

"Isn't it possible that many of the applicants for licenses have the same fallacious, out-of-date, or mistaken information that you have? They fill in the statistics with answers they believe to be true, but which could . . . actually . . . be quite inaccurate?"

"Well . . . no . . ."

"I don't mean obviously wrong, Mr. Means. But five or ten pounds off, an inch or two in height . . . can you guarantee that every one of the thousands of forms you have are one hundred percent correct?" Denman's voice had suddenly lost its friendliness.

"No," Means replied slowly, "sometimes somebody might make a mistake . . ."

"Exactly!" Denman referred to his notes. "You read into the testimony regarding Isham Reddick: 'Sex . . . male; age . . . 36; eyes . . . blue; hair . . . dark brown; weight . . . 175 pounds; height . . . 5 feet 11 inches.' " Denman glanced up from his reading and intently regarded the witness. "Now, Mr. Means, a few minutes ago you estimated my stature, but on the basis of your estimate . . ."

Cannon was on his feet. "Objection! Objection!"

"Isn't it possible Reddick was over six feet tall and weighed two hundred pounds?" Denman concluded.

"Your honor," objected Cannon, "I move the statement be struck from the testimony, and the jury be instructed to disregard it!"

"On what basis, Counselor?" asked Denman smiling.

"It is an opinion . . . purely hypothetical . . ."

"Sustained," agreed the court. The judge turned to the jury. "Please do not regard the last statement, made by Mr. Denman, as evidence in any way, and do not permit it to affect your decision."

Denman, however, was still smiling. He had built a smoke screen; how important it was, he couldn't tell.

Dr. Stanley Boss, the dentist, rather reluctantly returned to the stand. Denman stood beside the defense table, visibly sharpening up his weapons while the dentist was seated. Denman immediately launched his attack.

TWELVE

Those engraved printing plates worried me!
Plenty! I knew we had to get rid of them as quickly as
possible. In a strange hotel, it isn't customary to call a
bellboy, ask for a hammer, and then begin beating out
an anvil chorus on pieces of heavy gauge metal . . . in
the hope of destroying them. Merely possessing the
plates meant terrible trouble with the Treasury Department, in spite of their never having been printed from.

But even more dangerous, to my way of thinking, was
the unknown and unseen Greenleaf. He had arranged
with a great amount of time, and some expense, to con
Will Shaw into making them. If Tally was correct, he
had been in the house looking for the plates the night
the old man died. Now it was impossible to return the
engravings to the government without involving Tally—

because of the money Greenleaf had advanced through the checks she had endorsed. And then there was the next point, too. . . .

Suppose Greenleaf had been responsible for the old man's death? Wasn't it a probability that Greenleaf had struck him and knocked him downstairs when Will Shaw couldn't hand over the plates? Or possibly had struck Shaw first, and then with the old man unconscious had pitched him head first into the basement?

One thing was obvious, however; I must get rid of the plates immediately. And, furthermore, I had no intention of walking around the streets of Philadelphia, carrying them, while I found a place to hide them. Tally remained quietly in bed while I dressed. She looked worried. "Listen, doll," I said, kissing her quickly, "I'm going out for a while . . . stick around until I get back." She nodded. I put the engravings back in the closet, and hurriedly left the room.

Out on the street, I cut over toward the city hall, looking for a place to hide the plates, and where they might remain undiscovered for a reasonable length of time. Preferably until we had finished at the Lark and returned to New York. The streets were filled with people all of whom seemed to be watching me suspiciously. Walking along Benjamin Franklin Parkway toward the Art Museum, I approached the monument of George Washington on a concrete island surrounded by traffic. Within the grounds of the Art Museum, however, I found another statue and the place for which I had been searching. There's a bronze casting of a man with a raised spear, astride a horse, and it's called the Lion Fighter. Growing directly behind it is a well-groomed hedge, heavy and thick, with a tangled mass of interwo-

ven roots. By standing behind the statue, I could dig in
the roots and conceal the plates without anyone observing me. The plates, buried deeply enough, might remain
concealed for years—becoming corroded and ruined beyond any possible use.

I was anxious, now, to return to the hotel, pick up the
plates, and to come back and bury them. Hurrying
down the broad steps of the museum, I waved down a
cab and rode back to the hotel.

At the McAndrews, a newsie opened the cab door,
and I slipped him a quarter. He stepped back to the
sidewalk. "A nice day, Mr. Mountain," he said.

"That it is," I agreed. He was a thin, skinny little guy
with practically no shoulders at all, and the waddling
gait of a penguin. Several times, when it had been raining, he had hustled cabs for Tally and me and consequently we were on nodding-tipping-speaking terms.
For just a moment I stood beside him on the sunny sidewalk, and then it seemed a great flapping shadow covered the sun.

The newsie glanced up and, shouting loud senseless
words, shoved me back into the street.

There was a tremendous report like the slamming of a
door!

Death lay on the street beside me.

Stunned, the newsie and I stood there, stupefied, and
in those few paralyzed moments the sidewalk swarmed
with people, gathering from the streets and the buildings
and the cars to form a tightening circle around the hideous heap. At my feet lay a slipper, a small, black, velvet
bedroom slipper trimmed with gold.

It was Tally's slipper.

The tides lapping the beaches of all the oceans in the

world stopped running and for a moment stood still. Then ebbing, they piled back one upon another, rushing faster and faster in a great black tidal wave dredging up the sickly bottoms of the seas, sucking the sun from the sky. Within the black heart of the wave a great roaring began, increasing louder and louder, and the wave grew higher and higher until nothing remained but the presence of a sound so great there is no other sound, a blackness so deep there is no sight. And yet, somewhere there were loud voices, and soft voices, and voices in between.

And one face kept appearing before mine. A face I had never seen before . . . a large face, with dark close-set eyes and a heavy jaw. Finally, I could no longer hear all the voices—just the one voice. The voice that belonged to the heavy face.

The face belonged to a detective named Brockheim, and we were in my hotel room. Other men were in the room, too; some in plain clothes and some in uniform. It seemed as if everyone was there. Everyone, that is, except Tally.

"Come . . . come," Brockheim repeated, "it's been a shock. Come, come, Mr. Mountain, you must answer a few questions. Come, come, man, pull yourself together." One of the cops had discovered a partly filled bottle of Scotch in my drawer and poured me a drink. I drank it, but I couldn't taste it. "Come . . . come," said Brockheim.

Grasping the arms of the chair, I squeezed them. My fingers were lifeless—I was squeezing mush, whipped cream, the foam of beer. "Yes," I said finally, my voice coming from the void deep within me.

"That's better . . . that's good," said Brockheim.

"Tell me, Mr. Mountain, when did you see your wife last?"

"I don't know," I said.

"Come, come," Brockheim replied, "you were just returning to the hotel when your wife leaped from the window. You must have seen her sometime this morning."

"I don't know."

"Well then, how long were you gone?"

Among all the watches, I saw the apparition of my wrist watch as I had looked at it in the grounds of the Art Museum. "Two hours," I said.

"Good!" Brockheim replied with satisfaction. "When you left Mrs. Mountain this morning, what was she doing?"

"She was in bed."

"Undressed and in bed?"

"Yes."

"After you left, she must have gotten up and dressed, because she was wearing her street clothes when she jumped. Why? Was she going out?"

"I don't think so," I said numbly as the memory of Tally lying against the pillows returned to me. "But she might have decided to get up anyway. I was gone quite a while."

"How was she feeling when you saw her this morning? Did you have a fight about something?"

"No. We didn't fight. We never fought. . . ."

"Was she depressed about something? Anything?"

"I can't think," I said. "I'm all confused . . . it's hard for me to understand what you say. Let me go in and wash my face." Without waiting for Brockheim's permission I arose from the chair and stumbled into the bathroom. Pulling my tie loose, I unbuttoned my shirt collar; then turned on the cold water tap. Scooping up handfuls of water, I bathed my face and placed my icy hands at the base of my neck. When my head began to clear, the fog of unreality before my eyes slowly began to disappear. Drying my hands and face, I returned to the bedroom. "All right," I told Brockheim, "I feel better now."

"I asked you if your wife had planned to go out this morning?" Brockheim said.

"Yes . . . I remember you asked that. You said she was dressed in street clothes. But she was still wearing bedroom slippers."

"That's right," agreed Brockheim. "Now tell me what she was worried about? A woman doesn't jump out of a window on the spur of the moment."

This was the moment of decision! This was the point of no return. It was now that I told the truth . . . or never. Placing a cigarette in my mouth, I pretended to fumble through my pockets for a match. Before Brockheim could bring his lighter into play I walked over to the closet, opened it, and took a pack of matches from a jacket hanging there. My eyes touched the corner of the closet.

Tally's small bag containing the counterfeit plates was gone!

I returned to the chair and sat down. I knew that Tally had not jumped to her death—had not committed suicide. Not only was there no reason for her to do so, but it was impossible psychologically to reconcile the deed to her temperament. The final desperate act of suicide takes conditioning, over a long period of time, and Tally had given no indication of such thoughts.

The police, I knew, must also be considering the possibility that her fall was accidental. The two large windows at the end of the room were both wide enough and high enough to make it possible. Both windows had comparatively low sills, not more than twenty-four inches above the floor. The lower part of one window had been completely raised, sliding up to cover the entire top half of the frame, leaving a large wide opening. Suppose Tally had opened the window, leaned out—resting her hands on the sill—and her hands had slipped? As she lost her balance, was it possible that the momentum of the fall would pitch her out of the window? This would be impossible to prove or disprove as the outside cement sill would retain neither fingerprints nor palm marks.

One other fact remained; the big fact . . . the most important fact of all! The plates were gone. They had been in the closet when I left. Could Tally have dressed and hidden them somewhere in the hotel? It was a possibility although I doubted it. She was waiting for me to return. Then, if she hadn't gotten rid of them, Greenleaf had been in the room and taken them.

From this, it might appear that I had thought about the situation in detail, while attempting to stall off Brockheim. That's not the way it happened. Actually, all the possibilities seemed to flash before me in an instant of lucidity. In another moment, I had made my decision. I knew beyond doubt that it was useless to explain about the missing plates, and to accuse Greenleaf . . . whom I had never seen . . . and couldn't possibly identify, and against whom I had no proof of any kind. To admit existence of the plates, worth millions in counterfeit money, was to point a damning finger of motive to myself. Logically, the police might believe that Tally had hidden the engravings to keep for herself, and I had killed her to regain possession of them.

Although I had an airtight alibi . . . with the newsie . . . for the moment of her death, that did not rule out the possibility of an accomplice.

So in that second instant, as my eyes met Brockheim's, I said to him, "She'd been worried . . . well, not really worried . . . but distressed about her uncle's death. He died here in Philadelphia less than four months ago; he was my wife's only relative and naturally she felt very badly about it. Returning here to work depressed her, but not to the extent she'd take her own life."

Brockheim removed a stick of gum, peeled off the wrapper, and stuck it in his mouth. Chewing it slowly, he explained, "Trying to give up smoking. Doesn't work very well." He eyed me contemplatively and asked, "How long you been married?" I told him. "Newlyweds, huh?" he observed.

"Yes," I replied.

"Did she have any insurance?"

"Not that I know of . . . she might have had some before we were married. If she did, it couldn't be very much and she never mentioned it."

"You didn't take any out on her?"

"Not a penny."

"Sure about it?"

"Positive."

Brockheim shrugged. "I can find out." He relapsed to silence, and chewed his gum. After a few moments, he said, "The switchboard says you got a call this morning before you went out. Who was it?"

I looked at him. "Some joker in the show, I think.

Whoever it was just called to wake us up. Pretended it was a wrong number . . ."

"Oh?" Brockheim arose and ambled over to the window. "Seems there was another call later . . . after you'd gone. A very short one. Soon as your room answered, the connection was broken. Same joker?"

"Could be," I agreed. "You always find them in this business . . . in every show. They're not very funny."

"They never are." Standing by the open window, Brockheim stooped—leaning out to peer down the fifteen stories to the street. Bending further, he rested his hands on the sill, his hands and wrists supporting the weight of his body. "Was your wife a fresh-air fiend?" he asked, his voice sounding distant through the window.

"Not especially," I replied. Brockheim pulled his body back through the opening and dusted the palms of his hands. "She wasn't against fresh air, either. If she had a headache, or wasn't feeling well, she might have opened the window to lean out."

"Did she have a headache?"

"I couldn't say. We slept late this morning. Perhaps she just wanted a breath of fresh air."

"Yeah," said Brockheim. Walking back across the room he faced me. "You think it possible she jumped?" he asked.

"No." I was positive.

"Then you think she fell?"

"Yes. It had to be that way."

"Well," he said slowly, "we'll leave you alone now. There're some more questions I've got to ask around the hotel . . . and at that club where you're working. I'll talk to you later." He nodded to the men in the room, and they followed him through the door.

Instantly the room was deserted—a great square room, miles long and miles wide. Nowhere in the room was there a sound . . . and nowhere was there movement . . . except my fingers. After a while, I studied them and discovered they were doing a cull shuffle. In my hands, however, there were no cards.

I walked over to the dresser and picked up the bottle of Scotch.

THIRTEEN

The dentist's eyes, behind his rimless glasses, watched Denman with wary interest. Nervously he ran his hand through his hair and cleared his voice. The defense attorney approached him indifferently, his hands shoved in the pockets of his trousers. "Doctor, you said a patient known to you as Isham Reddick called because he had three teeth hurting; is that right?"

"That is correct, sir," Boss replied.

"Furthermore, you examined those teeth carefully and took an X-ray . . . but you could find nothing wrong with them?"

"I could find no reason for the teeth to be hurting him."

"After you told the patient this, what did he say?"

"He said they still hurt him."

"Following that first call, you continued to see him several times more. Did he ever say, again, that the teeth hurt?"

"I don't remember."

"But you remember everything else?"

Boss fidgeted uneasily. "When I saw him later, I was thinking about the new tooth. . . ."

"But didn't it strike you as strange that your patient told you his teeth were hurting. You told him nothing was wrong, and very cooperatively he never mentioned his sore teeth again?"

"No," replied Boss. "Sometimes teeth hurt because they are temporarily sensitive to extremes of heat and cold . . . then the condition passes . . ."

"So after you decided nothing was wrong with Isham Reddick's teeth, you proceeded to make a false one for him. Tell me, Dr. Boss, who brought up the subject of the false tooth?"

"I'm sure Reddick did, sir."

"Why are you so sure of that?"

"Well, the loss of it greatly affected his appearance. He needed it badly. The amount of time and labor that went into making the new tooth greatly exceeded what Reddick could pay. It was more important to him to have the tooth than it was to me to make it."

"You have implied, Dr. Boss, that you did Isham Reddick a favor in making the tooth for him, and I consider it very generous of you, I'm sure." Denman paused, then asked, "Have you a very successful practice, Doctor?"

"Yes, I should say so."

"A large one?"

"All I can handle," Boss replied.

Denman turned his attack. "Yet busy as you are, you

spent as much time . . . as much effort . . . as much skill in making this tooth for Isham Reddick, who couldn't pay for it, as you would for a wealthy patient?"

"I certainly did," Boss replied stiffly.

"Now, Dr. Boss, I don't deny that you made a tooth for Isham Reddick. I'm sure you did. But I'm not sure that you made by *hand* a tooth, specially colored, shaped, and shaded . . . a tooth different than any other tooth in the world." Deliberately, Denman looked the witness up and down, "Well, did you, Doctor?"

"Yes sir, I did!" Boss' lips set determinedly.

"Consider it well," Denman cautioned. "Isn't it possible that you found a stock tooth suitable to use? There are stock teeth of individual sizes and shapes, aren't there?"

"Yes, there are."

"So you could have found one which matched Isham Reddick's well enough in color, ground it down to fit . . . and have saved yourself a great deal of time and expense. Isn't that right?"

"No!" Boss denied it doggedly.

"Why not?"

"Because the patient is never satisfied with a poor job."

"But Reddick would have been better off, would he not? He would have a front tooth, one that looked reasonably well—which was something he didn't have before?" Denman was attempting to push Boss into admitting the use of a stock tooth. With such an admission, the dentist's identification of the tooth, as Reddick's, would be greatly weakened. However, Boss maintained tenaciously that the tooth he had made and fitted for Reddick was his own, and Denman was unable to shake his testimony.

Denman's examination of Mrs. Boss was cursory. She repeated her previous testimony that the laboratory report on Isham Reddick's blood had been type O. There was very little more that Denman could do with her. At the conclusion of his examination, the court adjourned for the day.

At ten o'clock the following morning Assistant District Attorney Cannon recalled Lieutenant Mikleson to the stand. "Now, Lieutenant, previously you have testified that on your first visit to the house on East Eighty-ninth Street, you examined the defendant's bedroom, the adjoining bath . . . and that pictures were taken of those rooms." Mikleson confirmed this statement, and Cannon continued, "When you searched the bedroom, what did you find?"

"I found a revolver in the second drawer of the bureau."

"Is this the same revolver?" asked Cannon.

Mikleson identified it. "Yes," he replied, "a .32, with one shell fired."

"Did you find anything else?"

"Yes, sir, I did. I found a piece of note paper folded and placed under a number of items of clothing in the same dresser."

"Is this the note?" Cannon passed a small sheet of blue-lined paper, approximately three inches wide and five inches long, of a type commonly used in pocket memorandum books. A piece had been torn out completely along one side.

Mikleson examined the paper and nodded. "This is the one. I identify it by my initials on it."

Cannon turned, addressing his next remarks to the jury. "I'm going to read what is written on this paper." He held up the slip and read in a clear voice: "Reddick . . . mt. 8500." Facing the judge, Cannon said, "Your honor, I offer this into evidence." Then turning back to Mikleson he continued, "Also in the possession of the defendant, you found a memorandum book. Can you identify this?" The prosecuting attorney handed a small leather-covered book to the officer who examined and identified it. "Thank you," said Cannon dismissing the witness.

Next recalling the handwriting expert . . . Alvin G. Hartney . . . to the stand, Cannon showed him the memorandum book. "You have examined the writings and notes in this book and have compared them to samples of the writing of the defendant. Would you say they are written by the same hand?"

"Yes," said Hartney. "The writing in the memo book is identical with other specimens of handwriting of the defendant."

"Here," continued Cannon, "is a sheet of paper . . . supposedly from that notebook. Have you examined the writing on it?" Cannon gave the blue-lined note to the witness.

"Yes," replied Hartney.

"Can you identify the writing?"

"Yes, sir. It is identical to both the writing in the notebook and the other handwriting specimens of the defendant."

"You would say, positively, they were written by the same person?"

"I would!" Hartney replied with assurance. Cannon excused him from the stand.

"Mary Deems," the clerk announced, and a middle-aged woman still retaining a trim and youthful figure made her way to the witness chair. Her round face was unmarked by lines, and she wore no make-up except lipstick. She identified herself as a house maid, in the house on East Eighty-ninth Street, having worked for the defendant. Dressed in a neat dark suit, she crossed her ankles, folded her hands in her lap, and continued with her testimony.

"You have said you were a house maid. Will you please tell us about your duties?" asked Cannon.

"Well, sir . . . actually I kept the house picked up, answered the door and the downstairs phone, and in the mornings prepared a light continental breakfast. . . ."

"Explain about the breakfast, if you will."

"I'm not a cook," she replied firmly, "but in the mornings, I'd make coffee, and warm up crisp rolls to be served with marmalade for breakfast." She nodded, thinking back. "When I was hired I said I wasn't a cook and I was told that there wouldn't be any cooking to be done. Breakfast, a real light one, was the only meal in the house. Sometimes . . . there might be a little private entertaining, but then a caterer would just send something in."

"Did you live on the premises, Miss Deems?"

"Yes, sir. I had a room in the upstairs servants' quarters."

"Were there any servants other than yourself?"

"There was Isham Reddick. He lived in, too. He was employed as a combination houseman-chauffeur."

"Was that all the help to run a large house like that?"

Mary Deems shook her head. "That was all the help that lived in . . . just Isham Reddick and me. There

was a couple . . . Mr. and Mrs. Lightbody . . . who
came in days to help. He was a super in another building
down the street. . . ."

"Just a moment. What do you mean by super?"

"Superintendent. He was superintendent, and janitor,
of a small apartment building down the street. He came
in every day to take out ashes, check the furnace, and fix
anything around the house that needed fixing. Mrs.
Lightbody, his wife, came in regularly to do the heavy
cleaning and vacuuming."

"I see. Now, returning to Isham Reddick. You said, a
few moments ago, that he was a houseman-chauffeur. I
understood that he also acted in the capacity of a valet.
Is that right?"

"Yes, sir, he did a little bit of everything." Mary
Deems was not inclined to argue definitions.

"Now, Miss Deems, you have been in service . . .
for how many years?"

The woman hesitated, "Since I was a young girl . . ."

Cannon was understanding. "I'm not going to ask for
a definite reply. Is it fair to say around twenty years?"

"Yes . . ."

"Good! Now in that time you've seen many servants
when you've worked for other families. How would you
compare Isham Reddick with other houseman-valet-
chauffeurs?"

The woman considered the question and replied
slowly. "Not very well, sir . . ." Her honest face was
worried with the idea of speaking disrespectfully of the
dead, "but he really didn't take an interest in his job. Of
course," she added brightly, "maybe he didn't like the
idea of doing so many things. Usually a valet is a valet
. . . and a chauffeur is a chauffeur."

"Did you get to know Isham Reddick very well?" Mary Deems blushed, and Cannon qualified his question. "I don't mean in any personal way, but did he talk to you very much?"

"No, sir. Not very much. Usually when he wasn't on duty, he'd remain up in his room. There was just the one time he ever acted very friendly. Once when we were alone, he asked me to go see a movie. Afterward we stopped and had something to eat."

"You remember that incident very well, Miss Deems. Is there any reason for it, other than it was the only time he ever took you out?"

"Yes, sir. There's another reason, too. There was a little restaurant near the movie up on Ninety-second Street. We stopped in there to get a bite to eat, as I said, and I was reading the menu carefully because I didn't want to spend too much of Mr. Reddick's money. I decided I'd just have a sandwich and a cup of tea and he said, "Go ahead and order anything you want. I've got plenty of dough.""

"Isham Reddick said, 'Go ahead and order anything you want. I've got plenty of dough,'" Cannon repeated. "By that, Miss Deems, you understood that he had plenty of money, is that correct?"

"That's what I thought he meant, although there was the possibility he was just joking . . . or bragging a little. Kidding him back, I said that I bet he didn't have an extra shirt to his name. He looked at me and said, 'What do you think of this?' He pulled a big thick roll of bills out of his pocket. He held them out in front of me for a minute, very proud like, and then put them back."

"Did Reddick tell you how much money there was in the roll?"

"No, sir. But when he held the bills up, I could see there were a lot of hundred-dollar ones among them."

"In your opinion, could there have been eighty-five hundred dollars in that . . ." Cannon was interrupted by Denman springing to his feet.

"Objection," Denman stated.

The judge agreed. "Objection sustained."

"All right, Miss Deems," Cannon said, returning to his witness. "After Reddick had showed you a large roll of bills, many in the denomination of a hundred dollars, what did you say?"

"Naturally, I wondered where he had gotten all that money. I knew it wasn't from his salary. . . ."

"Objection!" Denman shouted angrily.

"Sustained!" The court ruled.

"What did he say?" asked Cannon, addressing the maid.

"Well, first I laughed and said, 'Boy, you must have a private gold mine!' Then he laughed, too, and said, No, he didn't have a private gold mine. He was more like an undertaker—he knew where the bodies were buried."

"Let me get this straight now, Miss Deems," Cannon said deliberately, driving his point home. "Isham Reddick told you that he was like an undertaker—that he knew where the bodies were buried. Is that correct?"

"Yes, sir."

"And by that remark, you understood that Reddick was not talking about *real* bodies—but that he knew some important information?"

"That's right. That is what he meant."

"It hardly sounds to me like a man who could scarcely afford the cost of a tooth," observed Cannon. "Did it sound that way to you?"

"No, sir," the maid replied, "it didn't. It sounded like he had plenty of money."

"Was Isham Reddick wearing the tooth the night you went to dinner?"

"He couldn't have been," she said. "I remember there was a big wide gap in the front of his teeth—just like always."

FOURTEEN

In the magician's land of make-believe and illusion what one doesn't see is always there . . . only one doesn't see it until the conjurer is ready to show it. The silks are stuffed within the hollow egg, the flowers collapsed within the palm of his hand; the card concealed on the back of his fingers. But Death is the greatest necromancer of all; in a moment of inattention, he makes his sleight and palms a life, and one does not realize that the breathing figure is gone.

The illusion of life persists . . . you listen for the voice in the next room; you await the footsteps coming up the stairs—the well-known, well-beloved ones; you anticipate the turn of a profile in a busy restaurant, the tinkle of a laugh in a bar, the lovely swiftly moving legs on a busy street. The illusion is there still; yesterday has not yet become today. Today must never become tomorrow, because tomorrow will be too late.

Hope lingers on, the last soft breeze in the trees before winter; the last strain of music before silence. It is there before despair wilts completely the last bouquet of make-believe flowers, and Death takes his curtain bow before the black velvet drapes.

The delicate, well-remembered lips brush your cheek in the night, but in the morning there are only the twisted bedclothes beside you. In your own mind alone the voice remains; only behind your sleeping eyes does the face become reality. In the misery of the endless nights, the wretchedness of the matching days, hope vanishes. Then is the illusion completed! Because only then, is she gone forever. . . .

I didn't lose Tally in the street before the McAndrews that afternoon, nor on Locust Street . . . nor on any of the other little Philadelphia streets. She disappeared one night several months later in New York. I was lying on my back, on the sidewalk, in front of a bar on Eighth Avenue; I was lying there because I had been thrown out. I had been thrown out because I had been unable to pay for my drinks—and I couldn't pay for my drinks because I hadn't worked since Philadelphia. Thinking to myself without indignation what a cheap lousy joint to get bounced from, I lay there for a moment looking straight up into the sky. I could see no blue, no stars, no heavens. Only the murky haze . . . half translucent, half opaque . . . of blue neons and red neons, yellow fluorescents and green fluorescents; white Mazdas and amber General Electrics. They were all there in the murk above the street, mixed into a brown fog of quivering colors. Rolling over slowly on my stomach I pushed myself to my feet and staggered to the building—leaning against it for support. Wretchedly I spewed the cheap liquor back over the building in which I had drunk it.

That was the moment I decided to murder Greenleaf!

In the morning I went to see my agent. I had slept in my clothes for a week, my shirt was as filthy as an oiler's rag; I needed a shave, and I hadn't eaten in . . . I don't know . . . three or four days. I had to walk to his office as I didn't have the price of a subway ride, and I didn't think I would make it. Each block I was forced to sit down to rest. As I sat on the curbing, panting with exhaustion, passers-by walked around me in a careful antiseptic arc. Eventually I reached his office and I waited outside the door until he appeared.

"Sol," I said, "I want to talk to you." He nodded and opened the cubbyhole, helping me in. He is a little man with a round, compact potbelly. Seating me in a chair by his desk, he gave me a cigarette; the smoke gagged in my raw throat. "You've got to help me," I said.

"Sure, Lew," he replied sympathetically. "I heard about what happened in Philly, I'm sorry . . ."

"I need some dough. I'm broke."

"Sure, sure. I understand." His eyes brushed past my filthy clothes to search my face. "You all right now, Lew?"

"Yes," I replied, "I'm all right now."

"You got a good act, Lew. It don't make sense to throw it away. Even . . . as a single . . . I can keep you going pretty good. You got to lay off drinking, though."

"Sol," I said urgently, his little office swiveling before my eyes while my stomach cramped and crawled, "don't lecture me. Just give me some dough . . . let me get out of here!"

"How much you want, Lew?" He reached in his pocket and withdrew a thin, well-worn checkbook.

"I don't know . . . whatever you'll trust me for. I need it bad, and it isn't for drinking."

"Sure, sure," Sol agreed heavily. He scribbled a check and handed it to me. "Two hundred enough?"

"Thanks," I said, folding the check and stuffing it in my pocket. Swaying to my feet, I held onto the desk. "Now I can get back in my hotel room."

"When are you coming back to work?" he asked.

"I don't know," I told him truthfully, "I've got something important to do first. But in case I don't come back, I'll see you get the dough."

"Forget it, Lew," Sol replied, "it's for old times' sake. . . ."

A hot shower washes away many sins—at least the sins of dirt, grime, and grease. Back at the hotel, I showered, shaved, and slept the clock around. The following morning, in fresh clothes, I forced some breakfast into my protesting stomach. Although I was still lightheaded and couldn't concentrate for very long, I began planning to get Greenleaf. And each successive day, I continued to think about it, weighing the probabilities, considering the possibilities. Little by little, day after day, the idea began to go together. My most urgent problem, however, was money which I needed to complete my plans. And I needed it quickly. The money Sol had given me, after paying my hotel bill, left very little.

There was one fast way to get funds, and I decided to take it, although it was a dangerous and calculated risk. As soon as I felt better, and the shakes had left my hands, I looked up Max the bell captain. Tipping him, I said, "I've got a friend coming in from the sticks in a day or two. He likes a little action. Know where there's a game?"

"Craps?"

"No. Poker . . ."

Max gave it to me straight. "Sure this guy's a friend of yours?"

"Absolutely," I replied.

"I know a game, but a stranger might get hurt. Particularly, if there's any fast dealing. The mug who runs it ain't no Union Leaguer."

I shrugged. "I can't guarantee this guy's morals," I replied. "But he's been around. I kind of figure it's up to him." I stared straight back at Max.

Max lit a cigarette. "What the hell," he said, "it's no skin off my ass. What's this guy's name?"

"Tom Murphy," I said. "His father's name was Tom Murphy, and his grandfather's . . ."

"Yeah, I know," interrupted Max, "his name was Tom Murphy, too."

"I don't know how you guessed it, but you did."

"Okay. Tell Tom Murphy to ask for Jack at the cigar store. Tell him, I sent him." Max described a small to-bacco shop, near Times Square. "Ask for Jack before nine-thirty any night. The game starts at ten . . . it's a floater. Jack'll tell him where it's going to be."

The next night I contacted Jack. With the last fifty dollars in my pocket, I sat in a seven-handed game of dealer's choice, in the back room of a shoe store. It was a typical minor league, floating game. A consumptive and dangerous Greek named Steve operated it, taking a small percentage drag out of each pot. The other players were a used car dealer from the Bronx, a small restaurant owner, two out-of-towners attending a convention, a radio director, and a traveling salesman.

I played carefully and cautiously . . . not being able to afford any losses, and I played it straight. When the game broke up about four in the morning, I was seventy dollars to the good. For my purpose, the amount was just about right. It wasn't too much . . . large enough to cause comment . . . and yet Steve noticed it.

During the next two weeks, I sat in Steve's game every night; we played in hotel rooms, garages, back rooms of restaurants, record shops, haberdasheries, barber shops, antique stores, and any other place where an owner was willing to pick up a fast twenty bucks for the use of his premises. The players came and went; new faces every night—except mine. The Greek, of course, didn't care who won as his take was a fixed percentage from each pot. However, to be careful, I deliberately lost small amounts on two occasions, and indirectly brought it to his attention. At the end of two weeks, I was about five hundred dollars to the good.

One night, when the game had broken up, I said to Steve, "How about grabbing some breakfast at the automat?" He agreed and we walked down Broadway to Times Square. At the table, I put it right to him. "I want to make some dough, fast! I'd like to sit in a big league game. . . ."

Steve ate his Danish pastry without replying. When he had completely finished, he wiped his lips on a paper napkin. "You play a pretty good game. You make a little dough. What you want to lose it for?"

"I don't think I'll lose it," I said.

Steve shrugged. "Maybe not. But that's what they all think."

"All right," I said, "so I lose it. It's my dough. But if I win you get 10 percent off the top."

The Greek's eyes swiveled around to meet mine. He stared for a minute, then dropped them indifferently. "You're pretty eager," he said obliquely.

I agreed. "There's a good thing I can get a piece of on the West Coast. It's not going to be open forever. I either get some dough, quick, or forget it." I kept my voice expressionless. "You've got contacts, you know where the big game is . . . get me in it. I'll make it right."

"You said 10 percent."

"That's it."

He looked over my shoulder, not seeing me. "Maybe I can do something," he said. Abruptly he returned his attention. "How much dough you got going in?"

"Half a yard," I said.

"Not enough."

Now came the gimmick. This was the important pitch. He was right; with only five hundred dollars going into a big game, I couldn't hold down a chair. "Okay, Steve," I said, "I need some front money. You lend me another five hundred, and I give you another 10 percent."

"No dice. My five on the bottom, not playing." What he meant was that I'd bet my own five hundred dollars, and leave his on the table for show. If I lost my five, I'd cash in the chips for his money and return it.

"All right," I agreed reluctantly, "show and no play, but I'll only pay you 5 percent on it."

Steve arose from the table, pushing back the metal chair. "I'll see what I can get going," he said.

Three nights later, the Greek gave me the nod for the big game. It was held in the suite of a midtown hotel, located on the plush East side belt. Steve was with me for a number of reasons: to get me in, to watch his money, and to collect his 15 percent of any winnings. The drawing room of the suite was smartly and impersonally decorated with a false fireplace, huge antiqued mirrors, and weirdly designed modern lamps. A large oblong table had been arranged in the center of the room and covered with a piece of heavy green felt. Around the table were five players in addition to myself. Steve wasn't playing and he sat carefully to one side, away from the table where he could see no cards except mine. Half a dozen hard-faced men lounged around the room watching the game. The place quickly became blanketed with smoke notwithstanding the air-conditioning unit which was operating at top speed.

It was a strict game of five card draw with the deck and deal changing hands after each pot. Chips were twenty-five, fifty, and a hundred dollars. Who the other players were, I don't know; no one identified himself. But they were all experts.

As the hours crept by, I took it easy. By two o'clock we'd been playing over three hours—just long enough for everyone to be getting a little tired, a little slow with the eyes, a little slow with the reflexes. From the beginning of the game, I'd watched carefully and had detected no phony dealing. Unobtrusively, I checked the cards, at every opportunity, and could find no markings of any kind. The decks, six in all, were alternated regularly and in no particular order. The game looked to me like it was strictly on the square. There had been quite a bit of action with some big pots of three and four grand in them. Several of the original players had lost heavily and checked out; they had been replaced from the silent group of men watching the game.

I had been playing my cards pretty close to the vest and was a little to the good, and I continued to nurse along my chips, holding on, waiting for a break to come. In every game at some time, such a break occurs—either for good or for bad.

One of the original players was a heavily jowled man, with a broken nose, and black hair which he parted and combed in the middle. He'd won a few good pots during the game and had been betting his cards carefully, and dropping out often. As the night wore on, I kept getting a hunch about the fellow which I couldn't place. I continued to watch him; his hands were quick and sure; his heavy face impassive.

And then it came!

Heavy Jowls shuffled and offered the deck to be cut at his right. Casually picking it up with his left hand, his right hand covered the deck for a split second, and in that instant—with one hand—he completed the Ednase shift. It was done, literally, in the blink of an eye—and even then I couldn't have sworn he had done it. The Ednase is one of the fastest, smoothest gambling shifts in the world reversing the cut deck to its original position, and means just one thing. The dealer has stacked the deck.

This was what I had been waiting for. When I picked up my hand, I held three 8's and a pair of Queens. A full house. The betting opened and went around the table with four raises. Heavy Jowls had really set up his marks. Making my ante and raise, I sat there trying to figure out what Heavy Jowls held for himself. The other players called for their cards . . . dealer's left asked for two, which indicated three of a kind; the next player stood pat, which might mean a full house, a straight, or a flush; the player to my right took one . . . probably drawing to two pair. One thing was certain, in a stacked deck, the sequence is determined; it is important; break the sequence and you cause trouble. I discarded my three 8's and asked for three cards. The tiniest, almost invisible, twitch of surprise touched Heavy Jowls; he had planned for me to stand pat, too. The player to my left drew two.

Heavy Jowls, himself, checked his draw. At that point, I thought I had him pegged. He was holding four of a kind, and probably he would not bother to hold four extremely high cards . . . it wouldn't be necessary to do so, in order to beat out a full house or a flush.

Picking up my new cards, I looked into a Queen, and a 6 and 9 of Spades. The Queen and 6 had obviously been intended for the player to my left, as I had not been expected to draw.

Heavy Jowls knew that I was holding three Queens, a 6 and 9 of Spades—which was a weaker hand than I held originally. We were using a blue Bicycle deck.

As a rule, the packs used in professional gambling games are Bicycle Brand playing cards printed with medium-colored red and blue back-designs. These cards have become traditional . . . probably because they are very difficult to mark successfully. I'd come to the game with a load, both a red and a blue pack concealed under my coat, the cards distributed according to suit and number over my body. This was simple; I'd been doing it in my act for years.

I stole the fourth Queen from my load, and palmed

away the 6 of Spades while the original opener made his
first bet. The second man bet and raised, while the original opener checked out; the man to my right dropped
out; I met and raised; the player to my left dropped; and
Heavy Jowls met and raised.

This left only Heavy Jowls, the man second to his left,
and me in the game. Obviously Heavy Jowls held four of
a kind; the man to his left held a flush, as I had been set
up originally with a full house. We raised around again,
and the flush hand folded. Heavy Jowls and I stared at
each other across the table. I now had seven hundred
dollars of my own money in the pot. Squarely in the
middle, that was me. Heavy Jowls raised two hundred
and fifty; I met it and called. Behind me, I could hear
Steve's angry breathing as I had taken the two hundred
and fifty dollars of call money from his chips.

Heavy Jowls held four 5's.

I held four Queens!

Impassively, he pushed the pot to me. He knew . . .
and I knew, but he couldn't say anything. Picking up my
hand, I palmed out the extra Queen, sleighted in the
missing Spade, and mixed them into the rest of the dis-
cards. Heavy Jowls lit a cigarette. "Your face looks familiar," he said. "Are you a friend of Bill's?" His voice
was offhand.

"Yeah," I said. "I know him well." That was the tip-
off, of course—the round-the-world introduction of professional gamblers.

Heavy Jowls shrugged. "Haven't seen him lately," he
said.

The game broke up about an hour later. I tried no
more killings, playing the game straight, and stalling to
protect my winnings. Walking out of the hotel, I was

about three thousand five hundred dollars to the good. I peeled off seven hundred dollars . . . making it 20 percent for the Greek, and returned his five hundred show money. He grunted, and shoved it in his pocket. "I didn't like for you to use my show money," he said.

"You unhappy now?" I asked.

"No, but it wasn't part of the agreement." He pulled his gray soft hat down firmly on his head and signaled a cab. For just a moment he hesitated before getting in the door. "It was a good night," he said softly, then climbing into the taxi, he added, "but card mechanics don't live long."

"I've had it," I said.

He rode off down the street.

In my pocket, including my winnings and my original stake, was a little more than three thousand dollars.

Enough dough to get Greenleaf.

FIFTEEN

"Your name," asked Cannon, "is Gerald Lightbody. Is that correct?"

"Yes, sir." Lightbody identified himself as the superintendent of a small apartment building approximately half a block down the street from the house on East Eighty-ninth. He stated further under examination by Cannon that he worked approximately two hours each day in the brownstone. Early in the morning, he would check and fire the furnace and at that same time set out the trash cans for collection. Then later in the morning, he would return and put the cans back in the basement. In the evenings, before retiring, once again he would check the furnace, remove the ashes, and fire it for the night.

"You've been in and out of the furnace room many times. Are you very familiar with it?" asked Cannon.

"Yes, sir," agreed Lightbody. "Know it as well as my own face."

"Before the night of November twenty-second, last year, and the next time you saw the furnace room—several days later—were there any things missing? Familiar objects which usually were in that room?"

"Yes. There was a heavy wooden bench, and a piece of canvas about eight feet square. . . ."

"All right." Cannon thought a moment. "About the bench, what was it used for?"

"Sort of a workbench. Pound and nail things on it," replied Lightbody.

"Was it strong enough to support the weight of a man?"

"Yes, sir," testified Lightbody. "I've sat on it myself and smoked a cigarette."

"Was it long enough for you to lie down?"

"Just about. Never tried it, though."

"Now, about the canvas tarpaulin, what was it used for?" asked the prosecuting attorney.

"To put down on the floor, when there was a little painting to be done—so paint and turpentine didn't spill around and get all over things."

"And after November twenty-second, Mr. Lightbody," Cannon emphasized his words, "you never saw either the bench or the canvas again."

"That's right," Lightbody testified.

"Very clear," said Cannon. "Now those duties, which you told about, took only a few hours of your time. They did not in any way conflict with your other job at the apartment house?"

"No, sir." Lightbody was a small wiry man with heavy shoulders and large red hands. "Matter of fact, a lot of supers maybe hold a couple other little jobs like that. . . ."

"Were you ever asked, or expected, to do other chores?"

"Well . . . yes. Not very often, and they didn't amount to much. I usually kept the sidewalks and steps swept up. And once in a while, I'd fix something in the house . . . plumbing, or an electrical outlet . . . when it went wrong. Simple things like that."

"On these different occasions when you were around the house, did you ever see Isham Reddick?"

"Sure. I saw him a lot of times."

"Did you ever talk with him?"

"Yes. I talked with him quite a bit."

"Did Isham Reddick ever offer to help you with any of the chores you might be doing?"

"No, sir. Not exactly. He'd hang around and smoke a cigarette, and sometimes put out a hand to brace the ladder . . . things along that line. But he didn't believe in getting his hands dirty, that man didn't! If you ask me, he thought he was too good for the job!"

"Did he ever tell you that, Mr. Lightbody?"

"He sure did. He put on a lot of airs . . . well, like smoking Congress cigarettes. Special cigarettes they were, cost thirty-five cents a pack. And believe me, on his salary he couldn't afford 'em."

"Objection," Denman stated.

"Sustained. Strike out the last statement of the witness," directed the judge.

"Please continue, Mr. Lightbody," Cannon suggested.

"Well, this one time I came over to put in a little pane

of glass which had been broken, and me and the missus was going out later. To see some of her relations across town, and I was dressed up. It was on a Sunday, and I hadn't a chance to get my paycheck cashed, and I needed some money. I asked Reddick if he would loan me five bucks until Monday—when I'd get to the bank to get my check cashed. Reddick laughs and says sure, he'd lend me as much dough as I wanted. He pulled out a roll of bills and hands me a twenty! While he was doing this, he keeps laughing and I guess he didn't notice that an envelope fell out of his pocket. I picked this envelope up and hand it to him, noticing that a bunch of figures are written on it. Reddick takes the envelope, wads it up, and tosses it away on the steps to the entryway . . . where I was working."

"Did Reddick say anything to you at that time?"

"Well, I thanked him for the loan and he told me to forget it . . . real offhand like he was a big shot. It sort of raised my hair, and I said it was nice to know one rich man, anyhow."

"What did Isham Reddick reply to that?"

"He said he was rich, and soon he'd be richer."

"Let me get this straight, please, Mr. Lightbody. Isham Reddick said he was rich, and soon he'd be richer. Is that correct?"

"Yes, sir," agreed Lightbody.

"All right, please continue. What happened next?"

"Reddick went back into the house, and I finished up the job. As I was walking down the steps, I saw the wadded-up envelope laying on the stairs where Reddick had thrown it. It didn't look good there, so I picked it up. There wasn't any wastepaper container around, so I just stuffed it in my pocket and took it home to throw it away. When I got there, my missus wanted to leave right away—and I forgot all about it, until later." Lightbody paused for breath, then continued. "The next week the missus went through my pockets to send the suit to the cleaners. She found the envelope and showed it to me; she asked if I wanted to keep it, as she thought it belonged to me. . . ."

"When your wife found the envelope, what did she say to you, Mr. Lightbody?"

"She said, 'Is this anything important'?"

"What did you reply?"

"I replied that I didn't know what it was. I asked to see it, then I looked at it and saw the list of figures, and remembered Reddick had thrown it away. So then I said, 'No, this isn't important. I'll get rid of it.' I tossed it on top of the desk where I keep my old bills and receipts and stuff, and intended to throw it away. But it just slipped my mind until the police started asking me questions."

"When the police came to talk to you, you suddenly remembered the envelope with the figures on it, and you gave it to the authorities, is that right, Mr. Lightbody?"

"Yes, sir. That's exactly what happened."

Cannon held up an envelope, badly wrinkled, and handed it to Lightbody. "Is this the same envelope you picked up, after Isham Reddick had thrown it away?"

Lightbody inspected it carefully, then nodded. "Yes, sir. This is the same one. The cops asked me to mark it . . . right here." He pointed to his initials in a corner.

"Thank you, Mr. Lightbody," said Cannon. Turning toward the jury, he said, "I'm now going to read the figures on this envelope and offer it into evidence. On one side of the envelope is the name of Isham Reddick, his address, together with stamp and postmark. The name and address are typewritten, and there are no return name and address, on the envelope. On the reverse side are six amounts . . . figures written in a pencil. These figures are listed one beneath the other, and the first figure is preceded by a dollar sign." Cannon held the envelope before him and read:

$ 1,000.00
1,800.00
2,000.00
4,000.00
6,600.00
8,500.00
_____

"Beneath the last figure of $8,500.00 a line is drawn, but no total is entered. If you should care to know the total, I believe the figures make $23,900.00. Also, by the side of the figures, are the words, written in pencil 'and more to come.'" Cannon handed the envelope to the jury for examination.

Turning back to Lightbody, Cannon said, "There's one other point regarding which I would like to ask you some questions. You heard Miss Deems testify that on the evening of November twenty-second, Isham Reddick told her that the defendant, here, had instructed him to inform the help that they could have the night off, as well as the following day. Did you have a similar discussion with Reddick?"

"Yes, sir. The phone rang . . ."

"At what time, Mr. Lightbody . . . and the date please?"

"It was the early evening and we were just sitting

down to dinner—about six o'clock. It was the evening of November twenty-second. Isham Reddick called to tell me the boss said not to bother about the furnace as it was so warm, and to take the next day off as he was going out of town."

"So you didn't go back to tend the fire that night of November twenty-second, or the morning of the twenty-third . . . as you normally would?"

"No, sir. Reddick said to tell my wife the same thing about cleaning. And I told her."

Cannon excused Lightbody from the stand, and Denman reserved the right to cross-examine the witness later. The prosecuting attorney then recalled Alvin Hartney, the handwriting expert, to the witness chair. "Mr. Hartney," Cannon addressed him, "you have examined this exhibit," Cannon handed him the envelope with the figures, "is that not correct?"

"Yes, sir," replied Hartney.

"You have also examined other identified specimens of Isham Reddick's handwriting . . . a note which he wrote to a garage, a post card he once sent to Miss Deems, and other samples of his writing?"

"That is true. I have examined them carefully."

"Is the writing on the envelope written by the same hand which wrote the garage notation, Miss Deems' card, and the other identified specimens of Isham Reddick's handwriting?"

"The writing is the same."

"You can say without any doubt in your mind that Isham Reddick wrote the figures, and the other words, on the back of the envelope?"

"Yes, sir." Hartney was certain.

Cannon turned the witness over to Denman. The attorney for the defense took up his cross-examination. He carried his heavy horn-rimmed glasses in his hand, tapping them thoughtfully. "I've always understood, Mr. Hartney, that it's more difficult to identify figures than characters of the alphabet. Is that correct?"

"Well . . . to some degree."

"Will you explain 'some degree'?"

"Figures are usually written more uniformly than letters of the alphabet."

"I see. Now . . . in looking over the list of figures written on the back of this envelope, I find examples of the figures: 1, 2, 4, 5, 6, 8, and 0. The figures, or numerals, 3–7–9 are missing. On the post card which Isham Reddick wrote to Miss Deems there is the house address using the numerals 3 and 7 . . . and of course the numerals for Eighty-ninth Street. The only figure then . . . in common . . . between the envelope and the post card is the figure 8! Do you mean to tell me, Mr. Hartney," Denman demanded scathingly, "that you can determine . . . without doubt . . . on the basis of just one numeral?"

"There were other reasons," replied Hartney.

"What reasons? Certainly no more numerals! On the note to the garage, Isham Reddick simply scribbled a reply on the back of the bill. I'll read you his reply, and point out that it was undated. He wrote: 'This bill was paid day before yesterday.' " Denman paused, then continued, "Well, I'm waiting for an answer to my question. What are the other reasons?"

"On the envelope he added the words 'and more to come.' "

Denman repeated the words "and more to come," satirically. "In his post card to Miss Deems, Reddick simply said: 'See you soon. Home tomorrow.'" He paused, and then asked deliberately, "On the basis of his signature, the words: 'this bill was paid day before yesterday,' 'see you soon, home tomorrow,' and, of course, the single numeral number 8, you can identify the handwriting?"

"Yes, sir," Hartney replied definitely. "The words may be different, but the letters are the same."

"I'm not talking about letters," Denman interrupted. "I'm talking about numerals. The only numerals you know definitely Reddick ever wrote are 3, 7, 8, and 9. So how can you possibly tell me that he wrote the rest?"

"Yes, it's possible," Hartney retorted angrily. "He wrote other numerals, too!"

Suddenly, Denman remembered. Quickly, he dismissed the witness. Hartney looked mutely at the judge, and began slowly to rise from his chair. The judge watched him carefully, then said, "It is the duty of this court to discover the truth. I wish to put a question to the witness. Mr. Hartney, you have just said that Isham Reddick wrote other figures. Will you please tell the court what other figures he wrote, and where you saw them?"

Hartney looked straight up toward the judge. "Yes, your honor," he said. "When Isham Reddick made out his chauffeur's application, he wrote his age, height, and weight . . . and in these figures are included 1, 3, 5, 6, and 7. This gave me the numerals 1, 5, 6, and 8 in common between his identified handwriting and the figures on the envelope. These are more than sufficient."

"Thank you, Mr. Hartney," said the judge. Hartney left the stand. Denman ignored him, and asked permission to recall Gerald Lightbody. When Lightbody was seated, Denman considered him carefully. The attorney for the defense was uneasy. The evidence which in his opinion was at best highly circumstantial was, however, slowly tightening around his client. Evidence which should show, somewhere, a wide crack . . . and into which he could drive a wedge . . . seemed to become more solid as he attacked it. Denman hunched his lean figure forward, picking his way carefully, attempting to discredit Lightbody's testimony by establishing the witness's hostility.

"Mr. Lightbody, you testified in your own words that Isham Reddick 'didn't like to get his hands dirty.' Is that right?"

"That's right. He sure didn't!"

"In other words, Mr. Lightbody, because Isham Reddick wouldn't do the work you were paid to do, you thought of him as not wanting to get his hands dirty?"

"Well . . ."

"Did Isham Reddick ever ask you to do his work?"

"No," replied the superintendent.

"But you still prefer to sneer at Reddick? Tell me," Denman's voice was casual, "do you like to bowl?"

"Yes," agreed Lightbody, guardedly, "I bowl a little."

"And you go to an occasional movie?"

"Yes."

"Perhaps a ball game . . . now and then?"

"Once in a while . . ."

"So," Denman summed up, "you bowl, you go to movies, you see an occasional ball game. You spend an optional fifty cents here, a dollar there. Perhaps a couple of dollars, but you like to do it. Is that right?"

Lightbody squirmed uneasily. "Well . . . once in a while . . ."

Denman's voice cut in quickly. "It's all right for you to enjoy your pleasures, but when Isham Reddick spent ten or twelve cents extra for a package of cigarettes, because he liked them, because he bought Congress cigarettes, you accuse him of putting on airs. What standards do you use to measure people, Mr. Lightbody?"

Lightbody cleared his throat and crossed his legs uneasily. "Well . . ."

"Another question, if you please! It's Sunday, and you don't have any money. It's your own fault, because you have a check . . . but you don't get it cashed. You ask Isham Reddick to lend you five dollars. Reddick is pleasant and generous. Instead of giving you five dollars, he gives you twenty dollars! You said it raised your hair . . . and not only are you not grateful to your friend, but you try to read a sinister motive into the situation. Isn't that right?"

Lightbody, now red in the face and angry, shook his head. "No!" he shouted.

"What do you mean . . . no? In one breath you say Isham Reddick is laughing, and in the next breath you infer that he isn't joking when he says he is going to be rich soon." Denman realized that he was on a treadmill. He had no interest in painting Reddick as a friendly sympathetic character . . . other than to prove his client had no motive to kill him. At best, he was only leading Lightbody to give a wretched performance before the jury. Always, of course, there was the possibility the witness might lose his temper. Denman kept plugging at him, "So Reddick befriends you, helps you, lends you money—and in return you attempt to besmirch him in every way?"

"You didn't know him!" shouted Lightbody. "Sometimes you'd a thought he was head of the whole house. But not when the boss was around . . . then he'd crawl and bow around just as pretty as you please. Even that night he called me. 'You don't need to make the fire tonight. Take tomorrow off, too,' he says. Why, you'd a thought it was a paid vacation he was giving me. It didn't mean anything at all! There hadn't been a fire in the house for a couple days anyway, because it was so warm!"

Denman, who had turned away, suddenly swung around and faced Lightbody. "Did I understand you to say, that there had been no fire in the house for several days? And there was none on the twenty-second of November?"

"That's what I said," Lightbody replied, sullenly.

"Isn't it odd that Reddick should call you, deliberately, to tell you not to bother with the fire . . . when there was no fire?" Denman felt a rising surge of excitement. Perhaps he had finally found a thread; without knowing where it might lead, he would attempt to unwind it. "Did Reddick know there was no fire?"

"Sure, he knew it, but that was his way . . . just trying to be a big shot." Suddenly Lightbody dashed Denman's hopes. "It was just Reddick's way of putting it. He didn't have no authority to say nothing, unless the boss told him to." Lightbody shifted his eyes toward the defendant, then quickly moved them away.

Sixteen

Three thousand bucks . . . well, it was enough to get started after Greenleaf. During the days and nights, while I was getting back on my feet, I had thought of nothing else. I'd lie on my bed in the hotel room and think about him—trying to draw his face into focus. I never could do it; I couldn't even pretend. Always I would see his figure—the body of a man with a blank face. It reminded me of the paper cutout dolls which have figures completely clothed with hands and feet . . . but no face. You slipped the clothes over another little body with a face, and then the doll was complete.

Only one person I knew of had known what Greenleaf looked like; that was old Will Shaw and he was dead. Only one person I had known might possibly have recognized his voice; Tally. And she was dead, too.

Lying on the bed, I'd watch the room grow dark. Far below, the lights of the city would climb up the side of the building and crawl over the sill, inching their way stealthily up the walls. I'd lie on my back and watch the shadows flitting and flickering on the ceiling while the rest of the room remained in darkness. My mind would pick at the identity of Greenleaf, pawing and worrying the few bits of information I had concerning him. At first, I couldn't concentrate very long; my mind would wander away and all I could think was "Greenleaf . . . Greenleaf," over and over. But it didn't mean very much, because the word itself had no substance. I could just as well have been thinking "Atlantic . . . Atlantic" or "Pacific . . . Pacific." Suddenly, something would snap in my mind, and for a few minutes I could concentrate very hard and think very clearly. The ball of hate would roll around in my stomach until I could stand it no longer. I had quit drinking, so I'd go in the bath and draw a glass of water and sip it while I smoked a cigarette. In the dark the cigarette lost its taste and only the ember on its end would tell me it was alight. The glowing eye of it burning red to match my own hatred.

Over the days, and the weeks, certain things began to fall into place. Not all at once, but little by little. Obviously, of course, Greenleaf was not his correct name, but an alias. And an alias, unfortunately, which he had especially assumed in his relations with the old man. Greenleaf was a confidence man . . . the select, the aristocracy of the criminal world. He was far more intelligent, more cunning, more shrewd than the average criminal. Greenleaf was a new and assumed name, and one that would have absolutely no criminal record.

Secondly, he was utterly ruthless . . . a killer opportunist, rather than a premeditating murderer. Possibly the act of murder was distasteful to him; it might explain his selection of death by falling and accident . . . rather than by a lethal weapon. On this point, of course, I could not be sure; it was merely conjecture.

Lastly, I felt that Greenleaf worked alone. Most confidence men prefer to do so, except where a confederate is needed to arrange and color a specific situation. There have been instances where a number of con men . . . half a dozen to a dozen . . . have all worked together to pull off a big setup; but this is the exception. With trusting, old Will Shaw, he needed no help.

Undoubtedly, though, somewhere Greenleaf had one other man . . . a printer. He had to have a printer, and a good one, to print the false plates. This, however, was not unusual either. Every man in the confidence game has criminal printing connections somewhere; the con men need printers to make up phony letterheads, phony bill heads, fake stock certificates; worthless bond issues, and all the rest of the paper they hang. So, Greenleaf had a printer—someone to print up the beautiful authentic fives, tens, and twenties.

There was another point which was difficult to determine. Was Greenleaf passing the queer himself, or was he wholesaling it? A counterfeit wholesaler will buy up the queer money at ten cents on the dollar; resell it to passers for another markup; the passers, in turn, pass it as money and keep the difference. If Greenleaf was wholesaling it, I might never find him. If, however, he was passing it, himself, I might be able to catch him.

After thinking about it for a long time, I finally decided Greenleaf was passing it personally. Although wholesaling is faster, and makes a buck easier, it is far more dangerous! Because tremendous sums of counterfeit dough will hit different cities at the same time, the chances of its detection increase as the queer money passes through more banks and is seen by more tellers. This in turn adds up to the phony bills being detected more quickly by the Treasury men. With beautiful plates, such as Greenleaf had, he might go on safely for years, passing the money himself. With care not to flood the market, he could live forever . . . like a millionaire. Making only a split with his printer, Greenleaf would have no fear of other partners, wholesalers, and passers being picked up, possibly for another and entirely different crime, and squealing to the cops. It seemed logical to me that Greenleaf would pass the money himself.

After I had the money from the poker game, I went to see Dave Sherz. Dave operated an investigation and detective agency; before that, he had been captain of a squad of private guards protecting the wheel in a gambling house in Nevada. I'd worked there one season, a long time back, and knew Sherz from those days.

He remembered me and gave me a hearty handshake. "Sit down, Lew," he said. "How've things been going?"

"So, so, Dave," I looked around the office. "Where are the walnut-paneled walls, the oversexed secretary, and the dead bodies?"

Dave laughed. "You been watching too many movies," he said. He yawned, stretched his arms above his head, and leaned back in his chair—planting his feet on the desk. "This business is so quiet," he said, "I go to church baking sales just for the excitement."

"No murders?" I asked pretending surprise.

"Hell no. The cops would run us off, anyway. Nothing but suspicious husbands, more suspicious wives, and a few insurance investigations. . . ."

"Well," I suggested slowly, "perhaps you'd be interested in trying to dig up something for me."

"I'm interested in digging up anything, including flowers," he replied.

"You kept up with the bunco boys?" I asked. Back in the Reno days, one of Sherz's jobs had been to watch for sharpers, con men, and known criminals to keep them out of the club.

"Some," he said. "After I blew Reno, I hired on in Las Vegas and I've been in business for myself the last few years. Anyone you interested in particularly?"

"Just one guy," I told him. "His name is Greenleaf which may be real, but I doubt it. I don't know what he looks like, where he came from, what's his background . . . or anything else that's going to be very helpful."

"That ain't much," said Dave.

"The only other thing I have on him is that he was hanging around Philadelphia about a year ago. He was still in Philly up to a few months ago. He had a checking account in a bank there; what bank, I don't know. He signed checks which cleared using the name Greenleaf. I have no idea where he lived, or what his initials were."

"And that's all?"

"That's all."

"I can't place the name. Never heard of anybody in the bunco business named Greenleaf. I can check the police records for the name or alias."

"Okay," I agreed.

"Also I got a few respectable connections because of

my insurance tie-ups. I might be able to find something on the checking account in Philadelphia, although I can't guarantee it. Would that be of any help?"

"Anything would help," I assured him.

"I'll get on it," Dave said. He took his feet off the desk, and shook a cigarette out of a pack. Lighting it, he asked, "Any reason for me to know why you're interested in Greenleaf?"

"No," I replied, "there's not the slightest reason."

He shrugged. "Soon as I have anything, I'll call you."

I took out several bills, placing them on his desk. "Whatever the balance is, let me know."

Dave grinned. "For old times' sake, Lew, that's enough. Unless I have to hire a couple dog sleds for Alaska."

There was another point which I had been thinking about; it might mean something—or nothing, but it wasn't anything on which Dave could help me. However, a professor at Columbia University could; his name was Thurman Simons and he was a professor of Romance languages. Professor Simons was fluent in Italian, Spanish, French, and Portuguese. In addition to these, he was pretty handy with German, Dutch, and a few other assorted tongues. I called the professor on the phone, making an appointment to meet him the following day after classes. To my surprise, Simons was a comparatively young man . . . short, pudgy, and with brown colorless hair. He wore green sunglasses with pink plastic rims, and seemed absolutely incapable of sitting still. While we talked, he ran his finger around his collar, brushed his hair with the palms of his hands, nervously adjusted his sunglasses, shifted his position clockwise around the chair, smoked incessantly, and when there seemed nothing else to do, tapped the toe of his shoe on the floor.

Sitting down to talk to Simons, I made it clear that I wanted to pay for his services. He waved my offer aside, "If I can help you, I'll be delighted." Patting his hands together nervously, he added, "If you still insist, make a donation in my name to the Red Cross. But perhaps, after all, I can't help you."

"Well," I replied slowly, "it really isn't important . . . except in an extremely personal way. You see, Professor," I ad libbed as sincerely as I could, looking him in the eye and being unable to find his gaze behind the green glasses, "my wife died a few months ago. Before she died, she was in . . . well, a sort of delirium, and she kept repeating words which sounded like 'loon who ought to.' It meant absolutely nothing to any of us, and perhaps she was only making sounds . . . entirely meaningless, but sounding like that. Naturally, a death makes a tremendous impression on a family, and all of us have often wondered if she was trying to tell us something."

"Very sad, Mr. Mountain," Simons said sympathetically, "you have my condolences. I don't know if I can help, but I shall try. Tell me, did your wife speak another language besides English?"

"No. Not that I know of . . ."

"Hmmm." The professor flexed his fingers, putting them end to end forming a tent, then collapsed it. "Perhaps she had studied some language while going to school?"

I shook my head. "I honestly don't know, Professor. Perhaps in high school, although she never mentioned it." I paused and added, "The best explanation, after all, might be that she really was saying 'loon who ought to.' "

"Loon who ought to . . . loon who ought to?" Professor Simons tilted his head, repeating the phrase with small interjections of sounds and cluckings of his own. Behind his glasses, I would have sworn that his unseen eyes had rolled up in his head. He cocked his head to one side and appeared to be listening to himself. After a very long time, he said, "What you have told me about the phrase 'loon who ought to' very conceivably has been distorted in pronunciation. Perhaps your deceased wife may have given it a wrong accent and possibly . . . quite unknowingly . . . you have distorted it more." He waved his hands slightly. "Several possibilities come to my mind, the most obvious one being French. The French have a phrase meaning literally 'the one or the other,' and idiomatically meaning 'either.' "

"What is the phrase?" I asked.

"*L'un ou l'autre,*" replied Professor Simons. As he pronounced it, the phrase sounded like "lun-ooo-lowtra." "Does that help any?" Simons asked. Once again, in my mind I could hear Tally's voice telling me of her conversation with Greenleaf. He had called following Will Shaw's funeral, demanding the counterfeit plates. Tally frightened, and at the same time angry, denied having them and threatened to turn them over to the Treasury department if she found them. Greenleaf laughed, reminding her of the checks she had signed. He had said, "I'll pay you for them, or you might prefer another accident in the family." Then possibly, he had added "*l'un ou l'autre.*" The meaning of the phrase, as placed in his conversation, was logical: one or the other . . . either . . . take your pick. I turned to Simons, "I don't suppose we'll ever really know what she meant, Professor. But thanks for your help."

"I've done very little," Simons replied with a deprecatory shake of his head. "I'll think about it some more, and perhaps something else will come to mind. You might call me later in the week."

"Thanks," I replied. Shaking his hand, I said, "I'll drop a check to the Red Cross."

But I didn't call back the professor. After thinking over his suggestion concerning the phrase, I was convinced that he had hit the idiom right in the middle of the accent.

Several days passed before I heard from Dave Sherz. After he called me at the hotel, I dropped around to his office to see him. It didn't appear that he had moved from his chair since the last time I had seen him. Waving me to a seat, he pushed over a photostatic copy of a check. "This print is pretty grainy," he said. "We took it off of a microfilm negative, but it might be one from the guy you're looking for."

I examined it. The check had been written on the Philadelphia Mercantile Bank & Trust Company; it was made out to cash; was for the sum of thirty-five dollars; and had been signed by Derek A. Greenleaf. "We checked the banks pretty carefully," Sherz explained, "and settled on this bird. Other accounts under the name of Greenleaf, which we came across, didn't hold anything when we checked them. Some had been established for a good many years, others had permanent residences. This particular account—the one for Derek Greenleaf—ran for less than a year."

"When did he close it?" I asked.

"He never did, actually. The account was opened with

a cash deposit for one thousand dollars. He checked against it regularly with four checks a month, each check for thirty-five dollars. Finally after about six months or so, he just stopped writing checks. One day, he cashed a check for the balance in the account. That was that."

"What address did he give?"

"A number on Spruce Street . . ." Sherz checked a small book, and gave it to me. "You familiar with it?" he asked.

"Not that address," I told him, "but I know Spruce." It is a street of cheap rooming houses and light-house-keeping flats filled with a transient, restless population.

"Well," explained Sherz, "we looked up this number on Spruce. It was a typical crummy boarding house. The landlady's never heard of anyone named Greenleaf."

"The bank had to send him a statement each month," I said. "What happened to them? Were they returned?"

Dave shrugged impatiently. "I thought of that," he said. "But I suppose in a joint like that boarding house where the landlady had so damned many roomers she can't remember them, all the mail is just tossed out unless there's a forwarding address."

"What did you find out from the police records?"

"Nothing that fits," replied Sherz frankly. "The alias Greenleaf is unknown. Derek as a first name has been used a couple of times, but the times and places are wrong. A real smooth operator named Eddie Jackson, alias Derek Moore, used it in San Francisco. He's still in the can, and has been for three years, in California. Another old timer, Fred Hoskins, once used the name Derek Tone, but . . . hell, Hoskins is close to seventy-five years old and he's been going straight down in Birmingham, Alabama. Living with a married son . . ."

Picking up my hat, I walked to the door. "It was a good pitch," I said. I felt depressed.

"Lew," Sherz said, "I'm sorry there wasn't more. I didn't want to run up a bill on you. Do you want me to keep after it?"

I shook my head. "This guy is pretty fancy," I said. "Maybe it's the end of the road. If I need some help, I'll let you know."

Back to the paper dolls again. Here and there—a glimpse, a fragment of a pattern, but no man, no person, no face. A man using the name Derek Greenleaf, a con man with a thousand-dollar account in a bank to swing a deal, a man who used French phrases, a man who would kill an old man and a young woman. Today, right now, a man with the means and opportunity to make millions of dollars.

But still no face!

Sometime during the night, while I was asleep, the idea came to me. Subconsciously I worked it out, because in the morning I awakened with the answer. Rolling out of bed, I dressed hurriedly and rushed to Penn Station. There I caught a train to Philadelphia. I had breakfast on the train, and kept going over the idea in my mind. Sherz had told me that Greenleaf used a Spruce Street address when he opened the account in the bank. Greenleaf knew, of course, that the bank took microfilm records of all checks as part of its own accounting system, but it was important to Greenleaf to recover the canceled checks. He needed them for his own protection . . . to use as a threat against either Will Shaw or Tally. So, when he gave his address as

Spruce Street, he had some way of recovering the checks from there.

Dave Sherz had advanced the theory that the landlady probably threw out all the mail that wasn't claimed, or for which she had no forwarding address. This of course was possible, and if it was true made Greenleaf's job of recovering his mail quite simple. All he had to do was take it. Consequently, one had to assume that Greenleaf either lived in the rooming house—under another alias, or he lived close by in the neighborhood where he could pick up the mail without comment!

Arriving in Philadelphia at the Thirtieth Street Station, I telephoned the Mercantile Bank and got through to the personal checking department. I was informed that customer's statements were mailed the fourth of each month. Leaving the station, I took a cab to the address on Spruce Street. Approaching it, I had the driver continue to the corner where I got out. Walking back, I stopped in front of the number. It was a shabby four-story house refaced with imitation brick siding. A door, in need of paint, opened directly from the street into a cramped dark hallway. Overhead a weak light burned within a swirled brown and green glass globe. Against one wall, a heavy table stood beneath a chipped oval mirror. On the table were stacks of advertisements, newspapers, hand bills, and letters. The hallway branched into a Y . . . one dark corridor leading to the rear of the house, the other forming an extremely steep and narrow stairway to the upper floors. At that moment, footsteps approached from the rear of the corridor and a fat, red-faced woman dressed in a sleazy satin dress came puffing into the hall. She peered at me suspiciously, and in a strident voice asked if I was looking for someone. "Yes," I said politely, "I'd like to see the land-lady."

"I'm her," she replied, "and I don't want to buy noth-ing, and I ain't got no vacant rooms. So in either case, good-bye!"

"I'm sorry," I told her. "Your place was recom-mended to me by a friend of mine . . . Derek Green-leaf . . ."

"Who you think you're kidding?" she demanded bel-ligerently. "And what you think you're putting over? A little while back, another guy was sneaking around here asking about him. I told him I'd never heard of no Greenleaf and I ain't, neither."

That had been Dave Sherz or one of his men. "Miss," I said, holding my temper in check against the old bag, "I really do need help. I wish you'd listen."

"I don't like cops poking their noses in my business," she replied. "I run a respectable house, and I got a right to my own privacy."

"Yes . . . sure . . . certainly." I agreed with her. "But I'm not a cop. This is strictly something personal between Greenleaf and me."

"I told you I don't know any Greenleaf!" She turned and started down the corridor.

"Wait!" I said, withdrawing my wallet and taking out two twenties; I held them up so she could see them. "I'll pay for your time, if you'll help me. You're a business woman," I added quickly, "and I imagine you've had deadbeat roomers run out on you without paying their bills."

"Not any more I don't!" she snorted. "Now they got to pay in advance!" Perhaps I only imagined it, but the suspicion in her eyes dimmed a little.

"This guy Greenleaf owes me some money, and I need it," I said, throwing together a story. "I trusted him on credit . . . and he beat me out."

"Your own fault!" she said.

"Not entirely," I explained. "It was really my partner's fault. He advanced the credit. My partner died last week, and I've been trying to find Greenleaf ever since."

"Nobody ever stayed here by that name," she replied. "What'd he look like?"

"I don't know. I never saw him."

"Jesus! How'd you expect me to help you?"

"Well . . . think back carefully. For a period of six or seven months, each month about the fifth or sixth day a letter was addressed to this house. It was delivered in the name of Derek A. Greenleaf. Do you remember seeing it?"

"The same letter?" she asked.

"No. It was a different letter each month, but it always came about the same time. It would be in a large, heavy, brown envelope . . . perhaps like the banks use."

"And it was made out to a guy named Greenleaf?" She squinted her little pig eyes in thought. "Any letters supposed to have come lately?" she asked.

"I don't think so," I told her. "There's always a possibility of course. But I think they finally stopped coming about five or six months ago."

"I've been running this place for nearly fifteen years," she said, "and mail keeps coming for people I can't even remember. I've gotten in the habit of just running through the mail looking for my own name. I leave the mail there on the table, and the roomers can sort through it themselves." She waddled over to the table, puffing from the exertion, and searched through the pile of letters on its top, looking also among the old ads and newspapers. "There ain't nothing here for any Greenleaf," she announced.

"I think that proves he got it," I told her. "Otherwise, it would still be around . . . or you would remember seeing it. Particularly if all six or seven of the envelopes had accumulated." Pausing a moment, I said casually, "If he wasn't living here under an assumed name, then he must have come in to get it. Do you remember anyone who didn't live here—who stopped in pretty regularly? It would be a man, and he would have a good excuse if you talked to him. He probably always showed up during the first week of each month." There was always the possibility that Greenleaf had known one of the roomers who had passed on the mail to him. However, I didn't believe that Greenleaf would disclose his new name to anyone, if he could help it.

"I don't remember no one particularly," the landlady said. "The roomers, here, have friends of their own visiting. I see a lot of people. The only person I could think of wouldn't be the same man, because he was French. . . ."

"What!" I offered her a cigarette which she refused. Lighting one myself, I said, "A Frenchman used to drop around occasionally? What did he want?"

Pursing her lips, she thought carefully. "Come to think of it, he did drop around pretty regular . . . and usually sometime after the first of the month. I remember because he was always looking for a room . . . asking me for a vacancy. My roomers usually move out on the last day of the month, or the first day . . . if they're moving someplace else. This Frenchman would show up a few days too late every time. I recollect now, I told him to come around the last week of the month, but he never did. I never let him a room."

I thought it over. It made sense. Greenleaf evidently knew some French. A con man is always a good actor, and Greenleaf could fake an accent well enough, no doubt, to fool anyone as stupid as the landlady. He timed his visit to pick up the mail; and he was careful to inquire for a room—only when he was quite sure he couldn't get one. Undoubtedly, Greenleaf had no desire to be tied to the Spruce Street address in case anything went wrong with his plans. "What did this man look like?" I asked.

"He was a big man . . . taller and thinner than you." The landlady struggled to recall the impressions erased by time. "To tell you the truth," she said, "I didn't pay much attention. Thinking back on it, I'd say he was in his fifties. One thing I do remember though, he had a big nose." She nodded her head for emphasis. "Yes, he had a thin face, with a big nose . . . long, too, and gray hair. Dressed real nice."

I handed her the twenty-dollar bills. "Thanks," I said. "You've helped a lot. If you'd go down to the police station and look through some pictures to help identify this man, I'll pay you fifty more."

Her stubby fingers folded the bills into a tiny packet, and stuffed them into the front of her sweaty brassière. Once again her eyes had become suspicious, and she shook her head angrily. "I won't have no truck with the cops," she replied. "I was just helping you out neighborly. But I don't want nothing to do with the cops!"

Walking down Spruce Street, I felt good. A thin face, a long nose, gray hair, fifty years, tall and lean . . . all details added to the paper doll.

Someday, I'd cut the head right off that doll!

SEVENTEEN

Cannon, spinning the web of his case, was still concerned with the problem of motive. He was confident that he had impressed the jury concerning the corpus delicti; the evidence was, in part, circumstantial —but, in his opinion, indisputable. Sometime on the night of November twenty-second, or early in the morning of November twenty-third, a servant known as Isham Reddick had been murdered, his body dismembered and most of it destroyed through cremation in the furnace of the brownstone located on East Eighty-ninth Street. Not all evidence of the crime, however, had been consumed and there remained a severed finger with an identifiable print, a tooth, a handful of ashes, blood-stains on floor, canvas, and bench, a section of human leg bone; in addition to other miscellaneous evidence including the possible murder weapon—a gun and spent bullet, and the dismembering instrument—a bloody hatchet.

Cannon was convinced that he had established the fact of murder, and had identified the victim, as required by law. There remained, however, the motive. Why had the defendant killed Isham Reddick?

No murder is committed without motive unless the murderer is insane, and the defendant in this case, obviously, was not in such condition. There remained to be resolved then the reason behind the murder, and Cannon believed the motive was blackmail. The chauffeur-valet had been blackmailing his employer. Cannon had evidence indicating Reddick had collected nearly twenty-four thousand dollars . . . possibly more. Murder has often been done for less! Seeing no letup to his financial bleeding, the defendant had killed his blackmailer.

Regarding this particular point, a key certainly in his case, Cannon had spent much time, much work to buttress his theory. He next introduced three witnesses. The first to take the stand was Miss Beatrice Hyman, a saleswoman employed in a jewelry store located on Fifth Avenue in New York City. "Miss Hyman," said Cannon, "among the effects and possessions in the room of Isham Reddick was found a receipt—a sales slip which you identified as having been made out by yourself."

"Yes, sir. It was a receipt for three hundred and fifty dollars for a wrist watch I sold him."

"When was this?"

"According to the records in the store, it was October seventeenth of last year."

"Now, Miss Hyman," continued Cannon, "I'm going

to show you a photograph. Will you please identify it."
He handed her a black and white, glossy print.

Beatrice Hyman, a slim, efficient woman, looked at
the photograph carefully. "That is the same man to
whom I sold the watch," she stated.

"Did he give you his name?"

"He told me his name was Isham Reddick. And I
made out the sales record to that name."

"Now, you have testified that Isham Reddick purchased a wrist watch for three hundred and fifty dollars.
Do you consider that an expensive watch?"

"Objection," said Denman rising to his feet. "That
calls for an opinion." The court upheld him.

"Miss Hyman," Cannon continued undisturbed, "do
you sell many three-hundred-and-fifty-dollar wrist
watches?"

"Not many," replied the saleswoman.

"Do many of your customers spend a month-and-a-
half salary to purchase a wrist watch?"

Denman objected again, but this time Cannon argued
his point. Addressing the judge, he said, "I do not feel
that this answer calls for an opinion. Miss Hyman has
been selling watches, in this shop, for several years. As a
saleswoman, it is part of her job to determine, within
limits, what a prospective customer can afford, or will
spend."

"But she does not know the financial background of
each customer," Denman took exception.

The judge considered the arguments. Finally, he said,
"Proceed, Mr. Cannon, but cautiously."

Cannon returned to the witness. "Many of your customers . . . the persons who visit your store . . . are
wealthy, or at least well-to-do?"

"Yes, I believe so," Miss Hyman replied clearly.

"Do you have many customers of very little money?"

"No, sir."

"Now, if a man earned two hundred and fifty dollars a month, and bought a three-hundred-and-fifty-dollar wrist watch from you, would you think he was purchasing an expensive watch?"

"Under those circumstances, yes."

"You have less expensive watches to sell, do you not, Miss Hyman?"

"We have some watches starting at seventy-seven dollars; those are our least expensive ones, although they are still excellent watches."

"Did you show any of the seventy-seven dollar watches to Isham Reddick?"

"As I recall, sir, I did. I also showed him some at one hundred and fifty dollars, as well as two hundred and seventy-five dollars. But the one he wanted was priced at three hundred and fifty."

"He paid for it in cash?"

"It was in cash. And it must have been in large bills."

"Why do you believe the payment was in large bills?"

"Well," Miss Hyman explained, "most of our customers have charge accounts. Some of them pay cash, occasionally, and when they do it is usually with bills of large denomination. If Mr. Reddick had paid three hundred and fifty dollars in small bills, it would have made a good-sized pile of money—and I would have remembered it."

"And you don't remember Isham Reddick giving you a large number of bills?"

"No, sir. I don't. It was an ordinary transaction for

us." She paused, then added, "It was half a dozen bills at the most."

"One final question," said Cannon. "Do you sell many three-hundred-and-fifty-dollar watches to chauffeurs?"

"I wouldn't say we do," replied Miss Hyman. Cannon excused the witness, but Denman kept her on the stand for cross-examination.

"Miss Hyman," he addressed her politely, "do you ask strange customers when they come into your store, what they do for a living?"

"Of course not!"

"If I walked into your store, and happened to be . . . say, an engineer on a subway train, would you say to me, 'What do you do for a living?' "

"No, sir."

"Or possibly, Miss Hyman, you can tell at a glance what a man does for a living? If I walked into your store, you could take one glance at me and say, 'That man is a subway engineer'?"

"That isn't correct," replied Miss Hyman angrily.

"Then how did you know Isham Reddick was a chauffeur? Was he wearing a uniform?"

"No, sir. He wasn't wearing a uniform, and I didn't know what he did. I wasn't particularly interested, either."

"Then how did you find out he was a chauffeur?"

"Mr. Cannon told me, when he talked to me."

"So, until Mr. Cannon told you, you didn't know anything about Isham Reddick. As far as you know, you have sold watches, diamonds, and other expensive jewelry to chauffeurs—without knowing it!" He added, "If they weren't wearing uniforms. Is that correct?"

"I—I guess so," she replied.

Denman, having made his point, continued in another direction. "You mentioned, Miss Hyman, that the least expensive watch you have in your shop is seventy-seven dollars. Now, tell me what is your most expensive watch . . . man's watch, that is?"

"I can't be entirely sure, but I'd say several thousand dollars."

"If I wanted, couldn't I buy something more expensive?"

"Yes . . . on a special order."

"It would seem to me that a regular two-thousand-dollar watch should be good enough," Denman observed dryly. "But getting back to Isham Reddick, he bought a three-hundred-and-fifty-dollar watch—not a five-hundred-, or a thousand-, or a fifteen-hundred-dollar one. If he wanted a good watch, and had saved money for one, is there any reason he shouldn't have bought the three-hundred-and-fifty-dollar one?"

"No, no reason at all," agreed Miss Hyman. Denman thanked her, and she stepped down from the chair.

Mr. Dann, of Dann & Glend, Gentlemen's Tailors, impeccably dressed in a gray flannel suit, buttoned-down collar, and delicately knotted tie, somewhat fussily identified himself as senior partner in the exclusive shop which catered to many distinguished New Yorkers, as well as national figures. "Your shop is located on Madison Avenue?" asked Cannon.

"Yes," replied Dann, "we have been in the same location for over thirty years."

"Either you or Mr. Glend . . . your partner . . . personally take care of all your clientele."

"Naturally we have tailors who do the actual cutting,

fitting, and finishing, but Mr. Glend and I wait on our customers. This is strictly a personal business, and we would not consider hiring paid sales people." Dann glanced appraisingly at Cannon's suit, and what he saw, evidently, did not entirely meet with his approval.

"You recall selling three suits of clothes to a man using the name Isham Reddick?" Cannon handed Dann a photograph. "Is this the same man?" Dann identified it, and Cannon continued, "Will you please tell us, in your own words, what happened?"

Dann carefully crossed his flanneled legs. "The . . . ah . . . fellow came into the shop, and I waited on him. He said he was interested in buying some suits. I informed him that we made suits only to order. The suit he was wearing was a ready-made suit of very ordinary material, and I did not expect him to buy. On occasions, we have persons who wander into the shop, evidently under the impression that . . . well, we carry a stock of clothes. This, of course, we have never done. Usually when we tell them our prices, they leave very quickly."

"What are your prices, Mr. Dann?"

"Our suits begin at two hundred dollars. The prices vary depending on the materials selected and other details of the suits."

"When you told Isham Reddick this, what did he say to you?"

"He replied that he would take three suits. That day, he selected cloth for a charcoal gray, a medium gray, and a midnight blue flannel. Mr. Mat measured him. I told the customer that inasmuch as he had not yet established an account with us, we must request him to pay for the cloth and the cutting in advance . . . the balance to be paid when the suits were finished."

"Did Reddick object to that?"

"No, sir. He immediately paid us four hundred dollars."

"On that first trip, he paid you four hundred dollars? Did he pay you in cash?"

"Yes, before he left the shop," replied Mr. Dann, "he gave me four one-hundred-dollar bills."

"Do you remember the suit he was wearing when he came into the shop?"

"I remember thinking only that it was mediocre, although now I cannot recall the details. Actually, I suppose, there were no details to remember—it was that kind of suit." Mr. Dann silently sniffed his disapproval.

"You say a 'mediocre' suit . . . what would you say was a cheap suit?"

"Any mass-produced piece of clothing costing less than fifty dollars," Dann replied promptly.

"Did it surprise you that Isham Reddick bought your expensive suits?"

"Yes," said Dann, "he certainly didn't look as if he could afford them!"

"Objection!" Denman arose to his feet, and the judge sustained him. "No conclusions or opinions, please, Mr. Dann," he corrected the tailor. Cannon, however, had finished his examination of the witness, and the attorney for the defense took over.

"Mr. Dann," Denman opened, "I wish you would look at the suit I'm wearing. Do you consider it a cheap suit?" Denman turned slowly in front of the witness, walking up and down.

"May I take a better look at it?" requested Dann.

"Certainly . . ." Denman moved closer, standing before the witness. Dann examined the lapels quickly, and checked the buttons on the sleeves. "Well?" asked Denman, smiling.

"Your suit, sir," replied Mr. Dann with dignity, "was made by Meade and Thomas, tailors with a good reputation, and competitors of mine for twenty-five years." Shrugging, he added, "You paid at least two hundred and fifty dollars for it—and you could have done better."

A ripple of laughter lapped over the courtroom. Denman smiled and bowed to the witness. "Quite right, sir," he replied. "The next time I will come to see you." Mr. Dann nodded in agreement. "Now," continued Denman, "let's consider Isham Reddick's suits . . . which at two hundred dollars . . . must have been an excellent buy. Do you agree they were an extremely good buy, Mr. Dann?"

"Naturally," agreed Mr. Dann.

"You see nothing unusual in a man paying two hundred dollars for a suit?"

"I see it every day," the tailor pointed out.

"Even three suits at two hundred dollars is a good buy?"

"Excellent . . . an excellent buy. The suits last longer, look better when you change them often. Every gentleman should have at least a minimum of fourteen suits."

"Yes, I quite agree," Denman interrupted the witness. "Now, as I understand it Isham Reddick paid you four hundred dollars on account. Did he ever pay you the balance?"

"No, sir," replied Dann. "He came in for all the fittings, and then we heard nothing more from him. After the suits had been completed for several weeks, we called the number Reddick had left with us. When we asked for him, a policeman took the call. Later, the authorities came to see me."

"And you still believe the suits were a good buy?"

"Absolutely!" Dann stated with finality. Denman then dismissed the tailor. The attorney for the defense felt a growing depression; regardless of Dann's ready agreement concerning the good sense of purchasing quality clothes, he knew that the jury was not in sympathy with a chauffeur paying two hundred dollars for a suit, and purchasing them in lots of three.

Anthony Gillick, an employee of the Monterey Travel Bureau, had a high reedy voice. He identified the picture of Reddick as the man who had called on him the afternoon of November twentieth, of the previous year, in his place of employment at the travel bureau. "What did Isham Reddick want?" asked Cannon.

"He wanted to make a reservation for a flight to Paris on November twenty-fourth."

"Could you make a reservation for him on such short notice?"

"It wasn't too difficult," Gillick piped. "That time of year there's little tourist traffic. Besides he asked for a luxury flight."

"What is the difference in the price of tickets?"

"Regular coach flights are approximately one hundred and fifty dollars less than luxury flights."

"When did Isham Reddick plan to return?"

Gillick shook his head. "I don't know. He purchased only a one-way ticket. I told him he could effect a saving by buying a round-trip ticket, as long as he used it within one year. He said that he didn't plan to return."

"You mean that he didn't plan to return within one year?"

"No," replied Gillick, his voice climbing. With an effort, he lowered it again. "Isham Reddick said that he didn't plan to ever return."

"He told you that?"

"Yes, sir. That is what he said."

"Incidentally, Mr. Gillick, what was the price of the ticket to Paris?"

"Five hundred and seventy-five dollars."

"Did Isham Reddick pay you for it?"

"Yes, sir. In cash."

"Did you ever see Isham Reddick again?"

"No, sir. Twenty-four hours before flight time we called his residence to reaffirm his reservation . . . as is customary." Gillick paused and swallowed quickly, his Adam's apple bobbing. "It was . . . well . . . I was informed that Mr. Reddick was dead."

"Isham Reddick appears to have been a very busy man," Cannon mused aloud, elaborately watching the witness, "five hundred seventy-five dollars for a ticket . . . four hundred dollars for suits . . . three hundred and fifty dollars for a watch . . . that's thirteen hundred and twenty-five dollars. . . ."

Denman interrupted him. "Is this a soliloquy or an examination?"

Slightly exaggerating his motion, Cannon turned his attention to the attorney for the defense. "Oh, I'm sorry," he said, "your witness, Counselor."

Denman, heavily, began his examination of the new witness.

EIGHTEEN

Back in New York, I sorted out my facts.
Shuffling them and reshuffling them in my mind, I dealt
them out for examination. Sometimes they would fit,
and sometimes they wouldn't. Patiently, I'd reshuffle
them and begin all over again. I discovered I could think
better at night, particularly while riding the subway.
Very late, I'd board the last car in the train, on the
Seventh Avenue IRT. In the end car of the train, I'd
stand on the vestibule, at the rear, watching the back
hollows of the tunnels rushing past on both sides. The
lights flicked from red to amber to green as we roared
past, and the rails looked like long twining snakes
crawling back into their pits. There is no rocketing
rhythm, no clicking beat to a subway train, but in their

place is a rushing sense of destination . . . and my destination was Greenleaf.

Finally my facts were assembled, my conclusions reached. I knew that Greenleaf was tall, slightly over six feet; he was slender; had a large, long nose; gray hair; and he spoke some French. I did not believe, however, that he was French; Tally had never mentioned her uncle remarking about his accent . . . and neither had she. Greenleaf had deliberately played the role of a Frenchman for the landlady in Philadelphia. If Greenleaf really had been French, I believed he would have done everything possible to conceal it.

Greenleaf's physical description typed him to play three roles, and undoubtedly he had played them all at some time or other. There is a certain physical type which the United States, England, and France have in common. It is exemplified by a tall, lean, large-nosed man, and in America fits the conception of a Western cowboy. But with a change of accent, he becomes an English sportsman . . . or a French army officer. The British accent, particularly in the Eastern section of the United States, many times becomes difficult to distinguish from, say, Boston accents.

The use of a French phrase by Greenleaf, in his conversation with Tally, led me to believe that he had been playing the part of a well-educated Easterner (or an Englishman) when he had been conning Will Shaw. It was possible, because of the story he gave the old man concerning his Washington connections, that he had represented himself as being employed in some diplomatic capacity. Will Shaw, in his senile condition, might never have noticed his English accent if indeed Greenleaf had posed as being English. I couldn't be sure, although I remembered that Tally had once mentioned that Greenleaf didn't speak as a Philadelphian or New Yorker.

But Greenleaf, having secured the plates, I was strongly convinced would immediately adopt a new character . . . one as removed as possible from what he had been using—English or Bostonian, and French. Thus of the roles he had left, roles in which he was physically in character, only one remained for him to play.

A Westerner.

Not a cowboy, naturally, but someone from, say, Texas . . . Arizona . . . New Mexico; that general area.

I would begin searching for a tall, lean, gray-haired Southwesterner . . . but where? That was the problem; where would he go to pass the counterfeit money? Not to a small town, obviously, because a stranger with a great deal of money is always a person of speculation and curiosity. Furthermore, if there ever was a slip on a phony bill, it could be traced too easily in a small place.

I decided that if I were in Greenleaf's position and planned to start passing queer money, I'd do it in a large city—and a city in which there is a big tourist turnover. Automatically, that would be either New York, Chicago, or Los Angeles. This conclusion brought me face-to-face with another problem, and one that might decide whether I ever found Greenleaf. Was he planning to convert the queer into legitimate money, and in turn bank it; or was he planning to spend it, only as needed, for living purposes?

There was something about the shadowy Greenleaf . . . from what I'd heard, thought, and felt perhaps . . . that made me believe the man desired a certain respectability. His propensity for using foreign phrases, his enacting the role of gentleman were not much, certainly, upon which to base such a conclusion; but my feeling regarding the kind of make-believe roles he liked was strong enough not to be ignored. For this reason, Greenleaf would want a bank account. And this in turn meant something else: he would not be foolish enough to deposit counterfeit bills in a bank. Instead, he would pass his phony bills and bank only the legitimate money which he had received in exchange. New York is one of the few cities in the country where a man can buy a package of cigarettes, paying for it with a twenty-dollar bill, and not draw comment on the transaction, when he receives his change. In Greenleaf's operation, he could pass twenties all day, and never enter the same store twice. One other factor helped me reach my final conclusion. Most con men are suckers, themselves, for liquor, dames, and bright lights. New York's night life was the largest, the most gaudy, and it would appeal to Greenleaf. Converting money during the day for a respectable bank account and spending the queer dough lavishly at night . . . this, undoubtedly, was Greenleaf's dream of the best of all possible worlds.

In my reasoning, I had completed a circle. Right here in New York, right where I was, there Greenleaf was too!

Now, although I might not be able to recognize Greenleaf on sight, there was the possibility that he might recognize me. I didn't know if he had seen me in Philadelphia. He had seen Tally, and so far as I know, he might have looked me over while we were performing at the club . . . or at the hotel.

As part of my act, I had grown a mustache . . . a

small, dark military model. It is strange that when a man grows a mustache, it does not alter his appearance as greatly as a man, who has always worn one, alters his when he shaves it off. The first thing I did, naturally, was to shave mine.

Once, while I had been working in the carney, there'd been a big clem in a hick Southern town and I had lost my front tooth from a flying tent stake. As soon as I could, I had the tooth replaced with a false one on a removable bridge. I now took out the false tooth, leaving a wide gap in the front of my teeth. My eyebrows and hair are dark . . . an excellent combination for a stage magician, but easily remembered. However, I didn't want to dye my hair, because hair not only can be analyzed but it also requires a lot of work to keep it from looking phony and being detected.

I bleached my eyebrows to a lighter brown, which immediately changed the entire expression on my face. Most of my entire life I had worked with stage make-up as part of my job. One principle of make-up should always be remembered: keep it as simple as possible. A minimum is easier to maintain, day after day, and it's more difficult to detect. I kept it simple . . . lighter eyebrows, a missing tooth, no mustache. To this, I added a pair of conventional horn-rimmed glasses, with ordinary lens. The plain glass, however, had been ground around the edges to reflect concentric circles of depth, and appeared to be extremely strong.

In the clem I mentioned . . . the one where I had lost a tooth . . . one of the truck drivers in the carney, a man named Isham Reddick, had been killed. I had ridden in the cab with Reddick over many long dusty jumps, and during the endless, dull, night hours he had often talked. That night of the fight, the Southern cops had fired into the dark, and Reddick had been shot. The next day, without fanfare or publicity, he had been buried in a plain wooden box; dumped in a small Baptist cemetery on the edge of town.

But I remembered the name of the town where Reddick had been born, because it had been strange enough to make an impression. It was Rocky, Colorado, and his parents had moved away when he was still a kid. Sitting down, I wrote a letter addressed to the city recorder at Rocky. Enclosing a five-dollar bill, I wrote that my name was Isham Reddick, and I wanted a copy of my birth certificate. Ten days later, I received a small printed card, an official form which affirmed the fact of my birth on page thirty-three, volume twenty-six, of the city records, etc. It was signed by the recorder in office and . . . believe it or not . . . he returned three dollars to me.

It was as simple as that. I became Isham Reddick.

The best place to pick up the trail of Greenleaf, I decided, was in the bistros around town . . . the big-money, late-night spots. As I couldn't hang around the joints and ask questions without the possibility of alerting Greenleaf, I developed a good cover. Going to the City Bureau of Licenses, I applied for a license to drive a cab. It wasn't difficult, either; after filling out the application forms and passing the examinations, I was fingerprinted. Several days elapsed while the records were checked; I had no fingerprints on file, and evidently the original Isham Reddick had never had a record, either. The license was issued.

New York City has as many cab companies as it has pedestrians. I selected one of the largest . . . the Eastern-Circle Taxi Company, reasoning that it probably had a big turnover in personnel, and applied for a job as a night driver. It was a twelve-hour stint, from six o'clock at night to six o'clock in the morning, pushing around a heap, painted orange with purple circles on the fenders. The cab rattled and banged and steered with the ease of a Coast Guard cutter in ice. But I was the lowest man on the totem pole . . . the newest driver . . . and I had to take it. Hacking is a tough business, and let no one maintain differently. I pushed the hack around Manhattan, the Bronx, and Brooklyn during the early part of the evening. I needed the fares so as not to cut into my small capital, and also to show that I had been working when I turned in my mileage reports, and fares, to the garage in the morning. After midnight, however, I skipped all the fares I could. Instead, I'd pull into one of the cab lines outside the night spots; standing around I'd shoot the breeze with the other hackies, picking up a little gossip here and there, watching the customers leaving the club. Watching for a tall, lean guy with a big nose and gray hair! One by one the cabs worked their way up the line into first place position to take the next customer. As a rule, when I had reached second place, I'd take off for another club, and repeat the procedure— starting from the end of the line.

Each morning, I was just under the wire from getting fired. The money I took in on hauls in the early part of the evening didn't justify the loafing I did after midnight. I don't know why the company didn't let me go, except drivers were still pretty scarce . . . and possibly, I was the only sucker who would drive the oldest hack in the garage. Anyway, the night foreman kept me on, from night to night, but always with the threat of firing me the next day.

I saw plenty of prospects who might have been Green-leaf. Although they answered his description physically, they failed to hold up when I tried to check them. Either they were unknown at the club . . . and I figured Greenleaf would be a pretty well-known customer when I did locate him . . . or else they were too well and legitimately known. One night I thought I had found him . . . "That guy looks like a big shot," I told the doorman. "Who is he?" The doorman glanced at a tall, distinguished-looking guy with gray hair, and a flashy babe on his arm, and said, "He's a rancher."

"What's his name?"

"Cready. All I got to say is 'good evening, Mr. Cready,' and it's good for a ten spot."

"I guess he must have a pile of it," I said, acting impressed.

"You ain't kidding," replied the doorman. "Spends dough like he hates it. He's a big man back home."

I watched Cready climb unsteadily into a cab, the girl crawling in after him, clinging to the rancher possessively. "You know where he's staying?" I asked casually. I really didn't care about an answer, because in a minute I was planning to take off and tail him.

"Sure," said the doorman, "he stays at the Van Dyke-Plaza . . . he always stays there when he comes to New York." The doorman cocked an eye thoughtfully, "Must be four, five years now I've seen him coming to the club. When he's in town, he always stays at the Van Dyke-Plaza."

That was that. I shrugged, turning away to conceal my disappointment. It is fairly typical . . . in one way

or another . . . of all the other prospects I turned up
for Greenleaf. Naturally, when I found Greenleaf I knew
he would be operating under another name.

Somehow, though, I began to enjoy pushing that old
cab around the streets late at night. The hours . . .
staying up until morning . . . were a return to the pattern of my old life. Tally now seemed more remote; the
aching loss had gone. The hatred I felt for Greenleaf,
however, I had lived with too long to be able to lose it.
The desire for revenge burned as brightly as ever. The
gospel of my execration, the litany of blood I had recited
to myself too often. I had learned them too well to ever
unlearn them again. I was like a man who, only partly
believing in religion, ends up a raving fanatic!

Eventually, of course, I found Greenleaf. I found him
just as I knew I would find him. The first time I saw him,
he was slightly drunk standing beneath the canopy of
the Copabonga Club, arguing with a blonde floosie who
had come out of the joint with him. He gave her a gal-
lant bow, and pulling out a roll of bills unwrapped several from the outside. Stuffing the bills in the woman's
hand, he put her in a cab. Turning back to the doorman,
he shoved him another bill. The doorman saluted,
smiled, and said something before whistling up a second
cab. I was about the fifth cab in the line, and I was
unable to pull out to follow. Waiting a few minutes, I
climbed out of my hack and sauntered up to the doorman. "Who was that john?" I asked, lighting a cigarette.

The doorman, a seven-foot giant named Ozzie,
grinned. "A Texas oil man," he said. "Carries his own
oil well around with him." He unfolded his hand, and in
the palm was a twenty-dollar bill.

The excitement began mounting within me. "Wish to

hell I had him for a fare," I said enviously. "Does he come around often?"

"Oh . . . maybe once a week," said Ozzie.

"A regular?"

"Yeah . . . I guess so. Showed up here couple, three, four months ago. Something like that. Probably'll go back to Texas one of these days."

The time was right as far as Greenleaf was concerned. The masquerade was right . . . Texas and oil. "What's his name?" I asked.

"Mistuh Ballard Humphries," said Ozzie imitating a drawl.

"Well, shut mah mouf," I replied climbing back in the cab. I hung around the club for several hours waiting for the cab which had hauled Humphries to return. It didn't, and I decided that the driver had picked up a return fare. Knowing the number of the cab, and the company, I returned to the Copabonga Club the following night and the cab was in the line-up again. Walking down the line, I leaned against the cab door. Pulling out my cigarettes I offered one to the driver who took it, and stuck it behind his ear for future smoking. "Hey, Mac," I said through the window, "how was that Texas millionaire you hauled last night?"

The hacky, a little man with cramped shoulders, shrugged. "They're all the same," he said.

"Except some have money . . ."

"Yeah." A slow grin crept cross his wrinkled features. "This guy gives me a ten spot for the haul and I keep the change. . . ."

"How much was the haul?"

"Buck and a half over to the East Side."

"Uptown?"

"Yeah. Eighty-ninth Street. A brownstone . . . middle of the block."

"I know the street," I said, lying. "Bet I know the house, too. It's got a brass railing leading up from the sidewalk."

The cabby thought a moment, then shook his head. "Naw . . . no railing. This joint's got a big heavy glass door all covered with an iron grill."

"That doesn't mean anything, Mac," I said. "Lots of doors on that street look like that. I'll drive around tomorrow, and I'll bet you there's a brass railing going up the stairs."

He spat, disdainfully, through the window. "Naw. This house was the third house down from an apartment building. Same side of the street. No railing . . ."

"Okay," I agreed reluctantly, "maybe you're right." Walking back to my cab, I felt good, I felt positive—although I still had to nail it down. A little later, I got out again and strolled up to Ozzie. "Ozzie," I said to the doorman, "remember that Texas millionaire last night? What'd you say his name was?"

"Humphries. Why?"

"Well, I've been thinking. I'm getting plenty tired hacking, and I thought maybe this Mr. Humphries might want to hire a chauffeur. I'd like to hit him for a job."

"So, go ahead and do it. I ain't stopping you."

"How'm I going to? I just don't walk up to him when he comes staggering out and brace him for one. I got to be diplomatic. I figured if maybe I got a chance to haul him someplace, while we were driving along I might sort of start talking with him. . . ."

A party of four came out of the club and Ozzie busily

signaled up the first cab, opened the door, helped in each passenger, palmed his tip, and closed the door. I had lost his interest, and he grew impatient. "That's your problem, Mac," he said, "not mine."

"Okay, Mac," I shrugged. "I was going to make you a proposition. I'll give you twenty right now," I slipped two tens in his hand, "if you'll give me the chance to haul him the next time Humphries is here. If he gives me a job, I'll give you another twenty." Ozzie peered down at me from his altitude. "Incidentally," I asked, "do you ever get a nose bleed up there?"

He brushed my remark aside. "How do you plan to work it, Mac?" he asked.

"From now on, I won't get in the line-up," I explained. "I'll park down at the corner on the other side of the street. When he comes out, stall as long as you can before waving up the first cab. That'll give me time to get here, and pick him up on the cruise."

"The boys are going to be awful mad," Ozzie warned me.

"Tell the guy who loses the haul that I'll give him a ten. That ought to square it."

"Okay," said Ozzie grimly. He looked down again. "And don't forget my other twenty."

"If I get the job, it's yours," I assured him.

Humphries didn't show up again at the Copabonga all week. Each night I parked around the corner, across the street from the club, as if I'd been poured in the concrete. Every morning when I checked in, the night foreman raised hell, bawled me out, and finally one morning fired me. That night, however, he hired me back on again, and I returned to my vigil. At last, the following Tuesday night, Humphries showed up. He came out of the club about two in the morning, and this time he was squiring a slender, willowy brunette who was young enough to be his daughter, but who looked experienced enough to be his mother. Ozzie went into his stalling routine, and I slung the old cab into gear and roared up to the front of the club with the back door practically open.

Ozzie helped them into the hack, and Humphries with a broad Texas accent gave me the address on East Eighty-ninth Street. As the cab pulled away, he and the brunette began playing around in the back seat. After a few minutes of driving, I cleared my voice loudly; during the moment of silence that followed, I said, "Pardon me, sir, but you appear to be a well-educated gentleman."

The remark caught Humphries by surprise, and in the mirror I could see him straighten in the seat. In a loud, flat drawl he said, "Huh? What was that again, son?"

I repeated it and added, "If you don't mind, sir, I'd like some information, and I think maybe you can help me."

"Well, shore," replied Humphries. "If I can help out a fellow human, I'm always right happy to. . . ."

"It's like this," I said. "Earlier this evening, I was down by the United Nations Building. I picked up a gentleman and his wife . . . they were French, I think . . . and I hauled them uptown. The gentleman spoke some English, not very much, and when he got out of the cab he gave me a bill and told me to keep the change. It was a pretty good tip. I thanked him, and then he said something in French. I asked . . . what'd you say? He laughed and replied in English that he'd said 'don't mention it.' " Pushing the driver's cap to the back of my head, I continued, "Well, I been thinking about it, and I wish I could remember the way he said it in French. Would you, sir, happen to know any French?"

Humphries roared with laughter. "I'm going to tell you the truth," he drawled. "I'm right proud to say that I'm a graduate of Texas Christian University, in Texas."

"Yeah . . . sure," I said. "I've heard of it. They have great football teams . . . I've seen them in the newsreels. That's at Waco, isn't it?"

"Yore plumb right," Humphries agreed. "They got a great little ol' team. Well, as I was saying, I studied a mite of French at TCU and if I can remember correctly . . ."

"Oh, Ballard," the girl giggled admiringly, "don't tell me that you speak French, too! Why, that's wonderful . . ."

"Well . . . yes, m'am, I do," said Humphries preening himself. "And if I recall correctly what the driver heard his fare say this evening was '*il n'y a pas de quoi.*'" His delivery was abruptly weakened by a hiccough.

The girl attempted to repeat it after him phonetically, "eel knee ah paw duh qua." She clapped her hands. "I think that's cute," she said.

"Honey girl, I think yore plumb cute, yoreself," Humphries replied gallantly.

I was thinking other things. Here's a Texan who speaks French. And a Texan who was graduated from Texas Christian and who mixes it up with Baylor University. Texas Christian is at Fort Worth; Baylor University is in Waco. Drunk or not, no authentic Texan makes that mistake!

NINETEEN

The prosecution had closed its case the day before. Denman, counsel for the defense, had moved that the indictment be dismissed for failure to prove the defendant's guilt beyond a reasonable doubt. The jury had been excused during the argument between the two attorneys and, when the motion had been denied, the jury returned to the courtroom. "Will the court please instruct the jurors that the denial does not concern them, but is only the court's decision on a question of law?" Denman requested the judge.

The court so instructed the jury. "At this time, I also make my exception a matter of record," added Denman.

"Your exception is so recorded," agreed the judge. "Proceed please, Mr. Denman."

"If it please the court," said Denman, "I would like to

begin the defense tomorrow morning. It is now drawing near to the end of the afternoon, and I move the court adjourns until tomorrow morning."

Cannon did not protest the motion, and the judge dismissed the court, and retired to his chambers. Denman walked beside his client to a small private cubicle with heavily barred windows, located directly behind the courtroom. A uniformed officer stood outside the door. The attorney seated himself at a solid oak table with a badly scarred surface. His client, lighting a cigarette, walked moodily to the window which overlooked an enclosed air shaft. Denman was tired, and for a moment he sat heavily in his chair, his chin resting on his chest. Finally, raising his head, he said softly, "Sit down, Humphries. Let's have a talk." The tall, gray-haired man with a deeply lined face turned away from the window and walked listlessly to the table. He, too, sat down. "Listen," said Denman, his voice quiet and unemotional, "tonight we make a decision . . . and whether our decision is right or wrong will determine whether we save your life.

"Before we make that decision, I wish to do a little talking. Usually, I have my own ideas about the innocence or guilt of my clients. Whether a man is innocent or guilty is no personal concern of mine; it is my duty to see that he receives a fair trial, as defined by the country and state. I defend all prisoners to the best of my ability. The more I know about their cases, the better I can defend them." Denman paused for a moment, then said slowly, "But I'll be damned if I know what to think about you, Humphries!"

"I pleaded not guilty, didn't I?" Humphries replied.

"The man caught with his knife in his victim's throat

can also make that same plea," said Denman. "My personal belief is that you are hiding something . . . or someone." As Humphries began to object, Denman raised his hand, silencing him. "I've sat in this room many times before, Humphries. Look around it—how large is it? Ten by twelve feet? Two small windows with bars over them. Look at this scrubby table . . . two chairs . . . and a guard beyond that closed door. But this is elegant . . . a magnificent suite compared to what is waiting up the river. Yes, I've sat here before. How many times? Fifty . . . a hundred. I really don't remember, Humphries. Somehow over the years, all those faces began to look alike . . . some of them already tinged with the gray of the walled-in years to come, or with death stamped, early, on their faces. I mention this deliberately to frighten you . . . to put the fear of God in your heart. Don't you realize the position you are in?"

Denman hunched himself erect in his chair, pushing his legs out . . . straight and stiff . . . before him. "I've had men who came here, with an illicit fortune hidden away, who refused to talk. They gambled the chance that if they could beat the rap, they would walk out of here wealthy men. Some of them died in prison caught by the years, before they could get back to their money. Others took their last walk . . . shouting they would tell the truth, but then it was too late. A few have returned to find the money, and again be picked up by the police."

"I don't know what you're talking about," Humphries denied surlily.

"I don't either," came Denman's frank reply. "I'm not even guessing. But you haven't told me the truth . . .

you haven't told me the facts . . . you haven't told me anything! Humphries, you and I have sat for over a week while Cannon has beat us bloody with facts and witnesses. And what do we have? No alibi! No witnesses—not even a character witness. Tell me again, but this time honestly . . . was Reddick blackmailing you?"

"No!" Humphries brought his hand down hard against the table. "I've told you before! So help me God, he wasn't blackmailing me! He never asked me for a cent!"

"Suppose," Denman continued relentlessly, "he hadn't gotten around to it yet. Was there something that Reddick might have known . . . that he might have used for blackmail?"

Humphries did not reply immediately, an infinite part of a second elapsed before he denied it. "No," he shook his head. "He had nothing to hold over me . . ."

Denman ran his fingers, tiredly, through his hair. "Humphries," he pointed out, his voice laboredly calm, "look at the case Cannon has advanced. He maintains that you shot Isham Reddick in the furnace room with the revolver found in your drawer. After he was killed, you dismembered him . . . using the bench and the large canvas tarpaulin, and the hatchet. The body was consumed in the large furnace, and most of the traces and ashes were disposed of by you. He has even found traces of the ashes in your car. In evidence, he has Reddick's finger, part of his leg, his tooth, and possibly his blood. After the murder, he advances the argument that you cleaned up and showered in the basement bath. Now why did all this take place? Cannon maintains that Reddick was blackmailing you . . . he has evidence in your handwriting concerning a payment of at least eighty-five hundred dollars. Reddick was spending money like a sailor on shore leave. Where did he get it? Cannon says he got it from you. Witnesses have testified that Reddick, himself, implied he got it from you. Cannon has proved that you are not from Texas . . . have no business, and no traceable income. Where do you get the money that you have? Is that something that Reddick knew? Is that what you were paying him to hide?" Denman shook his head in disbelief. "And you want me to believe you aren't hiding something!"

"Cannon couldn't prove I had a criminal record," Humphries said.

"No," agreed Denman, "he couldn't. But there are plenty of individuals who have done something they don't want known . . . something which could land them in the prisons, if it ever came to light."

"I'm innocent," Humphries replied. "Reddick was a mad man. Stark raving mad!"

"And you want the jury to believe he killed himself . . . committed suicide, and then cremated himself in the basement?" Denman's voice was sarcastic.

"He could have gotten another body . . ." Humphries' voice was disbelieving.

"Don't be ridiculous!" Denman snapped. "Believe me, it's impossible to steal a cadaver; it's easier to get into Fort Knox. No, the prosecution has some pretty damaging evidence . . . but that isn't the question. What I want to know, Humphries, is why, WHY!!"

Humphries turned away helplessly. "I don't know . . ."

"Yes, you know, Humphries, but you aren't telling me. That's it, isn't it?" Humphries remained silent, although shaking his head. "All right," continued the attorney, "let's face up to the question we have to decide. Tomorrow, we start our defense. We have no evidence to establish an alibi for the night of November twenty-second and the morning of the twenty-third; we have no character witnesses; and we don't even have an alternate theory to advance concerning what did happen."

"I don't have to take the stand," said Humphries.

"Right," agreed Denman, "as a rule, with any kind of a defense, at all, it's better for the defendant not to testify. But damn it all, man, we've got to do something! With absolutely no defense, and if you don't take the stand, the jury is going to wonder why." Denman studied the brown painted wall opposite the table, his eyes tracing a feathery crack which ran . . . a narrow dark line . . . along one side of it. Heavily, he pulled himself to his feet, and walked around the table until he faced the wall. With one finger he traced the line of the crack, then plunging his hand into his pocket returned and seated himself.

"There're cracks all over the case," he said. "They're a mile wide in Cannon's evidence, but I can't plaster them up." Turning, he faced Humphries again. "Well, how about it? Will you gamble your life on the story you told me?"

"It's the truth," replied Humphries. "It's all the story I got."

"Are you willing to get on the stand and tell it? Afterward, Cannon is going to rip you apart."

"I'm willing, if you say so."

"Humphries, I don't want to say so. But, there's nothing else we can do. If just one of the jurors believes you

. . . or any part of the story . . . there's a chance. Our only chance."

The guard opened the door, and let Denman out of the room.

TWENTY

It took me about an hour to talk Greenleaf, or Humphries rather, into giving me a job. That first night, I drove him home, I played up to his vanity. Arriving before the house, I walked around to the rear door of the cab and helped him out—lifting his wallet off his hip as I did so. At noon, the following day, I was back at the house to return it. A maid let me in, and after a few minutes Humphries staggered into the living room, dressed in a silk dressing gown and looking miserable. He did not seem to recognize me.

"My name is Reddick, sir," I said. "I drove you home last night. Afterward, I found your wallet in the back seat of the cab. I'm returning it." I handed it to him, he received it blankly. Finally, he opened it and fanned through the bills. There were nearly five hundred dollars in tens and twenties . . . all new bills! I had counted them the night before.

"Why . . . thanks," he said. He regarded the wallet vacuously. "I hadn't missed it yet . . . just getting up. Terrible, bad night last night . . ."

"Yes, sir!" I agreed, looking around. It was a large room, with a high, lovely, old ceiling. The walls were hunter green, and a tremendous, ornately carved Italian marble fireplace dominated the room. Humphries walked over to an Empire chair, and sank into it. Picking out five bills . . . all twenties . . . he handed them to me. "This here's a reward for returning the poke," he drawled.

I shook my head. "Thanks, sir," I replied, "but that's too much. Twenty will be more than enough."

His bloodshot eyes looked at me with surprise. "Yore an honest man," he said.

"Yes, sir," I agreed, "I am. And you look like a sick one. Where's the kitchen, sir?" Humphries motioned toward the back of the house. Walking in the general direction he indicated, I found a large, white, little used kitchen with an electric refrigerator. Opening a can of tomato juice, I poured it out and spiked it with two spoons of Worcestershire, and added a dash of red pepper. When I returned to the living room, Humphries was seated where I had left him, his eyes closed. I shook him, and he took the glass and drank it. Sitting motionless for a moment, he swallowed abruptly and shook his head in a delayed reaction. He said, "Brother, I shore need that one . . . what a hangover!" He attempted to lift himself from the chair, then sank back weakly. "I'm shore grateful," he said, "now I got to get dressed."

"I'll help you upstairs, sir," I told him. As he began to

protest, I grasped his arm, pulling him to his feet. "I haven't anything else to do," I explained. Upstairs, while he stood stupidly under a shower, I selected a suit from his closet, laid out a shirt and underclothes. Later, helping him get into them, I said, "What you need, Mr. Humphries . . . a wealthy gentleman like yourself . . . is a good man to help out. If I may say so, frankly, I'm getting pretty fed up driving that hack. Tell me, sir, do you have a car?"

"No," he grunted, "too much trouble getting around this here city."

"Not if you have a chauffeur," I replied. "Someone to keep the car in good condition . . . and to drive you whenever you want to go." I paused, then continued, "And to pick you up, too . . . any place, any hour of the day or night. Why, it's the biggest convenience you can have, sir. You know, it's dangerous going around the city late at night . . . carrying as much money as you do."

"Hogwash," said Humphries.

"Not at all, sir. Someone to see you get home safe at night, someone to help around the house during the day. Such a man would be invaluable, sir. And, if I may say so, I'm just the man—and I'm available, too!"

Humphries looked haggardly in my direction. "You hitched up . . . married?"

"No, sir," I said brightly, although the bile was gagging in my throat, "I'm single."

"What about yore family, they live here?"

"No, sir. I've been working here a long time, but my home's in Rocky, Colorado."

"What's yore name again?" I told him: Isham Reddick. He frowned a moment, and I couldn't tell if he was displeased, or if it was just the hangover. After a while, he said, "I don't have many hired hands in this spread, Reddick. Just a maid, a cleaning woman, and a sort of handyman. Not too much of a layout, but maybe I could use another hand. How much you want to hire on?"

"Three hundred a month," I said.

"I'll give you two fifty, and yore room. I don't eat in 'cept for breakfast, but I guess you can rustle up enough to eat around here."

"Yes, sirrr!" I replied, quickly. "I'll take it."

That afternoon we went downtown to buy a car. I was anxious to see what he would do in the way of a splurge, but Humphries was cautious. Instead of buying a Cadillac, he settled for a smaller, medium-priced car . . . a black sedan with white sidewall tires. I wasn't surprised as it confirmed my suspicions. A man as wealthy as Humphries was supposed to be would not have hesitated to pay a high price. But Humphries had to pay for the car with a check, a personal one. It would have been impossible for him to pay in ten-and twenty-dollar bills, so he was forced to check against that legitimate account he was building up in the bank . . . and he didn't want to wipe it out. However, as far as I was concerned, he could have bought a rowboat and I'd have rowed him down Fifth Avenue.

That evening, I moved into the servants' quarters on the top floor of the house. With the door safely closed behind me, I was able to relax for the first time. I found myself trembling, both with hatred and triumph. I forced myself to remain quiet, although I wanted to pound the walls with my fists and shout curses down the stairs. After I regained control of my emotions, I thought about Humphries, analyzing what I had seen.

His eyes, although heavily lidded, were not large and they set deep within his head; the nose, long as had been described to me, swelled slightly at the bridge lending almost a predatory air; and his lips were a combination of both cruelty and sensuality. The upper lip was thin, straight, and very narrow, the lower full and heavy. Yet, unmistakably, the man had an appearance of distinction.

My greatest problem was not to give myself away. In my role of ex-cab driver and presently of chauffeur Humphries had accepted my disguise—if you could call it that. He gave no indication of ever having seen me before, and made no mention to a familiarity of appearance. I was convinced that he was entirely unsuspecting —although I do not believe that Humphries was ever trusting of anyone in his life. Determined as I was to kill the man, I was afraid that Humphries might read it in my face. Consequently, I went to great lengths to be servile—scraping and doing everything but touching my forelock. And he liked it.

Late at night, with contempt and loathing in my breast, I'd sit in my room, smoking, and consider the best possible method with which to kill him. While I would have enjoyed strangling him with my hands, making it as painful and lingering as possible, I realized such a plan had a drawback. Although Humphries was twenty years older than I, he was also larger and possibly stronger. But I liked to consider it anyway—as well as guns, knives, blunt instruments, and all their variations.

However, I was also determined to escape the consequences after I had murdered him. It would be little satisfaction to offer myself as another sacrifice to

Humphries after his death. No, I hoped to escape the law, and with this in mind I began planning a method by which to avoid the police after the killing. I determined to build Isham Reddick into a definite person, a concrete character; give Reddick a motive for killing Humphries; and then have Reddick disappear completely. While the police searched for Isham Reddick, the chauffeur with light eyebrows, smooth shaven, a front tooth missing, and wearing thick heavy glasses—I would simply, over-night, return to being Lew Mountain again.

It was, I believed, a good plan and I immediately put it into action. As I began to build up the background . . . a piece here, a piece there . . . I kept my eyes open for Humphries' other connection—the printer. Each day when Humphries went downtown, I'd drive him and usually he would get out somewhere in mid-town Manhattan. I'd try to leave the car, and get back in time to follow him, but as a rule this was very difficult to do. On several occasions, however, I did manage to pick him up near the place where I had dropped him. As far as I could discover, after trailing him all day, he concen-trated entirely on passing the ten- and twenty-dollar bills —buying innumerable, small, inexpensive little items which he often threw away after leaving the stores. And yet Humphries always had an inexhaustible supply of new bills. I had searched the house from top to bottom, attic to basement, to find the place where he concealed them. Searching an extremely large house is no easy task. It took me many hours as I could devote only a few minutes to it at any one time. Either the maid, a rather simple person, or the cleaning woman was always around and I had to be careful neither became suspi-cious.

The house on East Eighty-ninth Street had been rented, completely furnished, from a wealthy family living in Connecticut. Consequently, I didn't think that Humphries had access to the folderol of sliding panels, hidden rooms, and concealed passages. It was simply a large beautiful town house, and after my search I was convinced if Humphries had found a place to conceal the money, I'd have found it, too.

It took me some time, however, before I discovered how Humphries got his bills from the printer. Daily, while he was downtown, I'd go through his room and all his possessions. This aroused no comment from either Mary Deems or Mrs. Lightbody as I was doubling in the capacity of a semi-valet. I found no money in Humphries' clothes, or in his room, and I never came upon evidence of correspondence . . . or any other clue. Except once.

By Humphries' bed, there was a telephone which had a direct outside line; this was in addition to another phone in the house which had a number of extensions. Although this bedroom phone had no extension, there was nothing mysterious about it, and there was no secret about its number, either. On the table, beside the phone, was a tablet of paper. One day, I discovered tracings on the pad. The top sheet of paper on which the words originally had been written, had been torn off leaving an indentation on the sheet beneath it. Holding the paper up to the light, I could catch a slight shadow on the indentations. I read the word "Magarian—2:00." I put the pad back in its original position and went down to the bus terminal.

At the telephone booths, in the bus depot, is a collection of all the individual telephone directories for the boroughs of New York, as well as some of the neighboring cities in New Jersey and Connecticut. There were a number of Magarians listed, but no Magarian Printing Company. Obviously, there wasn't much more I could do about Magarian right then, so I returned to the house. I considered going to Dave Sherz for help, but by this time I decided I was too involved. Murder is a lonesome task.

As a rule, around ten o'clock at night, I'd pick Humphries up at a café after he had finished dinner, and drive him . . . with a girl . . . to a nightclub. After dropping him off, he'd instruct me to return at an appointed time. Instead, I'd park around the corner, away from the club, and then return to a vantage point where I'd spend three or four hours waiting for him to stagger out of the joint again. Most of the time, the girl would be so drunk that I'd practically have to carry her over my shoulder. The women were all pretty much the same . . . hard faced, sharply pretty, little chippies with predatory and acquisitive instincts well developed. It always surprised me that Humphries managed to meet so many, and eventually I decided that most of them were simply on lend-lease from call flats. Humphries often took the girl home with him, although sometimes he would slip her money in the car and then transfer her to a cab. On occasion, one of them would ride back to East Eighty-ninth with Humphries, and then I'd drive her home. Invariably, she would live in a cheap, walk-up flat, downtown.

When I did discover Humphries' method of getting money, it was a matter of an error on his part. I might never have found out, except Humphries went to a new club one night—one where there was no back entrance.

He and a girl had been in the club several hours. I was waiting down at the corner, as usual, when I saw Humphries hurry out of the entrance by himself. Grabbing a cab, he took off in a direction opposite to the one I was parked. His cab swung around the corner and disappeared, and by the time I reached the intersection, it was out of sight. I returned to my original location and waited. In less than half an hour, Humphries re-entered the club.

I could figure it out from there. The recurring patterns of clubs, and drunken girls. Humphries would get his companion high, excuse himself from the table, make his contact with the printer, and return. The girl, in her drunken condition, wouldn't know if he had been gone three minutes or thirty and would always be able to give him an alibi for the evening.

After that, I watched the backs or side entrances of the different clubs, and invariably Humphries would show up. He'd take a cab, and I would follow him. Driving for only a few minutes, and stopping in front of a drugstore or a restaurant . . . any place . . . and with the cab waiting, Humphries would walk in—and in a moment be out again. Back in the cab. Back in the club! It was that simple, and he never went near the printing plant.

I decided that sometime during the day, Humphries would call the printer and tell him the club he was going to attend during the evening. They'd arrange to meet at a place near the club, and the printer would slip Humphries the money as he walked past. I never saw the actual transaction, or the printer either, because of the danger in following Humphries too closely, and being recognized. After watching Humphries perform the cab and pickup routine a number of times, for caution's sake I stopped following him entirely.

It was with a degree of sardonic pleasure that I realized Humphries wasn't getting any real enjoyment out of his life. He worked hard during the day passing the queer money to pay the cost of running the house, and the salaries connected with it. And always he was working under the pressure and tension of possible discovery. Every night, he was back at a bistro, getting a floosie drunk, setting up an alibi, and contacting the printer. He had no opportunity to make friends or relax—except in drinking. Humphries was on a treadmill, running hard and fast in the same place just to keep even. Of course, he spent much money on clothes and personal jewelry, but after all where are the kicks—if only paid prostitutes and your valet can admire them?

Over the Fourth of July holiday, Humphries announced that he was going up to a lodge near Bear Mountain for a few days. I had to drive him up, and we edged our way in bumper-to-bumper traffic out of New York, cutting across the short slice of New Jersey, and then angling back into New York State again. During the drive, Humphries pulled a notebook from his pocket, scribbled on it, and handing me the piece of paper, drawled, "I'll call you to come fetch me . . . when I'm ready to leave. If anything comes up around the house, you phone me. Hear?" He indicated the paper. "That there's the number for up here."

"What might come up, sir?"

Suddenly irritable, he climbed out of the car impatiently, and I followed him carrying his luggage. "How'd I know what might come up? But if anything does, call me."

"Yes, sir," I assured him. Back in the car, I examined the note. Humphries had scrawled on it: "Reddick . . . Bear mt. 8500." Bear Mountain 8500 was the number of the lodge. He had written it across a small sheet of blue-lined paper—and I deliberately tore it across one edge. When I had finished, it read: "Reddick . . . mt. 8500." I carefully placed the paper in my pocket.

Returning to the city, I stopped at Duval's . . . a magicians' supply house on Eighth Avenue near Forty-fourth Street. Like all professional magicians' shops, it is located on the second floor of a building . . . to prevent nonprofessional trade from wandering in off the street. These places specialize in making up highly complicated productions and sell only a few great effects a year, although they also carry a stock of all the standard stage props. A little guy named Harry Lohr has always operated Duval's as far back as most magicians can remember, and I have regularly bought my mechanical stuff from him. In most of these shops, good regular customers are permitted to store their props . . . when they're not using them, or are out on the road . . . and the stores will keep them in good condition. When I had moved into Humphries' place, I had delivered my big theatrical trunk to Duval's, to hold for me. The store is open until late at night as many of its customers do not come in until evening. I slipped my glasses in my pocket, and kept my lip down over my missing tooth. When I walked in, Harry said, "How's the mechanic, Lew? You look different, kid."

"Just younger! I shaved off my lip-wig so I can practice catching that bullet in my teeth," I told him. This was a standard joke between the two of us. Some years back, an inventor had come up with a composition that disintegrated completely after passing through a quarter-inch pane of glass. A pellet made of the substance would pass through the glass, leaving a nice round hole, and then it disappeared without leaving any traces. A magician, with an authentic lead bullet concealed in his mouth, could create the illusion of catching the real bullet in his teeth, after a gun had fired it through the glass. It was a really great piece of business. The fellow who invented it sold the idea to Harry. Harry bought a supply of the stuff and showed it to me. I went for it. While I was rehearsing the act . . . building it up as a topper . . . I ran out of the material with which to make the composition, imitation bullets. Harry called the phone number the inventor had left but the guy had moved away. We couldn't locate him, and we never saw him again . . . and neither did anyone else. Because no one ever did the act. "Where do you have my trunk stored?" I asked.

"Third room back," Harry directed. "You can find your own way."

Passing through rooms filled with loaded shelves, built-in bins, costumes, masks, and a half century of collecting all the instruments of miracle-making, I arrived in a dark bare room, containing half a dozen large, metal-reinforced trunks. I had no difficulty recognizing mine. From it, I extracted a thick packet of stage money . . . not the ordinary green and orange fake stuff which you see in novelty stores, but a reasonable facsimile of real money both as to size and color. Naturally, the stage money was covered with "goon" writing . . . doubletalk words . . . and fake portraits. It could never be passed as real money, but magicians substitute the bills when they pretend to tear up a genuine five-dollar bill before the audience's eyes. From a short distance, it is difficult to detect a difference between the two. My trunk was crammed with a hundred other props, and finally I managed to get it closed and locked again.

Back in my room at the top of the house, I wrapped genuine one-hundred dollar bills of my own money, and a number of legitimate fifties around the roll of stage money. I had a wad of dough that would have impressed even a bank!

The following night I took Mary Deems out to a movie and to dinner. She was a nice person who didn't go out very often and was very anxious to be pleasant. Carefully, she ordered the less expensive items on the menu; my plans, however, called for me to flash my roll of bills and play the lout. I did, and the sight of the money hit her, hard. That was what I wanted.

Humphries had been away three days when on the morning of the fourth, I read a small item on page nine of the morning paper. The story said a man identified as Adrian Magarian, proprietor of the Inland Printing Shop, had been found murdered in his office. From what I read, the printing shop was just a small place located near Canal Street, and the police regarded it as another hold-up killing. Magarian had been struck down and killed by a blow on his head, and his shop had been ransacked. Judging by the position and briefness of the story, it was evident that Magarian wasn't very important.

I decided that the police hadn't found Humphries' counterfeit plates, or the story would have been page one! I wondered if Humphries had killed him . . . or had someone else killed and robbed Magarian. I was inclined to believe it was Humphries; it followed his pattern . . . no guns, no knives. Anyway, I decided to see what kind of reaction I could raise from him, so I called Bear Mountain 8500 . . . the number he had given me. When he got on the phone I said, "Sir, I don't know if this is important, but I thought I'd better call."

"Yes. What is it?" It seemed to me his drawl sounded a little forced.

"Well," I told him, "some man just called the house and asked for you. I said you were out of town. Then he wanted to know if I could put him in touch with someone named Magarian."

"Who?"

"Magarian."

There was a long pause. "Never heard of him," Humphries finally remarked. "Who was it called?"

"I don't know. He wouldn't leave his name."

"Is he going to call back?" Humphries attempted to sound indifferent.

"He didn't say."

After a moment, Humphries said slowly, suspiciously, "How come you called me?"

"You said to call if anything happened . . ."

"Well? What has happened?"

"Nothing," I admitted brightly, "except this guy . . . man called. I thought *maybe* it might be important."

"Well, 'tisn't," said Humphries, back in his old characteristic drawl again. "Incidentally," he added, casually, "I'm getting mighty tired of sticking around this here place. Ain't stepped a foot outside the door since I been here; guess maybe you better mosey up and get me . . . this afternoon."

"Yes, sir," I replied. I didn't mention the item in the

paper to Humphries . . . then or later . . . and he never said a word about it to me. However, I could never shake the conviction that Humphries had used his trip to Bear Mountain as an alibi, to slip back to New York to knock off Magarian. The facts were that Magarian was dead and, as I soon discovered, Humphries still had the plates.

That Humphries had known Magarian, and also knew that he was now dead, was proven by his acts of omission. For several weeks, until after the first of August, Humphries made no more sorties into the saloons and bistros. Then, abruptly, he began the old routine of sneaking out of the clubs at night, and I knew that he had found another printer.

In the meantime, I was still developing my own plans. As a motive for Isham Reddick to kill Humphries, I selected the motive of blackmail . . . with a reverse twist. Usually, it is the blackmailer who is killed, and not the victim. I would reverse the plot; as the blackmailer I would kill my golden goose. The cops would figure that I had pushed my victim to the end of his endurance, and to prevent him from turning me in—I had killed him. Flashing my roll of bills around the house, at every opportunity, I dropped hints and insinuations regarding the source of my wealth. Deliberately, I went out of my way to lend the caretaker . . . a prying ass of a man . . . money. To make the story better, I doctored up an envelope, with a list of fantastic figures including the number 8500 . . . and arranged for Lightbody to get it. I hoped it would give him something to remember . . . and to talk about . . . when the time came.

Although my three thousand dollars were dwindling

fast, it was imperative that I make my story convincing. The cops had to believe that I had taken Humphries for a big bank roll, and had spent it like a profligate. Making certain to leave a wide and easily followed path, I bought a solid gold wrist watch, jewelry, suits, sport equipment, and about everything else I could conceive; I couldn't be positive that the police would dig up all the purchases, but I knew they would trace some of them.

At one point, I nearly made a serious error. It was imperative I have a complete set of teeth the day I walked out of Humphries' house after killing him. The cops would be looking for a man with a tooth missing. Somewhere I had misplaced my tooth with the removable bridge. I couldn't remember seeing it since I had moved to East Eighty-ninth Street, and I couldn't find it. Consequently, I had to have another made. I realized the dentist might remember making one, and possibly inform the police. This would change their broadcast description of me, but I decided that it would take him several days to notify the police, and that would be enough of a start for me.

I called a dentist named Boss and went to see him. Attempting to remain as inconspicuous as possible, I stayed within the role of Isham Reddick—poor, hardworking chauffeur. Knowing that I would have to give an address and telephone number to his office, I was afraid to use a fictitious name in case Boss should call me to cancel an appointment. If he should become suspicious of me, he might remember me that much more quickly. He made me another tooth.

There was still a decision to be made concerning the method by which to kill Humphries. I had been so busy painting in my protective coloring that I continually postponed reaching a conclusion. Deciding, finally, that the best plan would be to strike when we were out of town, I determined to strip the body of identification and conceal it where it might remain undetected for a few days. This would give me even more time in which to disappear. Humphries, however, remained in town.

Shortly after the first of November, I began suggesting he take another short vacation, hoping that I might arouse some restlessness within him. Indirectly, I recommended a trip to Virginia, but he refused to rise to the bait. With each day, he seemed to become more taciturn and moody. When I had first found him, Humphries had been loud, blustery, and partly drunk most of the time. Since his return from Bear Mountain, in July, he had begun a slow deterioration. Possibly the idea that someone knew about his connection with Magarian worried him; or perhaps the strain of passing the queer, day after day, was wearing him down. The veneer of the open-handed Texan was getting very thin; occasionally his drawl would slip; and he took less interest in his appearance.

There was a certain satisfaction in watching Humphries break up, and because of this satisfaction, I continued to procrastinate. The idea that I should get him out of town, although a sound one, was based, subconsciously perhaps, on a premise to help postpone my final action. There were plenty of opportunities for me to walk into his bedroom at night, and simply put a bullet through his head.

But the decision was finally forced on me!

Humphries forced it himself. On the morning of November twentieth, he arose with his usual terrific hangover. The night before, at the club, he had been absent longer than usual, over an hour. When he returned, he had been carrying a very heavy package wrapped in brown paper, and securely tied. The girl he had with him had noticed his departure from the table, and they had argued about it in the car. Angrily, he had me stop and send her off in a cab.

Sitting on the side of his bed, eating aspirin, and sipping a pick-me-up, Humphries said, "Reddick, I've got some sad news. I've decided to close up this here house and haul stakes back to Texas."

"I'm sorry to hear that," I replied. Recalling the tightly wrapped package of the night before, I knew Humphries had secured the return of the plates. Possibly he felt that he had run his luck too long in New York, or perhaps he had printing troubles again. Either way, he was folding up.

"Yes," he said, "I'm going back. I'm planning to leave in a week. That's not much notice, but I'll pay yore wages for an extra week."

"What about Deems?" I asked.

"She'll stay on for the owner's family to keep the house open." For a moment, he whirled the liquor around in the glass, watching it intently, and not meeting my eyes. Finally, he said, "I'd . . . shore . . . appreciate it, if you didn't mention it until I'm ready to tell her myself . . ."

That was it. Humphries was planning to take a run-out powder and skip out from under his lease. He was afraid that Mary Deems might notify the owners. Momentarily, I couldn't understand why he had told me, and then I realized it was because of the car. Humphries was a wretched driver, and he needed me to sell the auto. "Yes, sir," I agreed, "I won't say anything about it."

That afternoon, I went down to buy a ticket for France . . . an airline ticket. I now planned to kill Humphries the night of November twenty-third. When the police discovered that Isham Reddick had bought a ticket for Paris, the news would confuse them for a day or two. Particularly, as I had not applied for a passport, the authorities would have no record, and they could not be sure . . . without detailed checking . . . that I hadn't slipped through under another name.

The next day, November twenty-first, I went through the motions of looking for someone to buy the car . . . driving it around to several car dealers . . . and repeating to Humphries the offers I had received. On the morning of November twenty-second, Humphries arose . . . earlier than usual . . . and sober for a change. He told me that he would be downtown all day, and wouldn't be home until late that night. I drove him down to Fifty-seventh Street and Fifth Avenue, where he got off in front of a bank. That evening, around dinner time, I pretended I had received a call from Humphries and told Mary Deems that she could have the night off, as well as the entire next day. She was very happy to go visit her mother who lived in St. Albans. I also notified the Lightbodys.

Mary Deems left the house around seven o'clock in the evening. At eight, I drove downtown and stopped for a sandwich; then I went over to Duval's. From my trunk I took a snub-nosed .32, a pistol which I had used while rehearsing the "catching-a-bullet-in-my-teeth" routine. On my way out, I asked Harry, "Do you have any bullets?"

"Blanks?" he asked.

"No, regular ones." I held up the revolver and forced a grin. "Remember this? I have another idea."

"Be careful, Lew. Don't forget that guy who got killed on the stage in London."

"Sure," I told him. "I just have an idea . . . for a shot-in-a-pillow illusion. I need some shells."

"I think I got some here, someplace," replied Harry. He began rummaging through the shelves, and eventually came up with a partly filled box of .32's. "Will these do?" he asked.

Shoving one into the chamber, I said, "Sure, they'll do great. How much?"

"Take the box," Harry said. "Nobody else wants 'em."

"Thanks, but I don't need that many." I filled the remaining chambers, and returned the box to him.

It was a little after nine when I arrived back on Eighty-ninth Street. The premises were dark, with the exception of a light I had left burning in the entrance hall. I went upstairs, first to my room on the top floor where I removed my coat and hat, then I returned to the second floor. The great house, suddenly, seemed sinisterly silent. Expectantly, it waited in the night, drawing its shadows around itself, clothing itself in darkness. The well of the stairway, which spiraled through the heart of the mansion, was a black void which sighed and rustled uneasily. Around me the deserted halls, the empty rooms were filled with the specters of all the murderers since time began. Each of my steps seemed to shake the walls to their very foundations, threatening to bring down the masonry in rubble.

At the end of the dark corridor, I opened the door to

Humphries' bedroom . . . the master suite. It is located along one side of the house, a locked door opening from the corridor into a small service hall. Grouped around the hall are several closets, and a large bath. Adjoining the service hall is an elaborate dressing room which, in turn, leads to the master bedroom. This is an extremely large room with a heavy fireplace at one end.

Somewhere in this suite, Will Shaw's plates were hidden. Humphries had concealed them here; and I intended to find them. Retracing my steps to the service hall, I began searching the closets . . . going through the boxes and built-in drawers, exploring clothing, shelves, and corners. Methodically, I examined the bathroom, looking under the top of the water reservoirs. In the dressing room, I explored closets, drawers, dressers, and commodes. Eventually, in the bedroom, concealed behind the logs stacked in the fireplace, I found them. Picking up the package, I walked to the bed and tore open the wrappings. There they were! The complete set of counterfeit plates . . . now stained with ink, but as perfect as the day they were made, as faultless as the moment I had seen them, with Tally, in Philadelphia!

"You lousy, sneakin' son-of-a-bitch!"

Whirling, I faced Humphries. He stood in the door connecting the dressing room and bedroom, and his face was twisted with fury. Rapidly he strode toward me, the wrinkles in his forehead bunched together, pulling the flesh across the bridge of his nose into a long, deep V. In the dim light of the shaded room, his eyes were merely opaque shadows.

My hands, reacting more quickly than my mind, flashed up with the .32. "That's far enough," I said.

At the sound of my voice, he stopped. His arms hung

loosely at his sides, and for a moment he peered at me—as if watching a stranger. "Reddick," he said hoarsely, "what do you want?"

"Step back about three feet," I said, "and then raise your hands in that respectable, old-fashioned gesture of hands-up." Complying with my command, he asked, "Who are you?"

"Well," I replied, "you've always called me Isham Reddick."

"That's not your name!"

"How about calling me Adrian Magarian? Perhaps I'm a reincarnation."

"God damn it! Stop playing cat and mouse. Who are you and what do you want?" He no longer even made a pretense of using his Texas accent.

"I'll tell you," I said, "suppose you call me Ath. That's spelled capital A-t-h."

"Ath? What kind of a name is that? Who do you think you're fooling?"

"No one," I said, "you least of all. My initials are D. E. My full and complete name, as far as you are concerned, is D. E. Ath."

Perspiration broke quickly across his brow. One second his forehead was dry, the next instant it was wet with a thousand little beads of sweat. "You're crazy!" he said, his voice croaking.

"Absolutely," I agreed. And at that moment I was crazy. My mouth was dry, so dry that it seemed necessary to form each word with my lips first—before attempting to pronounce it. In the back of my throat, I could taste the bitter bite of gall. Humphries quickly withdrew another step. "That's all right," I said benevolently as a Spanish priest lighting fagots at an auto-da-fé, "keep going. You and I are going to the basement. There, I shall kill you. I could do it here, but neighbors might hear the shots. In the meantime, turn around and keep moving." I motioned with the revolver, and turning with cramped, paralyzed movements he floundered from the room. I followed him. Stumbling down the stairs, he wavered through the hall and into the kitchen. "We're going to the basement," I explained, my voice so tight and rasping I could hardly speak, "because there are six shots in this revolver, and I'm going to put four of them into you. Slowly! The fifth I'll put in your head. The basement is nice and quiet . . . practically soundproof. I know . . . I've thought about it often."

Behind the kitchen loomed the back hall—and the stairway to the basement descended from there. Slowly, in slow motion, Humphries opened the door; his eyes were blind, unseeing . . . and distended with fear. "Switch on the lights," I ordered. His fingers clawed helplessly, scratching against the side of the door. Reaching past him, I switched them on myself.

Humphries began to descend.

I followed him.

TWENTY-ONE

Humphries raised his right hand to the oath, "I swear to tell the truth, the whole truth . . . so help me God!" As he seated himself in the witness chair, Denman approached him . . . in the quiet of the courtroom . . . and said, "I want you to tell the jury, and the court, in your own words exactly what happened between you and Isham Reddick the night of November twenty-second in your house on East Eighty-ninth Street." The attorney for the defense glanced at the jurors who were regarding both him and the defendant, impassively. "You will retell the circumstances exactly as you have told them to me, and I will not interrupt you —unless it is necessary to elaborate a point, or to ask a question. Now, Mr. Humphries, please begin."

Humphries sat quietly for a moment, staring into

space and, seemingly, hearing only part of Denman's words. Finally, after the attorney had ceased to speak and stood waiting expectantly, Humphries wrenched his attention back to the present, and looking over the heads of the jury began in a toneless voice.

"I had been downtown all day," he said. "I went to the bank to withdraw some money, and during the afternoon, I bought some things for a vacation I had planned. After a rather late dinner, I decided to return home, and not wishing to wait until Reddick could pick me up with the car, I rode home in a taxi. When I arrived home, I noticed the house was dark, except for a light in the downstairs' hall, and a light in my bedroom. This seemed strange to me, as the house should have been well lighted—and my bedroom dark. I opened the door with my own key, and walked in. Mary Deems was not around, although there was always the possibility that she was in her own room. . . ."

"You had not given her permission to leave for the night?" asked Denman.

"No, I had not!" replied Humphries. "I returned to the main hall and walked upstairs to the second floor, very quietly. The door from the corridor to the service hall of my bedroom was open and I entered it . . . passing through the dressing room until I could look into the bedroom. There I saw Isham Reddick rifling through my belongings. He had taken some jewelry, and at the instant I saw him, he had removed a large sum of money from a wallet I had left on top of my dresser.

"At the moment, he saw me, too. Instantly, he drew a revolver and told me to raise my hands. I was unarmed . . . entirely defenseless, and I did as he told me. I tried to reason with him, but he was a crazy man . . . yelling and threatening me."

"What did he say to you, Mr. Humphries?"

"He talked very quickly . . . almost babbling, and much he said didn't make any sense. Reddick kept referring to himself by the name of Ath . . . and he said his initials were D. E. And put them together, he was D.E.Ath . . . it was a nightmare! I told him he could have the jewelry and money . . . to take them and leave."

"In all the months that Isham Reddick worked for you," Denman questioned, "had he ever given any indication that he was insane, or subject to spells of unreasoning fury? Anything like that?"

"No," replied Humphries, "he wasn't the usual type of man you find employed as a chauffeur, though. Often he seemed . . . well, not quite disrespectful, but rather as if he was amused about something, or had a secret he was enjoying. However, he always did his work well enough. If I had thought for a moment that I had a . . . a lunatic on my hands, I'd have let him go immediately."

"All right," said Denman, nodding, "please continue."

"I thought possibly, as I stood there with Reddick pointing the revolver, that I might be able to escape from the bedroom. I was not far away from the door, and I tried to ease away, but he saw me. Suddenly, he ordered me to turn around and march to the basement. As you know, it's a large house and it requires a few minutes to walk from the second floor to the downstairs back hall . . . where the cellarway is located. It was quite dark, and on the way I tried to think of something to do, some way to escape; but Reddick was right behind me, with his gun, and he was raving every step of the way. . . ."

"Again, Mr. Humphries, can you recall what he said to you?"

"Yes. He threatened me with a slow death . . . he was going to torture me . . . shoot me four or five times."

"It would be an understatement would it not, Mr. Humphries, to say you were in mortal fear of your life?"

"I have never been so frightened!" Humphries abruptly removed the pocket handkerchief from his coat, and wiped his forehead. Returning it to his pocket, he removed it again to dry the palms of his hands. "At the top of the basement stairs," he picked up his story again, "Reddick ordered me to turn on the lights. That is the last thing that I distinctly remember. I knew I was walking to my death . . . to an execution . . . and each step down was less clear, less real. It is a long stairway from the back hall to the basement floor, and somewhere along the way I completely lost contact with reality. . . ."

"I wish you would explain that a little more," Denman interrupted. "You say that you lost contact with reality. Do you remember reaching the bottom step at all?"

"Yes," replied Humphries, slowly. "But only as an impression, not as an actual occurrence. Going down the stairs was like sinking into slumber . . . a grayness closed in over everything. My body worked mechanically . . . independently of my mind . . . there was absolutely no contact between the two. Eventually, my body reached the cellar floor, the last step, and at that point my mind went completely blank. Everything sank into darkness."

"That is all you remember of that night?"

"Yes, sir. That is all."

"What is the next event which you remember?"

"It was possibly twelve, or fourteen, hours later. I became conscious of a sound . . . a noise that kept repeating itself from far away. After what seemed a long time, I realized it was the bell ringing in the house. I aroused myself . . ."

"Where were you then? When you regained consciousness?"

Humphries shook his head, unbelievingly. "I was lying on my bed . . . upstairs in the master suite."

"Were you fully clothed?" asked Denman.

"No. I was wearing only my undershirt and shorts."

"Where was the suit you wore the night before?"

"It was hanging in the closet, I discovered later. There was a terrible aching . . . throbbing in my head, and I wondered why someone—Mary Deems or Reddick didn't answer the door."

"You mentioned Reddick. At that time, did you recall what had happened the previous night?"

"Not right then, sir. I simply got out of bed and put on a robe. Going downstairs, I opened the door . . . and there were the police."

"When you saw the police, what did you say?"

"I couldn't understand for a while why they were there. Then I suddenly remembered Reddick from the night before . . . how close he had come to killing me. Immediately, I thought he had run away and gotten into trouble. I thought the police were there because of him!"

"When they asked to come in, you let them in?"

"Certainly. I had nothing to hide."

From then, until noon, Denman painstakingly went over Humphries' story. He could only elaborate on the testimony as given; Humphries had nothing new to introduce. When he had finished, Denman studied the jury carefully as they filed out to lunch. Eleven of the faces were still impassive, but on one face . . . just one . . . Denman wondered if he didn't see a faint trace of credulity.

When court convened, again, in the afternoon, Cannon began his cross-examination. "Tell me, Mr. Humphries," he asked, "what happened to the jewelry and money Isham Reddick was supposed to be stealing when you caught him?"

Denman immediately interposed an objection, which was sustained.

"All right," Cannon continued, "you say Isham Reddick was stealing your jewelry, is that correct?"

"That is correct."

"Did you ever see the jewels again?"

"No. I didn't."

"The police found no trace of them. There were no traces in the house. Did you look for them?"

"I don't know . . ."

"You don't know?" Cannon pretended surprise. "You knew Reddick had them, but you didn't look for them again?"

"I—I didn't think about . . . he took it with him when he left."

"You had some other jewelry . . . which he didn't steal?"

"Yes. There was some left . . ."

"But you don't know what was taken? You only

know what was left behind. Could it have been the same jewelry?"

"No, sir."

"And the money? You testified that you had left a large sum of money home in your wallet?"

"Yes. Yes, I had."

"And earlier in the day, you had been to the bank to get more money? Why did you need all that money?"

"Well . . . I had planned a vacation . . ."

Because of Humphries' evasive and indefinite answers concerning the jewelry and money, Cannon was convinced the witness was not telling the truth. The prosecuting attorney continued to pound away at him, wearing him down, dogging his answers. Finally, Cannon said, "Mr. Humphries, you state that when you reached the cellar floor, the bottom step of the stairs, you completely . . . 'lost contact with reality.' By that you mean that you blacked out . . . lost consciousness?"

"Yes, sir."

"And after you blacked out, you do not remember anything for over twelve hours?"

"That's right. I don't remember anything."

"You don't remember killing Isham Reddick?"

"No, sir. I didn't kill him."

"You don't remember anyone else killing him?"

"No, sir."

"You don't remember dismembering Isham Reddick's body and destroying it in the furnace?"

"I didn't dismember him . . . and burn the body in the furnace."

"But you don't remember!" Cannon said.

"No, sir. I don't remember. But I didn't do it . . ."

"You don't remember anyone else dismembering Isham Reddick's body and cremating it in the furnace?"

"No. I don't!"

"You don't remember how the ashes got in the furnace, how the bloodstains got in the basement, how the fragments of the body were scattered around as if in a charnel house?"

"No, sir. I know nothing about it. I don't remember a thing. I only know that—I couldn't have done it."

"But you don't remember anyone else present in the basement that night, do you?"

"No."

"Absolutely no one?"

"No one. I don't remember anything until the next morning."

"In the morning you awakened in bed, refreshed from a night's sleep . . . after a miraculous escape from an insane killer . . . as you have described him?"

Humphries glanced helplessly at Cannon. He nervously tugged at his collar, and then with great effort clasped his hands, and forced them to remain quiet. The pressure of his hands, locked together, marked his knuckles with white.

"Was Isham Reddick blackmailing you . . . asking you for money?" Cannon pursued his questions relentlessly.

"No, sir . . ."

"You had no reason, then, to hate or fear Isham Reddick?"

"None . . . none at all."

"Did Isham Reddick have any reason to hate or fear you?"

"No, sir . . . except I caught him stealing."

"That was enough to make him want to kill you? Especially after you told him to take the money and jewelry—and leave?"

"Well . . ."

"Well . . . what?" asked Cannon.

"Isham Reddick was just crazy . . . that's all!"

"Was he crazy enough to kill himself, dismember himself, and then cremate himself? And afterward, clean up the mess?"

"No . . ."

"Then who killed Isham Reddick? Who dismembered him, and disposed of parts of his body?"

"I don't know," Humphries admitted, his voice hopeless, "except it wasn't me."

"This was a carefully planned, diabolically executed murder. Someone had to do it. To do it, someone had to be there. You were there, Isham Reddick was there. Was anyone else there?"

Wearily, Humphries retreated to his defense. "I don't know," he said. "I can't remember . . ."

As Cannon continued his ruthless questioning, Denman glanced cautiously at the one juror . . . the one he had noticed at the noon adjournment. Their glances met —the attorney for the defense, and the juror. Before their eyes parted, Denman was uncertain that he had ever detected a look of sympathy there.

TWENTY-TWO

The stairs yawned before us. The foot of the flight was washed in a reflection of light from the concrete floor, while the stairs, themselves, were wrapped in shadows. The descent was very steep, and a handrailing ran along the right side. I shifted the revolver to my left hand, my right grasped the rail as we descended. Just in front of me, Humphries' head was on a level with my chest, and his sweat . . . the acrid smell of fear . . . was heavy in the air. Its odor seemed to drive me into a deeper frenzy, and I thrust the revolver against the back of his neck. Slowly, legs moving in unison to the same macabre rhythm we marched down . . . step by step.

As Humphries reached the basement floor, he moaned loudly and stooping suddenly—straightened, a glittering, swirling arc of light flashing by his side. Instinctively I ducked, and thrust out my right hand to steady myself against the post at the foot of the stairs.

An instant later, the hatchet buried itself into the wood, and Humphries slumped forward to the floor!

I stood woodenly holding my position in the tableau. I looked questioningly at the gun in my hand . . . I couldn't remember shooting it. There was no smell of gunpowder in my nose, no echoing sound of a shot in my ears. And then I became conscious of warmth stealing over my right hand. Involuntarily, I moved my hand, holding it in front of my eyes. Part of a finger was missing from my right hand. Blood spouted from the severed flesh. The dismembered section was lying on the floor beside the post. Dazedly, I kicked at the motionless body of Humphries. He didn't move. There was no sensation, as yet, from my hand and I walked aimlessly around the furnace room, holding the pulse at my wrist, attempting to stop the flow of blood. The stream, however, seemed to clear my mind . . . and I began thinking again clearly and rationally. The cobwebs of hate, the clinging entangling skeins of insane anger which had twisted my thoughts for so long, disintegrated—dissolving finally with the falling drops of blood which marked my steps and crimsoned the floor of the furnace room.

Returning to where Humphries was lying, I knelt on the floor beside him. He was unconscious still, but I could hear the irregular sound of his breathing in the quiet of the room. Breaking open the chamber of the revolver, I found the shells intact . . . unfired.

With a sigh of relief, I realized I had not shot Humphries!

Humphries had collapsed from shock . . . from sheer fright. In one fast, frenzied, unconscious effort he had grabbed up the hatchet from the floor . . . a hatchet Lightbody used to split kindling . . . and had swung at me in a desperate attempt at defense. Even as he swung, he had blacked out through shock and hysteria; sometimes condemned criminals do the same.

Almost immediately I realized something else: here was a man who had committed three murders, or had been responsible for them, and had escaped punishment. But there was still a way by which justice could be served.

By my watch, it was then almost 10:30; the night of the twenty-second of November. I lit a cigarette, and sat down on the bottom step to think the situation over. The greatest illusions, I knew, are compounded equally by the things you see . . . and the things you don't see. Obviously, I could not leave my entire body, but possibly I could leave traces that seemed to prove I had left my entire body. The illusion must be of a murder committed . . . and almost entirely erased!

Picking up the hatchet, I walked into the next room, a semi-laundry, where the tool chest was kept. I pasted several hairs from my head to the blood on the hatchet, and wiping the handle on the sleeve of my coat, tossed it in the box. Next to the laundry was a basement bathroom. Standing over the wash basin for a minute or two, I permitted a trickle of blood to run down the drain and into the trap. Turning away, I splattered more stains around the cracks and corners of the floor—and then I was forced to stop. Already I had lost too much blood. With a piece of twine, I bound the finger as tightly as I dared, to stop the flow, and bandaged the end with a strip from my handkerchief.

My greatest fear was that Humphries might regain

consciousness. Under the basement stairs there was a small, securely constructed closet where logs for the fireplaces were stored. On the outside of the door was a heavy drop bolt. Lifting Humphries by his shoulders, I dragged him to the closet, and bolted him inside.

I returned to my room, upstairs, and found a pair of leather driving gloves. Slipping them on, I stuffed the empty finger with cotton; and put on a top coat. Taking the car, for the second time that night, I returned to my trunk at Duval's. Harry nodded to me, showing no surprise at my late return. From the big metal trunk, I removed Omar . . . my skeleton. God knows who Omar had once been. I had bought him complete, with wired joints, from Harry Lohr ten years before when I needed a skeleton for a comedy gag in a disappearing-cabinet act. Harry originally had purchased Omar from some long since forgotten magician, or supply house. Omar, however, was a real skeleton . . . and not a composition one. Removing the shin bone . . . the one reaching from the knee to the ankle, I broke off the ends where it had been wired through small holes. While I was returning the rest of the skeleton to the trunk, I remembered, suddenly, to look in a small built-in drawer in the top where I kept a lot of tiny gadgets such as springs, card-feeders, and release gimmicks.

Pulling out the shallow drawer, I discovered my missing tooth. I had packed it in my trunk, through force of habit, the day I had moved to Eighty-ninth Street. Slipping it in my pocket, I placed Omar's shin bone flat against the small of my back, holding it in position with my belt. After I had again donned my topcoat, it was impossible to detect. My hand was beginning to ache terribly, now, and I was anxious to get away. But there were still other calls to make.

I drove around town, looking for all-night delicatessens, carefully avoiding uptown and midtown Manhattan. Eventually, I found four of them which were open, and from each I bought five pounds of beef. Then with twenty pounds of meat, Omar's leg, and my missing tooth, I returned to the house.

It was after midnight when I arrived. Immediately, I built a great roaring fire in the furnace, and knocking apart the workbench, fed it to the flames; a large canvas tarpaulin, used for painting, also went into the fire . . . after I had carefully removed a small section which contained bloodstains. The pain from my finger raced high up into my arm; the stub swollen and angrily discolored from the tourniquet forced me to stop for a while. A great weariness weighed on me, and it seemed impossible that I would be able to complete all the effects called for by the illusion. My head whirled dizzily. I forced myself to climb to the upper floors of the house where I searched through the medicine cabinets. In Mary Deems' room, I found a bottle with three codeine pills in it. I took all the pills at once—and they seemed to help relieve the pain, or at least numbing me to the point where I could carry on. I also made another discovery, an important one. In the same medicine cabinet I found a small bottle of ether, which Mary used for cleaning purposes to remove spots and stains. I took the bottle back to the furnace room.

I kept the furnace roaring and forced the draft and at four o'clock the fire had pretty well burned through the bed of coals. I removed the ashes, shoveling them into a tub. Loading the tub into the car, I drove across town, and in front of a large apartment building, I left it concealed among a large number of other tubs filled with trash and refuse. On the back floor of the car, however, the imprint of the tub and the dust of the ashes remained on the rug.

Dawn was not far away. I looked in on Humphries, in the closet, and decided I had better take him upstairs while I still had the strength. When I touched him, he stirred uneasily. It gave me a shock. Hastily, I poured ether on the remnant of my handkerchief, and held it to his nose and mouth—praying to myself that I didn't smother him. He quickly became quiet again, and I immediately removed the cloth. Without another quiver from him, I alternately hauled, hoisted, and dragged Humphries upstairs to his bedroom . . . a long, difficult trip with the limp body of a man his size. Undressing him, I left him on his bed, and carefully hung his suit in the closet.

Back in the basement, I rebuilt the fire . . . but not so large as before. When it was glowing hot, I fired the revolver into a chunk of the beef and threw all the meat into the fire. It began to glow, then caught fire and burned with a thick, dark, black smoke. Eventually, it burned to ashy cinders, and I broke the mass up with the end of the poker, then shook the furnace to sift the ashes . . . both wood and meat . . . together into the receptacle below, where I had previously placed the charred piece of canvas.

Omar's shin bone I laid carefully on top of the mass of coals. The broken ends first began to burn. I permitted the fire to gradually envelop it, until the entire bone was blackened, and partly consumed. Then very carefully, I removed it from the flames placing it in the trash box, along with a charred end of wood from the bench.

Time was growing short now; the hours were running out. Partly paralyzed with exhaustion, I took a long drink from Humphries' stock of liquor. My mind was so benumbed with fatigue, that the whisky was absolutely tasteless. Lurching back to my work, I attached a garden hose to an inside connection and sluiced down the floor in the furnace room, permitting the water to stand in puddles and dry by evaporation. In the downstairs bathroom, I did the same. When I had finished, the floors were clean, but the damning traces of blood could still be found in the cracks of the floor!

Now, there were signs of life, noises, and activity on the streets outside, and I must make one final effort to hurry. As the last gesture, I placed the tooth that Boss had made on the coals, and when it had darkened I tossed it into the bottom of the furnace. The indisputable positive proof of my finger, I half concealed on the floor outside the furnace.

In Humphries' room, I buried the note . . . the one reading "Reddick . . . mt. 8500" . . . in a drawer of his dresser, together with the fired revolver, after wiping it clean of prints. Then I undressed, and in his bathroom took a shower . . . washing myself clean of dirt, ashes, and blood. When I had finished, I put on the same stained clothes again, as I did not want to leave them in the house.

Again, I climbed the stairs to my room on the top floor. Somewhat awkwardly, because I was forced to use my left hand, I darkened my eyebrows with a make-up pencil, and replaced my missing tooth; the glasses I put in my pocket to carry away. Carefully, I brushed my hair, making sure I left a few strands in my brush. Blood had soaked through the glove on my right hand, staining it; I put on a new pair again filling out the missing finger. The stained pair I stuffed in my overcoat pocket. Checking the room carefully, going through the drawers I removed all records except a few specimens of writing. Once more, I stopped in Humphries' room for a final look. He was still unconscious. Beside him on the bed where I had left them were the counterfeit plates. Wrapping the paper around them, I carried them away with me, to be destroyed later.

At the last moment, I stood within the main entryway on the ground floor, checking over everything in my mind: the hot furnace, the ashes, the bloodstains; the tooth, finger, and nail; the shin bone, the piece of bench, the square of bloody canvas; the hatchet with the blood and hairs; the hair in my brush; the blood in the drains; the ash-tub marks in the car; Humphries' note and gun in his drawer. I recalled the boasts I had deliberately made; the money shown to Lightbody and Mary Deems; the envelope with figures in my writing; the gold wrist watch; the expensive suits; the ticket to Paris. And, of course, the deserted house; Humphries unconscious for the night . . . with no alibi; no witnesses. And the final cynical beauty of *truth* itself. Humphries himself could never dare tell all the truth. Even if he knew the entire truth, his lips were partly sealed . . . or he would be exchanging one hangman for another; one executioner for his brother. Humphries' life had been built on lies; and he must continue to live it on that basis. His own truths would condemn him.

Yes, I was satisfied.

The illusion was complete!

TWENTY-THREE

Two weeks before, the verdict had been
returned by the jury. After nearly seventy-two hours of
deliberation, and argument, the jurors had reached a decision. They had reported it to the court. "Guilty," the
foreman announced in a firm voice.

And now the court was to pronounce the sentence.

Humphries stood before the judge, standing alone in
front of the high paneled bench. No longer was there a
crowd in the courtroom; no public, no spectators. Only
the members of the judge's court, Mr. Cannon, attorney
for the prosecution, and Mr. Denman, attorney for the
defense.

The spot, standing before the sentencing judge, is a
lonesome place. It is the loneliest place in the world.

The judge observed the prisoner before him, for a moment, then said in the age-old ritual, "Is there anything you wish to say before I pronounce your sentence?"

Humphries, raising his head, shrugged his shoulders hopelessly. He was wearing the same suit he had worn during the trial, but now it hung more loosely on him. His gray hair appeared whiter, and his long nose—projecting bleakly—looked like the bill on a ruffled bird. "No, your honor," he replied in a low voice.

"Very well," observed the judge. He lifted a paper from his desk and began reading the legal formalities as required by the State of New York. After a few minutes he put aside the paper and continued speaking, although he was no longer reading. "It is the opinion of this court that in many ways the case of the People of the State of New York versus Ballard T. Humphries has been a most unusual one. A jury of your peers has found you guilty of murder . . . a murder most reprehensible and compounded by the inhuman disposing of your victim's body after the crime. That such a crime was committed and executed appeared to be proved beyond a reasonable doubt to the duly impaneled jurors. You have heard the verdict. It is: Guilty.

"And yet the law is not untempered with justice. It is the duty of this court to discover the truth, and to see that justice is delivered within its jurisdiction. It is my belief that not all the facts and circumstances of this case have been discovered, disclosed, and explored by either the prosecution or the defense. Perhaps, in truth, such facts may not exist after all . . . regardless of this court's opinion, or if existing, will never be found and disclosed. But if they do exist, someday they may be brought to light. For that reason, this court has deliberated the sentence to be imposed. Hear it then:

"I hereby sentence you, the prisoner, Ballard Temple Humphries, to be delivered to the warden, or other duly authorized official, of the prison of the State of New York, located at Ossining, New York, during the week of May sixth, the next, and your person committed to him for all the remaining days of your natural life!"

The judge gathered his robe around him, arose from his chair, and retired from the courtroom. Denman reached the prisoner before the two armed guards had moved within hearing distance. The attorney placed his hand sympathetically on Humphries' arm. "You're lucky," Denman said. "You don't know how lucky you are!"

Humphries shook his head, blindly, and turned away. As he approached the guards, they took their places— placing him between them. The prisoner shuffled from the room.

TWENTY-FOUR

A magician with a finger missing is Merlin with a broken wand, a card mechanic with two thumbs. I traded my finger for the capture of a murderer, my future for a tube of grease paint in clown alley.

I have a copy of *Billboard*. It says the Big One is playing out West. The pennants are flying from the main top, the music is playing, the kids are laughing. Too long, now, I have been surrounded by the ghosts of the dead —Tally, whom I loved; Will Shaw, whom I never knew; and Magarian, whom I would have disliked.

And, of course, Isham Reddick. He died years ago, and then again just recently. And when he died the second time, Greenleaf died with him; not quickly, not suddenly . . . but a little bit each day.

It's time to shake the ghosts . . . the one I loved, as well as the ones I never knew. In the night, I hear the distant train whistles heading West.

I'm following them.

TWENTY-FIVE

In his cell, he walked to the window, standing beneath it, the few beams of light falling like dirty water over his hair. Humphries was unable to see out of the window, but he stood as close to it as he could.

He lit a cigarette, puffing it rapidly. Within his mind a question kept revolving. Day after day, night after night, it had spun there on an endless, never ceasing track. Who was it, he thought, who was it who was it who was it who was it who was it? Angrily, impatiently, he threw the cigarette to the floor and turned his face to the high-up window. "The lousy son-of-a-bitch!" he said. "Who was it that jobbed me? Who was it, who was it?" Turning he fell on his bunk. He rolled

over on his back, and in his mind the question
started going around all over again. Who was it
who was it who was it who was it who was it who
was . . .

Bill S. Ballinger is the bestselling author of more than a dozen highly acclaimed novels of crime and suspense. His books have sold more than ten million copies in the U.S., have been translated into eleven languages, and been sold in twenty-eight foreign countries. Born in Iowa, he worked in advertising, radio, and television. In addition to his novels, he is the author of fifteen motion pictures, over one hundred television scripts, and twenty-five short stories, and is a two-time winner of the Mystery Writers of America Edgar Allan Poe Award.

![HarperPaperbacks] **HarperPaperbacks** *By Mail*

MYSTERIES TO DIE FOR

THE WOLF PATH
by Judith Van Gieson

Low-rent, downtown Albuquerque lawyer Neil Hamel has a taste for tequila and a penchant for clients who get her into deadly trouble. *Entertainment Weekly* calls Hamel's fourth outing "Van Gieson's best book yet — crisp, taut and utterly compelling."

THE RED, WHITE, AND BLUES
by Rob Kantner

From the Shamus Award-winning author of THE QUICK AND THE DEAD. P.I. Ben Perkins takes on a case that strikes too close to home. When babies begin to mysteriously disappear from the very hospital where his own daughter was born, Ben embarks on a macabre trail of corruption, conspiracy and horror.

PORTRAIT IN SMOKE/ THE TOOTH AND THE NAIL
by Bill S. Ballinger

HarperPaperbacks is proud to bring back into print, after thirty years, a special two-in-one edition from the Edgar Allan Poe Award-winning author the *New York Times* dubbed "a major virtuoso of mystery technique." In PORTRAIT IN SMOKE, second-rate businessman Danny April is haunted by a beautiful woman. So is magician Lew Mountain in THE TOOTH AND THE NAIL. And both are involved in mysteries that seem impossible to solve.

RUNNING MATES
by John Feinstein

From the *New York Times* bestselling author. Investigative reporter Bobby Kelleher has just about given up the hope of ever landing the "big hit" —the story that will make him a star. Then the governor of ⎽land is assassinated and things start to change—quickly and

EVERY CROOKED NANNY
by Kathy Hogan Trocheck

In this high-caliber debut, Trocheck introduces Julia Callahan Garrity, a former cop who now runs a cleaning service in Atlanta. Sue Grafton calls this novel "dust-busting entertainment," and *The Drood Review* picked it as a 1992 Editor's Choice selection.

BLOOD SUGAR
by Jim DeFilippi

In the tradition of the movie BODY HEAT, this gripping suspense novel has just the right touch of sex and a spectacularly twisty ending. Long Island detective Joe LaLuna thinks he knows what to expect when he's sent to interview the widow of a murder victim. Another routine investigation. What he gets is the shock of his life. The widow is none other than his childhood sweetheart, and now, he must defend her innocence despite the contrary evidence.

COMING SOON FROM HARPERPAPERBACKS

For Fastest Service—
Visa and MasterCard Holders Call
1-800-331-3761
refer to offer HO661

FREE POSTAGE/HANDLING IF YOU BUY FOUR OR MORE BOOKS!

MAIL TO: Harper Collins Publishers
P. O. Box 588 Dunmore, PA 18512-0588
OR CALL: (800) 331-3761 (Visa/MasterCard)

Yes, please send me the books I have checked:

☐ THE WOLF PATH (0-06-109139-1) $4.50
☐ THE RED, WHITE, AND BLUES (0-06-104128-9) $4.99
☐ PORTRAIT IN SMOKE/THE TOOTH AND THE NAIL (0-06-104255-2) ... $5.99
☐ RUNNING MATES (0-06-104248-X) $4.50
☐ EVERY CROOKED NANNY (0-06-109170-7) $4.50
☐ BLOOD SUGAR (0-06-109106-5) $4.50

SUBTOTAL .... $ _____
POSTAGE AND HANDLING .... $ __$2.00__
SALES TAX (Add applicable sales tax) .... $ _____
                                    TOTAL: $ _____
* FREE POSTAGE/HANDLING IF YOU BUY FOUR OR MORE BOOKS!
Orders of less than 4 books, please include $2.00 p/h. Remit in US funds, do not send cash.

Name _____

Address _____

City _____

State _____ Zip _____   Allow up to 6 weeks for delivery.
                                    Prices subject to change.

(Valid only in the US & Canada)   HO661

WALK THE MEAN STREETS
WITH HARPERPAPERBACKS

THE PERFECT MURDER
Edited by Jack Hitt

Suppose you wanted to kill your unfaithful, wealthy wife. And you wanted to pin the blame on your best friend, the same one who's having the affair. Suppose you could ask five great mystery writers, such as Tony Hillerman, Lawrence Block, Sarah Caudwell, Peter Lovesey and Donald E. Westlake to create the perfect murder. Get ready for five fiendishly clever scenarios in the entertaining page-turner *Publishers Weekly* calls "a small masterpiece of cunning and deception."

THE QUICK AND THE DEAD
by Rob Kantner

From the Shamus Award-winning author of MADE IN DETROIT and THE THOUSAND YARD STARE. P.I. Ben Perkins has got his hands full. He's anxiously awaiting word on the birth of his first baby while busy juggling unfinished business with the mob. But when the body of a beloved priest is found missing from its grave, it is up to Perkins to unearth a host of shocking secrets that spell out a history of passion, betrayal, and murder.

A PERFECT DEATH FOR HOLLYWOOD
by Richard Nehrbass

From the critically acclaimed new author comes a suspenseful tale featuring private eye Vic Eton. An ex-LAPD detective, Eton is content to spend his days tracking down stolen movie equipment and taking his daughter fishing. But when a teenage prostitute is found horribly murdered, Eton is hired to search Hollywood's darkest and most unsavory corners to find the psychopath responsible for the grisly murder.

THICKER THAN WATER
by Bruce Zimmerman

From the Edgar Allan Poe Award-nominee comes a new thriller featuring San Francisco therapist turned sleuth, Quinn Parker, in another suspenseful adventure. This time, Parker's old pal, stand-up comic Hank Wilkie, invites him to Jamaica for a sunny all-expense-paid stay at the half-million dollar estate Hank has just inherited. It's just too good to be true.

THE WOLF PATH
by Judith Van Gieson

Low-rent, downtown Albuquerque lawyer Neil Hamel has a taste for tequila and a penchant for clients who get her into deadly trouble. *Entertainment Weekly* calls Hamel's fourth outing "Van Gieson's best book yet — crisp, taut and utterly compelling."

AVAILABLE FROM HARPERPAPERBACKS

For Fastest Service— Visa and MasterCard Holders Call

1-800-331-3761

refer to offer HO651

FREE POSTAGE/HANDLING IF YOU BUY FOUR OR MORE BOOKS!

MAIL TO: **Harper Collins Publishers**
P. O. Box 588 Dunmore, PA 18512-0588
OR CALL: **(800) 331-3761** (Visa/MasterCard)

Yes, please send me the books I have checked:

☐ THE PERFECT MURDER (0-06-109115-4) $4.99

☐ THE QUICK AND THE DEAD (0-06-104127-0) $4.99

☐ A PERFECT DEATH FOR HOLLYWOOD (0-06-109042-5) $4.99

☐ THICKER THAN WATER (0-06-109026-3) $4.50

☐ THE WOLF PATH (0-06-109139-1) $4.50

SUBTOTAL .... $_____

POSTAGE AND HANDLING .... $ $2.00

SALES TAX (Add applicable sales tax) .... $_____

TOTAL: $_____

*FREE POSTAGE/HANDLING IF YOU BUY FOUR OR MORE BOOKS!
Orders of less than 4 books, please include $2.00 p/h. Remit in US funds, do not send cash.

Name _____

Address _____

City _____

State _____ Zip _____ Allow up to 6 weeks for delivery.
Prices subject to change.

(Valid only in the US & Canada)

HO651